Praise for Meira Chand's novel, *A Different Sky*

"Chand proves herself a master of the modern Asian epic in this tale…she endows her characters with humanity and complexity, …grounding…their histories in solid research, and she offers a credible, compelling panorama of the tragedy and resilience, culture and individuality, political evolution, dissolution, and renaissance of 20th-century Singapore."

Publishers Weekly

"…a panoramic page-turner…This meticulously researched book is alive with engrossing detail, whether on the odour of Chinatown, the privations of a guerilla camp or the appalling rituals of foot binding."

The Guardian

"Historical fiction at its most complex and engaging…balances the communist groupings, Japanese occupation and emerging nationalism with skill… As history, *A Different Sky* is engrossing; as fiction, highly enjoyable."

Literary Review

"…the protagonists are richly and deeply drawn, the sights, sounds, and smells of Singapore are gorgeously rendered, and the principal characters' interwoven stories combine to form a compelling narrative."

Booklist

D1472979

SACRED WATERS

MEIRA CHAND

Marshall Cavendish
Editions

Other Marshall Cavendish Offices:
Marshall Cavendish Corporation. 99 White Plains Road, Tarrytown NY 10591-
9001, USA • Marshall Cavendish International (Thailand) Co Ltd. 253 Asoke,
12th Flr, Sukhumvit 21 Road, Klongtoey Nua, Wattana, Bangkok 10110, Thailand
• Marshall Cavendish (Malaysia) Sdn Bhd, Times Subang, Lot 46, Subang Hi-Tech
Industrial Park, Batu Tiga, 40000 Shah Alam, Selangor Darul Ehsan, Malaysia

Marshall Cavendish is a registered trademark of Times Publishing Limited

National Library Board, Singapore Cataloguing-in-Publication Data

Names: Chand, Meira.
Title: Sacred waters / Meira Chand.
Description: Singapore : Marshall Cavendish Editions, [2017]
Identifiers: OCN 999398171 | 978-981-4779-50-0 (paperback)
Subjects: LCSH: East Indians--Fiction. | Women--Fiction.
Classification: DDC 823.914--dc23

Printed in Singapore by Fabulous Printers Pte Ltd

With the support of

NATIONAL ARTS COUNCIL
SINGAPORE

To Cynthia vanden Dreisen,
with thanks

PROLOGUE

Some memories have the power to shape a life forever. Dim as shadows behind a curtain, shifting and uncertain, they are all the more menacing for that. When later in her life she remembered that day Sita was unsure of the details, she was only certain of the outcome. She still recalled the muddy skin of the water reflecting the sky above, hiding the darkness below.

She had been five or maybe six years old. She remembered walking with her mother beside the river, gathering wild herbs to make a poultice for grandmother's aching knee. That day, as she ran about the riverbank, her mother stopped and began to groan, low at first and then louder. Stumbling into the long grass they usually avoided because of snakes, she squatted down, partly hidden by the scrub, pulling up her sari as all the women did when answering the call of nature out in the fields. As her mother's cries grew intense, Sita ran forward. The vegetation screened but did not completely obscure a view of her mother, who was now moaning and panting like an animal. As Sita watched, she reached down and lifted up a bloodied mass from between her legs. Sita shrank back in shock; her mother's insides appeared to be pushing out unstoppably from her body.

'Amma!' Sita shouted, distress leaping through her.

Then, something moved and twisted and began to scream, and she saw that her mother held in her hands a creature with life and voice. Pulling a handful of soft leaves from a nearby bush, her mother wiped the child and, lifting the small curved knife she carried at her waist when they collected herbs, cut the cord that tied the baby to her. Eventually, holding the child in the crook of her arm, her mother stood up and walked towards the river.

'Where are you going?' Sita yelled, filled by new confusion.

'I must wash her clean,' her mother replied.

Wading knee deep into the water, she lowered the child into the soft lapping swell, holding her there, caressing her tenderly all the while with her one free hand. For a moment Sita saw the child in her mother's arms and the next she was gone, the tide lifting her free. Sita watched her float away, held briefly upon the rippling surface of the river before she sank slowly from sight, eyes open, a startled expression on her small face, uttering no cry of protest.

'Amma!' Sita screamed.

Her mother continued to stand in the water, her back towards Sita, unmoving. At last she turned, and Sita remembered her body, slack and flat beneath the old sari, emptied of its burden. She turned to look up at the sky and the sinking sun, and Sita saw the anguish in her face.

'Amma!'

She called out again, unable to understand what was happening. Then her mother was beside her, taking her hand, pulling her homewards.

'She was just a girl.' Her mother spoke softly, her voice thick and strange.

'The current is strong, it lifted her from my arms,' her mother explained in a more normal tone as they began the walk back to the village.

Sita stared at the river, awash with the light of the sky, the soft lap of waves cuffing the bank. The murky water had closed over her sister as if she had never been. It was a swift flowing river with a treacherous current, used by those too poor to properly cremate their dead. The fish in the river were large and plump from an excess of pickings on half-burned bodies.

'The *devi* will protect her,' her mother whispered.

In the house, they kept a picture of the goddess Durga, riding upon a tiger. Sita liked this picture, as much for the tawny tiger as the radiant goddess. The creature's amber eyes held her own, as if something special passed between them. Although Sita's heart beat fast from all she had just witnessed, it was comforting to think the goddess and her tiger protected her sister.

Releasing Sita's hand, her mother walked ahead, not once looking back at the river. In the distance the sky cracked open upon the dying sun, gold and crimson and purple. Near the village, the silhouette of a dead tree, struck by lightning long before, stood against the burning sky like a gnarled hand pushing up from the earth. Sita paused for a moment before the image, seeing it anew, then hurried after her mother.

1

There was the click of the door as Parvati left, and then the rap of her heels fading away outside the apartment. Soon the whirr of a descending lift was heard, carrying her down to where she had parked her car in the forecourt of the building. Amita turned to her mother, no longer able to control her irritation.

'Why won't you talk to her?'

She bent to wipe away a biscuit crumb clinging to Sita's mouth, aware of the unnecessary roughness with which she did this. As always, her mother's behaviour was unfathomable. Even the usually patient Parvati had given a sigh, packing away her notepad and checking her watch in a way that made it clear she thought the visit had been a waste of precious time.

The late afternoon sun streamed into the room and fell cruelly upon Sita's dark hair, illuminating a bed of white roots. Amita noted resignedly that soon she would have to help her mother cover this new growth, painting thick dye onto the brittle strands of hair, wrapping plastic sheets around them both, taking care to cover the floor with newspaper. Already, at the thought of these procedures her impatience grew. It seemed bizarre that, in her late seventies, her mother kept her hair resolutely black, while Amita in her early fifties rejected such artifice and welcomed the streaks of grey.

'You should let your hair stay white,' Amita reprimanded, still full of resentment.

Shifting her weight in an aged rattan chair, aware of Amita's tight-lipped frustration, Sita stared out of the window of her daughter's Clementi apartment, twelve storeys up from the ground, and wished she were a bird. She would not let her hair go white. It was nothing to do with revealing her age, as Amita thought. She could not tell her daughter that the colour white must be resisted in every way, no white blouse — no white nightdress, *no white hair*. She remembered the day she had made that vow.

Staring silently out of the window at the banks of trees and tall apartment blocks, Sita continued to ignore her daughter's agitation and imagined the elation a bird must feel, soaring free above the earth. Far across the town and beyond the nearby university where Amita taught, were the red-roofed shophouses and narrow lanes of Little India. Buried amongst them was the home she had lived in all her adult life and to which she could no longer return. Several months ago Sita had had a bad fall and, resisting all argument, Amita arrived to briskly pack up her mother's few possessions and move her into the Clementi flat.

'You can no longer look after yourself properly, or climb safely up and down those stairs,' Amita had announced, pointing to the twisting metal staircase that rose from the courtyard to Sita's front door.

A sudden low grinding announced the ancient clock on the wall was preparing to strike, and Amita allowed it four afternoon chimes before she trusted herself to speak again. Her mother had brought the clock with her from her old home when she moved in with her. Now, its crotchety clangs once again measured out her life as they had through her childhood. She hated the thing. As the last rusty reverberation died away she turned to her mother, hands on hips, annoyance rising within her.

'If you will not talk to Parvati, then you and all those other women in that army of yours will be forgotten. Is that what you want?' Amita reached to gather up dirty teacups from the table.

The cane chair creaked as Sita shifted her weight apprehensively. Parvati was writing a book about the Indian National Army in which Sita had been a recruit during the war. She had never spoken much to anyone about her time in the Rani of Jhansi Regiment, but now because of Parvati's book she was being questioned about things she had been careful to keep to herself. Memories rose up within her, painful as the hot dry earth beneath her bare feet when, as a child in India, she had walked to the village well.

Long ago, on the riverbank near that village home, Sita had seen a clam pried open and the soft flesh of its body scraped clean of the shell. That was how she felt about Parvati and the interviews. Soon, she would be forced apart, and bit-by-bit, memories would be extracted from her. Soon she feared she would be like those people whose minds were wiped clean by dementia, who no longer knew who they were. Her memories were a bundle of kindling she carried within her, to light for warmth whenever the need arose; she had no wish to share them with a stranger, disturbing the many things that lay comfortably buried. Once a memory was voiced it would no longer belong only to her. It had become a battle to keep things back.

In spite of her reluctance to be interviewed, Amita noted the trouble Sita had taken for Parvati's visit, wearing a sari instead of the usual slacks, putting on a pair of small gold earrings. She envied her mother her elegance and, when she could admit it, the much lighter complexion of her skin. When Amita was younger and people remarked on the dissimilarity between them, she took comfort in the fact that she had inherited the darker genes of the father she had never known. With an exasperated clatter, she piled the last teacup onto the tray. Her mother's stubbornness defeated her. Other women who had been part of the Rani of Jhansi Regiment were only too happy to talk about their experiences, many even called it the best time of their lives. Her mother, as always, had to be different, had to be difficult. When Parvati first told Amita about her proposed book, and heard that Sita had been a recruit in the Indian National Army, she could not contain her excitement.

'Your *mother* was a Rani in the Jhansi Regiment? That's incredible! History has neglected the INA women, just because they were women.'

During the Occupation, the Japanese military had formed a special force, the Indian National Army, from Indian POWs taken from the British Army. It was intended these men would spearhead an eventual Japanese invasion of India. Later, the legendary Indian freedom fighter, Subhas Chandra Bose, arrived in Singapore to take command of the INA, and formed a women's regiment.

'Any women of the regiment still alive are now getting really old. I *must* speak to your mother,' Parvati insisted.

Amita could still hear Parvati's words in her head as she picked up the tray and stalked off to the kitchen.

Sita continued to stare silently out of the window, as if unaware of her daughter's disappointment. Holding her face up to the sun she closed her eyes, feeling the warmth seeping through her bones. How the sun had burned them on the retreat from Burma, and in the jungle leeches had clung to their limbs! She remembered again the constant hunger, the fear of crocodiles as they forded a river. To speak about those long ago things was no problem for her; it was the fear of unwrapping experience that held her back. Layer by layer she would be forced to divest herself of memory, digging down through time to exhume each detail, and eventually they would reach the thing she had so carefully buried, the one thing she wished no one to know. If she began that unravelling, there would be no way to stop until she reached the end, and then her daughter would know the truth.

Soon, she heard Amita returning with a fresh pot of tea, her tread light but determined. Glancing up, Sita observed Amita's single-minded expression, and knew her ordeal was not yet over. Her daughter was as intellectually strong as any man, Sita thought, and she could not suppress her pride at Amita's fierce independence.

'It won't make any difference to the world if no one hears your story. But your life and everything you did will then be as *nothing*. Is that what you want?' Amita deposited a cup of fresh tea and a plate of her mother's favourite jam-centred biscuits on the table.

Sita shrank from the impatience in her daughter's voice, agitatedly smoothing the folds of her sari over her knee. Nothing. Her life had been shaped by that word. You are *nothing*, her mother-in-law had told her. We are *nothing*, Billi had insisted as they begged for alms in the street. You women are *nothing*, the Japanese had laughed. You were *nothing* until I married you, Shiva had told her. Anger rolled through her as it always did when these thoughts took hold of her. *Nothing.* The word remained alive within her when everything else was forgotten. Sita was suddenly aware that her daughter was waiting for a reply to her query.

The sun was now hidden behind banks of cloud. In the distance, the sea darkened beneath a sky suddenly leaden with approaching rain. Across that black water was the country from which she had journeyed, and to which she would now never return.

'Maybe you will learn things you don't want to know.' Sita heard the rogue words escaping her and was surprised. Amita paused, cup in hand.

'Talk to Parvati,' she urged, kinder now she felt a weakening in her mother, placing a hand on Sita's shoulder.

'Your life is my history, it's part of me. I have a right to know.' Amita's voice was soft with persuasion.

In the mirror above a worn sideboard Sita caught a glimpse of herself, an old woman, bent and cadaverous, her face unrecognisable even to herself, the skin drawn tightly over bones it should pad, loose where once it was tight. Her eyes moved to the thickset, middle-aged woman who stood by her side, remembering the baby she had once cradled and nursed. The colour of Amita's coarse grey hair, cut bluntly to swing about the base of her neck, contrasted strikingly against the deeper shade of her skin. Beauty was not a word ever wasted on Amita, but her strong square face with its darkly candid eyes was arresting. Energy sparked through her, lighting her up when her mood was good, drawing people to her. She had never married, and Sita found no reason to encourage matrimony when she looked back over her own experiences. It was better if a woman could be more like a man, self sufficient, one-in-herself, relying on no one, and able to look after an old mother, just as a son would have done.

'Soon I will be dead,' Sita admitted, seeing in a flash of clarity all the damage she might have done Amita by her persistent silence.

Old age was already upon her, but for decades she had lived a lie, and pulled Amita along behind her. The girl had a right to know the truth, whatever the consequences. She looked down at her hands, twisting a ring on her finger. The breath trembled through her as she tried to speak, and Amita bent low to catch her words.

'Tell Parvati to come again tomorrow,' Sita whispered, a sense of relief filling her as she spoke.

The next day Sita noticed Amita's pleasure when she made an effort to smile at Parvati on her arrival. In an attempt to set Sita at ease, Parvati waived her use of a digital recorder. She was some years younger than Amita, and her colleague in the Department of English Language and Literature at the National University of Singapore. Until recently Amita had thought of Parvati in the same way she regarded everyone in the department, with professional camaraderie. Then, a newly initiated course in Gender Studies required them to work closely together, deepening their association. They learned more about each other's families, confided minor personal details, and sought each other's advice on various topics.

Of dark-skinned Tamil ancestry, Parvati's forbears had arrived in Malaya from Tamil Nadu generations before as indentured labourers on the many rubber plantations in the country. That past was now long forgotten for her community, and Parvati was a respected academic. A slight woman of quick movement and bird-like intensity, she waited patiently across the table, notepad open and pen poised, ready to deposit Sita's words on the page.

Sita stared at her unflinchingly. The woman's thick curly hair was drawn tightly back into a pink band on her neck, from where it sprang free in a bushy tail. Her short cotton dress rose high on her thighs when she sat down, baring bony knees. What criteria determined which memories were of use for her book and which were not, Sita wondered. Sometimes she spoke at length and Parvati wrote nothing, and sometimes she said but a few words and the woman lowered her head and scribbled away at length. Whatever it was she wrote, Sita knew what Amita said was true, a mother's life is a daughter's history. She searched for the right place to begin.

'You never know when you do something for the last time,' she said, trying to put words to the recollections welling up within her now. A last glimpse of someone, the last closing of a door, a last word spoken; there was always the expectation that the moment would reappear, conversations continue, doors reopen, the festering emotions of a quarrel reignite or subside. Unable to frame these thoughts in words, she kept to the facts of that last day with Shiva, before they left separately for Burma and the war.

'It was raining,' she remembered. 'I wore a sari to please him, although by then I was so used to my army uniform, to wearing shorts or trousers. In the regiment, we all liked the freedom trousers gave us. In those clothes, we walked like men.' Sita gave a slight smile, moving her shoulders in an imitation of masculine swagger, remembering the pleasure of striding about.

Immediately, Parvati began to write and Amita leaned forward, her lips parted expectantly. Her spectacles, as always, slid down her nose and she quickly pushed them back up. Sita paused, her gaze returning to the window, seeing in her mind her old home in Norris Road, behind the nearby Ramakrishna Mission, with its ornate roof of domed pavilions. A spiral staircase twisted up to her front door, and a plant in a rusty oil drum stood beside it. If she had her way she would be living there still, in the room she had shared with Shiva, where she had brought up her child. Now, settled in her daughter's house, Sita knew at last that the past was a distant place, insubstantial and shifting as her memories, and felt bereft.

'I was quarrelling with him when we parted. I'm sorry now for that,' Sita confessed.

'It was war, you knew he might die,' Amita was unable to suppress the condemning edge in her voice. Instinctively, at any mention of her father she always found herself taking his side, although she had no memory of him.

'Even when death is all around, you never think it will come for you. We were given a day off to be together before each of us left separately for Burma.' Images spiralled up before Sita as she spoke.

'I wore a sari, not my uniform. I wanted to please him,' she repeated, anxious that these young women should think well of her.

Instead, she saw the slight rise of Amita's eyebrows, and knew she had made a mistake. Today's young women had different attitudes from those imbued into her. At times she noticed Parvati and Amita exchanging a conspiring glance, as if humouring her eccentricity, and controlled her resentment. What did they know of her life?

Yet it was not her mother Amita was thinking about as she raised an eyebrow, but her father. Why did her mother stress she had worn a sari to please her husband? In spite of his education, was her father's view of women a traditional one? Had he encouraged his wife to join the army or had he been against it? Was their marriage an arranged one, or did they marry for love? If he had lived, would he have urged Amita to marry? She had only one old creased photograph of her father. Shiva stood in the shade of a tree behind his pupils at the Ramakrishna

Mission School, a tall man with a narrow, intelligent face and a shock of thick black hair. To Amita's regret little more could be seen of him behind his pupils, and no other pictures had survived. He had been a teacher, an educated man, and she was sure he would have been proud of her position at the university, proud that she earned enough to look after her mother.

'Then we both left for Burma, for different destinations, by different routes, different trains,' Sita added hurriedly, not wanting the painful burden of memory thrusting up within her now.

The mirror reflected the back of Parvati's head. Sita observed the knobbly line of the woman's spine beneath the floral dress, the smooth curve of her buttocks and thighs, the bare protruding knees. The woman was at ease with her body, as was Amita, in spite of her weight. They did not know the shame associated with exposing their limbs in the way Sita had felt that first day in the Bras Basah camp. They did not know the shame she had felt at being a woman, or the far place from where she had journeyed.

*You have changed…you were nothing when I married you…*she heard Shiva's words again, and her bitterness deepened. All the old injustices hardened, pushing her down into the dark space that seemed ordained for her, from where she had struggled free. She could not assemble words as Amita did, using them like a sword to cut through attack or confusion. She wanted to tell these young women — because I have changed, you too could change, because I did what I did, you now do what you do. She did not know how to explain this, but she knew it was true.

And she knew too that at last she must put words to her story, if not for Amita, then for herself. To speak would be to experience again her experiences, to weigh them anew in her mind.

Before her on the table was a stack of old photographs she had found the previous night, in a box unopened for decades. She fanned them out on the table before her now, until she found the one she wanted.

'That's me there. It was the day Netaji came to meet us.' She stubbed a finger on the old black and white print, first pointing out herself, and then Subhas Chandra Bose.

'And that is Muni. She was my friend.' Her finger moved to the image of the slight woman standing beside her. As Sita stared at the image of Muni with her thin face and burning eyes, a sense of loss overwhelmed her. She returned her gaze hurriedly to the figure of Subhas Chandra Bose, whom they always called Netaji, Great Leader. He stood with his back to the photographer, surveying the girls lined up on a field before him in their uniforms of khaki shirts and jodhpurs, narrow caps set at a jaunty angle upon their heads, shoulders pulled back, heads held high. Sita's hand rested on the butt of the rifle at her side. Netaji's high polished boots and portly frame were instantly recognisable, and even now Sita remembered the glint of his spectacles, the smoothness of his voice, the faint scent of sandalwood soap as he stepped forward to speak to them. In the foreground of the photo, wearing dark glasses and the stripes of her rank, Captain Lakshmi saluted smartly.

Sita pushed another photo over the table to Parvati, who looked down at it with interest. In the picture a group of Ranis, guns held out before them, crawled forward stealthily on their stomachs, practicing the art of ambush. The scent of the hot dry earth and the crushed grass that stained their uniforms, came back again to Sita as she stared at the photo. She remembered the heat of the sun on her back, searing through her cotton shirt.

'We were practising guerrilla warfare. Wild lemongrass grew in the camp in Burma. We crushed it and rubbed the juice all over us to keep off mosquitoes. There were so many mosquitoes there.'

The scent of lemongrass had pervaded everything. The past rose up before her as she closed her eyes; smells and sensations she thought long forgotten she found her body had held onto, and released to her now.

'Shut your eyes. Think back. What comes into your mind?' Amita leaned towards her mother, her tone encouraging.

As Parvati picked up the photographs, examining them intently, Sita turned to the window to stare again across the urban sprawl of the town with its high-rise buildings interlocked with banks of lush green vegetation, to the distant view of the sea. Across the Black Water lay India, and somewhere in that endless continent was buried the village from where she had come, the hot dry earth cracked by the sun, hardened and sharp beneath her feet as pieces of broken ceramic, the water dry in the well in summer, the air plagued with the fever that took her parents one by one as they waited in vain for the monsoon, scanning the sky for clouds each day. A short distance beyond the village was the wide Yamuna River, immune to their every sorrow, touching them all in both life and death.

She saw again in her mind the dark water of the Yamuna, sombre as stone. The distant bank was far away, another country, with figures no taller than her thumb. The river pulsed with suppressed energy that came from deep within it, always moving, its thick scent filling her nostrils, expanding in her head. Upon its banks rested numerous small temples where ash-smeared holy men meditated above the fast flowing water, the religious minded bathed below, seeking blessings or redemption. On the stone *ghats* of temples cremations took place, the smoke of funeral pyres billowing up, the cooled ashes of the dead fed to the river. Women gossiped as they laundered clothes, fishermen hauled in nets of thrashing mercurial bounty, turtles rested in the cool mud of the shore while egrets stalked the shallows for fish. To all things, the river gave life and nurture. The goddess Yami, who lived in the river, was the sister of Yama, God of Death. Bathing in these sacred waters, grandmother said, freed a person from the torments of death. Sita remembered how she and her brother, Dev, had sat by the river after their parents died.

2
INDIA, 1932–1936

Sita sat beside her brother on a flat protruding rock, kicking her bare heels against the muddy riverbank. The sad weight of the day hung upon them.

Earlier, a fisherman had rowed them out midstream in his boat, along with a priest, Dev clutching the box of their father's ashes. Crowded with family, the craft sailed dangerously low in the water. While the priest chanted prayers, Dev, as the eldest son, scattered the ashes into the fast flowing current, a handful at a time. Mixed with the ashes were melted calcium deposits, and these floated on the water like small white stars before slowly sinking into the depths.

'Where does the river go to?' Sita asked as they sat together now. Dev was older than her and knew the answer to most things.

'All rivers flow into the sea. There, the Black Water waits for them. The creatures in the sea cannot live unless they drink pure river water.'

'What happens to Yami when she reaches the sea? Does she swim out into the ocean?' Sita thought of the river goddess, lithe and graceful as a fish, formless as water, long hair flowing about her.

'Yami remains in the river, that is her home. The ocean is the world of Varuna, god of the sea.'

Their village, Sagarnagar, stood on the bank of the great Yamuna River, and was named after a rich man who endowed the place with a small school and a well. The village was between the holy cities of Mathura and Vrindavan, where the god Krishna was said to have spent his youth. They knew no other home.

'What will happen to us now?'

Sita looked down at the river and thought of their father's ashes drifting through the muddy silt, food for a multitude of fish, mixing with the residue of the many other cremations that were scattered daily into the river. The Yamuna swallowed them all. There must be another river beneath the river, she thought, where the spirits of those tipped into the sacred waters swam with the river goddess. A place where she imagined her sister lived, whenever she remembered her.

In just a little over a year, they had lost both parents. Their mother died the previous year of a fever that visited the village at the end of the monsoon; doctors and holy men were powerless before the pestilence. Weakened by a new pregnancy, Sita's mother fell ill, and all they could do was watch her die. Grandmother kept a vigil beside her, praying to be taken first, but soon it was over. Too many people died too quickly, and the village temple was pressured by the constant cremations. Oil and wood had to be rationed, each allowance barely enough to render a body to ash. Half-cremated corpses were regularly being tipped into the Yamuna.

After her mother's death, the weight of the silent house was so great Sita and her grandmother grew mute beneath it. Sita took over her mother's duties, peeling vegetables, picking leaves off the stems of wilting coriander, grinding flour, churning butter, pounding spices, and cooking. Once these chores were finished there was always mending, sewing, the fetching of cowpats for the fire, work that kept her busy all day. Whatever Sita did, the sound of her mother's voice, singing the old songs of the millstone, echoed in her head and weighed on her heart.

Within the cool, muted light of the house where she spent her day, the bright square of the open door was always before her, the searing radiance of the sun suffusing the world beyond the threshold. Each morning the men of the house crossed over that threshold, Dev to go to school, her father to the shop. They walked out into the brilliance of the day, into a masculine world of commerce and complexity, leaving the women behind in the shadowy realms of the house.

A year after their mother died, their father came home with a gash on his hand from a rusty nail. The poison spread quickly through his veins, and soon he too sickened and died. The neighbours gathered around in shock, doing what they could. Dev was now the man of the house and the villagers helped him to arrange the cremation, contributing what little they could.

Kanta Aunty and her husband, Ashok Uncle, hurried over from nearby Vrindavan, just as they had done when their mother had died. Kanta Aunty was Sita's father's sister, his only surviving sibling, a plump woman who bustled around, finding fault with whatever and whomever she could. She had married a man who had grown suddenly rich in ways no one could fully explain, and now lived in a house in the middle of town with running water and an outside toilet. Her visits to her brother and mother were rare occurrences, and during each visit she never failed to complain in a loud hoarse voice of the backwardness of the village. Her husband, tall and gaunt, stood silently beside his wife, his eyes sliding about beneath lowered lids, never looking directly at anyone. Women did not attend cremations, but Kanta Aunty bribed the priest at the temple to load the pyre amply with wood, and instructed her husband to check that enough oil was poured on to burn the corpse properly to ash.

While the priest chanted prayers, Dev scattered their father's ashes over the water. Sita looked down into the darkness of the river, and the shadows of grey carp swarming beneath her, and she knew she was entering a new life. There was no way back to what had been, and what lay ahead was unknowable.

Now, as they sat beside the Yamuna in the dying light of the afternoon, Dev was silent, chin upon his knees, arms clasped about his drawn up legs.

'What will happen to us now?' Sita asked again, her eyes on the road leading out of the village, where the corrugated metal roof of her father's dry goods shop could just be glimpsed.

Each day, when school was over, Dev had joined their father at the shop, sitting on a high stool behind jars of biscuits and pulses and sugar, learning the trade. Stacked up around him were brushes and brooms, metal buckets, insecticide sprays, dustpans, matches, oil and wicks for lamps, mousetraps, rat poison and packets of tea.

'I am going to sell the business to one of the villagers. He is giving me a good price. You will stay with grandmother, and I will go to the Faraway Places, to Singapore, where it is said lots of money can be made. I will send money to you and grandmother from there.'

Sita stared at Dev in shock, remembering the men who had come to the village some months before. They rode a bullock cart strung with bright bunting, beating a drum as if to announce a wedding. They were labour agents from Mathura, who offered a handful of silver to any man who would agree to work in the Faraway Places. They shouted out the strange names of these places, Malaya, Singapore, Penang, Ipoh, and sang a song about how men had only to reach these lands for gold to fall into their hands. Dev was excited, but the men laughed and said he was too young to be sent to the rubber estates of Malaya. Yet, afterwards, one of them said it was possible for him to go by himself to Singapore and find work. The man told him that in the nearby town of Mathura, he could buy a railway ticket to Calcutta, and even recommended someone in that great city who would help him get a passage on a boat to Singapore.

'Don't go.' Sita shook his arm in alarm, but Dev stared resolutely at the distant bank of the river, at the small figures there going about their business.

In the following days, no amount of tears could dissuade Dev from his decision to go off to work in the Faraway Places. Grandmother kept repeating that those places lay across the Black Water, and crossing the *Kala Pani* would mean a loss of caste and identity, and an end to the possibility of a good reincarnation. And when, if ever, would they see him again?

'In those places the gods cannot protect you. Also, no water from the holy Ganges or Yamuna rivers is there to wash away your sins.' Grandmother's soft face was aquiver with grief, tears filled her eyes, already opaque with cataract.

Sita stood by her grandmother's side, feeling the old woman's pain, and seeing in her mind the endless expanse of rolling black water, a great beast that would swallow her brother and spit him out on some far shore, to be separated from them forever.

'The ships that carry us across the *Kala Pani* have large *matkas* of Ganges water on them. The holy river travels with us in those large pots, and the gods continue to protect us just as if we were still in India,' Dev assured the old lady, flashing a confident grin.

Soon grandmother and Sita were left alone. They watched as Dev, stooping beneath the bundle of belongings on his back, climbed into a farmer's bullock cart for the ride to the main road to catch the bus into Vrindavan. They watched until they could see him no more.

Neighbours came and went, comforting, supporting as best they could. Kanta Aunty visited, pressing money into grandmother's hand. At night Sita was unable to sleep, and lay listening to the old woman's soft breathing, and to the scuttle of rats and the rustle of insects in the roof above, wondering when she would see her brother again.

Now that they were alone Sita and grandmother slept together on a large string bed, and as the night descended, grandmother soothed them both by telling stories of the gods.

Grandmother was the keeper of history, a spinner of tales that could transport Sita into unknown worlds. Settled beside the old woman, head at rest upon the soft bolster of her breast, breathing in the comforting kitchen odours grandmother exuded, Sita stared up at a colourful religious calendar on the wall, depicting the *devi* on her tiger steed, and listened to the old tales. Best of all she loved the story of how the *devi*, the great Goddess Durga, came to be. Within the magic of the tale Sita could forget the sadness that surrounded her.

Above, from the calendar, the goddess gazed down upon them, her face radiant, the architect of her own life, not a passive participant as were mortal women. Her many arms held the tools of self-reliance as she navigated her way through her celestial world. According to grandmother, the *devi* was a no-child no-husband woman, and so could do the things she did.

As she told the *devi*'s tale, grandmother huffed and puffed at the appropriate times, her voice taking on the gruff tone of a deity, the whine of an evil *rakshasa*, or the strong but gentle voice of the goddess.

'There was a time when the great devil, Mahishasura, was terrifying the world. Whatever the gods did they could not defeat him. The battle went on without end until the gods decided to ask the Great Source, from which they were all derived, for help. They began to pray, and so great was the praying power of so many mighty gods, that at last it caused the *devi* to take form. She appeared in the distance, coming towards them out of the mists of the heavens. She rode upon a tiger, her face radiating light, her eighteen arms each grasping a different weapon in preparation for the battle ahead. The gods had been waiting for this moment, but now they looked at each other in confusion, not believing that in response to their prayers a female instead of a male god had materialised. Although they bowed politely before the *devi*, behind her back they grumbled bitterly, and joked about the impossibility of a weak female succeeding when they, with all their masculine powers, had failed. Let her go, let her try, let's see what she will do with that old devil Mahishasura, they laughed as they sent her off to do their work, happy for her to face death while they watched from afar.

'Now, the *devi* was well aware of their scornful laughter, but she ignored their rudeness. Understanding the great task that lay ahead, she searched within herself, calling forth all her inner power, her *shakti*, in a great rage of white energy that boiled and throbbed and fumed and blazed. At last all that energy spilt from her, causing the most ferocious part of herself to take a separate form. And lo and behold! That black-skinned creature Kali sprang forth from the *devi*'s brow, to help her in the great fight ahead.

'And so the battle began, and it was terrible. The *devi* fought and fought. Kali's long tongue sucked up blood and demons, devouring all their evil. And that devil Mahishasura tried all his old tricks. Every time he was killed he would take another form and jump up again to fight. If he was killed as a bear, he got up as a monkey, or a serpent, or a wall of fire. Then at last he got up as a buffalo, thickset and powerful, but slow on his feet, pawing the ground in rage. Seeing her opportunity, the *devi* sprang forward, and with one great blow finally chopped off his head, severing it clean from his body before piercing his heart with her sword. And at last Mahishasura lost the power to take a new form, and fell dead before the *devi*.

'Then, when it was clear the battle was over, the male Gods ran forward and praised the *devi* loudly.

'They acted as if they had never said a bad word behind her back,' grandmother said with a deep chuckle. 'So many powerful male gods, all of them strutting around the universe like brave warriors, and yet they could not defeat that wily old Mahishasura. The Great Force created a *goddess* to do their work for them, not another male god! That is how powerful a woman's *shakti* is.'

Grandmother liked this end to her story as much as Sita, and, looking up in admiration at the goddess upon the wall, they allowed themselves to laugh, but softly, so that the Gods, if they were listening, would not hear.

After he left the village, Dev wrote them the occasional letter from the town called Singapore. His few years in the village schoolroom had not resulted in any fluency of the written word, and his news came to them through a professional letter writer. Dev wrote that he had found a job as a *peon* in a large hardware and dry goods store in Serangoon Road, the place where most of the Indians in Singapore lived. As the shop sold many of the things similar to their father's stall, Dev was familiar with the trade. He also wrote that gold did not line the streets of Singapore, but with hard work he could go forward, making his way up in the hierarchy of the shop. His salary was more than he could earn in the village and, true to his promise, each month he sent a small amount to his grandmother.

Dev's letters were irregular, but Sita waited for the excitement of seeing them in the postman's hand. The village schoolteacher helped them reply to Dev, writing as grandmother dictated, and personally posting the letters for them. Each time their reply was sent off, Sita imagined the oceans the small square of paper must cross to reach her brother and how, finally, he would tear the envelope open and read the few lines written there, and know they thought of him still.

Nobody knew how old grandmother was, but after the death of her son and his wife and the departure of her grandson, her spirit no longer lit up her face, but remained inescapably wedged deep inside her. Often, she did not hear Sita speak, her cloudy eyes fixed on a distant place. Sometimes she talked as if the old days were still around her, and the family about to gather for the evening meal. She cooked for five when they were only two, and leftovers must be given to the fingerless leper or the untouchables in the village, who were always grateful for food in whatever condition. She grew thin and began to bump into things. Sita massaged the old woman's aching joints with coconut oil and steered her about, but one morning she failed to wake up. Sita ran to the neighbours, the priest and the doctor were called and confirmed that the old woman was dead.

A message was sent to Kanta Aunty, and she and her husband soon arrived. Once again after the cremation, they all rowed out into the river with the priest, to scatter grandmother's ashes upon the water. Ashok Uncle wrote a letter to Dev telling him of the sad developments, and instructing him to transfer the monthly money for Sita's upkeep to a bank account in Vrindavan. Since no one was left to care for Sita, Kanta Aunty was forced to take her in.

Sita had only been a few times to her aunt's house and did not know her cousins well. Neeta and Niti were not happy at her arrival and made this clear immediately.

'If you do not do everything we say the baboons will come for you,' they threatened.

In a nearby grove of swaying bamboo the creatures could be heard crashing about. Kanta Aunty joined in, her eyes alight with cruel mischief.

'At night they steal into houses and take away babies to eat, tearing them apart, limb from limb.'

So great was Sita's fear and confusion that she believed these tall tales. The baboons roamed everywhere around the house; they sat on the courtyard wall, ran across the roof and peered threateningly through window grilles, baring yellow teeth. A long barbed prod was kept in the house to keep the creatures at bay.

'We have no room for you here, and no money to keep you. We have taken you in only from the goodness of our hearts, and for my dead brother's sake,' Kanta Aunty told Sita.

'You must help in the house; I cannot afford to keep you like my daughters. Life in town is expensive, not cheap as in the village. Your brother sends but a pittance for your upkeep.' Kanta Aunty's brow furrowed disapprovingly.

Although her aunt and her family slept on cotton stuffed
mattresses on string beds, Sita was given a servant's rush mat
to lie upon. To everyone's surprise, she chose to sleep in a
storeroom off the kitchen, spreading out her mat beside metal
bins of rice and jars of lemon and mango pickle. Unbeknown
to her aunt, she chose this place because a calendar on the wall
with a bright picture of the goddess Durga, was similar to the
one Sita and grandmother had slept beneath. The *devi* sat as
always upon her tiger, face alight with benevolence.

From where she lay Sita looked up at the picture, and it
seemed the goddess smiled protectively down upon her. Sita
remembered her grandmother's story and knew the *devi* was
like no other immortal, moving easily between death and life,
darkness and light, the edge of existence and its centre. Much
as she missed a soft cotton mattress, Sita slept peacefully on her
rush mat beneath the gaze of the goddess.

In her aunt's house Sita learned anew how to cook and to clean,
but not willingly as she had beside her grandmother in the
village, sharing work with the old lady. Now, she was made to
understand she was a poor relative, and used as such. Stretched
out lazily on their beds, Neeta and Niti called for Sita to massage
their nubile limbs. To improve their complexions, they used
facemasks of almonds and rice soaked overnight, that Sita must
grind to a paste with milk and honey each morning. They were
educated girls, staying on at school until eighth standard, long
enough to increase their chances on the marriage market, but
not long enough to give them independent ideas. Kanta Aunty

herself had no education, but had seen the advantage a touch of learning might bring her daughters in a modern world.

Dev's letters now came to Ashok Uncle, and Sita was not informed of their arrival. Once, sure she had seen the Singapore letter-writer's distinctive script amongst the pile of post, Sita asked Ashok Uncle for news of Dev. With a sigh, he bent to retrieve a crumpled ball of paper from a metal rubbish bucket and gave it to her.

'You cannot read, so what will you understand? He is asking how you are; we are telling him you are well. It is rash and childish behaviour to go and live so far away when he has responsibilities still at home. If parents are dead then it is the duty of a brother to get a sister married. Instead, he is putting all responsibility on us.'

Sita smoothed out the crumpled paper, and just the sight of the letter-writer's intricately hatched script filled her with joy and grief. As her uncle said, she could not read what was written on the paper, but she knew Dev thought of her still. She took to checking the mail whenever she felt a letter was due, searching the rubbish bucket to retrieve Dev's discarded missive. Dev's letters, written on paper thin as onionskin, never stretched to more than one sheet, and Sita folded each neatly again and again until it became a small compressed square, easily secreted in a muslin bag and stored beneath her clothes. In her aunt's home, she lived only within the shape of each day, until the evening Kanta Aunty announced she would soon be getting married.

'A matchmaker has fixed it up for us. The money your brother sends for your upkeep is not even covering your food.

This is a good opportunity; the man is rich and is not asking for dowry. All he wants is to have a young wife. We have our own daughters to marry, we must first give dowries to them.'

'Does Dev *bhai* know I'm getting married? Have you written to him?' Sita's head reeled at the news, her heart fluttered with anxiety.

'Everything is finalised. By the time a letter is reaching your brother in Singapore and a reply is coming back, you will already belong to another house. Your brother will be grateful to us for finding you a rich husband.' Kanta Aunty laughed.

The sound filled Sita with a sense of finality, words of protest draining away inside her even as they formed.

'He is so old,' Sita whispered that night, crouched at her aunt's knee, remembering the visit of her bridegroom to the house earlier in the day.

She had been shut away in a back room, but a stolen glimpse of her future husband moving in the shadows of the house lingered with her. Her aunt looked askance at her.

'He is not yet fifty, and he is rich. His wife died only a year ago. His sons are already married and working; you will not be looking after small children. Remember, he is taking you without a dowry. You are already thirteen years old, old enough for marriage. Some brides are so young they must sit upon their father's lap throughout the wedding ceremony.'

Sita could not protest; she was dependent upon her aunt's charity and without voice in the flow of her life; she could remain forever in her aunt's house, no better than a servant, fetching, carrying, cooking, cleaning.

'I have done all this for my brother, your father,' her aunt remarked stiffly, acknowledging the righteousness of her deed.

'What will I call him, what is his name?' Sita implored, thinking again of the balding, large bodied man she had glimpsed. She pulled distractedly at her thick plait of hair, her nails bitten down to the quick. Her luminous eyes, the most arresting feature in her thin face, were filled with agitation.

'To you he has no name. You must call him, HE. Out of respect a wife never speaks the name her husband.' Kanta Aunty frowned in disapproval.

The intricate patterns of wedding *mehendi*, of flowers and birds and paisley leaves, covered Sita's hands and feet. The *mehendi* artists had come the day before to the house, and Kanta Aunty and Niti and Neeta had also had their hands painted, but only Sita, as the bride, decorated her feet. All night she had lain with her heels resting on a small stool and her hands unmoving at her side, so as not to smear the *mehendi* as it dried. In the morning, she washed off the henna, revealing the orange filigree beneath. She was told the name of her bridegroom had been secretly etched upon her, hidden within the elaborate designs, but what that name was she could not be told, for fear of bringing her husband ill luck.

Her aunt helped her dress in clothes gifted to her by her new in-laws. Sita was conscious of the silk sari with its crusty gold border, finer in quality than the sari her aunt had bought her, and unlike anything Sita had worn before; she was only used to the softness of her much-washed cotton shift or *kurta* and loose pyjamas. The sari width was made for an adult and, when draped about Sita's undersized body, the excess material had to be tucked into the drawstring of her petticoat, making a thick wad about her waist. Usually, her unruly hair sprang wildly about her shoulders, but now it was oiled and plaited and coiled high on her head, tamed for the life ahead. When at last she stood before a mirror, she did not recognise herself. The thin face and thick straight eyebrows, the bright eyes that her grandmother had said shone like two stars, her wide mouth — everything seemed changed. The severe hairstyle, the small gold earrings and the light chain necklace her aunt had given her, recast her in adult mould. She saw a reflection of the woman she would one day grow to be, an incongruous image superimposed upon her childish frame.

They piled into a horse drawn *gharry* for the journey to the wedding hall. Niti and Neeta giggled with excitement, and squeezed onto the seat opposite the adults with Sita. Kanta Aunty and her daughters wore items of finery superior to anything Sita owned, except the new sari from her in-laws. Her belongings were so few they were bundled into a carrying cloth and tied to the back of the *gharry*. Kanta Aunty, small and plump as a butterball, her deep-set eyes and determined chin resolute with purpose, took up most of the seat. Ashok Uncle, his long thin limbs folded together like a bundle of brooms, occupied much less of the seat. It was his habit to concede a greater share of the marriage ground to his wife; he seldom spoke, controlling her in the invisible ways a man had the power to invoke, a grunt, a frown, or a concentrated glower. His opinion was final and his wife grudgingly obeyed his orders.

A breeze blew about her as the carriage bowled along, and she listened to the clop of the horse's hooves rhythmically hitting the road. Inside her everything had stopped, as if she hung suspended in time.

'Your husband will give you a fine gold *mangalsutra* to put around your neck, to show everyone you are his wife,' Kanta Aunty informed her with satisfaction.

'Your husband will also give you a new name. Now you will belong to his family. Sita will die and you will be a new person. Maybe they'll call you Pushpa or Rukmini,' Niti giggled.

'Or Avantika or Ranjana,' Neeta laughed.

Sita was filled with panic. She did not want another name, imposing ownership upon her, killing that old self she knew so well. When her new family claimed her with a fresh name, would her memories remain intact? Would she still remember Dev and her grandmother? Would the images of her mother or father fade and die with the death of her old identity?

People swirled about them in the wedding hall, a blur of strange faces and voices. Sita was taken inside to sit alone in a dark corner, as if superfluous to the events taking place, while Kanta Aunty and her family waited outside to greet the bridegroom and his family. Soon, loud drumming and shouting announced the arrival of the wedding party, and eventually her aunt appeared to usher Sita forward amidst the crush of people. The sari dragged about her heels and she feared it would catch underfoot, pulling free of the petticoat and her waist. The silk covered her head and hung over her face, and she could see little as she was guided forward. As her aunt helped her to sit, Sita was aware of the great bulk of her bridegroom beside her.

At last the wedding rites began. The heat of the sacred fire spurted up as the priest began his ritual chanting, the sounds humming through the smoke of scented incense billowing about her. Sita kept her head down, conscious only of the man who would soon be her husband. At one point a bent and elderly woman approached, and Kanta Aunty, who sat close behind Sita, whispered that this was her mother-in-law. Then her bridegroom rose, and with his mother, bent over Sita. The sari still covered her face, and she could see little as her husband's large hands fumbled about her bare neck, securing the gold *mangalsutra* of marriage upon her. She caught the masculine smell of him, and the scent of raw onions on his breath.

At last Sita was helped to stand, to follow her husband around the sacred fire in the symbolic journey of matrimony. She was daubed with the red marks of marriage — the carmine *bindi* on her forehead and the *sindhoor* along the parting of her hair. At last her bridegroom placed upon her the wedding garland of sweet-smelling jasmine, making them man and wife. Her husband towered over her, she barely reached his chest, and the wedding sari, draped stiffly about her childish form, appeared to diminish her further. She reached up, struggling to loop the garland she had been given over his wedding turban. As he bent his head to accommodate her, she glimpsed the fleshy contours of his face.

He was an old man, grey-haired, his fleshy body as firmly bolstered as the horsehair sofa that stood in Kanta Aunty's house. His small eyes behind an upturned snout of a nose reminded Sita of the baboons that lived in the glade of swaying bamboo not far from the house. Trembling, she tried to back away, but came up against the press of people about her and knew there was nowhere to go.

Closing her eyes, she remembered her grandmother leading her by the hand to the temple on the banks of the river, and how in the dimness of that place, smelling of dank stone and incense, she had reached to touch the brass bell that called the gods; she remembered its quick sharp chime and how she had folded her hands before the image of the goddess, as her grandmother pushed her head down in obeisance. Tears filled her eyes at the memory, and she focused her thoughts on the *devi*, holding the image in her mind, praying for the strength grandmother always said the *devi* gave to those who sought her protection.

Even as she saw in her mind the goddess's glowing face, the weapons in her many hands and her tiger steed with its burning amber eyes, she heard a loud collective gasp from the people about her. At her side her husband staggered and clutched his chest, his eyes rolled up beneath his lids until only the whites were visible. As he lurched forward, his weight was thrown against Sita, almost knocking her off her feet. Falling to his knees in his bridal splendour, he writhed about, the gold turban tumbled from his head, his face turned crimson, then blue. A convulsion of loud and strangled sounds gurgled in his throat, foam bubbled from his mouth as he gasped for air. The wedding guests surged forward, shouting advice on how to handle an epileptic fit. Someone sat on the bridegroom's chest and held him down as he thrashed about, another thrust an old sandal beneath his nose, hoping the rancid odour of sweat and leather might revive the semi-conscious man, already choking on his tongue.

Sita drew back in horror until she could go no further, and stood flattened against a wall. Sliding down to sit on the floor, she covered her face with her hands, peering through her fingers at the writhing man. Eventually, there was silence. As she looked up the crowd drew back, and Sita saw her husband lying still on the floor before her. The wedding turban had rolled away, revealing the pointed bald dome of his head emerging from a ring of grey hair, like an egg from the warmth of a nest. Everyone turned to stare at Sita. The women began a loud wailing and as the lament rose about her, Sita knew her life had changed yet again, and that she was being blamed for her husband's death.

The body was placed on a bench and covered by a sheet. Beneath the shroud the mound of her husband's belly thrust up to the sky. The gold wedding turban that had rolled from his head was placed again upon him. Escaping the side of the shroud, the flowers of his wedding garland were still fresh and plump. Sita became aware of a low whispering of voices stirring through the crowd, like the sudden rustle of wind in a tree.

'As he lifted the sari, and her eyes fell upon him…'

'…devil…*shaitaan*…' The words were repeated about her.

'That creature has eaten her husband, has killed him,' a woman shouted.

People crowded about her, dragging her to her feet, their words beating upon her, neutering her of gender, now that she was a widow.

'Aunty,' she screamed, looking wildly about for her aunt, trying to twist free of the hands that now gripped her.

At last, through the crowd, she glimpsed her aunt with her husband and daughters, slipping hurriedly out of a door without a backward glance. The wedding was over and Sita was now the property of another household. Fate had unexpectedly turned her from bride to widow, but because the bridegroom had choked to death in the moments *after* the wedding rituals ended, and not in the moments *before*, Kanta Aunty was free of further responsibility for Sita, and a hundred witnesses were there to prove it. She knew it was the right moment to leave.

Even as Sita cried out, the women of her new family took hold of her, dragging her from the wedding hall, pulling her the short distance along the street to the bridegroom's home. Her hair was knocked loose, the plait unwinding down her back, pins scattering upon the road. The women pressed threateningly about her.

'You no longer need that,' her mother-in-law shouted, pointing to the gold *mangalsutra* about Sita's neck.

'No need for wearing jewellery ever again.'

She pushed her face close to Sita's, her eyes unhinged and wild. The loose skin of her arms, as finely creased as ancient silk or tissue paper, brushed Sita's lips as she fumbled with the catch of the necklace. Her breath, thickened by aniseed, beat upon Sita's face. In the shadows Sita glimpsed her father-in-law, slumped on a chair, silent with shock and grief.

As the *mangalsutra* was lifted from her neck, Sita instinctively raised a hand. The smooth gold still carried the warmth of her body upon it, and as she watched, the chain was returned to a blue velvet box that was locked with a tiny key. She imagined the ornament buried within the velvet, the heat of her flesh lingering upon it, leeching slowly away.

'Witch! devil!' Sita's mother-in-law cursed, and the women of the family chorused agreement.

'Most sinful of sinful creatures.'

Someone grasped her arms. The glass wedding bangles covering each thin wrist were smashed with a stone, the shards of coloured glass catching the light as they shattered about her, the ties of marriage broken as they fell.

'Now *this*, take it off.'

The women advanced upon her, pulling at the red wedding sari, ripping it from her body, stripping her down to her core. Another woman stepped forward to throw before her a widow's white cotton sari, bought hastily from a nearby shop.

'You'll wear this now until the day you die. A good woman dies before her husband.'

'*Amma*...mother...' she appealed to her new mother-in-law.

'*Aie Bhagwan!* What have we done that such a *shaitaan* should come to us?' Her mother-in-law muttered savagely, her eyes dark with fury.

Someone took hold of Sita again, and with a rough wet cloth began rubbing at the marks of marriage, at the red *bindi* that anointed her forehead and the *sindhoor* along the parting of her hair. Her palms were scrubbed repeatedly, but the intricate designs of bridal henna were already an indelible part of her and could not be easily wiped away.

'Now, *this*.' Her mother-in-law rushed at her again to lift the thick plait of hair off Sita's neck, thumping it down against her back.

Sita cried out in panic, realising what awaited her. Once more the women of the family surged about her. Pushed and prodded, half-falling, half-walking, she was propelled across rooms and down flights of stairs. The smell of sweat and attar of roses lifted off the angry women, and from their wedding finery the faint perfume of mothballs was released. Sita was dragged out of the house and into the blaze of the sun.

'You are nothing now, *nothing*,' the women screamed as they pulled her along.

In the small courtyard the barber, already alerted to his task, rose from where he crouched waiting in the shade of a tree, and came towards them. A stool was found, a towel was draped about her shoulders, water was brought in an enamel jug and the barber opened his bundle of implements.

'Careful,' Sita's mother-in-law warned as the man's blade and scissors flashed in the sun. The hair must be cut in one thick hank and as near Sita's skull as possible, for it would be given as alms to the local temple.

Soon it was done and the long plait of hair lay before Sita in a dented metal bowl, like a dismembered limb. The wedding guests stood in a silent circle about her, as the barber next set about shaving her skull. Sita's father-in-law observed her sourly from a distance, his lips tight, saying nothing before his wife's forceful ordering of events. On the high wall of the courtyard monkeys sat picking lice from each other's fur, oblivious of the furore below. A mangy pye-dog entered the courtyard through an open door, and settled to scratch itself near a water pump. The smell of cooking suddenly pervaded the yard as caterers heated great tureens of food to feed the guests who still swarmed about, preparing now not for a wedding but for a funeral.

At last, Sita put up a hand and felt the naked dome of her skull, sore and bleeding from the razor's rasp. Pulling the end of the cotton sari protectively over her head, she was aware of the rub of the cloth against her newly shorn skin. Immediately, her mother-in-law pulled the sari off Sita's head again, so that everyone could see her shame. Sita bowed her head, knowing she must endure this moment if she was to survive the day and all that lay beyond it.

Before nightfall, the bridegroom was cremated. Two heavy-jawed men, who Sita was informed were her stepsons, led male relatives from the house to the burning *ghats* by the river. There they would throw the first oil upon the pyre, igniting flames that would light up the darkening sky. The women waited at home, as custom demanded. From the nearby *ghats* the smell of incense, burning wood and roasting flesh drifted to them in the courtyard of the house. The women of the family tended Sita's grieving mother-in-law who, sobbing and beating her breast, continued to shout shrill curses at Sita.

'Die with him in those flames! In your next life may you bear only daughters, and never a son.'

Sita stood by herself. An evening breeze lifting off the river stirred the spindly tree in the courtyard; bats flew in and out of its branches. A brass water vessel stood on a wall beside her, a nearby lantern lighting its metal surface. Upon it Sita saw the mirroring of her own face. It must be her, she realised, for no one else stood there. Without the frame of hair, her eyes appeared enormous dark craters within a thin face. Her lips stretched grotesquely across her jaw, her nose appeared flattened, and the slight frame of her body in the white sari trailed away down the curve of the vessel, insubstantial as a ghost. The tonsured skull of the creature reflected to her was still stained by the red marks of marriage, the *bindi* and the *sindhoor*, as if her body clung to those marks, as it now clung to life. Eventually, the marks would fade, just as the painted swirls of henna on her hands would vanish, leaving her invisible to the world.

She wondered what would happen to her now; she was thirteen years old and a widow. Within the course of one day a husband had not only entered, but had also exited her life. His departure had left her an outcast, bound to a state of perpetual mourning, and she still did not know his name.

In the main house, the bridal bower, heavy with the perfume of flowers, the bed decorated with strings of jasmine, the coverlet scattered with rose petals, lay undisturbed behind a locked door. Sita slept that night on a rush mat in an outhouse near the servant's quarters, removed from her husband's family, her presence as a widow now polluting to all. In the morning, she was told, she would be taken to *that place* where from now on she would live, invisible to the world.

'You are nothing now; *nothing*,' her mother-in-law screamed as they led her away into the night.

'Without a husband, a father or a brother you are no one, nothing but a living dead thing.' The words echoed after her.

Beyond the outhouse, servants gossiped around a fire of burning cow dung, discussing the bridegroom's death, discussing marriage in general, and the events of the day. The dense sweet smoke perfumed the cool night air. Sita listened to their talk, her shaven head still sore from the abrasive rasp of the razor, neutered by the loss of her thick dark hair. A bright moon speared the dusty glass of a small window high in the wall. In the dim light Sita held up her hands, gazing at the filigreed pattern of wedding henna on the palms of her hands and feet. The henna had darkened, and she remembered her aunt saying that if the *mehendi* took well it was a sign that your mother–in–law would love you.

She shivered as she lay in the filthy shed, listening to the scuttle of rats and insects. Beyond the shame of it all, she recognised also with a pang of relief that she would not now have to endure her husband's touch. When he had lifted the sari from her face and she had glanced up at him for the first time and seen his loose lips, all she could think of was that moment when they would be alone, and he would move towards her. In that instant she had prayed to the *devi* for help, and had been heard. She had been protected.

4
Singapore, 2000

At the university, the lift was being serviced in AS5, the Arts and Social Sciences building, so Amita was forced to climb the stairs to the fifth floor and her room in the Department of English Language and Literature. The ascent, with the heavy appendage of the laptop and books, left her wet with perspiration, but on pushing open the glass doors to the department, the cool relief of air-conditioning surrounded her. In her room, she dropped her bags onto a chair and pulled out her laptop.

Parvati's room was a short distance down the corridor and, after setting up the laptop and looking at some emails, Amita made her way there, not bothering to knock before she pushed open the door. Parvati was at her desk, talking to a student who sat across from her. They gave her a startled glance. Amita shut the door again after a word of apology, and made her way back to her room.

Turning up the air-conditioning, she wiped the sweat off the back of her neck and opened the top button on her blouse. Nowadays, she always seemed to feel too hot or too cold. Nothing was helped by the weight she had recently gained and now tried to cover with looser clothes. Her weight was a lifelong problem she battled; neither fat nor slim, she just carried more flesh than was needed, and accepted by now that no diet would move it. When at home, Amita dressed carelessly in old jeans and baggy cotton shirts that gave her a masculine look. For the university, she wore stretch tops or soft blouses teamed with comfortable skirts of a longish length, or tailored trousers. On more frivolous occasions, she might choose an embroidered smock, but whatever she wore emphasised her preference for comfort and practicality.

Feeling cooler, she settled herself at her desk, which was positioned at right angles to the window across the narrow end of the room. The university sprawled across a ridge of low hills and her office in the department, no different from any other along the corridor, faced the tree-filled slopes between campus buildings. Before focussing on work Amita always took a moment to gather into herself the green view from her window, of wide canopied rain-trees, and the fulsome *angsana* and *tembusu*. At any hour, she had only to turn her head to this natural world, the sun aflame on the banks of foliage, to regain her sense of self.

There was plenty of work to be getting on with while she waited for Parvati to be free. She had a paper to write for an international conference in Delhi that she would be attending in a few months, and an essay to start for an American academic journal on the historic subject of *sati*. More pressing, she must also finish laying out the structure of the module, *Feminism: Text and Theory*, that she would be teaching in the coming semester and that must be uploaded online in the next few days. This was a basic introductory module for new students who, as expected in such a class in an Asian country, were exclusively female. Why were there no men, Amita always asked. She took care her classes always had a module on men and masculinities, yet no men ever came to hear it. It was the first question she asked her students as they assembled for their initial class. Where are our men? When she was a student in America, at Columbia University, there were always a few men in such classes, and some lectures on feminist topics were even given by men. Although things had advanced so much since she was a student there in the early 1980s, in conservative Singapore there were still subjects that simply could not be approached. In Western universities, where gender studies had moved into areas of unbounded complexity, much of what she taught in Singapore might be thought no more than fundamental. However, this was Asia, and more particularly, this was Singapore; she went as far as she dared.

Yet, at the beginning of each fresh academic year, she was heartened to see the minds of new students opening to absorb the thoughts she threw at them. In Singapore, her students were all young Asian women, Chinese, Indian or Malay, who, although modern in all outward appearances, were still subconsciously shaped by traditional cultures that valued women less than men. Recently, she had caught one of her young Indian undergrads in the canteen peeling an orange for a male companion and dutifully handing him segments one by one, holding each piece patiently in her fingers until he was ready to take it. Her friend was arguing with the boy next to him, and reached out for replenishment without even turning his head. The sight had incensed Amita, and she had walked determinedly up to the table and curtly instructed the boy to peel his own orange. He observed her in startled silence, while the girl met her eyes resentfully, without a glimmer of appreciation. Amita turned on her heel, uncaring of the apprehension or dislike with which many students regarded her.

Unusually, this morning Amita felt out of sync with herself. All she could think of was her mother, and each thought further soured her mood. The things her mother had revealed to Parvati about the use of infanticide by the women of her village, including Amita's own grandmother, had shocked her deeply. It was also an unsavoury coincidence that Amita had chosen the topic of female infanticide for the paper she was to present at the Delhi conference that had the theme, *Gendered Violence: Transnational Perspectives*.

She had been invited to give a plenary at the conference, and on the desk before her was the abstract she had written, entitled *Politics of Reproduction: The 'Missing Girl' in Indian Society*. Amita's name was well respected in the field of international feminist studies, particularly in the area of South East Asian women's writing. Over the years, she had attended several conferences in India, in cities where she felt little connection to her ancestors, but the thought of going to Delhi excited her. The north was where her parents came from, and she planned to take a side trip to Vrindavan and Mathura to find her mother's village, to trace her roots.

Beside the abstract on the desk was a photocopy of a photograph she had found in an Indian newspaper, of the bodies of three young sisters who had taken their lives to spare their poor and ailing father the need to find dowries for them. Hanging from a ceiling fan, each strung upon a separate blade, their heads slumped forward like broken flowers upon thin stems. Beneath this were separate print outs from a paper on female infanticide that Amita was preparing to quote from in her own paper.

> I examined a young girl with an advanced case of tuberculosis. I asked the mother why she had not done something sooner about the girl's condition, because at this stage treatment would be very expensive. The mother replied, "then let her die, I still have the burden of another daughter." (report by a public health physician, Ludhiana Christian Medical College).

Amita felt a great need for a cup of coffee, but her electric kettle was broken and she would have to wait for Parvati to make her one. Opening a drawer in her desk she pulled out a cereal bar from a supply she always had on hand, and tore off the wrapping. It was the last thing she should be eating, but she did not think she was capable of discipline this morning. She took a bite from the bar and her eyes returned to the papers before her.

> Statistics show that last year in India, 3 million girls or more went 'missing' at birth...
> Sex selection services now reach a poor, rural clientele in the back of a van...

Women reported that they killed their babies under
pressure from their husbands who would beat them if
they refused…

With a sweep of the hand Amita sent all the papers flying
off her desk, and watched as they floated down, scattering
about her on the floor. It was one thing to talk academically
and theoretically about female infanticide as part of her job,
and quite another to know that her grandmother was a serial
murderess, and her mother a chance escapee from that fate.
It made her furious and sad in equal proportion to know that
a woman would so easily kill her child. That the woman in
question was her own grandmother left Amita feeling tainted.

Soon she heard the sound of the student leaving Parvati's
room, and left her desk to hurry down the corridor again.

'Coffee?' Parvati asked.

Parvati refused to drink instant coffee, and always had
available a large flask of sweet milky coffee made from freshly
ground beans that she brought with her each day from home.
Amita had an electric kettle in her room and a jar of instant
coffee, but the element had burned out in the kettle and she had
yet to replace it, and Parvati knew this. Amita sat down in the
empty chair before the desk, biting her nails distractedly.

'Don't do that,' Parvati reminded her, and Amita nodded
obediently, picking up the mug of coffee Parvati placed
before her.

Across the desk, Parvati waited for Amita to speak, knowing
the signs of agitation well.

'It's upset me, all that talk yesterday of drowning that baby. I just can't write on infanticide for the Delhi plenary; can't stomach it now. I'll have to talk about something else,' Amita admitted. Parvati stared at Amita over the rim of the mug as she sipped her coffee.

'It was a long time ago, and nothing to do with you,' she reassured.

'Of course it is to do with me. My aunt was murdered, and I may have many more "missing" aunts for all I know,' Amita snapped.

'Why are you so angry?'

'I'm shocked to find I had a grandmother who regularly committed infanticide.' Amita tried to order her thoughts, wondering why indeed she was so upset about something so far in the past.

Traditional women of her mother's generation, Amita observed, feeling a familiar impatience rising within her, either meekly submitted to their fate or used feminine wiles and mule-like stubbornness to get their way. What she strove to impart to her students in the cloistered space of the university was that they now had choices their mothers and grandmothers did not have. They were the very choices Amita had worked to cement into her own life, deliberately practising what she preached. She was the agent of her own destiny, whole within herself, choosing lovers, but possessed by none. There were those who queried why she had never married or taken a partner, but her life was as she wanted it, and she felt no need for more.

'At that time, in a village, in a rural area, women lived with unbelievable cultural pressures,' Parvati's soothing voice interrupted her thoughts, but Amita was not ready to listen.

'It's still going on today. In the villages they suffocate newborn girls, drown them, feed them pesticide or poisonous herbs. I won't mention what goes on in urban centres; abortions after a scan reveals the wrong gender, sleeping pills in milk formula if they go full term. I've written about it extensively, as you know,' Amita argued in a rising voice.

'Everything was stacked against your grandmother,' Parvati reasoned.

Leaning back in her chair Parvati studied Amita, whose high-handed way with students had gained her a reputation. She always leaned towards exaggeration, throwing herself so wholly behind a viewpoint or position that her academic impartiality was in danger; Parvati hesitated to use the word 'obsessive'.

'Then, why did she not kill my mother as well?' Amita demanded. Parvati sighed and shrugged.

'Maybe your mother refused to drown quietly, or maybe your grandmother just couldn't find the strength to do it that time.' Parvati replied.

'Knowing my mother, she probably refused to drown without a fuss.' Amita laughed uneasily, picking up the mug of coffee before continuing.

'Its one thing to examine a fly under a microscope, and another to have it buzzing around alive inside your head! That's how this feels now, too close to home!'

As Amita sipped the coffee her eyes settled on the framed family photos on the bookshelves behind Parvati's desk, on a photo of Parvati and her husband and their two teenage children, smiling happily at the camera, arms wrapped around each other. Parvati's husband, Rishi, was an academic like Parvati, a professor in the Political Science Department at the university. In her present mood Amita had no wish to see Rishi's face, and turned her head away. Draining the last of the coffee in one long gulp, she stood up with such abruptness that Parvati stared at her in surprise. Then, with no more than a curt goodbye, Amita hurried from the room.

Each night Amita took care to leave her mother's bedroom door open and her own ajar, always fearing an emergency if Sita tried to find her way to the bathroom in the darkness. Sita slept restlessly, as did Amita, who now heard her mother call out in her dreams the name of her long ago friend.

'Muni.'

Amita remembered the slight, thin-faced woman in the photograph who knelt beside Sita at target practice, both of them staring in concentration down the barrel of a gun. What had they shared together in the war that her name should haunt her mother's dreams, Amita wondered. She listened to Sita toss and turn, to the laments of dreaming, a grief she knew had been stirred up by the conversation with Parvati. Yet, whatever the discomfort her mother must endure, Amita remained determined that Parvati's interviews must continue. Her mother's past was sealed in a silence Amita was determined to break.

Now, already into middle age, Amita's own experiences seemed to lack proper shape without a deeper knowledge of her mother's story. The meaning of her mother's life was in the challenges she had braved, and the choices she had made. Each life was shaped by its story, and until this point, Amita had never doubted the story she was trying to shape for herself. Yet, recently, and especially in these last days when her mother had begun the interviews with Parvati, she found herself filled with all manner of doubts. Was she just drifting through a role she had fashioned for herself, or was there a deeper meaning she must find in her life? Somehow, she felt sure that if she knew the truth of her mother's story it would provide her with an image, one way or another, of what her own life should be. From India to Singapore, child marriage to widowhood, to recruitment in an army, her mother's life appeared one of adventure and exception. Yet, as a child, the little she knew about her mother's life had been nothing but an embarrassment to Amita.

Her mother had been different from the mothers of her school friends, all absorbed in culinary matters and the birthing of children, the buying of gold and saris, and the running of their households. Her mother had no husband, had never developed the plump bolsters of hips and breasts that other mothers did, had never produced more children, or exuded the comforting odours of cooking and perspiration, and never laughed easily. Her mother did not share the interests of other women; her mother had been a soldier. Nothing could have been more outlandish. As a child, Amita never mentioned her mother's eccentricities. Instead, she found herself empathising with people who were orphans, who did not know who exactly they were. Like them, a piece of her seemed to be missing.

'Muni.' Her mother called out the name once more.

What long-ago terror had the two women experienced, Amita wondered yet again. The past was as much an illusion as the present, but in the darkness of nightmare time rewound, throwing her mother back into the dimension of her own inner space. The person her mother inhabited in her dream was a different person from the old woman who now dreamed the dream. Amita saw again the photographs spread out on the table, her mother's hand on the butt of the rifle, ready to pull the trigger, to acknowlege the recoil as the bullet left the gun; her mother had been prepared to kill. Perhaps she *had* killed a man. This thought did not sit easily with Amita. Yet, in the photograph, the knowledge of this power was everywhere in her mother's face, in the directness of her gaze.

'Muni,' the call came again.

Her mother seemed to retrace her steps to the same haunted moments in her past, a place she could not easily leave, whose vividness must equal the reality unfolding in her waking time. Did she smell again the perfume of lemongrass as she crawled forward with her rifle, and was her husband again beside her as she wandered the landscape of memory, Amita wondered.

Things moved forwards, not backwards, and what was done and lived through could not be undone, Amita reasoned. You just had to live with the consequences. She knew this fact now to her own great cost. The unfathomable movement of all she had so deliberately set in motion in her own life came forcefully before her now — her mother's dreaming, the resentful face of the student peeling an orange, Parvati, Rishi. Rishi.

5
SINGAPORE, 1939

At last they stopped before a shophouse in a busy street and Dev helped her out of the rickshaw.

'On Serangoon Road you will not believe you are in Singapore; you will believe you are still in India. '

Sita nodded, it seemed as Dev said; India appeared to be all about her in the familiar faces and familiar sights, in the smell of spices and incense, cow dung and jasmine. A priest hurried by, his brow smeared with ash in the lines of his religious caste, a bullock cart passed with a cargo of brightly painted plaster statues of the god Krishna. Then, another cart passed loaded with a strange fruit.

'Those are pineapples. Chinese people have become millionaires from this fruit,' Dev informed her.

Sita stared at the prickly balls; such fruit did not grow in India. In the dark recess of the many tiny shops about her, she glimpsed a goldsmith at work and a garland maker, bales of cloth and familiar brass cooking utensils, but the architecture around her was unlike anything she had seen before. There was also the presence of many Chinamen, such as their rickshaw runner. Everything was familiar, yet everything was strange.

Sita followed Dev through a narrow door into a dim interior, momentarily blinded after the sunlit road. Her brother began climbing the steep staircase inside the house, and Sita followed. People pushed past her on the narrow precipitous steps, almost throwing her off balance, while Dev climbed ahead without a backward glance. A confusion of sounds and smells assailed her, the distant clank of metal pots, the cries of a baby, the whirr of a sewing machine and the chanting of prayers. The perfume of incense mixed with the stale odour of food and spices, the stench of drains and old fermenting rice, all stewing together in the hot and airless house.

Sita felt suddenly faint with exhaustion. Although the long journey from Vrindavan to Singapore was over, her senses still reeled from her experiences, a myriad images jumbling together in her head that she could make little sense of as yet. From Vrindavan to Calcutta there had been an old train, plaintively blowing its whistle as it trundled across India's scorched plains. Sita had sat huddled before an open window, transfixed by the passing landscape and the rhythmic sway of the carriage. She barely noticed the black smoke that blew from the engine into the carriage, covering her face with a fine layer of soot, leaving a gritty taste on her tongue. She kept her eyes on the distant horizon, aware that she was now on her own, travelling deep into the world, just as Dev had done. Land was continually sucked away either side of the train. In the distance, fields and villages perched upon the horizon, but whenever these far places were reached, more fields and villages appeared upon yet another horizon, so that the train sped constantly towards a shifting destination at which it never arrived. Life itself, Sita had suddenly realised, might be just like this journey, rushing always towards a new horizon, a line that moved seamlessly as she moved, constantly evolving but never reached, always just beyond her.

At Calcutta she had boarded a great ship, and for days the swell of the waves pitched her this way and that. That voyage had been even more traumatic than the long train journey, and she did not want to think about it just now. Nor did she want to remember the widows' ashram in Vrindavan, where she had lived after her husband died. If it were not for Dev she would still be there. Somehow, she had reached Singapore and that was all that mattered. Above her on the stairs, her brother was now reaching out a hand to pull her up beside him as he stepped into a narrow corridor.

Dev held onto her hand, drawing her along behind him down the dim passage. From a half shuttered window at the far end, some light filtered through, revealing rows of small cubicles. Before most of the open doors a curtain was hooked up, but Sita could easily glimpse the tiny spaces behind, crammed with people and belongings. In one room a tailor and his assistant sewed busily, in another an *ayurvedic* doctor tended to his waiting patients, who overflowed into the corridor. In another, men slept on narrow shelves, head to foot, two to a bed, stacked up one above another, floor to ceiling. Dev turned into a room near the end of the corridor.

'What place is this?' Sita asked, her voice dropping to a whisper.

'This is my home. I share this room with two other men from

the shop, but they have moved out today to make room for you. I can pay for this room now because I am promoted to Number Three Assistant. Before my promotion, I was sleeping in the shop on the floor behind the counter.' Dev smiled proudly.

She did not know what she had expected, but the weight in her chest suggested it was not the dark cupboard of a room she now saw before her. Spreading a frayed checked cloth on a sleeping shelf, Dev instructed Sita to rest while he went to get a meal for them from one of the food stalls in the road below. Left on her own, she was suddenly overcome by the weariness of the day. Her sari dropped about her shoulders and putting up a hand she examined the short spikes of hair, measuring how long they had grown since she left the ashram in Vrindavan. For the first time in days she sat alone, and in the hot space of the tiny room memories engulfed her.

The morning after the wedding and her husband's untimely death, a *tongawallah* had arrived with a horse-drawn trap to take her to *that place*. Her mother-in-law's voice was hard with satisfaction.

'Only in that place can widows hide their shame. Just as my son is dead, you too are now dead to the world.'

Sita listened to the sound of the *tonga* wheels bowling along, and the familiar clop of horse's hooves that had accompanied her so recently on the journey to her bridegroom's home. The air rushed uncomfortably about her newly shorn skull. Soon the *tonga* entered the narrow twisting lanes of the old part of the city, and stopped at last. Her mother-in-law got down and rapped on a door in a weathered wall.

A wizened black dwarf of a man with an oversized head and bandy legs opened the door to them. Behind him towered a mountainous woman, tonsured like Sita, and dressed in a white sari. A short hawk nose dominated a fleshy face out of which glared small hooded eyes. The woman nodded and turned, her bulk balanced upon tiny feet, and they followed her and the black dwarf across a large courtyard. The singing of *bhajans* echoed about them, hymns Sita remembered her grandmother had liked to sing and, hearing the familiar songs again, a lump rose in her throat.

In the shade of a colonnade the other side of the courtyard, a priest sat at a table, upon which rested a ledger and a large metal cash box. He looked up, assessing Sita critically before turning to her mother-in-law. His sunken cheeks were covered by grey stubble and his dark face gleamed with perspiration. Immediately, with a curt nod to the priest, Sita's mother-in-law hurried away.

'Whatever you have you must give me now.' From beneath shaggy eyebrows the man's eyes squinted at Sita from different angles, it was hard to know which eye was looking at her.

'Join the other *mais* in there.' He gestured to a spacious hall in the building behind him.

Sita found a place just inside the door, up against the wall. The large room was filled by rows of white clad widows, heads covered, swaying together as they sang. The sweet sound of their voices filled the room. Sita closed her eyes and the music flowed through her, a lump swelled in her throat again as she remembered her grandmother singing.

Vrindavan was known for its many widows who all resided in the many small temples dedicated to the God Krishna, whose early life, it was said, had been spent in the town. Here Krishna had played with the *gopis*, the cowherd maidens, hiding their clothes as they bathed in the river, and romancing the most beautiful of them, Radha.

A young woman in the row in front wriggled back until she was sitting beside Sita. A down of soft hair covered her shorn head above a round pleasant face.

'Did *pujari* take money from you?' She asked, nodding in the direction of the priest and his cash box. Then, seeing Sita observing the growth of hair, she smiled.

'We shave our heads every two weeks. Tomorrow is the day the barber comes, and then even this bit of hair will be gone.'

Her eyes were steel grey and feline-like, and Sita could not stop staring; she had never seen anyone with eyes that colour before.

'If we *mais* sing it brings good luck to people; they earn good karma in Heaven by giving money for our singing.' The woman smiled again, revealing a narrow gap between her two front teeth, and continued.

'*Pujari* is always looking for money or things he can steal from us and sell. You'll get used to it here,' she whispered conspiratorially.

'I'm called Billi.'

'A *billi* is a cat, it's not a proper name.' Sita found her voice at last. Billi nodded in agreement and did not seem upset by this observation.

'Because of my light eyes, everyone says I look like a cat,' she answered, and then leaned forward with sudden insistence.

'Now sing. If we sing, we get food.'

'And if we don't sing?' Sita asked.

'No food.'

Soon Dev returned to the cubicle with their meal, the freshly cooked vegetables and rice parcelled up in banana leaves. Sita pushed her memories away, covering her head again with her sari, as was proper in the presence of a male relative, especially an elder brother. They ate in silence, Sita picking listlessly at the food without appetite, Dev shovelling it quickly into his mouth and then accepting without query the extra portion his sister offered him.

Looking down at the spicy aubergine, agleam with oil and spices, Sita remembered her shock that first day in the ashram at the blandness of the food. She would have liked to tell Dev about it, but suspected he would have little curiosity. He asked no questions about her marriage or her time in the *bhajanashram*, and she knew it was not that he did not care but that these things were already behind her, and were the kinds of things that happened to women and so were not of great importance. Even so, as she picked at the food before her, she could not help but compare it to the food in the ashram.

On that first day, she had queued beside Billi for a meal. The mountainous woman who had opened the ashram door to Sita, and whose name she soon learned was Roop, supervised the women, shouting orders to those serving out food from large tureens, pacing up and down on her tiny feet to see nobody was given too much. Sita held out a tin plate and observed in surprise the boiled rice and plain *dal* and vegetables doled onto it.

'Eat slowly, this is the only meal we get in the day,' Billi warned, observing Sita hungrily scooping food into her mouth.

'Only *one* meal? It is not even tasting good, no oil or spices in anything.' Sita stopped eating and stared up at Billi.

'We widows are dead things; we cannot eat 'hot' spicy foods that will stir up our bodies and stir up our feelings. No onion or garlic, no root vegetables and many other things,' Billi cautioned, looking up from her plate.

'And also no sweets,' she added, sadly shaking her head.

'Then, what *can* we eat?' Sita demanded, chewing more slowly.

'Rice, milk, some vegetables; we can eat only those foods that cool our body's passions. A widow's body must be weak and dry; dried out of all feelings,' Billi explained.

Now, the ashram seemed like a distant dream as she watched Dev eating hungrily. Over the years he had become a man, everything about him had solidified, his forehead was more prominent, his jaw firmer, his neck thicker, and he had grown a moustache. Gratitude welled through her; now that she was with Dev again, everything would be all right.

'Singapore is a good place,' Dev told her as he ate, not once raising his eyes from his food. His thickly oiled hair was parted in the middle, folding in two black wings either side of his head.

When they finished eating, Dev rolled up the banana leaves and directed Sita to take the rubbish to a bin outside the communal kitchen on the ground floor where, he informed her, there was also a latrine she could use. Sita made her way again along the corridor of cubicles and down the steep stairs. Dusk was already darkening into night and candles and oil lamps glowed behind the thinly curtained doorways, shadows stretched about her. Descending the stairs in the failing light Sita soon found the kitchen with its long sink and leaking taps. Several men stood cooking, stirring food in large woks over braziers, filling the place with pungent smells.

The kitchen opened into an air-well, a small courtyard where a square of night sky could be seen high above the house, embedded with stars. Stepping gratefully into the fresh air, Sita stood looking up at the sky. To one side she saw a stone-floored bathing cubicle, and beside it a latrine stall, before which stood the rubbish bin. There were also several large metal tubs for the washing of clothes, stacked beneath a tap. Tomorrow, Sita decided, she would wash her sari here, and also Dev's shirts and *dhoti*. Now that she would be living with Dev, she must also learn where to buy rice and pulses and vegetables, so that she could cook for her brother. Although Dev had not yet explained what form her life would follow in Singapore, as his sister he would expect her to look after him and his home.

When she returned to the cubicle Dev had already lit an oil lamp and she was aware of him observing her, his eyes in the candlelight moist and inquiring. The intensity of this assessment embarrassed her, and she pulled the sari further over her head.

Her mind was full of questions. Where was the market and where, after she had washed his shirts in the morning, could she hang them to dry? Glancing around the cubicle, she also wondered what she was going to do all day after she had folded up Dev's blanket and tidied his few belongings. Were there other women she could make friends with in the rooming house? Would the men he shared the room with return? And if they did, what would she do? As these thoughts ran through her head, Dev cleared his throat and began to speak.

'I have good news. Tomorrow you will be married. My friend Shiva will marry you.' Dev smiled, revealing fine white teeth.

Sita started in disbelief. The sari fell from her head, exposing her close-cropped hair, the alarm in her eyes. She wanted to speak but no words came as she stared at her brother in bewilderment. Dev took her silence as a positive response, and smiled again as he continued.

'Shiva *bhai* is an educated man. He is a teacher at the Ramakrishna Mission School and he is my good friend. Also, he is from Mathura, near our own village. He is from the same community as us, and so he is eating the same food as us and having the same customs.' He waited, but as Sita remained silent, he continued.

'In India Shiva *bhai* was a follower of Gandhiji. He believes in the Mahatma's idea of no dowry, giving education to women and getting widows who are still very young, like you, remarried. Because of these beliefs, Shiva *bhai* is prepared to marry you. For him marriage to you is an experiment in the new ways of thinking, of Gandhiji's thinking.' Dev gave another broad smile of encouragement, but as Sita continued to stare mutely at him he cleared his throat in irritation.

'When I first arrived in Singapore I went for night classes at the Ramakrishna Mission School, to learn more reading and writing. In Singapore if you want to get on you need a lot of reading and writing. Shiva *bhai* was my teacher. He has been like an elder brother to me, always advising and encouraging.'

'Why must I marry? Why can't I stay with you?' Sita interrupted, words bursting from her at last. Her brother frowned, taken aback by the query.

'How can you stay here in Singapore unless you are married? How will I keep you?' Dev's voice rose in exasperation as he continued.

'I have no money to send you back to India, and I have no money to keep you here. I was able to call you here only because Shiva *bhai* agreed to marry you. Even though your first husband died after the marriage ceremony was completed, he had still not touched you as a wife. For this reason only Shiva *bhai* agreed to marry you; you are still pure in your body.' Dev stared at his sister's lowered head.

'I am also an admirer of Gandhiji, but I would not marry a widow even if I had Shiva *bhai*'s great ideals.' He made no effort to hide his disapproval, wanting his sister to understand the enormity of the step his friend was taking. At her continued silence his irritation increased.

'All my money is gone in buying you a gold necklace and gold bangles for your new wedding. They may be gold plated ornaments, not solid gold, but from a distance all are looking the same and they cost me a lot. I have taken a loan from a Chettiar moneylender to buy you these things. It was also Shiva *bhai* who paid for your passage on the boat to Singapore. He paid this only because you were coming here to be his wife. Please understand; I could never afford to bring you here.'

Sita continued to stare at her hands, knowing all that was required of her was silent acquiescence; it was useless to protest. Dev's words pressed down upon her, and the thought of how hard he had worked to secure a future for her filled her with guilt.

'Tomorrow Shiva *bhai* will marry you,' Dev repeated firmly, rearranging the blue checked cloth on the sleeping shelf for Sita, spreading out another cloth on the floor for himself.

Dev fell asleep promptly, and in the darkness Sita stared down at him, her knees pulled up to her chest, her hands clasped tightly together. Her brother's breathing rose and fell steadily; in the distance she heard the cry of a baby, and then a tubercular cough. The scuttle of roaches and the scrabble of rats began. A mosquito whined in her ear. She did not want to get married again. Everything in her resisted the notion. She remembered her relief when her first husband died, and the thought that she would not have to endure his touch.

For the first time she wished she were back in the ashram, on her sleeping mat beside Billi. If only Billi were nearby to tell her what to do.

'Am I the youngest here?' Sita had asked as they lay side by side that first night in the stifling heat of the dormitory, the air dense with the odour of communal perspiration, and Billi had nodded.

'You are for now, but you never know who will arrive tomorrow. Roop has been here since she was six years old. Most of the *mais* were much older when their husbands died, but their children could not afford to keep them. A widow takes up space in a house, is an extra mouth to feed, and needs at least one sari a year. I've been here since I was seventeen, now I'm twenty-one. I liked my husband and he liked me, but he died in an accident. I was expecting a baby. The family looked after me until I gave birth. The baby was a boy, but he was born dead. My husband's family then blamed me for everything, for my husband's death, for the baby's death, and they sent me here.' Billi pointed to the sleeping form of a toothless old crone, snoring gently a short distance away.

'That is Maneka *didi*, she is the oldest person here. Nobody knows how old she is, seventy, eighty or maybe even ninety. She hasn't seen her son for years, but she's still hoping he'll pay for her funeral. That's what we're all saving for, our funeral. It is important they cremate us properly, with enough oil and with proper rites and prayers.'

As Billi spoke, Sita was filled by a sudden panic. In the darkness she stared up at a small window below the rafters, within which the moon moved beyond silver clouds. Inhaling the fetid smell of the lumpy pillow beneath her head, she touched the comfort of Dev's letters, secreted away under her blouse in a muslin bag.

'I want to write to my brother Dev.' Sita sat up suddenly in the darkness, filled by a sense of urgency. Dev might not know what had happened to her, her aunt and uncle might not have told him.

'*Pujari* will not like it, nor will Roop *didi*. You belong here now. Our connections to our past life are dead,' Billi replied, sleepy but firm.

The next day Sita summoned up courage to ask the mountainous Roop about writing a letter to Dev.

'He will come and get me and take me away,' Sita assured Roop, sure the woman would be glad to hear there would be one less mouth for the ashram to feed.

Instead, Roop *didi* raised her thin eyebrows, and her many chins shook as she laughed.

'*Pujari* will not allow it. He will not want to lose his little bird before he has taught her to sing.' Roop *didi* glared down at her.

'I am singing already,' Sita drew back, confused.

Roop *didi* laughed even harder, a low strangulated sound caught in the depth of her throat.

Now, in the shadows of her brother's home, Sita knew she would do as Dev advised. He wanted only the best for her, and there was no option but to accept the future he had arranged.

Once, in the night she awoke in panic. On the floor, Dev slept heavily. Gathering up her bundle of belongings, she stepped beyond the cubicle into the long dark corridor, filled with an urge to flee. In the darkness she could see nothing, not even the top of the stairwell. There was the scamper of rats, the cry again of a baby. For some moments she stood clutching her few possessions but then returned to the room, for where should she go, and what could she do? Settling back upon the shelf, she tried to absorb the knowledge that soon she would no longer be a widow, but a married woman once again. Listening to the sound of Dev's deep breathing, her thoughts returned again to the ashram.

Each day, in between the hours of singing, they went out to beg in the town for alms. From other ashrams, other widows joined them. The narrow streets of Vrindavan were filled by the pale spectral shadows of women, moving silently about, invisible to all but their own kind.

Once Billi had led them to a busy marketplace where a group of musicians and acrobats beat drums and rattled tambourines; the sound of a pipe floated to them. The people who gathered about the performers were immediately accosted by gangs of waiting beggars. Sita took a step forward, excited by the lively music and the sudden holiday atmosphere. Immediately, Billi held her back, and Sita struggled to be free.

'How will we get money from people if we sit so far from the crowd? Those beggars and the performers will get everything.' Sita shouted, pointing to the child acrobats whose skinny bodies contorted, turning cartwheels, twirling tin plates on sticks, juggling aubergines and carrots.

'Ssh. We cannot go any nearer,' Old Maneka shuffled forward, placing a hand on Sita's arm, drawing her back into the shade of a tree.

'Everyone will run away from you if you approach,' Billi told her briskly. Maneka nodded and began to speak, her lips working over her toothless gums.

'When I was first widowed I was not allowed to go out of my in-laws' house. I was not even allowed to draw water from the well because I would pollute it. Nobody served me food properly; my bowl was pushed towards me with a stick. Please understand, our presence is polluting to others.'

Across the road two dancers joined the acrobats and spun about, their colourful skirts billowing out around them. The sound of the pipe flailed about in Sita's head.

'If you accidentally touch anyone in that crowd, they will have to go and take a bath and say prayers of purification. Nobody wants you near them.' Billi spoke angrily.

'But they give us money to sing,' Sita shouted, tears running down her cheeks.

'Because we are the living dead, our word reaches God that much quicker,' Maneka chuckled through her toothless gums, her gnarled hand still gripping Sita's arm.

'*Beti*, sit down now and be quiet. Do not struggle against your fate. Afterwards, people will come and give you money so that they may become pure through our prayers. Then, you must cover your head and face, lift up your begging bowl to them and wait. Don't look up at people; don't catch their eye. That too is polluting, and upsetting for them.'

It was as Maneka said. After a while the band and the acrobats moved on and the music died away. Then a few people from the crowd looked across at the widows uncertainly, and began to walk towards them. Sita covered her head and lowered her eyes as Maneka had instructed, lifting her begging bowl above her bowed head. Soon there was the sound of a coin dropping into the bowl, then the clink of another upon it.

Now, in Dev's tiny room Sita listened to the sounds of the night, the wail of a cat, the bowling wheels of a passing rickshaw and the voices of men in the road outside. Fate had brought her to this strange place, and soon she would be married again. Soon she would no longer be a living dead thing, but returned to the world. Surely, she thought, this could only be good for her, and that was why Dev had arranged it.

6
SINGAPORE, 1939

The following day Sita waited for her bridegroom, the new sari pulled down over her face, the hanging pearl of the nose ring trembling as she breathed. Wedding garlands of fresh jasmine and roses were heaped on the sleeping shelf, the heady scent of the flowers filling the cubicle. Dev stood in the doorway, looking by turns expectantly at the corridor for a first sight of Shiva, then moving to stare apprehensively at his sister as she sat, head bowed, waiting mutely for her fate.

'Shiva *bhai* has no family; you will not have to adapt to any in-laws. In India his parents are dead, and the relatives who brought him up are also dead,' Dev reassured her in an encouraging voice.

Sita nodded, remembering the other marriage, the gifts, the sweetmeats and the loud trumpeting of the wedding band. This marriage was different. Her hands were bare of the decoration of henna, and her brother did not seem to think this important. It was a wedding arranged by two bachelors without a need to prove wealth or social status, and without any women to question its form. There were no elders, no musicians, no feasting or dancing. The unadorned shape of day loomed starkly ahead, its weight already pressing upon her.

'Will he change my name?' Sita asked, her voice little more than a whisper.

'He has said nothing of this to me,' Dev replied, his attention focussed on the imminent appearance of his friend.

Sita fingered the red sari Dev had bought her, remembering the stiff weight of that other wedding sari, the plait of hair in a metal bowl, the smoke of the funeral pyre. She took a deep breath, pushing those dark pictures from her mind. This time she had a name for her husband, and what was more, he was named after the great god Shiva, transformer and protector of the universe, and she must take comfort in this thought.

Soon there were footsteps, and Sita heard Dev welcoming the bridegroom into the room. Adjusting the sari over her head, Sita clasped her hands together in her lap, knowing the men observed her as they stood together in the doorway. Although her heart beat fast, all the thoughts in her head seemed frozen. As convention forbade her to lift her eyes, she focussed her gaze upon her bridegroom's bare feet in worn leather sandals as he stepped towards her, observing the clumps of dark hair sprouting from his wide toes, and his neatly clipped nails. They did not appear to be the feet of an old man, and this reassured her. Then she became aware of her brother speaking.

'Raise your head and look at him. He wishes you to do this, he does not think in the old ways. There is nothing to fear. He is my friend.'

In spite of her brother's encouragement, Sita hesitated, pulling the sari further over her face so that her bridegroom could see nothing of her. Dev sighed loudly, clearing his throat in embarrassment.

'Let us go,' Shiva announced at last, and Sita was sure she heard a note of impatience in his voice.

Dev picked up the garlands and the box of sweetmeats that would be used as an offering at the ceremony. Bending to take Sita's arm, he guided his sister out of the cubicle, down the stairs and into the hot sun of Serangoon Road. As Sita stepped forward into the road, a herd of bleating goats on their way to the nearby slaughterhouse milled about her. Their owner, an emaciated old man, at once began shouting and struck out at the animals with a stick. Dev gripped her arm, drawing her to the side of the road until the goats had passed. Although the sari still covered her head, Sita raised her eyes in that moment of confusion, hoping for a glimpse of her bridegroom, and was rewarded with the sight of a tall man, straight as a bamboo cane, striding ahead up the road determinedly. His long thick hair was pushed back behind his ears and curled at the end, but as yet she could see nothing of his face.

At last they reached the temple, and Sita fell back apprehensively, trailing behind her brother. Brightly painted sculptures of the deities crowded the temple's pagoda, and beneath it a pair of heavy silver doors stood open. Sensing her hesitation, Dev placed a hand upon his sister's shoulder and guided her firmly inside. A bare-chested priest received them and Sita was led to where Shiva waited for her, and settled herself on the cool stone floor beside her bridegroom. Soon the priest began his incantations, the sound building rhythmically as Sita and Shiva began the rituals that would make them man and wife.

As the chanting of prayers began, Sita knew her bridegroom observed her. Although she tried to make sense of what was happening, she seemed to move in a dream, and the heady perfume of jasmine filling her head appeared the only reality. She seemed to be reliving that first wedding, but when she lifted her head she saw before her a different man, and knew she was entering a new life. She wished Billi could see her now, and she tried to imagine her sitting nearby, whispering encouragement, as she did so often in the ashram.

Sita did not remember how long it was before she realised Billi sometimes went out at night, returning to the ashram as first light filtered through the dark sky. Soon, if she stayed awake, Sita noticed how often Billi was gone, and that other young girls in the dormitory were also mysteriously absent some nights. If she got up quietly and pressed her face to the bars of the window, she could see them leave the *bhajanashram*, passing out through the door in the high wall. Once she saw the great bulk of Roop *didi* hastening them forward, and then shutting the door upon them. In the silent street a curtained palanquin waited, and the women climbed obediently into it. Wherever it was they went each night they were escorted by *pujari*'s assistant, the black-skinned dwarf, Motilal. Billi dismissed all Sita's queries with amusement.

'You were asleep, you must have been dreaming,' she laughed.

In the end Sita asked the toothless Maneka as they ate lunch together when Billi was absent one morning.

'*Aie Bhagwan,*' the old woman sighed and shook her head. 'God saved me; I was past using when I came here. Sometimes it is good to be old.' Sita could make nothing of this answer and questioned further.

'Where do they go at night? Why are they taken away by Motilal?'

'There are many rich men in this town. One way or another we *mais* must earn money for God and the temple,' Maneka replied, her eyes resting on Sita with new empathy as she continued.

'Soon *pujari* will start to send you off too, and also call for you himself, just as he calls for the others when his need is great. *Aie Bhagwan*! *That* service too he expects in return for caring for us.' Maneka shook her head, smiling her toothless smile, unaware of the effect of her words upon Sita, who drew a sudden, sharp breath of understanding.

Within days the illness began, as if that one moment of comprehension at Maneka's side had penetrated Sita's body. Fever dried her lips and carried her dreams to high, strange places. Phlegm rattled in her chest, spluttered in her throat, exhaustion pulled her down deeper and deeper. Her skin turned yellow, her eyes burned, her head thumped. *Pujari* raged at her uselessness and the cost of keeping her, as she lay on her mat. At intervals Motilal or Roop prodded her with a sandaled foot to test if life remained. Billi fed her water and honey drop by drop, old Maneka massaged her head and held a wet towel to her brow.

Although it seemed that *pujari* was prepared to let her die, eventually, in the same palanquin in which Billi and the other young girls were carried away at night, Sita was hurried to a small clinic run by a charitable trust dispensing free medicine to the destitute. A lady doctor from a hospital on the other side of town visited the clinic regularly, and a queue of poverty-stricken people beyond the help of the MBBS failed ex-medical student who ran the clinic, waited for her.

At last Dr. Sen arrived in a battered rickshaw, wearing a brown homespun cotton sari marked with the dust of travel between the hospital and the clinic. As she stepped out of the rickshaw she recognised the obese bald widow from one of the *bhajanashrams* standing at the head of the queue.

'She is dying.' Roop pointed impatiently to Sita who lay in a bamboo litter, bloodless as a plucked chicken.

Dr. Sen bent to examine Sita's emaciated body, listening to the rattle and rasp of her lungs, feeling the feverish pitch of her temperature, and looked up angrily at Roop.

'Why have you waited so long? She must go at once into hospital; I will attend to her myself.'

Later, when they knew each other better, Dr. Sen told Sita how she had more than once, from this same ashram, as well as others in the town, been brought young widows with botched abortions, who were bleeding to death. She had tried many times to visit the women in the ashrams, to check on their health and living conditions, all to no avail. Only in extremis, if at all, Dr. Sen told Sita, was a widow ever brought to her. In the *bhajanashrams* secret practices of sexual abuse, never spoken of but known to all, were openly encouraged. Dr. Sen knew which rich men in the town availed themselves of these unfortunate women, but could do nothing to stop them.

The perfume of jasmine filled her head and, with a start, Sita returned to the present. The wedding ceremony was almost over and Dev was taking her arm and helping her to her feet. Her bridegroom now stepped towards her, placing the wedding garland upon her. She raised her head to observe him, and noticed his long fingered hands and his nose, flattened slightly at the end, as if someone had pressed it with a thumb. He was neither young nor old, and the warmth in his eyes reassured her. Her wrists were once again covered with glass wedding bangles; once again the marks of marriage anointed her, the red carmine *bindi* upon her brow and the bright smear of the *sindhoor* along the parting of her short hair. Observing these marks upon herself once more, Sita held her breath, instinctively waiting for her husband to drop to his knees, gasping and choking. Instead, the man at her side continued to stand before her.

From the temple, they began the short walk to Shiva's home in a lane off Norris Road, behind the Ramakrishna Mission School where he taught Hindi, and also some English classes in the mission's Afternoon English School. Dev strode ahead with Shiva while Sita hurried a few paces behind the men, one hand clutching the skirt of her sari, holding it clear of the dusty road, the other hand gripping the silk together beneath her chin so that the sari would not slip from her head. She could think of nothing but that she was a married woman again and the enormity of this fact filled her, leaving room for little else. As she walked, other thoughts began to press in upon her. Where did her new husband live, what would her life be like, what was *he* like? As she increased her pace in an effort to draw nearer the men her husband stopped, and to her surprise, turned back towards her.

'This is the school where I teach,' Shiva announced, pointing out to Sita a building crowned ornately on its roof by two dome shaped pavilions.

Sita glanced up at the structure, then hurried after Shiva as he turned into a lane beside the building. A stall selling coconuts stood on the corner, and the owner, a dark-skinned, pot-bellied man, stared curiously at Sita while greeting Shiva.

'That is Viswanathan. Every day he sells me a coconut.' Shiva said as he hailed the man. Sita stored away the information, already preparing to buy a coconut for her husband each day.

The alley they entered was narrow, but a strip of open land running behind the Ramakrishna Mission bordered one side of it, and gave a sense of space. The other side of the lane was lined with the tall back gates of a row of shophouses that faced into Serangoon Road. Shiva stopped at a gate before a jacaranda tree. Its purple blossoms were sprinkled over the road, and Sita stepped carefully around them as Shiva led them through the gate into the small stone-flagged courtyard of a dilapidated house.

'Here is my home.' Shiva pointed proudly to a spiral metal stair that led up to a narrow balcony and a door on the first floor.

Sita's heart beat fast as she climbed the twisting stair behind the two men. A straggly plant grew in a blue oil drum beside the door, and beyond the wall the jacaranda rose up, its purple crown overhanging the courtyard, almost brushing the spiral stair. A faint sweet perfume drifted to her, and if she reached out an arm she was sure she could touch the flowers.

'This room is separate from the rest of the house. It can only be entered by these stairs,' Shiva explained as he unlocked a bulky padlock and pushed the door open.

The compressed heat inside the small room engulfed them as they stepped inside, and the red tiled floor burned beneath their feet. Shiva hurried to throw open the window shutters. As light flooded the room the first thing Sita noticed were the stacks of books and newspapers piled up against each wall, pervading everything with the mouldy smell of old paper. A tin trunk covered with a brightly printed green cloth, a low Indian-style desk with a cushion before it and a couple of shallow backed stools were the only furniture in the room; a rolled up sleeping mat stood in one corner. A small space at the back of the room, little more than an alcove, appeared to provide a makeshift kitchen. Sita glimpsed an earthen water jar, kerosene stove and a shelf with a few glass jars, cups and plates.

'Usually I buy meals from the food stalls on the road,' Shiva explained, following Sita's gaze.

From under the silk veil of her sari, Sita looked hesitantly about and saw that her bundle of belongings had already been delivered, and stood in a corner.

'Make us some tea,' Dev ordered suddenly, taking command

of the situation, as if Sita must immediately prove her worth.

As the men sat down, Sita made her way to the kitchen area, looking hesitantly about. Picking up a small pan from the shelf, she turned the key in the earthen jar, and drew some water. Then, crouching down before the kerosene stove she tried to light the apparatus with a match she had found, waiting for the blue flame to spring to life, but nothing happened. A couple of metal tumblers sat on a shelf, beside glass jars holding sugar and tea leaves and another with cinnamon and cardamom, but there was no milk to be seen. Behind her the men's voices rose and fell in conversation as they waited for their tea. Weariness overwhelmed her in a sudden pressing weight; all she wanted to do was lie down on the floor and sleep. Although once again she had the status of wife, she seemed incapable of fulfilling the simplest of demands. For some moments she stood hesitantly in the tiny kitchen, then turned to where the men sat chatting, waiting for them to notice her. At last Dev looked up.

'Where is our tea?' he demanded with a frown.

'Milk…' she whispered, and at once her husband gave a self-conscious laugh.

'I forgot, no milk. And also no kerosene,' Shiva remembered.

Standing up, unfolding his long legs, he strode out of the door. Leaning over the balcony rail, he called to a servant boy in the courtyard below who immediately bounded up the stairs. Giving him a few coins, Shiva told him to bring tea from a stall in the street.

'Afterwards, I will show you where everything is,' he promised Sita.

The boy soon returned, carrying three tall glasses of milky tea on a metal tray. Sita served the two men and then crouched down in a corner and drank gratefully, the hot liquid coursing through her. It was the first thing, apart from a drink of water earlier, that had passed her lips all day. She had been too apprehensive to swallow the breakfast Dev had offered, and too ill at ease to eat after the wedding, when they had visited a roadside place. The light was fading, and beyond the window Sita glimpsed a patch of fiery orange sky. Shadows settled in the purple blossoms of the jacaranda tree beyond the window, the colour darkening, the light perfume drifting to her again as she sipped the tea.

Eventually, as Sita knew he must, Dev left, and she was alone with her husband. She listened to her brother's footsteps clatter down the metal stair and the thump of the gate shutting behind him, as he let himself out of the courtyard and into the alley. Shiva bolted the door for the night and unrolled his thin mattress on the floor, smoothing out a sheet upon it. Then, as she watched, he unrolled Sita's new mattress beside his own. Crouched in a corner, back up against the wall, head covered, heart beating, Sita wondered what would happen now, what was expected of her. A gecko clucked loudly above her on the wall. Shiva said nothing, ignoring her as he stretched out on the sleeping mat, turning down the oil lamp on the floor beside it, and yawning in an exaggerated manner. The wall pressed against Sita's spine, panic tightened her chest. In the darkness of the silent room she heard the scuttle of a rat.

'Are you going to sit all night in that corner?' Shiva asked at last, and the sound of his voice rattled through her.

The faint light of a streetlamp in the road outside eased the darkness in the room. Shiva stirred and then propped himself up upon an elbow, staring at her silently, as if unsure of how to approach her. In the weak light she made a careful inventory of him, observing the silhouette of his head, the large ears and square jaw.

'Come and rest here. We are both tired. I will not look at you.' He turned his back towards her, yawning again, as if to reassure her of his disinterest.

Her exhaustion was so great it robbed her of all will power. The need to lie down and close her eyes overwhelmed everything else. Making her way towards Shiva, she curled gratefully up on the mat beside him. She was almost asleep when he turned to her, and she felt his hand on her arm.

When at last it was done, the shock and shame of it filled her, even though it was over quickly. Sita stared at her husband, already asleep beside her on the mat, light snores escaping him. The scent of his hair oil, and the smell of his flesh filled her head. Her body echoed with shock, of the weight and force of him pressing down upon her, splitting her open. She had cried out in pain but he did not hear. At last, when it was over, he looked down at her, gently pushing the hair off her brow. She was sore and wet between her legs.

'You are now my wife,' he told her before he turned and slept.

In the dark room, she listened to the sound of his breathing and the strange noises of the street outside; the wail of a cat or a baby, the loud quarrelling of men in a language she did not understand. Through the window she could see a narrow slice of black sky dotted thickly with stars. This was her second night in the town, and already life had reclaimed her. Beside her Shiva turned and in the faint light, she stared at his sleeping face. He had made no mention of changing her name. Whatever had happened to her, whatever might await her, she was still the same person.

Standing on four truncated legs and with a heavy lid, Shiva's desk was the most important piece of furniture in the room. Thin lines of inset brass patterned the steeply angled lid, and gleamed dully in the sun. The desk was crammed so full of pamphlets and Shiva's writings that the lid rested upon a soft pad of loose papers. Shiva sat cross-legged on a cushion before it, writing industriously each day after he returned from the Ramakrishna Mission School. Shoulders hunched, his long nose just inches above his work, fingertips permanently stained with ink, he seemed to hear and see nothing once immersed in his writing.

Each day when Shiva returned from school, Sita made him tea, silently placing the thick glass tumbler on the floor beside the desk. He rarely looked up to acknowledge her or the food she prepared every evening, and she ate her own meal later when he was busy again at his desk. She took care to keep her head covered, as was proper before a husband, but sometimes caught him staring at her, as if in displeasure, and was filled with anxiety.

When Shiva was out of the room there was little for Sita to do. All their washing was given to a nearby laundry, and an old

Tamil woman came to sweep and clean. Each day Sita walked the short distance to the top of the lane, to the stall at the corner to buy Shiva a coconut. Vishwanathan greeted her warmly, and picked out the choicest nut from his daily delivery.

From the window of her new home Sita could see up the road to the back of the Ramakrishna Mission School and the strip of grassland behind it. The school was the centre of her husband's life and he spoke enthusiastically about it.

'Hindu monks from India run the school. Swami Bhaswarananda, the principal, has helped me. The mission does many good things, caring for the poor and sick, educating children and taking in orphans. Even the architecture is special, bringing together a little of all religions,' Shiva told her, pointing out the Hindu, Muslim, Christian and Buddhist motifs, as he stood beside her at the window on their first morning as man and wife.

Sometimes, the faint hum of children's voices drifted to her from the school, and Sita listened to the sound, nostalgia twisting through her at the thought of how, as a child, she had longed to go to the village school like Dev.

She remembered, when her mother was not looking, stealing out of the house, to run along the path Dev walked to school everyday, skirting the village and the muddy pond beside the temple where the buffalo drank. She ran past the great banyan tree, its roots hanging down like an old man's beard, past the hut of paper and twigs the fingerless leper shared with his hairless dog. She ran on breathless until she neared the school with its whitewashed walls and dark tiled roof. As she approached, the low humming that always emanated from the place grew louder, the rhythmic drone of children's voices repeating their lessons. The breath throbbed in her chest as she leaned against the hot wall of the schoolhouse, afire with the sun. Stretching up, she peered through the window at the rows of boys sitting cross-legged on the floor. Dev's brow was furrowed in concentration as he repeated the words written on a blackboard that the teacher tapped with a long thin cane. With her cheek against the burning wall, Sita absorbed the hypnotic chant. It throbbed through her like the buzzing of invisible insects, the magic mantra of rote learning.

Once, she told her father she wanted to go to school. Even now she recalled how the sour male smell of him, of work and sweat, of tobacco and dust and the raw edge of life's frustration, had closed about her.

'And who will marry you if you go to school? What in-laws will want an educated girl who will bring her husband an early death?' He grabbed Sita as she skipped playfully about him, and hit her so hard her lip began to bleed.

Then her mother was there, dragging her into the safety of her arms, curling her body protectively about her, taking the blows for her daughter. Sita felt the dull thuds reverberating through her mother's body as she pressed against her. Yet, they both knew they were deserving of this anger, because they were women. Sita could see their powerlessness in her mother's constant pregnancies, the way she hurried back from the well so that water was in the house for her husband before sunrise. She saw it in the commanding stance of men as they thrashed a bullock pulling the plough, as they gossiped in the shade of the trees, drawing on pipes or strong smelling *bidis*. She saw it in the way her mother shrank back against the wall, preparing to absorb yet another of her husband's meaningless poundings, the butt of his disappointment that life had not yielded him more.

Now, so many years later, as Sita listened again to the familiar sound of rote chanting coming from the Ramakrishna Mission School, she imagined her husband rapping a blackboard with a long cane, kind but firm with his pupils. Sometimes she caught a glimpse of him when he accompanied a group of young boys to the playground for a game of cricket. Once, a photographer had appeared and the boys gathered about Shiva under the trees, posing for a photograph. Standing behind his pupils, hands on their shoulders, Shiva smiled at the camera.

Some days later he showed Sita the picture, encased now in a thin metal frame. Sita examined the image of her husband, his bright intense eyes and the gleaming ebony hair springing away from his brow with a life of its own, and placed the photo on the shelf, between Shiva's shaving mug and a small bronze *nataraja* figurine. Within a metal ring of fire the god Shiva, after whom her husband was named, performed the cosmic dance of life, destroying the old in order to create the world anew, controlling the never-ending cycle of time. Each morning Sita performed a daily devotion before the god, placing a strand of jasmine or a blossom picked from the frangipani tree outside the window, in front of the statuette, and lighting a stick of incense each evening.

From the moment Shiva left for the school each morning, Sita's day was spent awaiting his return. When he came home Shiva settled immediately at his desk, busying himself with the writing of provocative articles for a local Indian language newspaper on the need for Home Rule in the country. Shiva also wrote pamphlets and flyers of inflammatory rhetoric, for distribution on the street corners of Little India, or at the nearby Indian Youth League where he lectured on India's history and culture, and the need for freedom from colonial rule. Occasionally, he looked up from his desk to shout, 'Tea' or 'Water!' and Sita scurried to fulfil his command. As he worked, Sita crouched silently in a corner, sewing or mending, content to watch her husband's hand flying over the pages as he wrote, listening to the industrious scratch of his pen. It was the same sound she had listened to every day from her hospital bed in Vrindavan, as Dr. Sen filled in medical reports.

On that day in Vrindavan, when she had been admitted to hospital, she had finally awoken and looked up into the face of the plump middle-aged woman in a homespun sari who had examined her earlier at the clinic.

'Ah! You're feeling better,' Dr Sen smiled, her round cheeks lifting, a dark shadowing of hair apparent on her upper lip. Fragments of memory returned to Sita as she struggled to make sense of where she was. The pain of breathing and the fury in Roop's face at the clinic were the only things she remembered as she looked up at the doctor.

Later, Dr. Sen placed a tray of food before her. Sita inhaled the aromatic smells and stared at the root vegetables she had not seen for months in the ashram, and at the oily pulses and the round sweet *ladoo*.

'I cannot eat these things,' Sita whispered, looking down at the taboo food.

'You are no longer in the ashram. Eat what you feel like,' Dr. Sen ordered, standing over Sita until the dishes were empty and she lay back replete.

In the days that followed, Sita ate and slept, listening to the chirping of birds in the trees outside. Dr. Sen had set up a narrow cot for her in a corner of the small office she occupied as Medical Director. Since Sita was a widow, Dr. Sen felt it best to keep her away from the other women in the general wards who, with their usual blind adherence to traditional ways, would inevitably complain about some form of the evil eye and other pollutions being cast upon them by contact with her.

Sita was more than happy to share the doctor's room. The sun pushed through the dirty window, and an ubiquitous religious calendar, similar to the one in Sita's old home and her aunt's house, hung on the wall above her bed. She stared up at the familiar image of the goddess Durga with her benevolent smile, riding upon her tiger, and was filled with new hope. Dr. Sen bustled in and out of the room between her crowded clinics, as did the nurses, mostly Anglo-Indian or lower caste girls who were Christian converts, and who came to take Sita's pulse and temperature, efficient and firm, but not talkative.

Only the sweeper, a woman of the *harijan* caste who cleaned the room, liked to gossip, and through her Sita learned something of Dr. Sen. As an Untouchable, the woman was forbidden to speak or look at those of higher caste, but she felt free to speak to Sita, who, as a widow now belonged to the living dead, and so shared the same status as all outcastes.

'The lady doctor is unmarried, living with her widowed mother and looking after her, just as a son would do. The lady doctor does more than any man. They say she has lived with Mahatma Gandhi in his ashram, cleaning his spinning wheel, writing his letters while he fasted to get the British out of our country. The Mahatma came to Vrindavan once and upset all the rich men because he stayed with our *harijan* people. The lady doctor also visits our huts, and cares for our children, asking no money from us.' The woman gossiped as she moved about on her haunches, swishing a mop of wet newspapers industriously about the floor with a broom of thin twigs.

Dr. Sen spent a few minutes with Sita in the morning when she arrived at the hospital, and in the afternoons sat at a small desk in the room, filling in forms and writing reports. Sita was happy to lie back in bed and stare at the woman, absorbing her powerful profile with its thrusting, well-padded chin and straight rod of a nose. Her sari was draped with practical grace about her short plump form, the *pallu* pinned up on her shoulder to leave her arms free. A thick roll of oiled hair lay in a heavy bun on her neck, like a coiled muscle waiting to spring. Sita put a hand to her own skull, and felt with surprise the soft sprouting of hair.

While Dr. Sen sat at her desk, people came in and out of the room to ask for direction on various matters. Dr. Sen dispensed orders in a firm voice and Sita noticed that no one queried her command, not even the male doctors and orderlies, who were clearly uncomfortable taking instructions from a woman, but were forced to recognise her authority in a position they thought should be filled by a man.

As Sita watched Dr. Sen busily filling in her reports, she wondered what must it feel like to have the power to read and write? Sometimes, she stared up at the sky, at the movement of clouds, and wondered at the endless space, and all that lay beyond her comprehension. The knowledge Dr. Sen possessed must be like seeing beyond the clouds.

'When will I go back to the ashram?' Sita whispered at last, after she had been in the hospital a number of days. She was beginning to feel stronger, and had found the courage to ask Dr. Sen the question that was now constantly on her mind.

'We will see.' Dr. Sen took care to reply easily, not looking up from the papers on her desk.

Dr. Sen had also been considering this very question. The black gnome from the ashram came regularly to ask when Sita might be collected, and she feared she could not put off the day much longer. She had spoken to certain people at the municipal level about Sita, but found most men were loath to discuss the matter, feeling in their hearts that things were just as they should be; the child widow was in an ashram as tradition demanded, and indeed where else should she be? Dr. Sen also knew that as a woman, and an unmarried spinster at that, she was seen to have no right to question men of rank about such age-old structures and beliefs.

As Dr. Sen industriously wrote her medical reports, Sita listened to the scratch of her pen until she could bear it no longer and the words spilled out from her.

'Will you write to Dev for me?'

'Tell me who is Dev and what you want to write,' Dr. Sen nodded, looking up from her papers.

Sita felt her heart lurch and reached a hand to her breast, only to realise she was in unfamiliar hospital pyjamas and that the pouch of Dev's letters was not on her.

'Your things are here,' Dr. Sen said, seeing her alarm, opening a cupboard beside the bed and retrieving the worn muslin pouch. Sita grasped it in relief; not only could she not read Dev's letters, but without the address inscribed upon them he was lost to her forever. She thrust the creased sheets into Dr. Sen's hand.

'What shall I write?' Dr. Sen asked, picking up a fresh sheet of paper, her pen readied above it.

When at last a reply to Sita's letter came from Dev, his shock at events was palpable and his thanks to Dr. Sen effusive.

'Respected Madam Doctor, send my sister here to me in Singapore. Ticket money I will borrow from employer or moneylender and transfer to you through some reputable person or bank. I was not knowing any of this; my relatives were not informing me of my sister's marriage or her husband's death. Too much pity for my sister.'

Dr. Sen was pleased with this reply. 'It shows your brother cares for you, and does not have the old-fashioned attitudes that hold this country back. He sounds like a fine young man.

Whatever awaits you, you will have a new life, and it will be better than this. Soon Mahatma Gandhi will see that laws are passed to allow young girls like you to remarry. Slowly things will change.'

'I do not want to remarry,' Sita said, her voice no more than a whisper.

The next day Dr. Sen opened a large atlas and showed Sita a map, placing a stubby finger on the great coloured landmass of India. Sita stared at the light and dark smudges that were craggy mountain ranges and huge barren plains, and followed Dr. Sen's finger as she traced a line to the many-pronged mouth of the Ganges, leaking out into the ocean. Dr. Sen pointed to a black dot that she said was the town of Calcutta, from where Sita would set sail for Singapore. Leaving the solid body of India her finger journeyed over the blue emptiness of the ocean, to a distant tongue of land, beneath which rested a miniscule point that she said was the island of Singapore.

'Very small,' Sita whispered, appalled at the expanse of ocean between India and the faraway speck at the bottom of the page.

'Very small,' Dr. Sen nodded in agreement as they stood looking down at the map.

'But your brother is there,' she reminded Sita.

'My brother is there,' Sita repeated, happiness flooding through her.

Now, as Sita watched Shiva's pen moving over the page, these memories were as distant as a past life. Hidden behind the veil of her sari, Sita stared at her husband's narrow face, the high-ridged nose and firm, well-shaped lips, and felt she discovered him anew. She noticed how he pulled at his ear lobe, knocking the end of the pen against his teeth as he sought to dredge up a word. She noticed the length of his eyelashes, the small hairs sprouting from his nostrils and each ear. His skin had the glow of soft leather, and his hair was always neatly combed. Each night she lay beside him, opening to him, silent and unmoving, accepting the things he did to her. It was only then, in the darkness, when he turned to her for that act of the night that no wife should refuse, that she showed him her face, as his hands explored her body. Passive beneath him, she ran her fingers over the animal softness of his back and breathed in his musky masculine odour, that had become for her the very scent of the night.

Sita also drew strength from the knowledge that both Dr. Sen and Shiva were followers of Mahatma Gandhi. The great man's name was like a lifeline. She recalled a picture she had seen once of the half-naked Mahatma, bald and wizened, holding a staff in his hand. Dr. Sen had said that any person who believed in the ideals of the Mahatma could not be entirely bad; it was proof of character that they held such high ideals.

As the days unfurled, a routine set in; she became used to the sight and feel of her husband, and to the strange intimacies demanded by her new life as a wife. People sometimes came to their home to talk or seek Shiva's advice, and Sita served these guests tea and biscuits as he taught her, and listened to her husband's conversations about politics and the freedom of India.

Sometimes Shiva looked up from his desk to read her something he had just written, his eyes resting upon his wife, waiting for her response, but Sita did not know what to say, how to reply. Her heart beat wildly at such moments of scrutiny and she bowed her head, feeling his displeasure at her silence, hearing him return to his work with an exclamation of impatience, and knew she disappointed him.

One evening he returned with a newspaper and sat down at his desk, reading intently. When she bent down to place his tea beside him he looked up and gripped her arm.

'There is news of war in Europe. Our Indian soldiers in the British Army will be required to fight against the Germans. This is not right. They should not fight as part of a foreign army for another people's cause. Our people should fight for their own country, for India.' He stared searchingly into her face and she drew back, unable to understand the real meaning of what he said.

Eventually, he released her and she returned to her mending, sewing a button onto his shirt as he sipped his tea, yet uncomfortable because she felt his gaze upon her, and knew he still observed her critically. Finally, he put down the newspaper and turned abruptly to her, his voice rising in exasperation.

'Have you no voice?' A muscle clenched in his cheek.

Sita drew back in shock, the needle pricking a finger in her confusion.

'Say something! Ask me a question, anything,' he ordered.

Putting down her sewing, she looked up and met his eyes. Her heart fluttered nervously in her throat, but however hard she tried, no words came to her, and she grew desperate. She was sure he would hit her now, just as her father had so frequently hit her mother. Instead, he continued to sit at his desk.

'Try! Let me hear your voice.' His tone was more kindly now.

She searched for words that might please him. The image of Dr. Sen came into her mind and then the bald and wizened Mahatma Gandhi. It was because of the great man's ideals that Shiva had embraced the experiment of marrying her.

'Are you following the Mahatma?' she whispered, pushing the words out at last.

'*The Mahatma?* My wife has a voice! And asks an intelligent question.' Shiva slapped his knee, incredulous. He had expected her to ask if he wanted tea or food; instead she spoke extraordinary words.

'What are *you* knowing about the Mahatma?' he asked, puzzled. Behind the veil of her sari, he could see little of her face.

'Dr. Sen was living in Gandhiji's camp, she wrote Mahatmaji's letters for him. Write me please a letter to Dr. Sen,' Sita whispered.

She waited, but he did not reply, and when she looked up again he was back at work and the scratch of his pen filled her ears once more. Overwhelmed by having spoken so much, she was sure she had displeased him, but at last Shiva put down his pen and turned to her again.

'I will not write a letter to your Dr. Sen,' he told her, observing her shrouded form crouched in a corner against the wall, waiting mutely for his pleasure in a manner that annoyed him.

'You can write it yourself.' He watched her start in surprise and knew the bewilderment she must feel.

'I will teach you.' His voice softened. An idea was taking root in his mind and he moved from his desk to sit down before her.

'Take that sari *pallu* off your head,' he ordered, but in her confusion she only gripped the cloth more firmly beneath her chin.

'Let me see your face properly.' He reached out to push the drapery back over her short curly hair.

'Please understand, I do not like the old forms of respect, we live in modern times. How will India move forward if we keep such old ways? Women must be educated, must live their own lives.'

Already, he regretted his rashness in throwing himself into marriage with this unknown woman, an illiterate child. He was late in marrying, but he had always thought that when the time came he would marry a teacher like himself, an educated woman to whom he could talk of intellectual matters, and who would share his dreams. Now, he wondered at his mad moment of idealism. How could he have thought one woman was as good as another in the role of wife? When Dev told him that widowhood doomed his sister to live her life forever as an outcast, he became angry at the brutality of the old traditions. Just that day he had heard the Mahatma speaking on the radio. *Be the change you want to see in the world*, Gandhi had said, and the words had stayed with him.

Now, staring down into Sita's face, he was taken again by the unusual luminosity of her large eyes and the round, soft lips.

At thirty he must appear an old man to her and, moved by this thought, he put out a hand to touch her cheek, aware that she cringed from him like a frightened animal.

'I will not hurt you. You are my wife. You have left your old life behind, and in this new life you must learn new things, become a new person. I will be your teacher, and you will be my pupil.'

He had been so determined to align himself with Gandhi's thinking and to take on the challenge of social experiment, that he had given little thought to the woman he was marrying. Now, he saw that, just like him, she too was a bundle of thoughts and experiences that had carved their design upon her.

Overcome by embarrassment at his scrutiny, Sita pulled the sari over her head again, but Shiva held her hand and the cloth fell from her shoulders, revealing the shape of her breasts beneath the tight blouse. Shiva continued his examination of her, his eyes travelling over her face and then the contours of her body.

'Your hair is growing, soon it will be long again.' He got up to fetch his small shaving mirror from the shelf.

Placing the looking glass in her hands, and feeling the warmth of her fingers about his own, he watched her stare at herself. She was a fragile, small-boned animal that must be persuaded to trust. He knew she was pleased by the growth of her hair, the new fullness of her cheeks, the reassurance that she was once again a woman.

'You are a real Sita, just like the goddess,' he told her softly, surprised when tears filled her eyes.

'You are not to cover your head before me any longer. And you must talk with me,' he added, and she nodded mutely in promise.

All she wanted was to please him, but the things her husband said overwhelmed her. It was as if she stood before an ocean and was ordered to cross it, even though she could not swim.

There were things she needed for the kitchen, a new pan, a new spirit burner to cook on, bowls, spoons and ladles, a pestle and mortar, spices, pulses, rice. Shiva was a bachelor and had bought all his food, even tea, from the stalls on the road near the school; he knew nothing about the implements needed to cook a meal at home. Dev announced he would take Sita to his shop where, he assured her, all these things and more were available.

As she hurried along Serangoon Road beside Dev, he pointed out the local sights, the mosque, the temple, the racecourse a short distance from the road, the Youth League where Shiva spoke to young men each week, the market, the slaughterhouse, the parrot astrologer with his caged birds and pack of cards, the Chettiar money lender, the barber, the herbalist. The sun was hot on her head, and sweat collected in the small of her back. In the heat rotting piles of rubbish fermented, the fetid odours mixing with the scent of cowpats left in the road by wandering cattle.

Soon Dev turned down a side street to stop before the open recess of a large shop with a dark and cavernous interior.

"This is where I work," he announced with a proud smile, pointing to a large sign that was nailed to the wall above them, on which was written in faded letters, Krishnaswami and Sons.

Sita followed him into the shop, cool after the heat of the road. Baskets and brooms and buckets for sale hung on long strings from high rafters. Shelves lined the walls, packed with polished metal utensils, pans and long handled *tawa* on which to cook *dosai* or *chapati*, water *lotas* of all sizes, steel tumblers, plates and jugs, spirit stoves and kerosene lamps. One section of the shop was given over to religious figurines of varying sizes, and brightly coloured framed pictures of the gods covered a wall. Marble pestles and mortars, wooden rolling pins, dusters and mosquito nets, spoons and knives and mousetraps; the place was packed with merchandise, and busy with shoppers. People pushed against Sita, assistants hurried about calling out in loud voices the items required by customers, and *peons* scurried up and down ladders to storage areas above the shop, searching out requests. The place was all noise and bustle.

One end of the shop stocked dry foodstuffs, pulses and spices, rice and sugar, and pungent odours thickened the air. As she trailed after Dev picking out the things she needed, he introduced her to the other assistants. Then, putting a *peon* in her charge to collect the things she needed, he busied himself in serving waiting customers. Soon Sita amassed a large pile of items, and the young *peon* ran with each piece to the accounts desk and the wrapping table. As she made her way to the desk for a final reckoning, Sita passed the wall hung with pictures of gods and goddesses; Ganesh, Krishna, Shiva, Kali, and more. She searched the bank of frames until she found the *devi*, sitting as ever upon her tiger, face radiant, weapons at the ready, suffused by light.

'That also,' Sita ordered the boy, pointing to the picture, watching him take it down from the wall. Her heart lifted as she watched him place the goddess on top of her pile of purchases.

Although her mother eventually quietened and slept, Amita lay awake. There was little need in her tenth floor apartment for air conditioning, the cross ventilation was good and the ceiling fan moved lazily above her. The lights of the town outside eased the darkness in the room, and in the dim light she stared up at a large damp stain that had been growing over the last few days on the ceiling above her bed. The upstairs flat must have some leakage again, and she would have to battle for repairs and painting with the owner, an elderly Chinese, who made his dislike of Indians clear. The stain had built up, and seemed, as she stared at it, to take on a menacing shape. She could make out the curved back, the bulbous head and the budding limbs of a dark incubus, and turned away determined to ignore the sinister image, willing sleep to come.

Across the corridor her mother moaned softly again as she dreamed. If sleep could so easily tease out buried memories from her mother, then she too must be wary of unguarded moments and the things she might unwittingly reveal. The image of Parvati came forcefully before her and, alone in the darkness, she had nowhere to hide.

In the past, unknown to her mother, Amita had had a

couple of long affairs with male colleagues at the university, married professors, both of whom had eventually terminated the liaisons. Amita had drifted into these relationships because that was what experience of life appeared to demand, and stayed in them apathetically, surprised at her own indifference when each affair finally ended. Then, just a few months ago, Rishi appeared.

The irony of the situation was painful; her best friend and confidant was also now her lover's unsuspecting wife. Her own vileness sickened her. She had only slept with him twice, but such infrequency of involvement did not ease her guilt, and although Amita watched for signs, Parvati appeared unsuspecting. She continued to consult Amita on departmental issues, continued to share her flask of coffee. Did Parvati choose not to see what was before her, was she used to Rishi's philandering ways, or did she perhaps no longer care, Amita wondered. Although ignorant of the labyrinthine ways of marriage, Amita was acutely aware of the feckless nature of the friendship she now offered Parvati. The situation knotted tighter within her each day, often filling her with an irrational desire to confess to Parvati, to beg for absolution, but that would heal nothing, she knew.

Amita switched on the light and threw off the thin quilt; if she could not sleep, it was best to work. Just that day an email had come from a friend in New York, a well-known Indian academic who would also be at the coming Delhi conference. Amita had promised to write a paper for a volume of a prestigious American academic journal the friend was guest editing. "Everyone else's piece is in but yours. Get it to me pronto please.

We have to go to print!" the friend had written. The publication was a special volume entitled *Indian Woman: Warrior or Victim?* Amita sighed. Time had run out and she would have to rehash some old piece or cobble something together from various past papers.

With a sigh, she sat down at the desk and opened her laptop. Pulling up relevant documents, she began trawling through them for inspiration. It had been suggested she write on the old subject of *sati*, the immolation of a widow on the husband's funeral pyre. This repugnant practice, although outlawed a century earlier, was still relevant in the context of modern Indian attitudes towards women, and some isolated cases had even been known to occur in recent times. It was not Amita's choice of subject; she was doing a favour for a friend. The lighted screen drew her in, and she began to cut and paste from the documents she opened, promising herself she would find a way to recast it all the next day.

> ...the Hindu male traverses his life through four ascending stages... Woman as wife is indispensable to a man's status...as a woman, a wife has no access herself to the final stage of asceticism. Trapped in the misfortune of her female body, a woman is denied entry to Heaven, which remains the sole prerogative of men...

Feeling suddenly hungry, Amita pushed her chair back and padded over the tiled floor to the kitchen. In the passageway she always left a nightlight on, a small bulb pushed into an electric socket outside her mother's room. Sometimes, she awoke to hear her mother wandering around, and worried that she would stumble in the dark, or worse. Amita's bare feet made no sound as she passed her mother's open door, pausing briefly to check the peaceful rise and fall of Sita's breathing. A surge of freedom filled her at the knowledge that her mother slept. She was not used to living with anyone, and the constant sense of another presence in her home, even if it was her mother, appeared an invasion of privacy. Her space and time were also eroded by her mother's inevitable demands. At the university, it was all about students, teaching, lecturing, marking and, before her mother moved in, she had often worked through part of the night to keep up with her own writing, especially at weekends, when she could sleep in the next day. In the academic hierarchy it was necessary to write and publish, publish, publish. Now, the evenings were dented by the needs of her mother, and frustration grew within her.

In the kitchen, she made a mug of Milo and opened the tin in which she kept biscuits. Inside it there were only her mother's favourite jam centred cookies that Amita found too sweet. Opening a packet of plain crackers, she stood by the window, staring out over the town as she sipped the hot drink. The diffused radiance of the lights below yellowed the sky and obliterated the stars. The town had grown into a modern metropolis since she was a child. Then, the night sky felt like an actual presence in her life, a black pincushion of luminosity, dense with the infinite depth of the universe. Sitting on the spiral stair of their Norris Road home, Amita had felt her own smallness beneath it. Yet, at the same time, she had also sensed the possibilities life might offer if she could only set herself free of her mother, and the claustrophobia of the room they shared together. Now, so many years later, as she squinted up at the thin gauzy clouds drifting before the moon, she realised that life was not waiting to be found and claimed somewhere in the future. Life was being lived at each moment, and she was in a state of constant becoming. A state that must now include Rishi.

She first met Rishi as Parvati's husband. Sometimes, at the end of the day, if their times coincided, he came up to the English Department from his own room in the Political Science department to collect Parvati, and go home together. Amita knew little more of him until, in the process of setting up the new gender studies course together, Parvati had invited her home for dinner.

It had been a cheerful, wine-filled evening. Amita sat contentedly at the dinner table with the family, successfully engaging Parvati's withdrawn sixteen-year-old son, Arun, and gaining the begrudging respect of her fourteen-year-old daughter, Anu, by her knowledge of Japanese manga and their heroines, a genre Anu was currently obsessed with. Amita's detailed knowledge of this abstruse subject had been gained from one of her MA students, whose thesis was on the depiction of women in Japanese manga. Fleetingly then, within the warmth of this family, Amita wondered for the first time if she had missed something by not marrying and having a child, and the thought had surprised her.

With Rishi, a tall, fleshy man with an endearing smile and ready affability, there had been easy banter as he attempted to educate her on the subject of wine, about which he had considerable knowledge. She found him an attractive man and he was attentive, but there had been no special chemistry. As they talked about his work, Parvati sipped spasmodically on her wine, snatching up her glass from the table as she ran in and out of the kitchen, seeing to the food.

Rishi's specialist area of study and research was Complexity, Adaptive Systems and Evolutionary Theory. Amita listened closely as he talked about understanding the interrelationships between microscopic processes and macroscopic patterns, and the evolutionary forces that shape all systems. She kept thinking of how the concepts he spoke about could be fitted into her own feminist gender related subject, and how she could tweak part of a paper she was writing for a forthcoming conference in Amsterdam to incorporate something of these ideas. Even as her mind processed these thoughts, she noticed how his eyes lit up as he spoke, how his upper lip was fuller than the lower, and how the words tumbled from his mouth. Her interest in his subject, even if for her own ends, added a depth to their interchange. Rishi appeared pleased with the questions she asked and the interest she showed in matters he was passionate about.

'Oh, you're both getting on well. It's not often in this house he finds such a good listener,' Parvati teased, placing a hot dish of baked macaroni before them, her brow damp from the blast of the open oven door.

The unexpected edge to her tone made Amita look up. Parvati's eyes were fixed upon her husband with such measured intensity that Amita drew back, conscious suddenly of how her interest in Rishi's conversation might appear. Yet she knew the censure, so light it barely weighted the air, had nothing to do with her but rose from some toxic vein in their marriage.

'I was just thinking of how all this could be applied to a paper I'm writing for a conference in Amsterdam.' Amita hastened to distance herself from the situation, hoping she had not inadvertently upset Parvati.

'*Contemporary Ethnography Across Disciplines*? I'll be there too,' Rishi announced, and she stared at him in surprise.

With an effort Amita put an end to these recollections and returned her attention to her laptop. Her mother still slept peacefully as she guided the cursor to the next cut.

> …as widow the woman must regress…self immolation becomes the extreme case of the general law… The *sati* widow is…often pushed and poked into the fire with long stakes after having been bathed and ritually attired and drugged out of her mind…

In each new course she taught at the university, she always included something of the subject of *sati*, to illuminate the roots of traditional Indian attitudes towards women. There was a novel she listed for her students to read, by a modern Indian novelist, a woman whose own great-grandmother had committed *sati*. The book described the horror of a young son sent on an errand by his widowed mother, who returns home to an empty house. Some premonition drives him to the riverbank where he sees a blazing pyre and realises that, in his absence, his mother has been forced by her in-laws to become a *sati*. Amita clicked the mouse on a passage she always quoted to her students, and added the cut to her list of passages.

> He saw his mother fling her arms wildly in the air, then wrap them about her breasts before she subsided like a wax doll into the flames.

The words stared up at her as she pasted them onto her list, the image formed indelibly in her mind. Years ago, when she first read the novel from which she was quoting, the scene had touched her deeply. Now, remembering the curses thrown at her own mother by her in-laws, a sense of outrage filled her.

'Die with him in those flames! In your next life may you bear only daughters, never a son.'

The words still echoed though her, close and personal now, not the words of a distant novelist in a distant country, to be taught impersonally in an academic course, but a curse heaped on her *own mother*. Remorse ran through her; the things her mother had survived did not bear thinking about. What right had she, Amita, to complain about the small issue of sharing her space, and the dent in her privacy?

The next day Sita's lessons started. Shiva came home from school with a slate and chalk, and excitement throbbed through her as she watched him write the Hindi consonants on a large new notepad.

Ka – Kha, Ga – Gha, Ta – Tha, Ja – Jha, Da – Dha…

Then, picking up the slate, he pressed the chalk against it, and copying from the notepad, quickly drew a graceful character before giving the chalk to Sita. Each time she tried, the chalk-stick broke and crumbled into her lap. Soon a cloudy dust covered her fingers and clothes.

'Don't press so hard. Relax.'

Shiva placed his hand upon her own and gently guided her. She was aware of his arm around her, his breath on her neck, the grip of his fingers. Eventually, she managed to form a meandering shape and waited for his praise.

The following day after Shiva left for school, and once her domestic chores were done, Sita took up the slate and the chalk, full of suppressed excitement, but found she was unable to remember what sound each character made, or in what order each stroke must be drawn. Soon, her hand was cramped from gripping the chalk, her clenched jaw ached with tension and she was ready to cry with frustration. When he returned that evening Shiva looked at the squat and ugly shapes on the slate and paper, and laughed.

'You will learn, soon it will be easy.' He spoke gently, patting her arm.

Before he left for the school each morning he gave her work to show him by night. Her practice must be done in chalk on the slate, and then a fair draft was to be written in pencil in a lined exercise book. She wanted his praise more than anything and, hurrying through her chores, devoted most of the day to her learning. Slowly, the symbols became recognisable and she began to form them more easily. She imagined each character as a dancer, the stem of the body erect, arms akimbo or flung out at odd angles, legs bent or curled or pointed straight. Slowly, if she thought of them like this, the dancers assembled each day before her in familiar poses. As time went by, she also began to recognise words in Shiva's newspapers and books, and was filled with the pleasure of achievement. Slowly, she began to read. It was as if holes had been punched in a thick curtain, revealing the light beyond. Somehow, she had passed through an invisible membrane into another world.

At night now Shiva liked to light a cigarette and talk as he smoked. Stretched out beside her on their sleeping mats he inhaled lazily on his cigarette, occasionally flicking the ash into an old condensed milk tin beside him. From outside, the scent of the town drifted to them, of excrement and spices and night flowers, and the rotting odours of the blood-filled drains around the nearby slaughterhouse. Sometimes, the smell of the sea blew over to them, and the odour of drying sardines. She sensed that before she came into his life he had been lonely in this room and that now, even though she lay silently beside him and did not always comprehend the things he confided, it was enough that she was there. The sight of his tall slim frame, his firm lips and deep-set eyes filled her with gratitude; he had returned her to life.

The things he described as they lay together each night opened a window onto new worlds for Sita. It was just like the long ago comfort of lying beside grandmother on the string bed, listening to her tales of the gods. She especially liked it when Shiva spoke about Mahatma Gandhi. Because of Dr. Sen's close proximity to the Mahatma and the things she had recounted of her life with him, it was as if they spoke about a mutual friend. Sita was happy to listen any number of times to Shiva's account of the Salt March, the famous protest march in which Dr. Sen had also participated. She listened, enthralled by the vistas opening before her as she journeyed through the story.

'Gandhiji set out from Ahmedabad for Dandi on the coast with seventy-nine volunteers. At Dandi the Mahatma intended to gather salt on the beach and relieve the terrible burden of the salt tax that was breaking the backs of the poor. As they walked, people from the villages along the way ran to join the procession, until it became two miles long. At last, after a march of twenty-four days, the Mahatma reached the sea and bent to pick up a lump of salt from the beach, and all those with him did the same.' Shiva lifted the cigarette to his lips, inhaling contemplatively. The sweet scent of tobacco surrounded them.

'The following week a storm of revolt swept across India. The word *salt* had acquired magic power. Everyone began gathering natural salt, picketing liquor shops, burning foreign cloth, acting in civil disobedience against the government in any non-violent way they could. Many were arrested and imprisoned, many also were killed.'

Sita's eyes focused upon her husband with such concentration that everything else seemed to vanish in the dark room but the smouldering tip of his cigarette, igniting fiercely each time he inhaled.

'I deeply respect Gandhiji, but his non-violent ways can never get the British out of India. They laugh and call him a half-naked *fakir*; they have no fear of him. The only man the British fear is Subhas Chandra Bose.'

'Who is this Bose?' she whispered, struggling to understand.

'He too, like Gandhiji, is working for India's freedom, but in a different way. Gandhiji wants no violence. If the British wish to kill us then we must lie down before them and allow them to do this, he says. In contrast, Subhas Babu says violence can only be fought with violence. Blood must be shed for us to gain our freedom.' Shiva raised himself on an elbow and looked down at his wife.

'I came under Subhas Babu's spell as a young man. I went to hear him speak, and was immediately enthralled. He is a man to follow to the ends of the earth; that is his magic.' Shiva's voice had a faraway note.

'And then?' Sita asked, looking up into her husband's face, knowing he was opening a secret part of himself to her, that something important but wordless was being exchanged between them.

His body was warm against her, the dense perfume of his tobacco unlocked in her head and she reached out to touch his warm flesh, breathing in the male odour of him.

Pushing a strand of hair off her brow, he had to admit to himself that her rapt attention pleased him. He was getting used to her presence in his life, the hot tea she had ready when he returned from school, the meals she prepared for him. She was like soft clay, unformed and his to mould in whatever way he chose.

'And then?' Sita shook his arm gently.

'In India I was a teacher, but secretly, like so many young men, I belonged to a group fighting for Home Rule. Like Subhas Babu, we believed blood must be shed for freedom; it could not be gained by peaceful means, as Gandhiji advocates. We learned to make bombs and shoot guns. We learned how to blow up Englishmen.'

'And then?' she whispered again, trying to comprehend the things he was telling her, shocked at this revelation of his violent past.

'Englishmen were killed by the bombs we made, and the police started hunting for me. Along with many others, my picture was pasted on the walls of railway stations, marketplaces and telegraph poles. The police caught some from my group, who gave them my name.'

As she listened to her husband, Sita remembered again the first time she had seen an Englishman. It had been the mango season, the fruit hanging in golden orbs from the trees, its perfume pervading the village, filling the night. A few small mangoes were piled on the counter of their father's shop, and he gave one each to her and to Dev. There was also the treat of a biscuit with a sticky jam centre, and they sat in front of the shop to eat this feast. The juice of this particular mango was tastier than its stringy flesh, and Dev showed her how to rub the fruit between her palms until the flesh was soft. Then, they made a hole in the top of the fruit and sucked out the sweet liquid.

Suddenly, she recalled, the earth had begun to vibrate and on the horizon a cloud of dust appeared. Sita looked up at her father but he showed no panic, calmly continuing to weigh out *gram*, sliding it into cones of newspaper. A gritty wind now blew about them and a drumming pulsated in their ears. Within the ochre cloud of dust bearing down upon them a figure could be seen astride a horse, crop raised high, berating the animal. Sita glimpsed cheeks the colour of fire, bleached straw for hair and eyes glassy as rain. She flattened herself against the shop as the whirlwind passed. At last the thud of hooves grew fainter, and the whipped up dust settled upon them in a powdery layer.

'That was the *angrezi* tax Collector Sahib,' her father announced, staring grimly after the horseman and the accompanying entourage of carts that trailed behind him at a slower pace.

'Once, in a village that could not pay its taxes, he hung a

man who protested, and left him strung from a tree for days. The rotting flesh could be smelled from a mile away.'

Hearing such tales, Sita had always imagined the Collector Sahib to be a man of darkness. Yet, the figure that had just blown by on the back of the wind appeared, by an absence of colour, to have the attribute of ghosts. Heart pounding, Sita turned to her brother. The mangoes they held were now covered in grit, the sticky jam biscuit had fallen to the ground and was already black with ants.

The sound of Shiva's voice returned her abruptly to the present and she leaned towards him, filled with awe at his bravery in opposing people like the Collector Sahib, who hung men from trees so easily.

'My parents died when I was small and my uncle and aunt brought me up. When I became a wanted man, my uncle got me onto a ship coming to Singapore. He was a supporter of the Ramakrishna Mission in India, and because of him the Mission in Singapore gave me a job in their school here. They asked me no questions.' Shiva lay back on the pillow.

'Your parents...tell me about them,' Sita whispered.

She had not dared to ask about his parents before, but now she wanted to know everything about him. She turned on her side to face him, placing a hand upon his arm, feeling the solidity of his flesh under her fingers, feeling her own audacity.

'They were killed, shot.'

She drew a quick breath, unable to hide her shock. Shiva was silent, and in the dark she watched the glowing end of his cigarette and understood, from the flare of intensity, that he drew upon it with hard emotion.

'They were killed at Jallianwala Bagh.' The words left him in a rush, the cigarette glowing fiercely as he exhaled.

'What is this Jallianwala Bagh?' she whispered.

'It is a place where terrible things happened. It is a garden where hundreds of unarmed people, peacefully attending the festival of Baisakhi, were deliberately fired upon by the British army. My parents were amongst the dead; more than a thousand died. They were visiting friends in Amritsar, and were taken to see the garden. They need not have been there at all,' Shiva replied, his voice low and harsh. He pulled again on his cigarette, and Sita watched the tip ignite then fade then ignite angrily again.

The intensity in his voice frightened her, but as she listened to her husband's impassioned voice, the rightness of the Indian struggle swelled within her just as she knew it swelled within Shiva, and the blood pulsed wildly through her.

'If I have to die to avenge my parents' death, I will do so.' Shiva's voice was savage.

'Like me, Subhas Babu also escaped from India and from the British, who had placed him under house arrest. He fled in disguise to Germany, where he is living now. He is meeting Hitler there, to ask for his help to free India from British rule. Hitler is a powerful man,' Shiva added.

The smell of tobacco filled her nose. She was not listening so attentively now. Instead, her mind was full of the story of his parents' death, the violence that had broken his life. Beneath the

talk of guns and bombs, she sensed he was a gentle man whose
life had been cruelly shaped, aligning him to his destiny. Sleep
was heavy upon her, and she battled to keep awake, hearing his
voice now at a distance.

'In Europe a great war has already begun and Germany will
win it. Japan is also advancing through China. These countries
are our friends; they will help India get its freedom,' Shiva
assured her, stubbing out his cigarette.

The night enclosed them, and outside the rasp of crickets
and the crash of thunder gave way suddenly to the steady pelt
of rain.

All the while, as her mind grew and changed, so too did her
body. She suspected that now a child was growing within her.
Each day she placed her hands over her belly and thought of
the beating heart that might be within her, struggling to live.
In Shiva's shaving mirror she viewed her face for change, but
could find none. Her mind was full of the memory of her
mother's permanently swollen shape, but looking down at her
own body, nothing was detectable. She had not yet told Shiva,
and could not understand why she stubbornly held back news
that she knew would delight him. Nothing had ever belonged
so wholly to her before as this secret, and she wished to share
it with no one as yet, not even her husband. The changes in
her body and its cycle had not alerted her immediately to what
was happening; the knowledge had come to her unexpectedly,
through Old Usha at the Ramakrishna Mission School.

Five orphaned boys of five or six years old had recently come under the care of the Mission, but had yet to be integrated with other orphans into the mission's boys' school. Shiva suggested that as only basic reading and writing was needed to prepare them for class, Sita might pass on her own recent learning to the boys, and the school had agreed. She was to start the next day.

The five urchins waited for her, sitting on a mat in a small bare room, each with a slate before him. Scrubbed and clothed by the mission, heads shaved to rid them of lice, the boys were bright eyed and curious. Sita settled on the chair behind the desk, a box of coloured chalks before her, uncertain of what to do, or how to start. The children observed her silently, a band of bright eyed mice. Then suddenly they were jumping about her, pushing against each other and shouting.

'Can we have yellow chalk?'

'Can we draw a cat?'

'Can we draw a pig?'

She wanted to laugh, but instead ordered them to sit down. Turning to the blackboard balanced on a rickety easel behind her, she began to draw some of the characters she now knew so well. Behind her the boys chattered excitedly, testing the chalk on the slates. As they tried to copy the script, they were immediately entangled in the same difficulties from which Sita had so recently struggled free. She knew just how to help them.

'Make a picture in your mind. Think of the characters as dancers, like this, like that.' She flung out a leg then an arm, balancing on one foot, and the children laughed.

Throughout the lesson Sita was aware of Old Usha, a squat, ebony-skinned woman in charge of the children, who crouched in a corner of the room, staring fixedly at Sita from small eyes in a deeply pouched face. Her worn, russet coloured sari melted into her dark skin so that she appeared as if carved from mahogany. She had been with the school for longer than anyone could remember and worked in a general fetching and carrying capacity. It was said she had strange powers, and knew the art of black magic and prophecy. Everyone called her Old Usha, although she was no more than middle aged.

Finally, the hour of tuition was up. The boys shouted boisterous goodbyes to Sita and ran towards the door. Usha waddled after them but paused, turning back to Sita before she left the room.

'Already you are two months, three months?' She stood squarely before Sita, her eyes travelling down her body.

Sita started, staring into Usha's deeply bagged eyes, shock running through her. It was true, she knew it now; the woman had seen what she could not yet openly acknowledge.

'You must eat salty food to get a boy, no oranges and also no yogurt. Later, come to me, I will tell you if it is a boy or a girl.' A large inky wart lodged in the crevice of a nostril, but her smile was kindly and it lit up her face.

A boy. Usha knew she must concentrate on making a boy. She must eat the right foods, say the right prayers, she must focus all her thoughts on creating a boy, denying room within her to a girl. Was this, she wondered suddenly, what her mother had done, willing male life into each pregnancy. She saw the river beside the village again, smelled its muddy odour as it voraciously swallowed each female offering, and knew the same fear her mother had felt each time she was filled with a child, the fear that she carried a girl.

Her parents had been married as children. Her father had been seven years old, and her mother five, and she had gone to her parents-in-law's house after her first bleed. From the time she was physically able to, her mother had produced a child at regular intervals. The gap of a few years between Sita and Dev was because no intervening sibling had ever lived for long. Sita remembered several small brothers who ran briefly through the house before they died of one infection or another. She could not clearly recall a single one of these brothers; they all seemed to merge into one. Yet, even after all these years, she still saw the tiny, squashed face of her sister in those brief moments she had glimpsed her.

Now, on the day Usha confirmed what Sita already knew, an older knowledge floated up within her, unasked. Her mother had killed her sister. And, if she had murdered that girl-child, how many more had she felt forced to silence at birth, Sita now wondered, holding the child down beneath the water until she was still, freeing her from the hate loaded against her because she was a girl. Her mother had known that a girl was always better off dead.

Within days of realising that she carried a child, the war Shiva spoke about in faraway Europe edged its way nearer towards Singapore. The Japanese were advancing through South East Asia, territories falling to them like a row of dominoes. Japanese reconnaissance planes flew continually overhead, the red rising sun visible on their fuselage before they vanished into the clouds.

Each evening Shiva listened to the radio, to broadcasts from All India Radio, Radio Saigon, Radio Tokyo and the BBC, whatever he could tune into. The room was filled with the crackle of static and the voice of the news announcer, sometimes loud and clear, sometimes fading into the ether from which it had emerged.

'They say Singapore is a fortress, and the British will quickly defeat the Japanese if they try to attack. But already the Japanese have occupied much of China, already they are marching across Asia, and nobody is able to stop them.' Shiva held his ear to the radio.

The announcers spoke mostly in English, a language Shiva spoke but Sita did not understand. Occasionally, he remembered to translate the disembodied voice of the broadcaster for Sita.

'I will also teach you English — then I will not have to translate like this all the time,' Shiva complained lightheartedly.

Outside, the distant rumble of thunder was heard, and in the stifling heat of the room beads of sweat collected on Shiva's forehead. Sita stretched to pick up a paper fan, waving it gently before him as he returned his attention to the radio, twiddling the knobs, trying to find a station that might give more news, but receiving instead only a wall of static. At last he gave up the battle with the radio, and stretched out on the floor. The cool breeze from the fan Sita waved over him was a welcome relief, and he glanced up at his wife in approval. He found himself looking forward to her attentions when he returned to the room, and the food she cooked for him. She had a bright and inquiring mind, and her efforts to read and write and the quick progress she had made filled him with satisfaction. As he watched her small hand in the light of the lamp, waving the paper fan tirelessly back and forth for his comfort, he realised with pride that she wholly his creation.

The room was dark now except for the glowing pool of light surrounding the oil lamp. The smell of the burning wick filled Sita's nose, and Shiva's voice flowed over her as he talked about the Japanese advance. Although she tried to understand the events unfolding in the world, she could not focus on the things Shiva explained. Her mind kept slipping away, forming the same thought over and over again, like a mantra deep inside her. Make a boy, make a boy, she willed her body, closing her eyes to better project the thought into the depths of herself.

Each day after Shiva had gone to school, she put a fresh flower before the picture of the *devi* and the dancing figure of the god Shiva, and lighting a stick of incense, bowed her head in prayer. In her metal frame Durga sat as always, perched upon her tiger. The morning sun filled the room, intensifying the vibrant colouring of the picture, giving the tiger new depths. Its tawny stripes and amber eyes, glaring at Sita from a lowered head, blazed with fire. A boy, Sita prayed. Let me make a boy.

With the increasing threat of war and the Japanese advance, air raid practices became compulsory. In the beginning Sita had pinned a thick cloth over the window as the law demanded, but now she did not bother. As they had no electricity and only burned an oil lamp, she did not know what it was they were supposed to black out. Who would see their one small light from so high above? A ripple of fear ran through her, and her heart pulsed as one with the heart of the child. Everything within her was turned inwards around the new life she carried. She thought again about the war that threatened to engulf them. Bombs might drop upon them and their existence end tomorrow, and Shiva would still not know he was a father. Yet, until she was sure she carried a boy, she could not tell him her secret.

10
Singapore, 1941–1942

At first the troubles escalated slowly. As December ended and January began, incendiaries fell upon the city with growing intensity. Sita stared up each night at the wheeling searchlights roaming the great space of the sky. They thrust open the darkness with needles of light and filled her with increasing unease. Sometimes now she could feel the baby turn, a faint flutter against her heart. Each night she prepared to tell Shiva the news the following day, but each day passed into the next and the weeks went on. Each week she resolved to go to Usha to put an end to the torture and to determine, by whatever dark art the woman practised, whether she carried a boy or a girl.

Japanese planes now roared endlessly over the island in perfect formation, like a flock of migrating birds. Shiva watched in fascination as bombs were detached from the underbellies of aircraft to fall earthwards, like streamers taking flight in the wind. In the distance there was the crack of anti-aircraft guns or the thud of the bursting bombs. The Indian area of Serangoon Road did not at first experience the rage of the bombs. This was put down not to luck, but to the fact that India, like Japan, wanted to see an end to colonial rule in Asia, and it was believed that the Japanese military understood this.

'That is why the pilots are not bombing our Indian area,' Shiva said, voicing the conviction all Indians now held.

'Nothing will happen. The Japanese are Asiatics like us Indians; they are helping us to chase the British out of Asia,' he assured Sita each morning as he left for the Ramakrishna Mission; the school was still open, even though many others had closed down.

The odour of death soon permeated the air. A pall of sulphurous smoke from the oil burning at the Sembawang naval base blackened the sky and made Sita hug her secret closer in new fear. Now, even to voice the existence of the child seemed to expose it to danger. Sita's slight frame hardly showed the presence of the baby, hidden beneath the drape of her sari. Only Old Usha at school scrutinised her roundly on the days she went in to instruct the five urchins, shaking her head, muttering in disapproval. Each time the class ended, the woman hung back, always with the same advice, staring up at Sita, who stood a head taller than her.

'Now you are big enough, now I can tell you. If it is a girl, then I can help you get rid of it. Then I will tell you how to get a boy for the next time.'

Sita pushed past the woman, and ran.

As the weeks went by the bombing increased, and soon the Ramakrishna Mission School decided to suspend all lessons. Many families had already evacuated, and the school similarly sent its children to safety in outlying areas.

As February began, the Japanese drew near the island. During air raids the residents of Serangoon Road ran for shelter to the covered colonnade of the five-foot-way fronting the blocks of shophouses. Destruction in other parts of the city soon revealed that these buildings were more of a danger than a refuge, and people made for the open land of Farrer Park and the presumed safety of the racecourse. It was thought that the Japanese would not waste valuable bombs on open land, and nobody used the trenches there, surrounded by sandbags and sodden with rain. The Indian flag was raised boldly upon the grassy expanse of the park, to let Japanese pilots know there were Indian civilians below. A large part of Sita's life now seemed to be spent running from her home to the park.

The days slid terrifyingly one into another as the bombing continued. Shops had closed, boarded up against looting. Chinese of the coolie class had fled the city to the relative quiet of the rural areas, and labourers were now almost impossible to find. So relentless had the bombing become, and so frequently did the air raid sirens wail, that in the confusion it was difficult to determine if raids was beginning or ending.

At the Ramakrishna Mission the monks remained on the premises, as did the five urchins and Old Usha, who would soon leave to join the other children, now housed in a far corner of the island. Sita continued her lessons with the boys, although around them the school's rooms now lay empty. Each day she battled with growing exhaustion, her limbs and head aching continuously. It took all her strength to hide how she felt from Shiva. During lessons Usha continued to sit in her corner, staring at Sita.

That day Sita left the school for the short walk home, her limbs heavy, each step an effort to push herself forward. As she crossed the school compound towards the gate, a pain ripped through her with such violence that she gasped aloud. When the spasm subsided she struggled on, but as she neared her home, a further convulsion doubled her up. As it seared through her, the air raid siren began again, and almost immediately she heard the thunder of bombers approaching. As she climbed the spiral stair, her head reeled and a wave of nausea swam through her; the planes droned low over the roof of her home as she pushed the door shut behind her. Then another pain gripped her and, looking down, she saw blood running over her feet.

Curled up on the floor, she willed the child to stay within her, but already she knew it had leaked away, cell by cell, the very parchment of life seeping from her. The secret she had held so close to her, the words she had not been able to say, spilled from her now in anguish. As she cried out in the empty room she was conscious again of the siren's shriek. Then, suddenly, the earth shuddered beneath her with the impact of a bomb. Outside, the jacaranda tree buckled and bent, its feathery branches blown wildly about by the blast, before it cracked and fell. The earth shook again and she heard the screams of animals in the nearby slaughterhouse, and then the screams of men. She could not move, and blood flowed from her unstoppably.

Shiva burst through the door with a cry and ran to where Sita lay. He had heard the bomb drop as he left the school, and knew his wife had gone home before him. The missile had hit the slaughterhouse, tearing the limbs off cows and goats,

loosening roof tiles and blowing out doors in the buildings on
Serangoon Road. Shiva saw the fallen jacaranda outside his
house and feared for Sita as he ran. Old Usha hurried behind
him, shouting incomprehensibly. As Shiva entered the room he
saw Sita curled up on the floor in a pool of blood. Behind him
in the doorway Usha sized up the situation and, pushing Shiva
out of the way, bent to Sita.

'She is not dead. Only baby is gone,' she told Shiva, seeing
that he thought his wife was the victim of the bomb, and then
she ordered him out of the room.

In the midst of her pain Sita was aware of Usha's presence,
and knew by the firmness of her hands that she had assisted
in such situations before. Usha leaned over her, pressing down
upon her, and Sita felt her body respond with violent spasms of
pain until all the life it had held was gone. The woman pulled
the wet bloodied sari off her, and brought a bowl of water to
sponge her clean before covering her with a sheet. On the floor
a distance away, Sita saw a sodden mass of bloody newspaper,
and knew it contained the raw membrane of her child. Usha
followed her glance.

'It is still early. No soul had entered into it yet. Only in the
seventh month does a soul enter, before that no ceremonies are
required. I will see it is disposed of.' The woman scooped up the
mess, tipping it into the metal bowl that she pushed firmly to
one side.

'It was only a girl, so better it came out early. Next time I will
help you get a boy,' Usha comforted, rising to her feet.

Sita stared at the bowl of bloody newspaper, and for

a moment saw that other bowl from so long ago, and the dismembered plait of hair. She began to sob, and knew that a shame similar to the shame she had known on that distant day would take hold of her now.

Then Usha was gone and immediately Shiva was in the room, standing over her, his face distorted by anger.

'You *did* this,' he shouted. 'Why did you not tell me?'

She was confused and could not answer. Shiva's voice rose louder with each word.

'That old witch is known for these things. Women go to her to be rid of a child. Why have you done this?'

Whatever she said in the weeks that followed the miscarriage, Shiva persisted in the conviction that Sita had deliberately got rid of the child. At night he no longer told her stories that opened windows for her into the world, no longer encouraged her writing and reading, no longer enquired about the urchins at school. He ate silently and slept with his back towards her, absenting himself from her life. About them sirens and explosions accelerated, the air was thick with smoke. They ran to Farrer Park less and less, taking their chances wherever they were. Bombs rained down everywhere now, and they were resigned to the possibility of sudden death.

Krishnaswami and Sons remained open but most of its assistants had fled to the suburbs, resulting in a promotion for Dev, along with added responsibility. His hours at the shop increased, but any free time was spent with his sister, sharing a meal and chatting with Shiva.

Often now, on the short-wave radio, they tuned in to Azad Hind, the new Free India radio station that had begun transmitting from Germany. Frequent broadcasts were made from Berlin by an Italian diplomat by the name of Orlando Mazzotta, who spoke passionately of plans to free India from British Rule, his deep melodious voice filling the room.

'The overthrow of British power in India can, in its last stages, be materially assisted by Japanese foreign policy in the Far East...'

Rumours swirled about the identity of this mysterious diplomat, and it was rumoured he was Subhas Chandra Bose in disguise. Shiva was stirred to a great pitch of excitement each time he heard the man's voice.

'It is him, it is Subhas Babu speaking. Everyone recognises his unmistakable voice. He is using this disguise for safety, so that the British will not pursue him.' Shiva adjusted the knob of the radio as the voice began to fade.

'This is the time to remind our British rulers that east of the Suez Canal there is a land inhabited by an ancient and cultured people...deprived of their birthright of liberty under the British yoke...'

The deep voice wrapped briefly about them again before it was sucked into a band of crackling static from which it could not be retrieved. Shiva thumped his fist on the desk in frustration.

'The Japanese are just across the water. Soon the British will be forced to surrender,' Dev reminded him.

'The Japanese are Asiatics, like us. I will welcome them,'

Shiva replied, his hand adjusting the knob of the radio, hoping for the return of the mysterious Orlando Mazzotta.

Crouched before the small stove at the other end of the room, Sita heated a pan of spicy tapioca. It was increasingly difficult to find anything to eat other than the ubiquitous tapioca that grew easily on the smallest patch of land. Listening to the conversation, she kept her eyes upon Shiva, hoping he would look up and include her; day after day since the miscarriage, he continued to ignore her.

Much of the room was now taken up with a metal-topped cage, a Morrison type shelter that Swami Bhaswarananda had given them for Sita's protection. It had open wire netted sides and a mattress in it, and they slept beneath it for shelter each night. Even in that confined space, pushed up close against him, Sita still felt Shiva's resistance.

In the evenings, when he returned home, Shiva settled cross-legged before his desk and, by the light of the oil lamp, immersed himself silently in his writing, erecting a further wall between them. Depression overwhelmed her, pulling her down into a black well. At night she could not sleep, and by day was listless and without energy. In the evenings she sat quietly in a corner with a pile of mending, a newspaper spread before her or her new English alphabet primer on her lap, practising the letters in an exercise book, determined not to react to Shiva's cold exclusion of her. Yet all the while she was alert to the scratch of his pen, the echoing croak of bullfrogs in the open drains outside, the whirr of crickets, the distant clank of empty milk churns or the voice of the school janitor gossiping with friends across the road. Worst of all was the nightly wail of mating cats, a noise that had not bothered her before. She knew Shiva heard it too and that the calls, so like the cries of disconsolate babies, awoke in them both an anguish neither could speak about.

She had not told her husband the miscarried child was female, preferring not to admit to the shame of making a girl, but the knowledge moved through her. Her tossing and turning each night worked loose distant memories; she saw the small pinched face of her sister again, before the river consumed her. And she remembered also a woman on the boat that had carried her over the waters to Singapore, a memory that was lodged within her forever, and rose now to fill her mind again.

Dr. Sen had paid extra to secure Sita a berth in the dark and suffocating bowels of the ship, in a cabin with six other women and their children, travelling to join husbands in Penang or Singapore. Male passengers slept above on the open deck, and during the day the women were obliged to join them there. At night the ship heaved and ploughed its way forward, creaking as if it's very sides would split. In the hot airless space Sita listened to the seasick moans of women and children, breathed in the odour of oil and brine, the rank stench of bodies and vomit. By day, battered by breezes and the undulating swell of the ocean, travellers sat crushed together without decent facilities, sleeping, defecating and eating their food in a makeshift manner. Day after day the wind whipped Sita's face and the taste of salt encrusted everything. Pressed into the small space of the deck, enduring the fierce blaze of the sun and the sickening pitch and roll, the women had to queue along with the men for the use of a single stinking toilet. The door would not close securely and the women looked out for each other, standing guard when one of their own was inside.

Before turning into the open sea, the ship made one last stop at an Indian port. Here, further indentured labourers going to work on the rubber plantations in Malaya were taken aboard. The vessel stayed out in deep water and the labourers were rowed out to the ship in small boats. Sita stood with others on the deck, leaning over the rail to watch the proceedings. The sea was choppy and the boats, crammed mostly with men but also a couple of women and two small children, rode high over the waves, rearing and diving. A rope ladder was thrown over the side of the ship as the boats approached, bobbing about beneath the hull. The men went first, one by one, grasping the ladder with difficulty, struggling for each foothold on the swaying rope as they ascended. Soon, all the men were aboard the ship, and only the two women and children were left in the boat, sobbing in terror as they looked up at the ship looming above. With threatening shouts the boatmen drove them towards the dangling rope, while high above spectators peered silently down over the rail of the deck. Two young boys of ten or twelve, with their mother close behind, and all driven by the liquid fear of death climbed quickly aboard, like monkeys swinging determinedly up the rope.

The remaining woman, clasping a baby strapped to her breast and with a fat bundle of belongings tied to her back, now attempted to scale the rickety ladder. Her husband, already safely aboard the ship, looked down from above, shouting encouragement. The woman gasped and moaned as the ladder swung this way and that, hanging on as best she could. Sometimes, daring for a moment to lift the arm encircling her baby, she used both hands to pull herself up a further step but, in spite of angry urging from her husband, she soon came to a halt. Sita saw the straps securing the infant to her body had loosened and, paralysed with fear, she leaned against the rope suspended between life and death, her husband shouting frantically from above.

For some moments the woman refused to move, sobbing and calling for help. Eventually, her husband climbed over the side of the ship and descended again down the rope. Reaching a point a few feet above her, he bent and extended a hand. At last the woman took her arm from around the baby and reached out to her husband. In that moment the tying cloth slipped, releasing the baby, who plunged down into the sea. With a scream the woman jumped after it, hitting the water with a splash, floundering about, the bundle of belongings tied to her back bobbing about like a great white egg. Screaming and thrashing, the woman sank quickly, the weight of the sodden bundle pulling her down. Then her head broke the surface of the water again as she flailed about, unable to reach her baby, who tossed upon the waves a distance away. In that last moment she raised her head to appeal to her husband high above her on the ladder, but he was already scrambling up the rope to the safety of the deck. Soon the water drew them under, the faint shape of the child was seen drifting lower and lower in the water, until at last its small body was lost in the depths. There was nothing now to be seen of the woman. The oily membrane of the sea had closed over them both, like a curtain dividing one dimension from another. In the sudden silence the sea could be heard once more, slapping against the bow of the ship.

Soon, Sita remembered, she had felt the deck vibrate beneath her feet as the engines started and the ship prepared to move forward. A distance away on the deck the new widower sat in stunned silence, a crowd of fellow passengers about him.

'It is God's will,' a passing deckhand commented.

'There are many young girls on those rubber estates; in no time he will get another wife and child,' a man near Sita shrugged.

As the ship moved into new waters Sita stared into the churning wake opening behind the vessel like a trail of crumbled quartz, and drew a breath. In her mind she saw the woman again, her loosened hair spread out upon the surface of the water like a mass of dark weeds. In that last moment she had looked up at her husband, but he had already turned his back upon her, leaving her to her fate.

Now, as she stared at the silent Shiva and listened to the industrious scratch of his pen, Sita felt a rush of unbearable grief for that unknown woman and infant, and for her own lost and unformed child.

The Japanese were now just across the narrow strip of water separating mainland Malaya from Singapore, and the new and terrifying noise of shelling was heard, like the whirring of a giant cicada. All Sita's aching grief reverberated to the sound. Shiva was out all day, working now as a volunteer with the Indian Passive Defence Corps. The wounded and homeless of all races crowded a hospital tent set up on the Farrer Park field. Shiva left early in the morning and returned exhausted late at night. With a truck and a couple of other volunteers he drove to distant parts of the city, tracking down food supplies, bringing in the aged and wounded of all races to the Farrer Park tent. The empty classrooms of the Ramakrishna Mission School were also turned into emergency accommodation for the growing numbers of homeless people in the city. As the air raids intensified, casualties mounted, and Shiva was forced to speak to Sita again.

'We need volunteers at the field hospital. You can assist the nurses as a dresser, we need everyone to help.' Shiva spoke stiffly, but the plea in his voice was clear.

New energy throbbed through her the following day as she walked up Norris Road beside Shiva. As they reached Farrer Park, Sita was surprised to see a huge tent of the kind usually erected for marriages in the middle of the green. Shiva ducked beneath the open flap and Sita followed. So great was her relief at the resumption of communication with Shiva, that she had given no thought to what work in the hospital might involve, and was unprepared for the crowds of wounded lying on makeshift pallets or blankets, men, women and children, Indian, Chinese and Malay, all massed together in misery. Cries, groans and the screams of babies filled the place. People, who she presumed were doctors or nurses, hurried about, shouting orders. She was unprepared also for the compressed heat of the place, the fetid human stench of blood and bodies, the chaos of distress.

They made their way to a small wiry woman who was dressing the wounds of a line of waiting patients.

'Do you know any first-aid?' The woman asked Sita, when Shiva introduced her.

'I will look and learn.' Sita replied, surprising herself at the confidence she heard in her voice.

Beside her, Shiva nodded approvingly before turning away, making his way to the men waiting by the truck beyond the tent, and the day's work ahead.

Soon Sita was working long hours, leaving with Shiva early each morning, and returning home late at night. Every day she faced an endless variety of wounds, and learned to recognise when infection had set in, and how to deal with the maggots that quickly colonised suppurating injuries. She supported the elderly who stumbled wearily about, and managed the small children running wild through the tents. Commandeering her five small pupils from the Ramakrishna Mission School, she set them to organise activities for refugee children in the nearby school premises, suggesting they teach the script and numerals they had learned from her to those younger than themselves. The urchins took to the task with zeal, distributing slates and chalk, rapping on blackboards, shouting out commands.

People milled about Sita, confused and frightened. Absorbed by the appeals for help from those in need, she was stretched in new ways, and forced to assert herself. Soon, to her surprise, she found herself taking control of situations, giving directions, feeling her own fear ebb away, her voice projecting from her with new strength. At times she felt she could no longer recognise herself.

Many of the people she met each day, Chinese and Malays, she had had little contact with earlier, and had no language of communication. Yet whatever their race, everyone, even the Indians spoke to each other in bazaar Malay, and she began to pick up words, soon learning enough to give routine orders or make basic enquiries in this strange language. English was also heard, and she made an effort to store the strange new phrases away in her head, glad she had persevered with the alphabet primer Shiva had given her, and could already read and write some simple words.

Eventually the bombs and the shelling stopped abruptly, as Singapore's colonial government surrendered to the Japanese. The unexpected silence was unsettling and menacing.

'We must stay inside,' Shiva said, repeating the advice he had heard on the radio and been given at the field hospital.

He listened for the daily news bulletins on the radio, but all he heard now were heavily accented Japanese voices telling him Singapore was liberated from the tyranny of British rule.

The Japanese victory had an immediate effect upon Azad Hind broadcasts from Germany. On the day of Singapore's surrender, Subhas Chandra Bose threw off his disguise and announced what everyone had suspected, that it was he who had been speaking to the world incognito from Germany under the name of Orlando Mazzotta. Shiva was ecstatic as Bose's deep voice filled the room, for once miraculously clear of static.

'…I have waited in silence and patience for the march of events and now that hour has struck, and I come forward to speak. The fall of Singapore means the collapse of the British Empire, and the end of the iniquitous regime which it has symbolized, and the dawn of a new era in Indian history…'

Sita listened to the powerful and melodic voice, and it did not matter that she understood little of the English he spoke. The hypnotic tempo of his voice was enough. Shiva leaned in close to the radio and once the broadcast was finished, sat back in a daze.

'In Germany people now call Subhas Babu Netaji, great leader. In Germany they have their Fuehrer, we have our Netaji.'

Later they ate some parathas made from tapioca flour, the dough hard and chewy. Outside, the roads were deserted and silent. Occasionally the sound of marching soldiers or an unnerving burst of gunfire was heard. They ate the parathas slowly, savouring each mouthful, not knowing how many days they must wait in their home, or where food would come from tomorrow. As they finished their meal, Dev, who had now moved in with them, offered the advice that was being circulated throughout Little India.

'If Japanese soldiers stop us, we should say we are *Indo*. This is the Japanese word for Indian. On the mainland, Japanese soldiers have not mistreated Indians in the towns they have captured. They only mistreat the Chinese, who are fighting against them in China. We Indians are of less interest to them and they usually leave us alone.'

'All Japanese know the name of Mahatma Gandhi because, like the Japanese, he is fighting against the British. They hold him in high regard,' Shiva added, putting the last morsel of paratha carefully into his mouth.

Through the night they dozed, alert to every sound, disturbed by shouts and the tramp of marching feet. As morning broke, Shiva could stand the tension no more. Looking out of the window, he found nothing untoward. When he turned on the radio only Japanese music and propaganda slogans was heard.

'Let's see what is happening. Perhaps we can find some food, or a tea stall,' he said to Dev.

'Don't show yourself at the window. We will not be long.' Shiva ordered Sita.

She watched the door shut behind them and retreated to a corner, crouching down between the wall and the metal cage of the Morrison shelter that, until the day before, had appeared to offer some security from death. Now, overnight, the dangers they faced had changed. The stories of Japanese soldiers came back to her, of their cruelty and disregard for life, the rape of women and the callous beheadings. Outside, the silence was broken by the call of a *koel*, and she was suddenly conscious of how hungry she was, and that she needed to use the latrine downstairs in the yard. Finally, she could bear it no longer, and against Shiva's orders, stood up and made her way to the window. The road was deserted and, looking over the courtyard wall and up the lane, she glimpsed the familiar dome-shaped *chhatris* on the roof of the Ramakrishna Mission.

The sound of shouts was suddenly heard. Stepping back out of sight, she watched a group of Japanese soldiers turn from Norris Road into the alley. They ambled forward, stopping before each firmly locked door, shouting in frustration when they could not enter. Soon they arrived at the gate of the courtyard below. Shiva had left it unlocked and Sita stared in horror as the soldiers kicked it open, and peered curiously inside. Crouched below the window, she listened to the rough incomprehensible voices as they entered the yard and paced about, her heart beating painfully. Crawling behind the iron table shelter, she crouched down in a narrow space against the wall, wedging herself in between stacks of books, making herself as small as possible. Downstairs, the voices grew louder, the men shouted across the courtyard to each other, opening doors, entering other homes in the building. Sita heard the screams and shouts of her neighbours. Then, there was the metallic echo of footsteps on the spiral stair, coming up towards her. She closed her eyes and covered her head with her arms.

Bursting into the room, they surrounded her, grabbing her roughly, pulling her up. Their guttural voices bounced about, loud and incomprehensible. They had been on the march for days, through jungle and swamp, and their filthy uniforms hung in tatters upon them, their faces were unshaven, and their rank odour pressed upon her. One of them pinioned her against the wall with the end of a bayonet, moving the tip of the blade up to her breast, pricking her flesh through the thin cloth of her blouse. All the while they laughed, lips drawn back upon wide square teeth, and she remembered the fangs of a cornered rat she had once seen in her aunt's house, imprisoned in a trap. She remembered then what Dev and Shiva had said.

'*Indo.*' Her voice was no more than a whisper.

'*Indo.*' She took a breath and yelled out the word as loud as she could.

For a moment they glanced at each other and she saw the surprise in their faces, the sudden uncertainty.

'*Indo.* Gandhi. Gandhi. Gandhi.' She repeated the name like a prayer, at the same time raising her eyes to the picture of the *devi* on the shelf across the room.

'*Gundi?*' The man with the weapon bent towards her, repeating the word, but whether his tone was cautionary or encouraging she could not tell. After another quick exchange of glances the bayonet was withdrawn.

'*Indo? Gundi?*' Tossed about in their thick rough voices, the words were almost unrecognisable. The man with the bayonet now stepped back, staring at her with a thunderous frown. Then, with grunts of angry frustration, the men turned away, pushing out through the door. Their voices grew distant as the metallic echo of their footsteps retreated down the spiral stairs. With a groan of relief Sita sank to the floor, too chilled by fear to cry.

11
SINGAPORE, 2000

Amita and Rishi travelled separately to Holland on different flights on different days, and met as the conference started. Since they were the only two delegates from Singapore, they formed a natural bond, hailing each other from afar, discussing their papers together and gravitating to the same table at meals. Rishi knew many more of the international delegates at the conference than Amita did. His ability to make people laugh, his exaggerated gestures and endless stock of anecdotes made him popular with everyone. Free of the presence of his wife, his personality expanded. Amita saw how attentive and openly flirtatious he was with women, and how they responded. Women she respected for their academic prowess and self-determined lives dissolved before him in an indefinable way, engaging with him, smiling into his face with uncharacteristic coyness. With Amita, Rishi adopted a companionable stance, even confiding once or twice about the uneven tempo of his marriage, embarrassing her with such confidences. He was also a shrewd and perceptive academic with many publications to his name, and his work was widely recognised and respected. The seminar room was crowded for the reading of his paper, *Complex Adaptive Systems: The Known, the Unknown and the Unknowable in Asian Societies*.

Amita also had a good audience for her own paper, *Complicity and Resistance: Gender in the Politics of Migration*. She had a special interest in the subject of female Indian migrant workers, especially those who in colonial times had come as indentured labourers from India to work on the rubber estates of Malaya. Many of those women had joined the Indian National Army at the time her own mother had joined, sharing the same experiences, fighting for the same cause.

The weather was so bad that a sightseeing trip was cancelled and Amita and Rishi spent the afternoon in the Rijksmuseum instead, looking at paintings by old Masters. Most of the conference delegates had gone to a new blockbuster exhibition at the Van Gogh Museum. The towered and turreted Rijksmuseum was presenting a small but treasured exhibition of van Eyck masterpieces, lent by several international museums. Rishi was more interested in the Rembrandts and Vermeers on show, but Amita was determined to see the van Eycks. She had never forgotten the portrait of a man and his wife seen in the National Gallery in London on a visit there long ago.

It was the last day of the show in Amsterdam. With pamphlets and audio guides they entered the exhibition rooms, keeping close together. There were no more than twelve pictures in two rooms, works of marvellous detail, density and stillness. Amita stood before the portrait, *Man in a Red Turban*, thought to be a self-portrait of van Eyck, the audio told her. Beside it was a portrait of the artist's wife, Margaret, a handsome woman in a copious white headdress agleam against a dark background and her red dress. She stared out of the canvas, frozen in time, her face filled with stoic resignation-patient and benign. Then, across the room Amita noticed the picture she had come to see, a fifteenth-century portrait of an Italian merchant and his wife in the Flemish city of Bruges. When she last saw the picture Amita was a student and on her way to America from Singapore. Just as she had so many years ago, Amita stood transfixed before the painting, feeling she had transcended time, stepping into another dimension.

The merchant Arnolfini and his wife, standing hand in hand beneath a brass chandelier, inhabited a rich and secluded world. The man in his wide black hat, and the woman in her voluminous green gown, an excess of material held up over her stomach to hide a possible pregnancy, were surrounded by symbols of fertility-oranges on the window sill, a wooden statue of the patron saint of childbirth, Saint Margaret, on the bedpost finial. On the wall in the centre of the picture was a concave mirror that, the audio informed Amita, might represent the eye of God.

Now, she stood before the painting at a different time in her life, and saw different things. The pregnant woman was positioned beside a bed while the man stood next to a window, a threshold beyond which the outside world was glimpsed, and where the merchant Arnolfini would have lived his life. From his expression he appeared a passionless, self-contained man, aware of his wealth and position. Beside him his pale wife, eyes dutifully downcast, meek and hesitant, seemed the prisoner of an interior world. Her hand lay lightly upon her husband's palm, accepting of her fate with him, whatever it may be.

Given as she was to critical analysis, Amita did not understand why this ancient portrait affected her so deeply. The couple stood frozen forever on a day in their lives, a moment that must have seemed to them both fleeting and eternal, just as the moment Amita now inhabited, standing before them so many centuries later, felt to her equally transitory and yet unending. Where could you live your life, Amita wondered, but in the container of each day? The space between her and the long-ago couple, living their fourteenth-century day seemed suddenly to fuse into the same unending universal day. The same cyclical occurrences boxed the couple in, just as they now encased Amita so many centuries later. Who were these people, unknowable, yet no different from her? What were they thinking, the meek woman and the self-contained man? It was doubtful the woman had a lover waiting for her, but the man possibly had a mistress. They fulfilled their prescribed fourteenth-century roles, just as Amita fulfilled her role as a single fifty-two-year-old woman of her time, set on defining herself in opposition to the world.

Rishi had wandered off to inspect the other paintings and now sat on a bench in the middle of the room, reading the catalogue, waiting to go on to the Vermeers. As Amita made her way slowly around the remaining pictures, she noticed an American family wandering through the tall narrow rooms in tandem with them. Two sandy-haired and freckled children, a boy and a girl of perhaps ten and twelve years old, were lissom reflections of their parents and moved quietly at their side. The father stopped before each picture, explaining it to the children, who did not carry audio guides.

Amita sighed as she observed them, feeling a hollow space open up within her, a space that life should have filled, and had not. Eventually, she joined Rishi on a bench in the middle of the room as he read the catalogue and listened to his audio guide. The American family were still absorbed in the pictures and Amita followed their progress, unable to ignore them, yet unsure why she felt so drawn to them, except that they seemed to be all that a family should be. Their world appeared far from the rough-edged, intractable shape of her own life, and Amita felt solitariness twist within her.

She had never actively looked for a husband, never desired marriage or children as a life purpose, as her peers all seemed to do. Yet now, with Rishi companionably beside her, she wondered if she had made a mistake, if this was how marriage might taste, wandering together through the rain and the autumnal slush of fallen leaves beside the canal, sharing all they had shared that day, not only the close proximity of an umbrella but the warmth of shared interests, deciding where and what they would eat, waiting discreetly for each other whenever a bathroom was needed. The family she now studied so intently would probably take them as husband and wife.

If she were married to Rishi, Amita found herself wondering, which of them would their unborn children resemble? Would Rishi guide and tutor them in the same intelligent way that the father in the gallery was doing? Even as these nebulous thoughts formed in her mind, the absurdness of her fantasy reared up before her, along with vivid images of Parvati and Rishi's children. As she thrust away her toxic musings, anger and sadness rushed through her. She had made her choices and must live by them.

In the hotel, their rooms were only a few doors apart. Rishi had promised to give her a copy of his paper, and on the last day of the conference they walked upstairs together at the end of the evening, for her to collect it from him. Amita drank only socially and usually not much, but after several glasses of wine at the farewell dinner the world appeared pleasurably expanded, lightness filled her head. Rishi opened the door and she followed him into his room. The curtains were not drawn and rain beat against the window, a flash of lightning slit open the sky illuminating the darkness. He did not switch on the light but turned to her in that moment. She made no effort to resist, even when she felt the softness of the bed beneath her, but folded him into herself, eager, voracious, already locked into the blackness of desire, a darkness she knew too well. She thought fleetingly of Parvati, but the image was too distant to prevail. Her body was already intent on its own perverse path, and even as he filled her she knew this was what she wanted, what she had waited for, and even if life denied her many things she would not deny herself this.

In the morning she awoke in her own bed, and only vaguely recalled the stumbled return to her room. Struggling into consciousness, she was flooded by the horror of what she had done and the knowledge that nothing would make it go away. Yet, even as guilt consumed her, her mind threw up complex rationalisations. What she had done she had done for herself; Rishi was no more than the vehicle she needed. She was not in love with him. Love or infatuation would mean she trespassed into Parvati's domain, and this she had not done. There was no emotional involvement, but she was unsure if this made what she had done any better or worse.

She clung to these thoughts as she forced herself to get up, to shower and dress, to face the prospect of seeing Rishi again at breakfast. It was a one-off thing, she comforted herself, it would not happen again. When she came down to breakfast she found Rishi had already left on an early flight to Frankfurt, where he was to present another paper. His departure filled her with such relief that her hands trembled and she could not hold her coffee steady. Sitting alone at a small table, her fingers clasping the hot cup, relief flooding through her at Rishi's absence, there was already an unreality about the incident. It was something to be left behind in the distant city she was about to depart, and nothing to do with her day-to-day life.

12
SINGAPORE, 1942–1943

Singapore was now renamed Syonan-to, Light of the South in Japanese. The word was strange in everyone's mouth. Living conditions in the city were chaotic. There was so little food it was rumoured people were eating grass, rats, snakes; decomposing bodies on the road were a common sight. Yet mynah birds still settled on the sprouting green stump of the jacaranda, hoping for the crumbs Sita once fed them. Now there were no leftovers, they ate every last morsel themselves. The birds would survive, she thought, war did not lessen the worms in the ground or the number of grubs in a tree, cicadas still shrieked in the foliage and crickets strummed in the undergrowth. Life continued in this other dimension, while in the humdrum element she occupied, everything had stopped.

Since the Japanese had entered the town, the streets were deserted. The monsoon rain fell in sheets, flooding roads with muddy rivers through which those who dared to venture out must wade. The odd cart trundled along; figures hurried beneath the five-foot-way, always watching for soldiers. The Japanese army tore down the first-aid tent on the grassy expanse of Farrer Park and sent its patients home. Japanese soldiers were everywhere.

Like every other woman, Sita stayed out of sight. Families were hiding their daughters in cupboards, the fear of rape was so strong. Chinese women blackened their faces with mud or soot to appear as ugly as possible. Sita's bare arms were thin as twigs, the flesh gained after her marriage was now whittled away. She was always hungry, everyone was; food and its daily acquisition occupied them all, and sitting alone for long stretches of the day, boredom was now as great a torment as hunger.

Slowly the situation improved and within three months of the surrender, life became more normal, some shops reopened under Japanese licence, some doctors and dentists returned to work, some buses reappeared on the roads. Change was also felt in other ways. At the Ramakrishna Mission, Swami Bhaswarananda was abruptly dismissed by the Japanese military, and instructed to return overland to India. The crowd of homeless people who occupied the mission's empty classrooms was relentlessly driven out. The mission was to be turned into a Japanese language school.

Shiva, along with everyone else, had been forced to hand in his radio to the authorities for 'fixing'. No foreign news station could now be heard, which meant no balanced news of the war and its progress could be gleaned. Japanese English language broadcasts only reported unending Japanese military successes and there was no way to know if this information was true. Shiva found a job with a military construction unit, recruiting and supervising men to repair the bombed and ramshackle British army camps. There was little transport to these camps, and often Shiva was forced to walk long distances to check on the progress of work on broken fences, and bombed roofs and barracks. He was a tall gaunt figure, ribs visible, the soft pouch of his cheeks now reduced to hard bone.

Things were not good for Dev either. Krishnaswami and Sons, like all other shops and businesses, had been closed to await a trading licence from the Japanese authorities. Dev had also found a job with a Japanese building contractor, and was gone for days at a time to distant parts of the island on construction projects, often sleeping in the makeshift dormitories erected on site, returning exhausted and covered in dust and dirt. He came home only intermittently, and Sita saw little of him.

Shiva had been out all day since first light, and Sita waited for the sound of his foot on the stair. At last she heard him returning, a heavy bumping sound accompanying each step. As he threw open the door the night carried in a cloud of mosquitoes and moths and a stench of drains. Shiva stood before her, breathing hard from his climb, clutching a parcel the size of a small child that was wrapped in filthy sacking. He thrust the package towards her, with an apprehensive smile.

It was difficult to guess what the hard angular shape might be, and her heart beat with excitement as she pulled off the last of the wrapping. Shiva stood beside her while she gazed down upon an old wall clock with a long brass pendulum.

'I found it in the black market. I gave a man books in exchange, the plays of Shakespeare in leather binding. Now you will learn to tell the time.'

By the slight tremble in Shiva's voice she knew it had not

been easy for him to part with his books. A rush of tenderness filled her as she gazed at her husband; no one had ever given her a gift before. If Shiva had asked her what she wanted, she would not have known what to choose. Now, this wondrous thing, commanding time and ordering the day was before her, no gift could have been more perfect.

At her feet the round glass face of the old clock reflected the light. Shiva stooped to pull the machine upright, opening the glass door to the pendulum and giving the metal prongs a slight push. Immediately, the clock came to life. Sita listened to the metallic tick of its heart, and watched the rhythmic swing of the metal weights, unable to explain the joy surging through her. Soon Shiva found nails and a hammer and a strong hook, and fixed the heavy clock securely upon the wall. As he stepped off the stool he turned to her and she saw the new energy in his face, and knew something had happened.

'The camps I am repairing are to be used for the Indian POWs the British Army handed over to the Japanese military at the time of the surrender. The Japanese are forming these men into a new army that will free India from colonial rule. It is to be called the Indian National Army. With the help of the Japanese, it will invade India, and liberate it. Already today I saw Indian POW soldiers entering the new camp.'

Sita nodded, still gazing at her clock, that was now preparing to strike the hour. A laboured grinding began deep within the belly of the instrument, and soon it coughed out some surly clangs. Sita clapped her hands in pleasure. The clock's light ticking would be forever near her, breaking the solitude of her day. Perhaps she too would now move forward like the hands of the clock, regardless of what lay ahead.

'Did you hear what I said? An Indian army is being formed. It will free India from British rule,' Shiva repeated impatiently.

Months passed, the year changed and life under the Japanese became a wary routine. Soldiers were seen when least expected, and their arbitrary behaviour filled everyone with fear. Each day after Shiva left for work, and if the area was free of any military presence, Sita walked to the top of the alley where, at the junction with Norris Road beside the Ramakrishna Mission, the pot-bellied Vishwanathan had returned with his coconut stall. A relative of Vishwanathan's, an old Tamil woman with the deeply lined face of a polished walnut had now joined him, selling the fresh produce she and her husband grew on an allotment near Kranji. Sita bought two small aubergines and an onion from Savitri, and a coconut from Vishwanathan.

'At least in this war, if nothing else, the trees continue to give us coconuts.' Vishwanathan laughed, his fleshy face perspiring in the heat, as he handed Sita the nut he always kept for her.

When she returned home, she poured the coconut milk into a tall glass for Shiva to drink later. Chopping the white flesh of the coconut finely, she stirred it into the chopped fried onion and aubergine with a spoonful of the precious spices she hoarded, and cooked it slowly on the primus stove. It was better than anything she had tasted in days, but when Shiva returned in the evening he ate quickly and without comment, preoccupied, his eyes overly bright, as if he had a fever. At last he told her his news.

'Yesterday Subhas Chandra Bose arrived in Singapore. He has come to take command of the Indian National Army. The Japanese asked Hitler to send him to us. Our Netaji arrived yesterday in Singapore! Can you believe it! The route from the airport to town was lined with our people, all waving flags of welcome. I heard him speak yesterday at the Cathay Building. Thousands and thousands of people were there. Those of us who had tickets were inside the building, but hundreds more stood outside to hear Netaji accept command of the Indian National Army. It was the most wonderful day.' His thin face blazed with excitement.

During the months of the Occupation, the Indian National Army had been firmly established as a force, and Shiva avidly followed its growth and news. Yet within months of its formation, the army collapsed, beset by problems of leadership.

'They say the Indian National Army will begin recruiting civilians. When they do that, I am going to join.'

Sita drew a quick breath, knowing in that moment that her life was changing, that Shiva's gaze was already now fixed on a world beyond the life they lived in their small room. Remembering how his parents had died, she knew this was what he had waited for, and that nothing could stop him joining the new Indian army when the time came.

'When I join I will come back every few days to see you. And of course, Dev will be here with you,' he promised, seeing the expression on his wife's face, and the effect his news had upon her.

Sita nodded silently, knowing protest was of little use. Looking down at the food on the banana leaf before her, at the aubergine cooked so carefully and with such expectation, she knew she could not eat it now.

Soon, the call Shiva waited for came, and he immediately began packing his few belongings, anxious to start his new life. Sita watched him piling books on top of a clean *lungi*, shirt and vest, pushing everything into an old cloth bag. Soon it was done, and he swung the bag up onto his shoulder. At the open door he turned, silhouetted against the bright morning light, a dark shape on the luminous threshold of a world waiting to absorb him.

'The training is only for a short period. The camp is nearby, at Newton Circus; I will be back soon,' he assured her before he disappeared, clattering down the spiral stair.

She listened to his steps getting fainter, then the sound of the gate closing behind him as he let himself into the alley. Behind her the clock began a metallic whirring, preparing to spit out its hoarse chimes. She listened to it strike as she shut the door and turned back to the empty room.

The next morning Sita returned to her usual routine, stepping out into the alley to make her way to Vishwanathan's stall for a coconut and whatever vegetable Savitri had saved for her. As she walked up the alley she noticed the strip of grassy land behind the Ramakrishna Mission was now stacked with long bamboo canes of the kind used for scaffolding. Turning the corner into Norris Road, she saw that the Mission building was undergoing repairs before opening as a Japanese language school, its façade already shrouded in a trellis of bamboo. Half-naked Tamil labourers clambered up and down the flimsy scaffolding, agile as primates, metal bowls of cement balanced easily on their heads, their dark limbs a stark contrast to the pale walls they industriously whitewashed. The Chinese coolies who would previously have done this work had fled the town as the Japanese arrived, and Tamil labourers now monopolised all such jobs. There was the loud scrape of spades as they mixed cement under the direction of an Indian supervisor. As Sita paused to watch, the sudden sound of Japanese voices startled her. A military truck drew up noisily before the Ramakrishna Mission and five or six Japanese soldiers jumped out.

'Get down, sister.' Vishwanathan shouted as Sita approached, gesturing her to the safety of his stall. As Sita ran forward, Savitri reached out to grasp her arm, pulling her down under the stall, where she crouched unseen behind a pile of fresh coconuts.

'No one can see us here.' Savitri whispered.

Her deep-set eyes had the knowing gleam of a friendly reptile as she peered into the road around the coconuts. Pressed close to the bony warmth of Savitri's body, the dusty scent of her worn cotton sari filling her nose, Sita was suddenly reminded of old Maneka at the *bhajanashram*.

The soldiers had no interest in Vishwanathan's stall. They strode across the road to the Ramakrishna Mission waving their bayonets, ordering the labourers off the scaffolding with loud guttural commands. The workers' supervisor, a short burly Tamil, dared to voice a polite protest and was slapped in the face and pushed to the ground for his trouble. As soon as the Japanese appeared, passersby disappeared, and the street was suddenly empty. The workers were now climbing down off the scaffolding to huddle fearfully together beside their abandoned shovels and cement. The soldiers, short men in puttees, dusty uniforms and peaked caps, strode about, herding the labourers closer together with blows from the butts of their rifles. Naked except for filthy loincloths and ragged turbans, mute with fear, the men watched as one of their group who had tried to flee through an open window was beaten until he bled.

The soldiers shouted incomprehensible orders, pushing and prodding the labourers until the men were forced to shuffle forward, stumbling over each other in terrified confusion, a burst of further blows moving them slowly towards the junction of Serangoon Road. They passed so close to Vishwanathan's stall that Sita could see the burnish of sweat on their naked torsos, the floury dust of cement clinging to their arms, and the whites of their terrified eyes. Powerless beneath the relentless blows, the men were as trapped as the goats driven regularly along this same road to the slaughterhouse. Eventually, they turned the corner onto Serangoon Road with its traffic of trundling carts, rickshaws and bicycles, and were lost from sight.

Once the soldiers had gone, a shocked populace emerged again into the road, looking up at the empty lattice of scaffolding and down at the half mixed pile of cement. Vishwanathan stepped forward to gaze along the empty road, while Savitri pulled Sita to her feet, shaking her head in distress. The supervisor reappeared to assess the remnants of his remaining workforce, who were now creeping forward, bruised or bleeding.

'They have taken all your young men,' Vishwanathan called across to him, glancing at the elderly crew now gathering together, visibly shaken by their experience. The supervisor nodded grimly, dabbing his cuts and bruises with the end of his *dhoti*.

'These men are good only for mixing cement. They are taking labourers from everywhere they can, to work on a great railway they are building from Burma to Siam.'

The supervisor turned to the trembling men who still remained, ordering them to climb the scaffolding and take over the work of the younger men, who were now marching along Serangoon Road towards an unknown destiny.

13
SINGAPORE, 1943–1944

There had been no rain for days. Dust thickened the air, heat pressed down upon the town, stewing noxious odours in open drains. Sita's head ached. On the wall the old clock continued to tick, measuring out each day that Shiva was gone. He had not come home since his recruitment, and without him Sita's life was adrift and anchorless. Poring over his books, choosing random volumes from the stacks along the walls, she continued with her own learning of both Hindi and English, looking up new words in Shiva's many dictionaries.

Smoothing out the cloth on her lap, she returned to her sewing. A Japanese woman, a teacher at the Japanese language school that had taken over the Ramakrishna Mission, had come knocking on doors, requesting women to volunteer to make shirts for orphaned children. Cloth, needles, thread and a pattern were supplied by a women's charitable organisation. Sita readily agreed to help, remembering the five urchins who were now in a distant orphanage at the other end of the island, and might be the recipients of just such a shirt. The woman gave her a small amount of money for the labour. It felt good to earn a wage, and the notes in her hand filled Sita with pride.

As the old clock began its usual hoarse breathing before

gathering the energy to strike, there was the sound of steps on the spiral stair. Shiva threw open the door, filling the room, a stranger she did not recognise. Sita's heart thudded in shock. He had left her wearing a worn checked *lungi* and singlet vest, old leather sandals on his feet. Now, he stood before her in a smart khaki uniform, brass buttons agleam on his belted jacket, a narrow cap settled upon his head. Good food filled out his cheeks, a sense of purpose smoothed away anxiety, and his eyes were bright.

'These were given to me by a Japanese officer,' Shiva thrust an armful of fruit and several packets of biscuits into her hands, speaking as if he had returned from a day's work and not after days of absence.

The room was suddenly full of the unfamiliar, of the man her husband had become and the unknown world he now inhabited. The smell of a medicinal soap drifted from him, and his long thick hair was shorn so short his ears stuck out from his head in a way she had never noticed before. Turning silently towards the kitchen, seeking a moment to absorb the shock, she went to make tea, knowing this was what was expected of her.

'I have come here only to get you,' he called after her. She turned back towards him, struck again by the excitement pulsing through him.

'Soon Netaji will speak at the Padang. I want you to hear him.'

There was no way to refuse, and she quickly gathered up her hair, twisting it into the usual tight knot, while he waited impatiently. At last she was ready and he pulled her after him down the spiral stair, across the courtyard and out of the gate. Soon they reached Serangoon Road and then came into Beach Road, walking quickly towards the green expanse of the Padang, where Bose was to speak. The briny scent of the sea, filled with the stench of drying sardines on the beach in front of the fish market, carried over to them. Sita trailed behind her husband, surprised by the number of Indian men and women walking in the same direction. People streamed into Beach Road from Selegie Road, Dhoby Ghaut, Bencoolen Street, Middle Road and Bras Basah. Above her the sky was heavy with rain, but the crowd converging on the Padang appeared undeterred.

'Netaji.'

His name was on everyone's lips, tossed from one person to another. Sita hurried to keep up with Shiva's determined stride. The *attap*-roofed hutments and peeling shophouses were left behind as they reached the colonial heart of the town, with its churches and municipal buildings, the parliament, the cricket club and the clock tower of Victoria Hall. This area was strange to Sita, and she looked around in awe.

Bordering the Padang along St. Andrew's Road stood the imposing neo-classical edifices of the Supreme Court and City Hall. On the steps of the City Hall a raised platform decorated with red and white bunting had been erected. Huge Indian and Japanese flags were draped over the walls of the building behind. Sita gazed at the soaring Corinthian colonnade, and at the mass of people collected on the huge field of the Padang. Shiva crossed the road and plunged into the waiting crowd, pulling Sita after him, pushing his way forward like a

swimmer through choppy water. Dev was waiting for them a
short distance from the red and white platform from which
Subhas Chandra Bose would speak. Seeing Shiva in his INA
uniform, people respectfully made room for them, and Sita sat
down beside Dev.

'I must join my regiment. We will march before Netaji, he
will take the salute,' Shiva explained, and hurried off.

In the distance the INA regiments could be seen assembled
at the other end of the Padang, awaiting the arrival of their
new commander, but it was impossible to pick Shiva out from
amongst the mass of khaki-clad soldiers. Sita turned back to
Dev, who was explaining to her how Subhas Chandra Bose had
reached Singapore.

'From Germany, at the request of the Japanese, Hitler sent
Netaji to Tokyo by submarine. The journey took many months.
All that time he was buried deep beneath the surface of the
sea. Halfway to Japan, in the middle of the ocean, the vessel
surfaced and Netaji left the German submarine and transferred
to a Japanese submarine. Then, once again, he lived deep under
the water for many days until he reached Tokyo. There the
Japanese requested him to take over the Indian National Army,
and sent him here to Singapore.'

Sita gazed at her brother wide-eyed, imagining the long
journey beneath the ocean, seeing the impossible feat, the man
walking on water like an immortal from one dripping vessel
to another. She imagined the storm-tossed darkness through
which he journeyed deep within a briny universe. In her mind,
she saw him surface again into the world, rising from the ocean

like the god Varuna on the back of a sea monster, water rolling from his gold armour, the sun forming a halo behind him.

A stir rippled across the packed field as an open-topped car approached the Padang, passing the parliament and the Cricket Club to enter St. Andrew's Road, moving slowly.

'The Japanese Prime Minister, General Tojo, has also come to Singapore with Netaji,' Dev explained.

A pennant with the red and white rising sun of Japan flew from one side of the car, and on the other, stamped with the image of a pouncing tiger, flew the orange, white and green pennant of Azad Hind, the country that soon hoped to be called Free India. The flags flew like coloured fins on the head of the vehicle, which drew to a halt before City Hall. From one side of the car General Tojo, a small and insignificant looking man with a short moustache, climbed out, and then the powerfully built Bengali emerged. At the sight of Bose wild cheering erupted from the waiting mass of people.

A tall thickset man of military bearing, balding and bespectacled, Bose exuded authority and energy as he turned to acknowledge the crowd, striding up the steps of City Hall behind the Japanese prime minister. People roared and surged towards him, but the police and Japanese soldiers armed with rifles advanced, pushing everyone back again onto the field. Waiting Indian dignitaries now stepped forward to garland Netaji, and soon his head was half buried in flowers. A young Indian woman dressed like a man, in army uniform, was amongst the people garlanding Bose. Netaji was guided to a seat and, as Sita watched, the uniformed woman sat down beside him. A narrow military cap was set stylishly upon her dark shoulder length hair, and she gazed out at the crowd from behind dark glasses, straight-backed and assured.

'Who is that?' Sita asked.

Dev did not know, but a man beside them overheard the question and leaned towards her.

'That is Captain Lakshmi. She is the only woman in Netaji's cabinet, and she is also a doctor living in Singapore,' he informed her.

The sun broke free of the clouds to shine upon the Padang, turning the brass buttons on Bose's uniform to points of fire, gleaming on his high polished boots. A confetti of petals from the garlands still clung to his uniform. With the appearance of the sun, new energy throbbed through the crowd.

'Netaji! Netaji!'

Around Sita everyone was shouting now. Dev and the men beside him were waving their arms as they roared out Netaji's name. Women were also shouting unashamedly. A great wave of sound rolled about the field, sweeping everyone up, growing louder and louder, filling Sita's ears and beating in her chest.

'Netaji! Netaji!'

She too was now shouting his name, hearing it reverberate through her again and again.

'Netaji! Netaji!'

Her pulse quickened as she gazed up at the man on the platform. Bose held up his hand and the crowd quietened as he began to speak, his powerful well-modulated voice rising and falling rhythmically, projecting across the Padang. Reaching out to adjust the microphone, he paused, and in that moment a bolt of hot energy rushed through her. Then his deep, smooth voice curled over her again, shutting out all else.

'Comrades! Let the battle cry be *Dilli Chalo!* Onwards to Delhi! How many of us individually will survive this war of freedom, I do not know. But we shall ultimately win…I will be with you in darkness and sunshine, in sorrow and in joy, in suffering and in victory…

'This must be a truly revolutionary army…I am appealing also to women…women must also be prepared to fight for their freedom, to fight for independence… Along with independence they will get their own emancipation… Give me your blood and I will give you freedom.'

As he finished speaking there was a brief silence, no one moved. Then all at once women began rushing forward, pushing past Sita, breaking through barriers, some with babies in their arms, all shouting, *we will fight, we will fight for the freedom of India.*

Sita found she too was on her feet, following the crowd of women. Dev pulled on her hand, trying to hold her back, but it seemed her heart would burst with all she was feeling. Breaking free of her brother she ran towards where Netaji stood high on the dais above her, his face exultant, head thrown back.

We will fight; we will fight…

She screamed out the words. She would fight for India; she would fight for him. Then there was the cold touch of steel on her arm, and rough hands grabbed her as Japanese soldiers with rifles confronted the women, forcing them back. Above her Netaji continued to smile, his gaze focussed distantly upon the crowd, his hand raised as if in blessing. She was near enough to see the soft crease of the boot about his ankle, the stout metal buckle around his waist, the gleam of sweat upon his broad cheeks, his full and sensuous lips. Then, Japanese soldiers fenced her in, driving her back, step by step.

A bugle sounded and on the dais Netaji turned, drawing himself up to salute his new army. The sun was gone and clouds darkened the sky once again. In St. Andrew's Road the massed regiments of the INA began to move forward, marching smartly past their new leader as he took the salute. As the march-past ended a flash of lightning was seen and the whip of thunder was heard. It started to rain, and people hurried to disperse.

Leaving Shiva on the field with his regiment, Sita and Dev walked home, heads down against the rain, each lost in thought. The excitement of the afternoon still burned through Sita. She could not recall Netaji's features clearly or even the things he had said, much of which she had not understood, but the power of him remained within her and would not let her free. He was a golden man, a leaping tiger, who had entered her at a thrust.

Give me your blood and I will give you freedom. The words spun through her and were part of her now, as was the fierce rightness of the Indian struggle. She would fight as they all would fight, until freedom was won.

In the following days energy throbbed within her in a way she had never experienced. Tossing and turning through the night, she woke well before dawn to watch the first grey light spread through the thin curtain. Suddenly, she dared to do things she had never done before.

Ignoring Shiva's explicit orders not to touch his precious books, she set about dismantling the towers of paper stacked against each wall, dusting each volume, even disposing of those so badly devoured by silverfish that only pages of lace remained. She sprayed insecticide in every corner of the house. All the while she thought of Netaji, hearing his voice, seeing the shape of his balding head, the gleaming boots, his tall and upright form. Her body ached with the thought of him.

Within days of the rally on the Padang, it was announced that a women's regiment had been set up at Bose's instigation and would be part of the Indian National Army. Captain Lakshmi would command this new regiment, named after the legendary Rani of Jhansi, a spirited princess who had fought against the British in 1858.

'Who is joining the regiment?' Sita asked Dev, trying not to reveal her interest.

'Only some young girls without family responsibilities,' Dev replied.

'Should I join?' Sita asked, watching his expression for a sign she might explore such an action.

'You are a married woman. How can you join?' Dev frowned in disapproval.

Within a few days the opportunity Sita waited for arrived. Two girls going from house to house, hoping to find recruits for the Rani of Jhansi Regiment, knocked on her door. As soon as Sita knew the purpose of their visit, the words rushed from her, as if someone else was speaking.

'I will join, I will fight.'

Elation filled her as she spoke, as did apprehension. It was the first time she had made a decision about her own life, and the raw power of such daring amazed her. The girls told her about a meeting at which Netaji was to speak about the newly formed regiment.

'You must come,' the girls entreated and Sita nodded, knowing the decision was already made within her, even as she wondered how she would find the place.

In spite of her apprehension, it was not difficult to find Waterloo Street, and the venue was easy to identify by the number of people gathered before the entrance. No one stopped her as she slipped inside.

The room was crowded with mostly women, and Netaji had already arrived. Sita found a place near the door at the back of the room. Netaji stood on a raised dais, an unmistakable presence, tall and uniformed, his face dominated by heavy framed spectacles. A shaft of light fell upon him, polishing his balding head. He began to speak, his voice commanding yet intimate, as if he spoke to each one of them individually.

'You all know the part our women have played in the freedom movement in India…sharing the burden with men in our national struggle…facing imprisonment and persecution, insult and humiliation…'

In the silent room Netaji's voice flowed through her. As always, some of what he said she did not understand, but the words came from a place deep within him and, closing her eyes, she felt their touch.

'If there is anyone who thinks it is an unwomanly act to shoulder a rifle, I ask them to turn to our history and the brave women of our past.'

Some words stayed with her, others were lost. She was conscious only of the force of the man before her.

'I know what our women are capable of, and therefore I say without exaggeration that there is no suffering which our brave sisters are not capable of enduring.'

As the meeting ended, Sita slipped out from the hall, wanting to get away as fast as she could, to be alone. As before, her body throbbed with unfamiliar energy, strange thoughts and emotions surged through her. Netaji's face was before her as she walked home, his voice echoing within her. His words filled her and would not be silenced.

14

It started to rain as they set off from the house for the walk to the Bras Basah camp. A sudden downpour emptied down upon them. Water sluiced off the protective canopy of the umbrella Shiva held over them. Sita leaned nearer her husband as the rain splashed about them, the hem of her sari dragging wetly around her ankles. Her few belongings, tied up in a bundle and carried by Shiva, were already soaked. She was supposed to report to the camp in the morning, but it was now afternoon. She was late because Shiva had insisted she wait for him to take her to Bras Basah. Even now, as they walked towards the place, Shiva's resentment at her decision to enlist soured all exchange between them. She had expected him to support her; she had expected him to be pleased. Instead, there was only his disapproval.

'You did not discuss this with me. I am your husband.' Shiva chided.

'You were in your camp. You did not come home, so how could I speak to you?' she replied.

The enormity of her decision and her husband's displeasure was heavy upon her as they walked together under the dripping umbrella. Shiva was seldom openly angry, assuming instead an expression of sad disappointment, withdrawing into silence.

She would have preferred some naked aggression, of the kind she had witnessed as a child and to which she knew how to respond. Yet, even as she gazed at Shiva's stony face, something unyielding pushed her on.

'Most girls joining this regiment are unmarried and not having family obligations,' Shiva insisted.

'I want to fight like you to free India,' she whispered.

'Soon, I will be forced to salute my own wife,' Shiva glared down at her.

As abruptly as it started, the rain eased and then stopped. They reached the domed edifice of St. Joseph's Institution and turned off Bras Basah into Waterloo Street. Shiva collapsed the umbrella as they passed the school and the camp came into view. The young female guard behind the gate looked up as they approached. Sita hung back, suddenly nervous, now that the reality of her decision was before her.

'He can't come any further with you,' the girl told Sita as she unlatched the gate.

'I am an INA officer,' Shiva announced in a loud voice.

'This is not your camp,' the girl replied, ignoring him and beckoning Sita forward.

Shiva stepped away tight-lipped, and walked off with no more than a curt nod of farewell. Sita stared after him, expecting him to glance back at her, but he strode resolutely towards the main road and was gone.

'Hurry up.' The guard held the gate open impatiently.

The girl wore shorts that ended just above the knee, and Sita stared at her bare legs in growing uneasiness. She was aware, as the gate thudded shut behind her and she took her first step into the camp, that she had waited for this moment, yet a sudden agony of indecision now filled her. Perhaps she was wrong, perhaps she should have discussed her decision with Shiva; perhaps she should still be at home. She turned back to the gate, but the girl had already thrust the lock firmly into place.

Sita's damp hair, coiled loosely on her neck, now began to uncurl, hairpins falling over the bundle of belongings she clutched tightly. The girl in shorts, her waist neatly belted, observed Sita silently, not bothering to hide her distaste. Then another uniformed girl, holding a clipboard of papers and with the stripes of rank on her sleeve, hurried across the open ground towards them.

'All the other girls in your group of new recruits reported here this morning, you are very late!' She ticked Sita's name off her list, after an assessing glance.

'I am Lieutenant Bhatia, and I'm your platoon commander. Follow me, all new recruits must first see Captain Mehra.' In spite of the initial complaint, she now smiled at Sita in a friendly way.

Like the guard, Lieutenant Bhatia wore shorts, her bare legs ending in thick socks and stout shoes, a soft brimless cap upon her cropped hair. As she turned to follow the girl, Sita was filled with growing trepidation; she too would now have to wear these same clothes; she too would soon look like a man.

The great space of the parade ground stretched before her, sodden with rain. In the distance, newly built barracks stood next to an older brick building. Sita hurried after the officer who walked smartly ahead, trying to avoid the many muddy puddles, the sodden hem of her sari dragging along the wet ground, hair trailing down her back, the damp bundle of belongings bumping against her thigh. Sita's eyes kept returning to the officer's bare legs as she marched smartly ahead of her.

Captain Mehra looked up from her desk as Lieutenant Bhatia entered and saluted. The captain was dressed in the same khaki jodhpurs Captain Lakshmi had worn at the Padang rally, jacket neatly belted, brass buttons and buckle agleam. Sita was acutely aware of the picture of dampness and dejection she must project as she stood before the officer.

'You are a soldier now in the Rani of Jhansi Regiment. Stand up straight; don't bow your head like that. Get her out of that sari and into uniform quickly,' she ordered, and then turned back to Sita.

'This time next week I don't expect to recognise you,' she predicted briskly as she dismissed them.

Lieutenant Bhatia led Sita down a corridor and turned into a storeroom with shelves of khaki uniforms. She began pulling out items, measuring things up against Sita for size. The heat in the room was stifling, sweat pooled in the small of Sita's back.

'You can call me Prema when we are not on duty. We wear shorts and shirts for everyday, Jodhpur breeches and bush jackets for marches. Netaji designed our uniforms on his submarine journey from Germany.'

Short hair curled from under her cap around a broad-boned face. Everything about her was bright, her manner direct and warm, her cheeks dimpled as she smiled.

'Three platoons form a company; one platoon has up to twenty recruits. Your platoon is made up of two squads housed in adjacent barracks. Each squad has fifteen girls. Your squad has a lot of Tamil girls from the rubber estates in upcountry Malaya. Most of them are malnourished, but we'll soon fatten them up here,' Prema threw out information in a casual manner, speaking quickly as she piled the uniform into Sita's arms, deep lines creasing about her eyes when she smiled.

Sita tried to grasp the military information Prema tossed to her; she knew nothing of the rubber estates in Malaya, or the people who worked there. Through a small dusty window high above the shelves, a shaft of strong afternoon sun streamed in, falling on Sita and the clothes in her arms. Its warmth moved through her, the smell of starch drifting up from the crisply folded uniforms.

Prema strode out of the building and onto the wet parade ground again, making her way towards the newly built barracks, and Sita followed. Stopping before one of the wooden huts, she threw open the door upon a long narrow room of mosquito netted bunk beds and wooden lockers. The astringent odour of newly sawn wood and fresh paint filled Sita's nose. Prema reached to turn on the ceiling fans, and the air was stirred.

'The others arrived early and chose their bunks, but this one's not yet taken,' Prema said, pointing to a lower vacant bed.

'And that is your locker. Get changed quickly and join them outside. Major Pandey does not like latecomers.' Prema pointed through a window to a line of girls being drilled on the parade ground.

Alone in the hut, Sita looked about. The makeshift feel of the place seemed to confirm she would be there only temporarily, that her life was not changing in any permanent way. Placing the pile of uniform on the bunk, she fingered the thick cotton garments. A wave of panic passed through her, how would she wear clothes that revealed her body so extensively? She had never shown anyone her legs before, not even her husband had seen so much of her naked. Whatever she did with him was in the dark, and even then she kept as much of herself as she could decorously covered; her husband may be familiar with the feel of her naked body, but not the sight of it.

Holding up the stiff and ugly shorts, she considered how such a garment was to be entered and secured. It seemed best to pull the shorts up first beneath her petticoat, and then unwind the sari after the garment was in place. This way she would be covered if anyone glanced through the window. At last it was done and she unhooked her sari blouse, pulled on the khaki shirt, tucking it into the waist of the shorts, and buckling the leather belt about herself. There was no mirror in which to see her refection, but looking down, her eyes went first to the bony protuberance of her bare knees, and embarrassment curled through her; although she was dressed she felt naked. Finally, she pushed her feet into the thick rough socks and heavy walking shoes and, plaiting her hair into two braids, settled the narrow cap on her head. Unsure of what to do with the wet sari, she placed it on top of the lockers.

Through the window the group of marching girls could be seen; an untidy phalanx of thrashing limbs, obeying the loud boom of Major Pandey's voice. Sita walked towards the door, knowing that when she stepped out of the hut nothing would ever be the same again. Used only to light leather sandals, the heavy shoes weighed her feet down, her heels knocked against her toes, and she feared she might trip over. It was bad enough that her breasts had no veiling, but the shame of her bare legs sticking out of the wide-legged shorts was worse than anything else.

'Late!' Major Pandey yelled as Sita approached, indicating that she should fall into line behind the others.

'Chin up. Shoulders back. How will you hold a rifle? How will you face the enemy? I have just two months to make soldiers of you. Two months!' Major Pandey's throaty voice pressed upon them, interspersed with sharp blasts blown repeatedly from the whistle around her neck.

'March! One two. One two. Chin up. Legs straight.'

As they marched around the parade ground it was impossible to avoid the puddles. Cold muddy water splashed up Sita's calves, wetting her socks and heavy shoes.

'Chin up! March.'

Sita threw out her legs one after the other. The breath quickened in her chest, her arms thrashed through the air, her limbs moving with a momentum of their own. They were about thirty girls and all, like Sita, appeared equally awkward and self-conscious. Many were of Tamil origin, but they did not appear like the more prosperous Tamils seen on Serangoon Road. They were from the labouring community, the daughters of men such as those she had seen on the scaffolding at the Ramakrishna Mission, who had been rounded up by the Japanese. The girl marching in front of Sita was so thin her uniform hung voluminously upon her, and her legs appeared no more than dark wiry sticks emerging from her shorts. The plaits of hair, swinging about her shoulders as she marched, seemed thicker than her limbs.

'Right leg. Left leg. One two. One two,' Major Pandey strutted smartly before them. Whatever leg Major Pandey called for, the thin girl in front of Sita always lifted the wrong one. Many other girls, Sita observed, did not seem to know right from left. As a result, the platoon was disorganised, however determinedly they marched. It began to rain lightly again and the girls slowed down, looking up at the sky and then at Major Pandey, expecting to seek cover.

'Will the enemy wait for the rain to stop? March. About turn. Shoulders back.' Major Pandey blew savagely on her whistle.

At last it was over, but when they returned to their barracks Major Pandey ordered them all into Sita's hut and followed them inside. The girls lined up before the bunks and Major Pandey strode up and down, rapping at the metal frames of the beds with the end of her baton. The thin girl with thick plaits of hair stood beside Sita and hung her head, staring down at the floor. Major Pandey came to a halt before her.

'Is this my right hand or my left hand?' The Major raised a hand and prodded the girl with her baton. The girl did not answer.

'What is your name?' Major Pandey demanded.

'Muniamma,' the girl whispered, continuing to stare at her feet.

'Look at me. Answer the question.'

'What is right? What is left?' The girl whispered.

'Ah! You do not know. Those of you who are illiterate will get an education here, on Netaji's orders. All Ranis of the Jhansi Regiment should be able to read and write.'

'Which side is right?' Major Pandey pointed her baton at another girl, who also stared mutely at her feet.

'What is your name?' Major Pandey demanded again.

'Muniamma,' the girl replied.

'Another Muniamma?'

Prema, who had followed them into the barracks, hurried forward.

'These girls are from the rubber estates up country. Plantation managers are European and cannot remember Indian names. To them they are all just women, just workers; they see no need to name them. Muniamma means, girl. Only at home in their family do they have names, Muniamma this or Muniamma that,' Prema explained. Major Pandey's frown turned to an expression of perplexity.

'We cannot have such things here. How will we know who they are?' The Major's voice softened as she continued.

'Here we will call you by the name they gave you at birth in your family. Understand, here each one of you is a person and important to us. You are not cattle.'

Major Pandey beckoned Prema forward and instructed her to write each girl's name on her clipboard list. Shivani, Valli, Ambika, Rashmi, Vasanthi, Aarthi, Hemavani, the girls called out their names. At last only the thin girl who had marched in front of Sita was left.

'Muniamma,' she replied in a low voice when Prema pressed her.

'Do you not have another name?' Major Pandey frowned and raised her baton, tucking it beneath her arm.

The girl shrank back against the bunk, forced to explain why she had no other name, and Major Pandey bent forward to catch her whispered words.

'I have no mother or father. The family I live with on the estate did not give me a name. To them I am always just Muniamma, although their own daughter has a name.'

'Then I suppose you will have to remain Muniamma,' Major Pandey shook her head sadly.

'You. Latecomer.' Major Pandey resumed her fierce stance and waved her baton at Sita.

'Right hand, left hand.'

Sita raised each hand correctly as Major Pandey demanded, thankful that through her husband's help she now had some education and knew about such things. Major Pandey nodded approval, then glared again as she looked at the girls, all of whom had hair of some length, plaited or bunched or coiled into a bun.

'These hairstyles will not fit under a military cap. No time in the regiment for combing and oiling long hair. No time for vanity when you get to the front and the enemy is waiting. It must be cut.'

A soft ripple of consternation was heard. Major Pandey stepped forward to poke her baton beneath Sita's chin, forcing it up. The skin beneath the Major's eyes was more darkly pigmented than the rest of her fleshy face, and gave her an owlish look.

'Cut.' Major Pandey withdrew her baton from Sita's chin and waved it at the other longhaired recruits.

'Follow me,' she ordered.

They trailed out of the barracks behind her, crossing the damp parade ground into the main building. The Major walked with a swagger, her broad buttocks beneath the pull of khaki drill trousers moving up and down like pistons. She led them to a large bare room stacked with chairs and ordered them to seat themselves in two facing rows.

'Scissors. Newspapers,' she demanded, turning to Prema.

Prema disappeared from the room and soon returned with several uniformed recruits holding long-bladed scissors, brooms and an armful of old newspapers for the conscripts to tuck about their necks and shoulders. As they waited for their haircuts, exchanging apprehensive glances, Major Pandey stepped forward to address them.

'Netaji gives us all a choice; he does not insist you cut your hair, but it is better that you do so. We are given the same training as the INA men and also wear similar uniforms. We cannot think of ourselves as women now. We are, first and foremost, soldiers. Everything we do now, we do for the freedom of India. *Jai Hind*,' she added, before turning from the room, leaving Prema in charge.

As the girls with the scissors stepped forward to begin their work, Sita was conscious of a disturbance at the end of the row. Leaning forward, she saw the thin girl, Muniamma, give a cry of protest, pull off the newspapers draped about her, and run from the room.

'There's always someone who won't cut her hair,' Prema sighed, stepping up to stand behind Sita, brandishing her scissors.

Prema began to unravel Sita's plait. The hair she had taken so long to grow and that hid a life she was at pains to forget, was now spread about her shoulders. Sita gave an involuntary shudder and Prema paused in surprise, raising her eyebrows in query.

'It will be over quickly,' she reassured.

Sita nodded, unable to explain the sudden grip of the past upon her, the white sari thrown at her feet, the dismembered braid of hair in the metal bowl. Her whole life seemed to swing before her as the scissors flashed and clicked. Prema pushed her head forward, and Sita felt the cool touch of steel on her neck.

'Don't move. I don't want to cut you,' Prema warned.

Closing her eyes, Sita listened to the clip of metal as strand after strand of hair slithered down over her body, brushing against her bare knees. The breeze from a standing fan in a corner of the room swept over her, blowing wisps of hair about the floor. Looking down at the pile of soft curls at her feet, she remembered that other time, the resistance she had exerted as her head was shaved. The realisation came to her that this time was different from that previous cruel tonsure. The thick hair now being sheared away held her to a life she was voluntarily discarding. This time the severing of her hair was not a death or a neutering, but a rebirth.

'There! Now you can look.' Prema reached for a mirror that was being passed around, handing it to Sita.

For a moment Sita did not recognise herself. A stylish cap of hair swirled about her head, just covering her ears. A dart of excitement ran through her as she touched the bare nape of her neck, not now in shame but in exhilaration. Leaning back in the chair, she stretched out her legs and gazed at her shamelessly naked knees, her heart beating at the thought of all that now lay ahead.

It was dusk. Through the window of the barracks Sita could see lamps lighting up behind the trees around the parade ground. Bats flew up from beneath the roof of the main building. She remembered the bats in the village, their comings and goings from the trees each night, and how they hung by day like black seed pods under the eaves of the house. Now, the heat of the barracks pressed upon her, filled by the sound of buffing brushes as they all concentrated on cleaning their boots. Sita's fingers were covered with brown shoe polish, an ugly dark line of it ingrained under her nails. Each night, Prema instructed, they would be required to clean their boots. Crouched down on the floor before their bunk beds, this task now absorbed them all. They had each been given a wooden box containing brushes and cloths and polish to be kept in their lockers.

The girl called Muniamma sat beside Sita, and it appeared she was also the occupant of the upper bunk under which Sita would be sleeping. Head bent low over her work, scrubbing at her shoe in a concentrated manner, the girl did not lift her gaze like everyone else, to exchange a word or a smile, constructing the first links of friendship. She made no effort to acknowledge Sita, who worked beside her. The boot in her hand was spread so thickly with polish that the whirls of the brush were clearly seen.

'Too much polish, you must take some off, then it will shine,' Sita advised in a low voice.

The girl gave her a startled look, but nodded and began silently wiping off some of the polish with a rag. The hair she had refused to cut fell forward over her shoulder in a single thick plait.

'My husband is also in the INA. He showed me how he cleans his boots, otherwise I too would not know,' Sita confided, but the girl did not reply.

Muniamma's waist was so small an extra hole had been punched in her belt to hold up her shorts, the bones stuck out all over her. A dark scar ran down one cheek and another patterned her arm. A thin gold chain that she fingered nervously hung around her neck.

'On the plantation we were always barefoot, only sometimes we wore sandals. I do not know anything about wearing shoes.' Muniamma spoke at last in a whisper, her eyes dark with intensity. As they worked, Prema strolled up and down the barracks, issuing instructions. Fit from training, the muscles of her body were hard and compact.

'You must learn to look after your kit; shoes and buckles must all be polished. Soon you will get your rifles and be taught how to clean them, and tomorrow you will learn how to make up your beds.'

'Why don't you cut your hair?' Sita whispered to Munniama after Prema had passed.

There was now a thick streak of shoe polish on the girl's thin face. Sita wondered how she would have the strength to become a soldier, and felt a rush of sympathy for her.

'My head was shaved once,' Sita confided.

'Why did you do that? Did you have lice? Was it for religious penance?' Muniamma paused in her polishing and stared at Sita.

'I was a widow.' Sita kept her voice low.

Even as she spoke, she was shocked at herself. Why was she sharing things she had been at pains to keep from the world, with this sullen girl? Muniamma gave a gasp, and her eyes widened. Sita looked down at the shoe in her hand, already regretting her words; it was as if she had allowed a stranger to see her naked.

'But now I am married again,' Sita reassured her, and Muniamma nodded, as if something was sealed between them.

'The only good thing I have ever had was my hair. That's why I don't want to cut it,' Muniamma whispered, returning the confidence.

Most of the girls had already finished polishing their boots and were placing them beneath their lockers. Sita gave a last rub to her own shoes, and then picked up Muniamma's remaining blacked but unpolished boot and began buffing it vigorously. Still struggling with the first boot, Muniamma threw her a grateful glance. Prema was now marching back down the barracks, inspecting the laid out shoes.

'I have been placed in charge of you. Don't let me down. I will be accompanying you to the camp in Burma once you finish your basic training here,' she told them.

'Burma?' Muniamma whispered, looking up in new terror.

Later, washed and changed into regulation pyjamas, they slipped into the rows of bunks, pulling the mosquito netting about them. Muniamma was not in the room as Sita settled herself into the strange bed, and her eyes were closing when the girl reappeared, shaking her into wakefulness.

'I cut it. Please see.' Muniamma pulled excitedly at Sita's arm.

Sita sat up and stared at Muniamma, who danced about before her now. Swinging her legs over the side of the bunk, Sita stared at the short hair now curling irrepressibly about her head. She gave a laugh and pulled Muniamma to her, feeling the girl's body crushed against her own, aware that Muniamma's thin arms returned the embrace.

'Because of you I told Prema to cut it. It's good it is gone. It's all because of you,' she repeated.

'Now we are both new people. Everything bad in the past is gone with our hair,' Sita's eyes filled unexpectedly with tears.

She knew nothing of this strange girl to whom she had already disclosed her deepest secret, but felt bound to her in a way she could not explain.

'You are now a new person, so you should have a new name. I'll call you Muni,' Sita decided, as the girl climbed the ladder to the upper bunk.

'Muni,' Muniamma repeated, sounding pleased.

The wire mesh of the upper bunk creaked with Muni's weight. Settling down in the narrow bed again, Sita thought

about Shiva and wondered if he too lay in a similar bunk in the
Newton Circus camp. The barracks were hot and airless and
she listened to the sound of breathing from the sleeping girls;
a cough, a snore, the creak of metal as someone turned, the
smell of close packed human bodies. It reminded her of the
bhajanashram and, although the comparison comforted her, she
wished that Billi were nearby, to guide her through the new
world she was entering.

Above the odours of the crowded room, the light scent of
freshly sawn wood and paint still lingered in the newly built
barracks, underlining the sense of adventure filling her now.
She was on the verge of new experience, and everything around
and within her was changing. By the side of her pillow she had
propped up a miniature picture of the *devi* she had bought, to
keep near her in the camp. A faint light from a lamp outside
lifted the darkness. She could just make out the form of the
goddess, the radiance of her face and the dark shape of her tiger
with its burning eyes fixed upon her in this strange place.

15
Singapore, 2000

'When is she coming?' Sita asked every few minutes, fidgeting at the table as they waited for Parvati to arrive.

'Soon,' Amita replied.

The three hundred and sixty degree turn her mother had made, now asking continually about Parvati, annoyed her unreasonably. It had disturbed Amita to learn at the last interview, that her mother was a child widow when she married Amita's father, something she had not known before. Even though she understood her mother had had no choice in the matter of her marriage, nor a voice in the shaping of her life at that time, even though she was married and widowed on the same day, it still angered Amita that her mother had mentioned none of this to her before. The memories Sita was now revealing to Parvati were things she should have shared with her daughter, Amita thought. As at the last meeting, Amita noticed the extra care Sita took with her appearance, the loose comfortable trousers topped by a bright chiffon blouse with a loose bow at the neck that she had not seen for a while.

Waiting impatiently at the table, Sita's eyes were bright with expectation. Spreading out some new photographs she had unearthed, she gazed at them intently, sometimes lifting one to her nose as if it released a secret perfume, as if she could enter again those frozen moments in time. She was surprised how the loosening of memories, teased from her initially with such difficulty, sprang from her now with ease.

Her gaze settled on a large pot of white orchids before the window, the long bare stems tied to thin sticks to support the fleshy weight of the flowers. The only things Sita liked about her daughter's home was the transformative beauty of these flowers, and the endless sky-scape beyond the window, light changing by the hour, majestic with cloud, dark with tropical storms. There was not an hour, however, when she did not long for her old home, cramped, grimy and overrun with cockroaches, but familiar as her memories.

She stared out of the window across the distant buildings of the university, in the direction of Serangoon Road. A conservation order now protected the buildings of Little India, and tourists crowded the narrow streets. Yet, unlike the tawdry commercialisation of Chinatown, Little India was still a lived-in place. Vegetables and fruit were bought from roadside barrows, jasmine garlands bedecked the flower vendor's stall, hardware, sari and jewellery shops flourished, the parrot astrologer ministered from a street corner to a regular clientele, the huge wet market reigned at the end of the road. The high-rise buildings of modern Singapore ringed the place, but could not encroach. She closed her eyes to visualize it the better and knew she would never return.

At last Parvati arrived, giving Sita a kiss before pulling notebooks from her bag. Already a routine was established between interviewer and interviewee. Now Sita spoke rapidly and without reserve, and Parvati made notes, writing swiftly, head down, as if she were taking dictation.

When Sita presented her with the new photographs, Parvati clapped her hands in pleasure, moving nearer to Sita to examine them better. Standing behind them, Amita stared down in irritation at the two heads drawn together over the photographs, and felt excluded. Pulling a chair up to the table, she sat down on it with deliberate force. Everything in the day conspired to annoy her. When she had finally slept the night before she had dreamed of Amsterdam, and awoken with a headache that nothing seemed to relieve. The residue of that nightmare and all it dredged up within her continued to shape her day.

On Amita's return from Amsterdam, Parvati hurried up to her in the university, her unsuspecting face full of welcome. It was all Amita could do not to turn away. Instead, she bit down upon a rush of guilt and smiled, and reported that Rishi had read a good paper at the conference. The intolerable feelings overwhelming her could only be balanced by the degree of affability she showered upon Parvati. As bad as the culpability now consuming her was the slow burn of desire Rishi left in her body, which she seemed powerless to control.

At the university, she continued to work with Parvati as if nothing had happened. Weeks went by before she saw Rishi again on a Sunday afternoon, buying bread with Parvati at an artisan bakery she had gone to in Tiong Baru. The meeting was breezy, and when Parvati insisted they all have coffee, she readily sat down with them, surprised at how easy it was to focus solely on the moment.

The following week Rishi contacted her, and she knew she had been waiting. They met at a budget hotel on Bencoolen Street. She went without a backward glance to where he waited for her. Even as she hailed a taxi, the blatancy of what she was doing shocked her deeply, but a woman within her whom she did not recognise now pushed her forward and would not let her free.

It was only afterwards, as he dozed, lying heavily upon her, his bare fleshy shoulder pressed uncomfortably against her jaw, that she looked beyond him to the window with its view of high rise buildings, and knew she could not continue with the deception, that to do so would destroy her. Across the oceans, in the provisional world of Amsterdam, nothing had seemed rooted in actuality. Here, in Singapore, but a short distance from where the unsuspecting Parvati went about her day, it was not possible to continue with such a base charade. Amita gave Rishi a push, struggling free from under him, gathering up her clothes, holding them before her nakedness, the decision already strong within her.

'I should not have come. It is not right.'

'What about Amsterdam? It didn't seem wrong to you then?' Rishi rolled over to stare up at her.

Censure edged his words, and she knew when he observed her he saw an aging spinster, ripe for the taking, fleshy and awkward, intellectually adept but naïve before the worldly negotiations such situations demanded. Yet, he would be wrong, she thought angrily. She was not naïve, he knew nothing of her past, and she was not about to tell him. All she wanted suddenly was to be free of him, free of guilt to live her life anew.

'These things can be arranged, you know; no need for anyone to get hurt.' He propped himself up on one elbow, staring at her.

'It's nothing to do with arrangements. Parvati is my friend.'

Even as she spoke, standing naked before him, and trying to hide that nakedness behind the clothes bunched up in her arms, she heard herself shifting angrily to Parvati's defence. He shrugged and sighed resignedly, rolling again into the comfort of the bed, turning his bare back towards her.

Later, in the taxi on her way home, the scent of him still upon her, the horror of her duplicity burst so violently within her that she thought she might be sick. She heard the censure again in his voice and knew he held himself above any blame. She had conspired in her own humiliation, betrayed a friend and thought she could place her actions beyond the parameters of all their lives.

For days afterwards such a presentiment of her own evil doing filled her that she thought of resigning from the university and finding a job abroad. At every opportunity she avoided Parvati, diving into a convenient door in the department if she saw her coming, taking unaccustomed routes along alien corridors, until Parvati asked in distress, what had she done wrong that threatened their friendship? There was no option but further concealment, pushing her secret deeper within her, a large stone she was forced to carry. Yet, as the months passed, the misery of that ill-considered meeting in Bencoolen Street eased. Amita was surprised that guilt could be managed so effectively as she stepped inside the different compartments of her life, as if one was not linked to the other. Now, when Parvati sat with her mother, Amita found she felt almost nothing.

At the table Sita searched amongst a pile of photographs, and at last found the one she wanted.

'Here, see. This was during our training, before we left Singapore for Burma. I am there, and that is Muni beside me.'

Amita stared down at the photos spread out on the table; she had seen them before as a child but had not understood their significance. Peering over her mother's shoulder, she gazed at the faded image of a line of young women at target practice, crouched down on one knee to support the weight of the heavy guns they thrust before them. She recognised the slight figure of Muni, whose uniform seemed too big for her. Head lowered to a thick-barrelled gun, Muni's expression was determined as she waited for the command to fire. Beside her, Sita bent in a similar pose, eyes intent upon the distant target. Her narrow military cap, tilted at a rakish angle, reflected the confidence radiating from her. Her mother was enjoying what she was doing, and had probably been a good shot, Amita thought.

'Did Netaji come to see you training?' Amita asked, seeking a way to insert herself into the closed circle that Parvati and her mother now seemed to form. Sita shook her head.

'In Singapore we did not see Netaji while we were training; he was already in Burma. We kept hoping he would come, but he did not. We saw him only when we arrived in Burma, at

Maymyo.' As she spoke of Subhas Chandra Bose, Sita's eyes filled with emotion.

'We were all in love with him. He was our Krishna, we were his *gopis*.' Her voice was low and full.

Amita gazed at her mother in embarrassment, seeing the naked sentiment in her face, hearing the wistful sigh.

'But you had a husband,' Amita heard the primness in her voice, the absurdity of her comment.

'Maybe Netaji was the romance we never had. We were all in love with him,' Sita repeated, lowering her eyes.

Amita's embarrassment intensified. Something about her mother still mystified and frightened her, as it had during her growing up. That part of her mother she had needed most as a child, from where she sought approbation and love, had always seemed elusive.

Staring again at the young woman in the black and white photographs, a woman who resembled her mother and yet was not her mother, Amita wondered at the journey Sita had embarked upon so long ago. As a young woman, her mother had an uneven beauty, a mobile face with thin cheeks, large luminous eyes, a wide mouth and a determined chin. There was also an overlay of shy innocence in her expression; an expectation that life still had more to give than to take. Yet the experiences that awaited her had dulled and dispersed that light, and Amita was determined to know what those experiences were.

Why, Amita wondered, should it discomfort her to think her mother had secrets or hidden emotions, or that she had once been young, with a body that must have throbbed like her own, with needs and desire? She herself had a life her mother knew nothing about. She knew to her own cost that secrets were a way to survive, a way not to remember, a way to forget. Such reasoning did not help her discomfiture. However well she knew her mother in an everyday sense, an unknown woman lay buried within that known person. If a chink in her mother's armour were prised open, Amita thought, she had no idea what she might find.

Amita fell silent, recognising that part of her growing irritation with the interview came from knowing Parvati was already making use of the Rani of Jhansi Regiment material she had prised from Sita. She was presenting a paper at a workshop organised by the Institute of South Asian Studies in the university, *Past and Present: Voices of South Asian Women in Malaysia and Singapore*, and reading the same paper again for the Gender Studies module in their own department. She had also lost no time in planning her book on the subject, and it had already been accepted for publication the following year by the university press. She was doing well out of Sita, Amita thought, but immediately checked this professional spite. Why could she not be more forgiving of her mother?

Maybe her Uncle Dev, who had been some years older than his sister, and had lived not far from them in Singapore, could have told her more about her mother, but he had died many years earlier. He had two daughters, and Amita remembered him as an indulgent father, always trying to balance his wife's iron discipline. After his death, the family returned to India, and there was little contact between them and Amita and Sita, who had never got on with her sister-in-law, Rohini.

She remembered a visit with her mother long before, to her Uncle Dev's house. He was a good-humoured man, who enjoyed gently teasing his sharp-eyed wife about how she had not given him a son, but only daughters. Amita remembered how he reminisced with her about events when her mother, Sita, had been born.

'Your grandmother got a good beating for producing another girl and not a boy, and for not getting rid of the baby at birth. Sadly, such things happened in the village in those days. Father was always beating Mother for everything, and after baby Sita was born he shut her out of the house for one full week. Our neighbours were good people and they gave Mother shelter, looking after her and also pleading with Father. Grandmother and I begged him every day to let her come home. I worried about what would happen if Father did not take her back. I imagined her living on the street like the fingerless leper in a hut of paper and sticks, and mad dogs attacking the new baby and carrying her off to eat. Mother could have drowned the baby in the river, or fed her poisonous berries, as so many women did, to be rid of girl babies. But for some reason Mother clung onto Sita and would not let her die. At last, the pleadings of Grandmother and I prevailed, and Father told me to bring Mother and the baby back into the house.'

This memory returned to Amita in a sudden jolt of recollection. As a child, listening to her uncle speak, the images his words produced had haunted her for years; mad dogs attacking babies, the drowning of new-borns, the fingerless leper, the poisons brewed to kill a child. The images faded as Amita grew, buried beneath the expanding texture of her life. Now, she realised in a rush of surprise, her grandmother had found the courage to resist a cruel and ancient practice, enduring abuse and shame and threatened abandonment for the sake of her girl child, her own mother, Sita.

Turning away from her mother and Parvati, Amita made her way to the kitchen. The light aroma of Indian spices floated on the air, a smell that permeated the flat nowadays. Her mother liked her Indian food and cooked it every day, whereas Amita lived on pre-cooked snacks or meals quickly thrown together, and used few spices. She was always careful to switch on the exhaust fan over the stove, which her mother constantly forgot to do. Already, there had been several complaints from her Chinese neighbours about the smell of Indian cooking. Her mother dealt with this by sending them plates of delicacies, and for the time being the protests had ceased. Joyce, the part-time Filipina help Amita now employed since her mother came to live with her, chopped up the vegetables, onions, garlic and ginger for Sita, and cleared up after the cooking was done; the kitchen was clean and a meal was always waiting for Amita when she came home each night. She was grateful for this, but a piquant scent of food was now permanently in the air, and Amita did not like it. It was yet another reminder that her space was no longer her own. As she picked up the kettle, filling it with water and lighting the gas, the sound of Parvati's voice drifted to her from the living room.

'The women recruits in the army were from so many different places and communities, how did you all communicate?'

'Netaji wanted to see unity in India, not everyone divided by religion and language and food and caste. We had Hindi lessons, and that is how we communicated, in Hindi. Those who could not speak it learned fast. Hindu and Muslim ate together; there was no segregation. We were one community, we were all sisters,' Sita explained.

On a counter in the kitchen Amita had piled up old newspapers to give the *karanguni* man who came each week, ringing his bell and calling for recyclable things. There were also a few disintegrating books her mother insisted on bringing with her when she moved, that had once belonged to Amita's father. Amita had disposed of everything she could in her mother's cramped home before moving her to Clementi, but the trauma of relocation had finally demolished these few frail books. Tattered pages slid from shrivelled spines, and Amita had quietly tied them up for disposal. Her mother would never notice, but although she was now beyond the need of her father's books, she stared at the desiccated bundle nostalgically as she waited for the kettle to boil. There had been a time when her father's books had meant everything to her.

As a child, the only way she felt she could know her father was through his books, stacked up in tall piles against the walls of their home. The titles were varied and included scholarly volumes on Indian history and culture, health, science, astronomy, mathematics, literature and military history: *History of the Indian Mutiny*; *Handbook of Chemistry and Physics*; *Advanced Mathematics*; *Decisive Battles of the World*; *Great Expectations*; *Napoleon's Military Strategies*; *The Bhagavad-Gita and Modern Life*; the list went on and on.

They had all been bought from second hand bookshops, her mother told her, already well thumbed when Shiva purchased them. Over the years they had yellowed further, the smell of age and mould lifting off them as Amita turned the pages, the paper brittle, devoured by silverfish, bindings cracking. Amita did not see these things, nothing had mattered to her then but that these books had belonged to her father, a legacy he passed to her. It had been her ambition then to read all the volumes in the room, to share the journey of knowledge her father had made through his reading, to know him through his books.

They had only one photograph of her father, that sat in a frame on a shelf in the room. He stood with his pupils in the schoolyard behind the Ramakrishna Mission, a tall thin man with a high, intelligent brow, deep-set eyes and a shock of thick hair. As a child, she felt closest to him when she untied the loose bundles of writing that lay in his small desk, beneath a lid of inlaid brass. She took the thin sheets of paper in her hand and stared at the dark patterns of dried ink, at the words that came directly from her father's mind to spill upon the page. In the same way as her mother now held old photographs to her nose, as if to draw in the ether of the past, so she too as a child had held those desiccated pages to her nose, breathing in her father's spirit, the smell of dried ink, metallic as blood, filling her head. There were notes in English, and others in Hindi, all written with a fine nibbed pen. Some pages were splashed with ink, on another the round stain of a cup base was seen, and one precious sheet was stamped with the inky print of her father's thumb. Unknown to her mother she had taken this ghostly keepsake for herself, folding it small, hiding it in her biscuit box of trinkets and knickknacks, opening the box to touch it each night before she went to sleep.

Her mother was not a loquacious woman, she was not given to gossip, nor did she have many friends. Their neighbours were always helpful, conscious of the needy status of a widow with a child. Sugar, flour, a cup of milk were easily borrowed, and if the electricity tripped or a pipe was blocked, help was quickly forthcoming, but people rarely dropped in just to chat, and her mother did not linger in the common courtyard exchanging pleasantries with the other women in the building. Mother and daughter led a solitary life, focussed upon the necessities of each hour, as if such focus were a means of survival, and in a way it was, Amita thought now. One moment grew out of another, one hour bled into the next, time passed, things were achieved.

Amita had had a good education. The Ramakrishna Mission helped generously, recognising her brightness and aptitude for study. It was these abilities that got her into an elite Christian mission school, one of the best in Singapore. Yet at school she felt her difference, and never invited anyone home. The privileged Chinese girls who lived in spacious houses, or even those lower down the economic scale, who resided in government subsidised housing blocks all lived more lavishly than Amita and her mother in their one small room. Only Amita's brain kept her above water, top of the class in everything.

Later, she won a scholarship to a university in Perth. The Ramakrishna Mission found a charitable sponsor to pay her airfare and support, and she worked as a waitress and tutored other students to make ends meet. For postgraduate studies she transferred to New York, to Columbia University, on another scholarship. Once again the Ramakrishna Mission found her financial support, and again she worked at tutoring and odd jobs to pay her way. She would have been happy to stay on in America after she gained her PhD, but anxiety over her aging mother drew her back to Singapore. She owed everything to her mother. In those study-filled nights of childhood, her mother had silently carved out the way ahead, seeing a future for her daughter that Amita appreciated only now.

At her desk in her cramped student accommodation in New York, Amita would think of her old home, seeing again the silhouette of her mother against the light of a standing lamp with a rusted metal shade. She saw her mother's upright back as she sat rooted on the other side of the table, marking school books, embroidering, mending, always there as Amita studied. The mute force of her determination pinioned Amita to that table. No man ever intruded into their solitary companionship and, presided over by the *devi* in her tin frame on a shelf above them, their world appeared adequate. In far away New York, Amita had only to visualise this long ago scene to apply herself anew to her study.

The kettle was boiling, but Amita always waited for a full whistle to sound before lifting it off the gas ring. A shaft of afternoon sun flooded into the small kitchen, illuminating a swirling cloud of dust motes. Her life was like one of those spinning specks, Amita thought, no more than a grain of dust amongst millions of others, yet, compared to her mother's life, her own life appeared ordinary. As these thoughts ran through her, Amita was filled with a rush of empathy for her mother. Trapped by life's contortions, her mother always turned to her gods, to the *devi* who, although an immortal, was also a woman like themselves, single and put upon, but without a man to command her, one-in-herself and strong of purpose. For Amita no such comfort existed, no god waited for her, she could not pray with conviction. The void before her seemed too great, too dark, and words fell heedlessly into it. She was forced to rely upon herself.

Opening a cupboard, Amita took out three mugs and a teapot, setting them on a tray. She opened a new packet of her mother's favourite jam centred biscuits and piled some on a plate. She wished she did not have to hear Parvati's voice, stirring within her a sense of her own worthlessness, and was glad when the whistling of the kettle interrupted her thoughts. Picking up the tea caddy, she heaped a spoonful of leaves into the pot and watched the boiling water splash down upon them. Her headache had returned, and the tiredness that dogged her recently persisted. The weight she had gained was no help, and she decided she must think of trying to lose a few kilos.

Probably she had got to that age, she thought resignedly; her periods had been irregular for the past year or more, and non-existent the last few months. Researching the subject of menopause on the Internet, she learned that fatigue, mood changes, hot sweats and irritability, besides much more, were all to be expected. That her body should have the power to act in such an evasive manner, independent of her will, was frustrating.

A visiting American professor in the department, an attractive, buoyant woman in her mid-fifties, had told her the secret to her energy was Hormone Replacement Therapy, and that the advantages of taking it far outweighed the disadvantages. Most doctors, certainly in America, regularly and easily prescribed it, she said. No need to dry up like an old prune, the woman laughed. That such a drug waited to steer her away from decrepitude heartened Amita considerably. The following week, she decided, she would go to the doctor and demand to be put on HRT. Picking up the tray she marched back into the living room, determined to take herself in hand, and put the recent past behind her.

In those first days at the camp Sita slept soundly, and woke each morning to the powerful feminine scents of the warm hut, an odour reassuring in its familiarity, and for a moment there was a vague sense that she might still be in the *bhajanashram*, with the comforting presence of Billi beside her. Then the sharp note of the bugle broke upon her and in the bunk above, Muni stirred. The barracks were still in darkness but already birds in the trees outside welcomed the dawn, and Sita listened to their riotous affirmation of the new day.

Then there was the rush to the toilets, to the washroom, to the lockers, everything happening at once but in an organised manner, for they were all now used to the military precision of the day, who went first, who went next, the speedy pace of ablutions and dressing, the making of their beds. Within a short while they assembled on the parade ground for the raising of the tricoloured flag of Azad Hind, orange, white and green, the Free India for which they were all fighting now. As it made its graceful ascent up the flagpole, the tiger at its centre stirred briefly, and Sita silently acknowledged the *devi*.

Then the hour of physical exercises began; sit-ups, push-ups, squats and crunches, ten, twenty, fifty, eighty, followed by running, round and round the perimeter of the parade ground until several miles were covered. There was also an obstacle course of challenging rope constructions they must scramble up and down, and the vertical course with its swinging logs and ladders to be traversed. Then, exhausted and starving, they lined up with their metal cups and plates at the canteen for breakfast. At first the physical demands of military training seemed impossible to fulfil, but they were surprised at how quickly their bodies strengthened and their muscles hardened. Soon, they cohered as a group, drilling and marching smartly in unison, inhibitions and inadequacies dropping away as their abilities improved.

The routine of camp life left no moment unoccupied, and was organised to train not only their bodies but also their minds. Some hours each day were given to the learning of Hindustani. On Netaji's order, they learned the language in Romanised script; it was thought a knowledge of this script would be useful in learning other languages later, and also promoted national unity in a country with so many ethnic divides and vernaculars. As a group, they communicated mostly, if imperfectly, in the common language of bazaar Malay that most of them already knew. There were also lessons in political history and geography; they learned why they were fighting the battle for India's freedom, how they had been colonially enslaved, and the history of the Indian National Congress. They were also taught the theoretical side of military training, battle strategy and the ways of ambush in guerrilla warfare. An officer from one of the men's camps came to instruct them, and for a while Sita hoped that Shiva might also appear, for these were the subjects he taught at the Newton Circus camp, but the men who came were officers from the Seletar camp and did not know of Shiva.

It pleased Sita that most of the Tamil girls from the rubber plantations, knowing that she knew Hindustani, turned to her for help as they learned the language, and she found herself once again in the role of teacher, especially to Muni.

'I have never had a chance to learn anything before; everything will change when I can read and write,' Muni leaned excitely over the upper bunk, peering down at Sita in the bed below.

Often, they sat side by side on the edge of Sita's bunk after lights out, and with a torch went over the words learned that day, until they were solidly wedged in Muni's mind and she recognised them at a glance. She was quick to absorb whatever she was taught, and Sita understood only too well her need to swallow knowledge whole. In Muni, she recognised herself before Shiva came into her life, and realised again how much he had changed her. As the weeks went by, Sita watched the amazement grow in Muni's face as she wrested meaning from a hidden world she had never expected to access. Her expression changed, new confidence filled her, and she stepped forward when earlier she would have hung back.

'It is because of you,' Muni gripped Sita's hand as they sat in the dark, side by side on the bunk, a circle of torchlight illuminating the open book on Muni's lap.

In the class on Indian history they learned the story of the legendary Rani of Jhansi, the namesake of their regiment. The

widowed and headstrong princess, privileged and emancipated
to an extraordinary degree in a bygone time, ran her husband's
state of Jhansi after his death. When the British tried to annex
the state in 1858, she rejected the cloistered status of widow
and emerged to lead her army into battle. With her infant son
tied to her back, she rode at the head of her force, but was soon
martyred to her cause.

Pictures of the fearless Rani on her leaping steed, hair flying
free beneath her helmet, armour-clad and with shield and sword
brandished before her, stirred them all. Yet, while the other girls
were full of admiration for the courageous Rani, Sita's attention
was always drawn to the child strapped to her back, forced to
confront a destiny in which he had no choice. Why had she
taken her son into battle? The smallness and vulnerability of the
infant's terrified face peering around the figure of its ferocious
mother never failed to fill her with horror. The image floated up
before her at unexpected times and would not let her free.

Only after dinner, when their shoes and kit were polished,
could they relax. Often, discussions were organised or improvised
concerts took place, but usually they just sat informally together
to chat in the barracks, which now had the comfort of home.
They were at ease with each other, all the divisive differences of
class and caste, of language, customs and community had fallen
away and the multiple Muniammas had each evolved into an
individual identity. Deep-voiced Valli was so badly troubled by
flat feet that the camp doctor fitted her shoes with supports.
Ambika's eyebrows met above her nose and her flat hair was
pinned behind ears that had exceptionally large lobes. It was

whispered that Kamla's mother must have been raped by a White plantation manager, her skin was so fair; a custom made uniform had to be ordered for Aarthi, to fit her generous hips and breasts; the facial tick that had troubled Shivani through the first days in camp had almost vanished; Vasanthi no longer bit her nails and proudly displayed to them all the new growth. One by one each girl came into focus, as they settled in together.

Forthright Valli's deep voice constantly filled the barrack as she practised her newly acquired Hindustani.

'Is that right, *akka*?' She shouted, checking with Sita's superior knowledge of the language.

'*Akka*, you're the best friend I've ever had,' Muni told her, in the torchlight over their language book.

The word *akka*, elder sister in the Tamil of the plantation girls, resonated deeply with Sita. Just as she had once called Billi *didi*, elder sister in Hindustani, she was now seen as a mentor by these plantation girls in the same way. She remembered the security she had felt with Billi beside her, and knew this was how these girls now felt with her. Although they were all about the same age, they were in awe of her because she was married, because she appeared educated, because Shiva was an officer in the INA. No one had shown her such deference before.

At the end of each day Sita's newly drilled muscles were sore, her mind full of all she had learned. At night she dreamed strange dreams, that she crossed great rivers, pushing against currents. She dreamed wild animals chased her, that armies chased her, that her grandmother chased her, that even the *devi* on her tiger chased her. In every dream she seemed to be running, and woke in her bed to the darkness of the barrack, her body damp with sweat, heart pounding. On the narrow bed she turned and gazed into the safety of the dark room, conscious of Muni's light snores from the bunk above, and knew everything within her was shifting and growing.

Sometimes Prema joined them in the evening when she was off duty, entering the barracks in a flurry of energy, the screen door slamming behind her, exuding a strong smell of the lavender she used to repel mosquitoes. They each had their favourite repellent, and the strange medley of scents in the hut, of citronella, lemongrass, *neem*, eucalyptus and also the stench of the garlic oil Vasanthi insisted on using, filled the air with pungency, but only Prema used lavender, and it defined her difference.

'Bats can eat one thousand mosquitoes in a night, so it's good there are so many in the trees outside,' she told them, sitting on a bunk while they gathered in a circle at her feet.

Prema knew everything, and a casual hour with her always revealed some inner workings of the regiment, or an intimate glimpse of their as yet unknown future.

'I should already be on my way to Rangoon, and then the new camp in Maymyo, but instead I stayed behind to take charge of you all and accompany you to Burma. The first batches of recruits are already getting advanced training there,' Prema told them.

'What is Burma like?' Vasanthi asked.

'Beautiful. The new camp at Maymyo is near the front line at Imphal. It is high in the hills and much cooler than Singapore,' Prema explained.

'The front line?' Sita asked, the words conjuring up a narrow white path running through a jungle.

'It is where they are fighting. The Japanese are pushing forward towards the Indian border, and our Indian National Army is fighting beside them. Together they are pushing back the British army,' Prema revealed.

'How were you recruited?' Someone asked Prema.

'My parents didn't want me to join Netaji, but I heard him speak and I knew immediately that I would follow him anywhere. I was wearing gold earrings and when Netaji asked everyone to donate to the cause, I rushed forward to give him my earrings. A journalist took a photograph and my parents saw it in the paper the following day. They were shocked, but they could see how determined I was to join up, and eventually they let me go.' Prema laughed.

'When will we see him?' Sita asked. She had expected to see Subhas Chandra Bose in the Bras Basah camp and hoped each day he would appear, just as she hoped Shiva might also suddenly stand before her in the classroom.

'Netaji is in Maymyo, near the front, with the troops. You will see him there,' Prema replied.

Maymyo. The word was spoken often now. The place waited for them on a horizon towards which they crept closer each day.

'It is time to make proper soldiers of you. Tomorrow you will be issued with your weapons,' Prema informed them one day.

The Armoury was a padlocked shed at the far end of the parade ground. It sat apart from the other buildings, as did the

Magazine, a further locked shed a distance away, where they were told ammunition was kept; bullets, powder and grenades. Standing alone in an area that was off limits, these unassuming wooden sheds exuded a mystique out of all proportion to their humble appearance. Armoury, Magazine; the strange names rolled around Sita's mouth like unwieldy stones. Within them, secreted away, the very essence of war lay hidden.

The next day they marched towards the Armoury, to be issued with rifles for their first target practice. An officer from one of the men's camps, Captain Ganguly, with the fat cheeks of a beaver, had come to instruct them, and strode smartly ahead with Prema, who unlocked the heavy padlock securing the shed. The door opened on rusty hinges, revealing a dark and windowless interior.

The place was lit by electric light, the weapons stacked upright on rack after rack around the walls of the hut. When her name was called, Sita stepped inside the hot airless place, into a forest of metal trunks. The harsh smell of ammonia, oil and cleaning solvents surrounded her, and she realised this must be the odour of war.

Captain Ganguly took a rifle from the racks and handed it to Prema, who then placed it in Sita's hands. Looking down at the smooth satin wood of the butt with its gentle patterning, Sita was surprised at the weight and presence of the thing, and wondered for the first time, how would she hold it, how she would shoot from it.

'These are magazine loading rifles with five round chargers. Think of your rifle as part of you now. In war it is as important as an arm or a leg to your functioning. Everything we train you for is found at the end of that gun. The same weapon will always remain with you; look after it well. You are your weapon, your weapon is you,' Captain Ganguly told them.

For the first time, looking down at the gun, Sita realised that what she held in her hands was a killing machine, and she was being trained to kill. The realisation shocked, dismayed and also surprised her, for she had not understood this clearly before. She had been carried away by the rush to enlist and join Netaji's army, by the excitement and romance of the venture, and overlooked the fact that the business of killing was integral to military life. It was at the heart of Netaji's grand speeches, at the heart of Shiva's need for revenge, at the heart of what she was doing in this camp. All the high talk of laying down your life for India meant only to kill, or be killed. When she stepped through the gate of the camp that first day, she had not realised to what extent she was entering an alien world. All she had wanted in her life was change, and the chance to follow Netaji.

'Balance is everything. Align your shoulders to the target; left foot to target, elbow to body,' the instructor roared.

There was also, it seemed, no substitute for real bullets. After some sessions of dry firing, and learning the intricacies of their weapon, they were ferried to a nearby firing range where they were to shoot with live ammunition.

'There is no substitute for marksmanship. No substitute for the weight and speed of a real bullet leaving your weapon; that is why you will not be shooting with blanks,' Captain Ganguli yelled.

They lined up to face the targets, wooden blocks pasted with the monochrome image of a man. Captain Ganguly strode up and down, shouting commands.

'You will shoot in all kinds of weather. Watch the wind flag on the pole to your left to adjust your aim.'

'Until the target nears, keep your trigger finger on the trigger guard. Left arm to body; take aim. Do not blink. Do not jump.'

The unwieldy weight of the gun on Sita's shoulder made it difficult to find a comfortable grip.

'Shoot.'

Nothing prepared her for the explosion in her ears, or the recoil of the gun that ricocheted through her body like a heavy weight rammed against her, throwing her back. The gun was a live thrashing thing in her hand, and fell with a clatter at her side. There were screams, and she saw that she was not the only one who sprawled on the ground amidst the crackle of gunfire.

It was not easy, but by the end of the afternoon she could hold the gun steady and shoot, although she was unsure of where the bullets landed. The recoil blasted through her each time, the gun punching painfully against her shoulder, but she clung onto the rifle, determined. With each shot the sense that she was taming a wild thing grew stronger, and at last she was rewarded by seeing the paper target at the end of the range ripped by her improving aim.

'Clean your weapon carefully and it will serve you well,' Prema told them later, instructing them how to oil the gun and scour the barrel with a brush and rod before they returned it to the armoury.

That night in her bunk her shoulder ached sickeningly and a large dark bruise spread across it. She could not lie on her side, and in the barrack most girls cried with the pain. In the bed above, Muni whimpered, but Sita gritted her teeth and made no sound, knowing this pain must be endured. Once it was behind her she would own her gun. It would be her thing and its power would be part of her, as nothing had been part of her before. In her mind she saw the target again, torn by the bullets she had managed to place accurately. If it had been a real man, she was aware her badly placed bullets would not have killed him. Lying in her bunk she wondered if, when the time came, she would even be able to kill. Could she learn to take a life, even if it was the life of an enemy?

Once, long before in the village she remembered a rabid dog. The villagers had managed to corral it in a corner, and a man with a gun had come. The dog snarled and barked and jumped at the fencing around him, but the man raised his rifle and without hesitation shot the creature dead. It slumped to the ground and Sita still remembered her horror as she stared at the lolling tongue, the foaming mouth and open eyes, staring now into nothingness. One moment the creature was viciously alive, and the next it was gone from its mad-dog life. The villagers had stared at the body in shock, but the man with the gun had shrugged and, with a half-smile, turned away.

Now, as she recollected the incident, Sita understood the gunman's casual gesture before the awed villagers, and knew that same authority would be part of her once the weapon was in her control. It had been nothing to the man to take that dog's life. A strange excitement thumped through her, just by the touch of the gun she was changed.

As the weeks of training went by, the gun appeared to lessen in weight, and she handled it with greater ease. The sense of the bullet leaving the gun and speeding towards its target filled her with pleasureable satisfaction; and her aim was always sure. Just as Captain Ganguly had predicted, their weapons become part of them. They learned to throw themselves to the ground while holding their rifles, to catch a tossed gun, and to shoot as they ran.

Eventually, bayonets were fitted to their guns for a different kind of practice. The gleaming knife filled Sita with a discomfort she had not felt when using bullets. Now, on the parade ground of the camp, straw dummies were set up for them to attack. Some were stuck solidly into the ground on a wooden strut, but others swung freely from a rope, as if to dodge attack. The dummies were painted with rudimentary faces, black slashes for eyes and nose and a grinning lopsided mouth, confronting the recruits in a defenceless row.

'Imagine the enemy is ready to kill you. Aim for the stomach. Grip your weapon with both hands. Charge,' Captain Ganguly yelled.

At last, it was her turn. Sita heard the order and sprinted forward, feeling the weight of the gun in her hands, the blade at its tip glinting in the sun. Each bound brought her closer to the waiting target, its makeshift face alight with inane welcome. She must stab the bayonet deep into the straw innards and, closing her eyes, she imagined the blood that would spurt in a real situation, the blade striking bone, the intestines spilling out; the cry of pain. As she ran she raised her eyes and saw the sky, the green bank of trees, heard the call of a *koel* and the cry of a food hawker from the road, the impatient honk of a car, and wanted these things to gather her up and lift her free of the earth so that the moment she ran towards would never come. Then, the grinning straw face was before her, and she slowed her pace. The sheer solidity of the straw body surprised her, the bayonet refused to penetrate, and the gun slipped in her hand.

'You're dead!' The officer roared as she turned away.

To Sita's surprise, it was Muni who excelled at this simulated killing, more than anyone in their squad. Muni, whose bayonet appeared disproportionate in size to her slight frame, charged forward each time with an aggressive yell, eyes on the target, unwavering in her commitment to the task. She stabbed as if her life depended upon it, the blade disappearing deep into the straw. Where she got the strength to do this, Sita did not know. Afterwards, she caught sight of Muni's face, and found it filled with such an expression of exaltation that she turned away, feeling she had glimpsed something in Muni that she had no right to see.

17
SINGAPORE, 1944

The hard metal quilting of the grenades reminded Sita of the pineapples she had seen on her first day in Singapore, a day that now seemed long ago.

'They say a woman cannot throw a grenade. You must learn to, because if you make a mistake you will kill yourself,' Captain Ganguly told them.

For practice, they were given empty grenades without a pin, and although it seemed no more difficult than throwing a ball, many did not make it over the wall into the burned earth of the grenade pit.

'If these were live grenades, you would be dead. Reach further, throw harder,' Captain Ganguly roared.

'In Burma your training will continue. There they will give you the real thing. Are you going to blow yourself up when you get there?' he asked, shaking his head.

Soon route marches began twice a week, and in spite of their hardened muscles, these were difficult for all of them. They must carry a loaded rucksack of fifty or sixty pounds. Eventually, these would be filled with kit, but for now they must load them up with bags of sand. Once full, the heavy sacks could not easily be hoisted up onto their backs. They must sit down to shoulder the load and then stand up. It surprised them all, the amount of weight they could carry, if it was on their back. Rifles positioned across their shoulders, they were ready at last for the march. They were transported to the far end of the island where thick jungle and undergrowth predominated, where snakes and large monitor lizards basked in the sun, and mosquitoes swarmed about them; they were all on quinine. From these places, the platoon must walk back to the Bras Basah camp along predetermined routes that they had to find with a compass.

'In war, more than shooting and combat, you will have to march. You are receiving the same basic training as your INA brothers. At the front, your brothers are forced to march under load, all day, all night, along mountain roads and through thick jungle, pushing forward against the enemy through rain and drought, uphill and downhill. The first thing an army must learn to do is to march. March. We march to liberate Delhi. *Dilli Chalo!*' Captain Ganguly shouted.

It was an ordeal of heat and biting insects, of thirst and no rations or rest, of aching muscles and the heavy loads they had to carry. At first it seemed relatively easy, five miles in the morning under the fiery sun was managed with ease, but quickly the distance was increased to ten, twenty, twenty-five miles. The straps of the heavy sacks sank deep into their shoulders, the barrels of their rifles burned hotly in the sun as they strode forward like men in their heavy boots.

'In action a forced march may be a tactical necessity. Then your life may depend on your ability to march; thirty-two miles in twenty-four hours, even forty miles in eight hours may be asked of you,' Captain Ganguly informed them.

The singing of military songs kept them buoyant. Sita liked the hard beat of their boots on the road as they marched; the rhythm of their stride pushing them on mile after mile, everyone moving as one under the heat of the sun. They were one seamless body with many legs, like the giant centipedes Sita remembered in her childhood home. As they marched they sang:

Kadam kadam badhaye ja! Khushi ke geet gaye ja
Ye zindagi hai qaum ki! Tu qaum pe…

Valli had a voice that rang out above everyone else, deep and strong as a man's, leading the tempo. The singing emptied them of emotion. Sometimes they even sang in English, a language they did not understand, random incomprehensible verses taught to them by the drill sergeant, the words rolling strangely on their tongues:

Lay me down in the cold, cold ground
Where before many more have gone…
Or,
It's a long, long way to Tipperary. It's a long way to go…

Sita did not know what the words, cold, cold ground meant, or where far away Tipperary might be, but it did not matter. The beat of the rhythm pounded through her body as she stamped her feet down on the road, shouting the words to the heavens, emptying her body and mind. The platoon marched three across and Muni was always beside her, her voice soaring up beside Sita's own, her face alight as they sang. Sometimes, she turned towards Sita and caught her eye, and Sita knew the same unloosed emotion sparked through them all.

Then, once daytime foot marches had become routine and they could cover any distance, night marches were introduced. Whatever the ordeals of sunlight, they must now march through a black world drained of sight and colour. The easy rhythm they were able to attain by day was impossible by night, and they could no longer sing as they marched. The night demanded stealth and restraint. Marching was slower and more focused; they must avoid stumbling in the dark, or bumping into each other, relying heavily on a compass and the moon for direction. Although they all carried torches these could not be used, as in any action they would alert the enemy to their presence. They followed Prema's single lead torch and the dark outline of those marching ahead of them. They kept closer together, only the hammering of their boots on the road breaking the silence, binding them together. In the darkness, the black jungle pressed upon them on either side of the road, alive with the noises of nocturnal animals, of hoots and snufflings, and the occasional crack of breaking branches. As they marched, Sita noticed Muni staring fearfully into the undergrowth, and gradually edging out of formation, moving closer to Sita.

'Its all right. We are all together,' Sita whispered reassurance.

Even as she spoke, Muni stumbled on the rutted path, falling to her knees with a groan. The formation did not stop but moved on, flowing around Muni's prone form like water about a rock. Sita stepped out of rank to stand at the side of the road until the platoon had passed, and then crouched down beside the trembling Muni. Within a short distance, Prema called the platoon to a halt, aware of the disturbance behind, and walked back to the injured Muni.

'Stay here with her. When we get back to camp I'll send a truck to pick you up.' Prema shone her torch on Muni's swollen ankle before turning back to the platoon.

Soon the dark phalanx of bodies was gone, the sound of their marching boots growing fainter and fainter until at last there was only silence. In the coolness there was the fresh earthy smell of vegetation around them, the perfume of the night.

'How long will it take?' Muni whispered.

The night was full of sounds. From behind the dense wall of the jungle, strange whooping cries were heard, as was the sawing of crickets, a flap of wings, and frequent movements in the undergrowth. Muni whimpered and edged nearer Sita.

'These are the places where *pontianak* live,' Muni whispered, shivering in fear of this ghostly apparition.

'That is an owl or some other night bird. I am here with you and we have our torches,' Sita reassured her, flashing the beam of light about the empty road.

'See, there is nothing here, no ghost, no *pontianak*,' Sita insisted, the need to reassure the frightened Muni giving her a courage she knew she might not otherwise feel.

'If you have your eyes open when a *pontianak* is near, they say she will suck them out of your head,' Muni whispered.

'They live in banana trees,' she added, looking into the darkness trying to discern if any of the offending trees grew nearby.

'No banana trees here,' Sita told her firmly, swinging the torch beam about.

Soft cries came again from the impenetrable undergrowth, and Muni clutched at Sita, who replied calmly.

'On your plantation, just like in my village, the night is full of sounds. There is no *pontianak* here, and we will keep one torch on all the time to keep any animals away.'

'In darkness like this on my plantation, the trees grow so thickly together that men have been killed, and nobody knows who murdered them. My father was killed like that. He quarrelled with another labourer, who stabbed him one night in the dark, but because of so many trees nobody saw anything. They found his body in the morning. It had rained in the night and he was wet and cold. Already ants filled his nose and ears and crawled under his eyelids. I remember it still.'

In the torchlight, Muni's face was a mask of craggy shadows, and she nervously fingered the thin gold chain she always wore around her neck, its tiny pendant, no bigger than a teardrop, set with a sliver of ruby. They were not allowed to wear jewellery in the regiment, but Muni refused to give up the chain, and in the end Prema told her to keep it hidden beneath her shirt.

'This chain was my mother's, and before that my grandmother's. My mother put it on me before she died. It is my good luck charm; I am never without it. It keeps me safe. It will keep me safe now from the *pontianak*,' Muni confided. The darkness seemed to give her the courage to talk.

'When my mother died of malaria after my father was murdered, the English Manager Sahib of the estate told one of the workers' families to take me in. I had a brother. He was sent to one family and I to another."

'My brother came to work in Singapore and when my grandmother died he called me here,' Sita admitted, simplifying her story but feeling the need to share a confidence in return. Muni nodded in the darkness.

The perfume of night flowers carried to them, a bird shrieked in the trees, and in the sky the moon pushed free of thin clouds, its silver light spilling onto the road. Muni continued to talk, her voice rushing on.

'My adopted family did not like me; they wanted a boy, they wanted to have my brother, not me. I was thin and weak, but from a small age I was doing all the cleaning work in that house, and then weeding work also on the estate. Weeding is children's work, but it is hard; your back hurts so much.' Muni pulled out a handkerchief, wiped the sweat from her brow and rubbed the cloth over the back of her bare neck.

'I cannot get used to being without my hair; it was the best thing about me. Everyone said my hair was beautiful, but when I washed it I had to be careful no White Sahib or Indian Manager Sahib on the estate was near when I dried it in the sun. If I saw a sahib I ran and hid myself immediately.' Muni's voice dropped.

Under the torch the tiny ruby on her pendant glowed. When she began whispering again Sita leaned forward to catch her words, at first not understanding what the girl was trying to tell her.

'You cannot refuse to go to the English Manager Sahib, or to the other white Sahibs who work for him, or even our own Indian Supervisor Sahibs. If any of them is wanting you, you must go.'

Muni's voice was almost inaudible, and as she spoke she rolled the gold chain between her fingers. Sita sensed they were crossing a line into buried territory and sat silent, waiting. In the darkness the cries of a night bird came again, there was a stirring through the undergrowth as a creature made its way about its nocturnal world. Sita had propped up the lighted torch on a stone, and the safety of this pool of light was comforting.

'One of the Indian Manager sahibs called for my family's oldest daughter. Her father owed the Sahib money and could not pay it. They did not want her to go to him and so they sent me instead. They said in the dark the sahib would not know or care which girl it was. He was old and fat and his face was so black. I hated to go but they made me. I was so young, I had not yet begun my bleeding.' Muni spoke in a rush as if afraid the words would get stuck inside her if she stopped, and Sita listened in distress.

'How did you become a Rani?' Sita asked, not wanting to hear any more about Muni's life on the plantation.

'When the war started, all the White English Sahibs ran away. The Japanese came but they did not know how to run a plantation. Soon everyone was going to Singapore, trying to find work. Some women came to the estate to find recruits.

They said if you join the Indian National Army you will be safe from the Japanese and you will get food and a better life. Already, everyone knew about Gandhiji and his fight against the British; we had his picture in our home. Like Gandhiji, Netaji is fighting for India and I am happy to die for him.' The words rushed from Muni, tears filling her eyes.

'I have never told anyone these things before. Now you will hate me,' Muni added in a whisper.

'There are also many things I have never told anyone.' Sita put an arm around Muni's shoulders, drawing her close.

They sat in silence, Sita absorbing the revelations Muni had made, wanting to reassure her that these secrets were safe with her. She searched for another confidence of equal weight to offer as proof of this.

'I had a baby once. It was a girl, and born too early. They say there is no soul until seven months, but I felt her turn, I felt the beat of her heart. And then she was gone; I could not keep her safe inside me. After that my husband was different towards me.' She had not realised until she spoke that the grief of that time was alive in her still.

Muni reached out and grasped Sita's hand and held it tightly in her own. At last in the darkness, a car was heard approaching.

Eventually, their months of training were over. Shiva was there at the Passing Out Parade, but Netaji did come to take the salute, as they had all hoped. Later Sita walked with Shiva out of the camp onto Waterloo Street, and remembered the rain on the day she had arrived, remembered her apprehension and his resentment. Shiva's regiment was preparing to leave for Burma some days before Sita's, and they had been given leave to spend one day together before they both left for the front. She walked beside him, the smart jodhpurs and shirt of her uniform showing off her hardened body, and knew he was assessing her out of the corner of his eye. Without realising it, she no longer aligned her steps a pace or two behind, but strode forward beside him.

During the months in the camp she had not been home, and was relieved to find nothing had changed. The Ramakrishna Mission stood as before, its ornate rooftop divorced from the busy comings and goings of the Japanese language school below. Vishwanathan and Savitri still sat behind the stall at the corner and greeted them, piling coconuts into their arms. The alley was quiet and the courtyard of the house deserted as they climbed the spiral stair to their room. Shiva produced his key and removed the hefty padlock from the front door. The plant in the oil drum was now a mass of shrivelled dead leaves.

A pungent odour of rot and mould surrounded them as they stepped inside the room. In a basket in the kitchen Sita discovered two decayed potatoes she had forgotten to throw out before she left. She hurried to open the window and to wind up the clock that had stopped on a distant day at eight minutes to three, some months back. Everything was familiar, and yet everything was strange, as if she were seeing it for the first time. The room had shrunk, and she seemed to no longer fit it as before. The towers of books and periodicals padding the walls weighed her down, fettering her to the place once again.

Shiva immediately sat down at his desk and called for tea, making it clear he expected everything to be as before, even though they had yet to bring up water from the tap in the courtyard. In their absence, roaches, rats and geckoes had moved into the room, and their droppings were everywhere. Sita picked up a brush and pan and began clearing the dirt, then hurried down to bring up water, hearing again the familiar metallic ring of her feet on the spiral stair. Setting the water to boil, she remembered the first time she had tried to make tea for Shiva, and the sense of shame at her failure, even though it was his fault that there was neither milk nor kerosene. Everywhere she turned she saw her earlier self, and realised the extent to which she had changed.

In an effort to please Shiva, she changed out of her uniform, pulling a sari out of the old tin trunk in which she stored her things. Shiva made no comment as she tied it about herself. The long skirt brushed about her ankles again, and the freedom her jodhpurs gave her, a freedom she had grown so used to, appeared irretrievably lost. She stared at the folded uniform on top of the trunk, and it seemed to belong to another person, from whom she was temporarily estranged. It frightened her then that in this room the old self reached out, trying to reclaim her, and possess her as before. She kept her eyes firmly upon the folded khaki jodhpurs and willed herself to be patient until the next morning, when she could again be the person she had become.

Later, Shiva went to buy them a meal from the food hawkers on Serangoon Road. When he returned with the usual warm banana leaf packet, she was careful to give him all the old deference, laying out the food before him, serving him first, and bringing him, as always, a bowl of water in which to wash his hands. Yet, something about her seemed to upset him, and he stared sullenly ahead.

As night came upon them, she lit the oil lamp, and laid out the sleeping mats. The thin wadding of the bed and the pillows were damp and musty, and she breathed in the unpleasant smell and coughed. In the dark the scuttle of rats was heard. He lay down beside her and she tensed, knowing what he would ask of her now. The light rasp of his breath touched her face, and she smelled garlic in his mouth, felt the movement of his hand upon her thigh, and prepared for his embrace. Lying on the damp mat she felt separate from her husband, conscious only of herself. Although she wished not to displease him, something within her was intent now on controlling what she gave or did not give to him.

'Even this now you do not want? I am your husband; this is my right. Why are you angry?' His resentment alarmed her, and also took her by surprise. She was not aware that she was angry.

'You have become arrogant,' he shouted, drawing back from her, and she was further shocked.

'I am doing everything I did before,' she protested, feeling the beat of his breath upon her. Above them the old clock began its wheezy gasps, preparing to chime ten o'clock.

'You have changed. You are doing the same things, but not in the same way. You are not even walking the same as before,' he spoke bitterly above the hoarse clanging of the hour.

'You were nothing when I married you.' His accusation fell heavily upon her, but did not hurt her in the way it would have, before.

His hand was on her shoulder, forcing her back. Gripping her arms so that she could not move, he laid his weight upon her with a roughness that was new, his anger mounting with his desire. Soon it was finished, but as he pulled away from her she felt her body stir, and tried to hold onto him, unable to control the strange convulsion rippling through her, making her cry out beneath him. Afterwards, he stared down at her, as if she embarrassed or even repelled him, but she found she felt no shame.

In the morning he spoke stiffly, sitting cross-legged before his desk, drinking the tea she had silently placed before him.

'I'm with the 3rd Division, and it is said we will be going to the front line, near Kohima and Imphal. That is where Netaji will enter India; that is where we will invade. I may not return. You could be a widow once again.' He held up a hand to silence her protest.

'This is the reality of our life. You are my wife, and I do not want you to face hardship again. If anything happens to me you should know I have already paid many months' rent in advance to keep this room. You will not be without a home. If I live I will get a soldier's pension, if I die you will get that same pension. In the camp we have talked about these things. Also, Swami Bhaswarananda has promised me the Ramakrishna Mission will always help you.' He stared at her fixedly, as if trying to imprint her face on his mind, to carry with him wherever it was he was going.

Sita was silent, contrition as painful as the guilt welling up in her. She wanted to move towards him, for what use were the strange feelings that had overwhelmed her the night before when they may never see each other again, but the emotions knotting within her held her back, and she sat silently where she was.

18
BURMA, 1944

For the first part of Sita's journey to Burma the platoon's transport was a convoy of old cattle trucks. A strong smell of animals lingered in the vehicles, and crumbs of dry dung encrusted the metal floor. The long journey through the green world of the jungle and the rubber estates of Malaya passed easily, as they sang and laughed. When the sound of enemy aircraft was heard, the trucks drew to the side of the road under the camouflage of trees until the danger was passed. As she had promised, Prema was with them.

At last they reached Ipoh and left the vehicles, making their way to the railway station to continue the journey by train. Striding forward, arms swinging, they marched smartly, backpacks now heavy with kit, rifles across their shoulders. They walked with the swagger of men, sitting with their legs apart or with an ankle crossed boldly over a knee. Everyone they passed knew who they were, and that they were going to fight for India's independence. As they crowded onto the platform the stationmaster, a wizened old Indian with a luxurious moustache, saluted as he hurried towards them, shouting enthusiastically

'*Dilli Chalo!*'

'*Dilli Chalo!*' they shouted in reply.

Further down the platform they noticed Japanese guards observing them disapprovingly, and they quietened. Drawing closer together, they waited as Prema walked over to the ticket office to inquire about the train that was to transport them across the border into Burma. She returned grim-faced.

'*That* is our train.' She nodded towards the rusty shuttered wagons of a stationary goods train. The stationmaster, who had followed them down the platform, shook his head in concern.

'You must not ride in that death trap. These wagons are used for taking supplies and prisoners to the Japanese camps, to work on the railway in Burma. No light, no air; prisoners die. Go home,' the old man advised, casting a wary glance at the Japanese guards.

'We cannot go back. We are soldiers,' Prema told him.

Alerted to the situation, the Japanese guards strode forward and began pulling back the heavy doors of the wagons, waving the ends of their rifles about in a threatening manner, ordering the women to get in.

'*Haite kudasai. Hayaku!*'

'Get in,' Prema ordered in a low voice.

'Don't look at them,' she added, turning away from the Japanese.

One by one they climbed into the wagons, suddenly aware of their vulnerability as women. The doors were slammed shut upon them, leaving them in semi-darkness. A barred space at the top of the wagon let in some air and light. As soon as the door was shut, the heat radiating from the metal walls of the carriage became intense. The train had waited all day in the sun, and was hot as a branding iron.

Pushed uncomfortably up against each other in the stifling heat, they thrust their rifles and kit into whatever space could be found in the wagon. Crouched beside Sita, Muni fanned herself with her cap. Sita opened the top buttons of her shirt, and found a handkerchief to place under her collar to absorb the sweat flowing down her neck. They waited, but the train showed no sign of moving, and eventually Prema stood up and with some help pulled back the heavy door. At once the Japanese soldiers rushed forward to slam it shut again.

'*Dame*. No,' they yelled.

'It will be cooler when we move.' Prema encouraged them, glancing up at the open slits at the top of the wagon.

Soon water and toilet facilities were needed. They pulled back the door once again to protest, and finally a rusty bucket and an enamel pail of water with a drinking cup were given to them. They drank gratefully and, making room for the bucket in a corner, used this one by one. Soon the bucket was full but when, in the hope of stepping out to empty it, they prised open the door, it was slammed shut again upon them.

Finally, with a tremor and a grating of metal couplings, the train jerked suddenly into life, eventually settling into a slow trundling gait. From the narrow vent at the top of the wagon a soft wisp of air stirred about them. The engine's plaintive whistle floated to them and the sense of movement at last was cheering. Their own feminine odour, baked to a rank and powerful smell in the wagon, was overwhelmed by the stench of excrement from the filthy pail. At times the wagon rocked dangerously, throwing them to the right or left, slopping the stinking contents of the bucket onto the floor to gasps of distress and disgust. Instinctively now, they concentrated their energy on enduring the journey, hoping that by nightfall their destination would be reached.

'Let's open the door now and empty the bucket while we are moving,' Prema suggested once the train swung freely along, but they found the doors locked.

Eventually, after some hours the train stopped, the doors were opened and the girls tumbled out into the fresh air. They found they were at a transit stop, a Malay village of *attap*-roofed huts. Japanese troops were everywhere. The most pressing need was for a toilet, and water to drink. A Japanese sergeant appeared and led them to a large hut built on stilts, and showed them also a primitive latrine with rush walls, that gave some privacy.

In the hut they rested, stretching cramped limbs. Village women served them a meal of rice, spicy vegetables and fish and they ate hungrily, aware all the while that they were objects of curiosity both for the villagers and the Japanese troops, neither of whom had seen women in uniform before, carrying guns. After a couple of hours they were ordered to climb back into the wagon to continue their journey, and found the bucket had been emptied and cleaned.

The carriage was cooler now that the sun had set, but they were still pressed uncomfortably against each other, and any sleep was fitful. As the train huffed and puffed its way forward, they tried the doors again, and finding them unlocked, pulled them wide open. Cool air blew in upon them now, and the relief was intense. Outside, nothing could be seen in the darkness, the vast black net of the sky stretched above them, alive with stars. In the early morning, they stopped once again at another transit point, where they rested and were fed, as before. They were told they were crossing the border into Siam, and when they were herded back again into the wagons they saw that a camouflage of palm fronds and tree branches had been tied to the top of the train, and knew the danger of bombing must await them.

The train went forward more slowly now, for the narrow track swung through hilly country, increasing the rolling motion of the wagons. Much of the time the track followed a distant river, but sometimes it curved inland through thick vegetation or narrow passes blasted out of solid rock. In places the hillside met the river, falling sheer into the water a distance below, the line winding terrifyingly along a narrow ledge hacked into the face of the cliff, and they held their breath until level ground was reached again. At some points the track appeared barely finished, crossing the river on what appeared to be makeshift trestle bridges. A constant view of the water refreshed them as the train chugged along.

Sita sat near the door and held her face to the breeze, filling her lungs with the dense earthy smell of the thickly forested land. Muni slept beside her, head resting on Sita's shoulder. The sooty smoke of the engine blew in upon them, and the mournful keen of the whistle filled Sita with nostalgia, as she recalled the ride from Vrindavan to Calcutta long ago.

Below them, at a lower level, they saw large bands of

workers, half naked in the sun, still working on the construction of the railway. In some places rough camps of rudimentary *attap*-roofed huts were seen. Many of the men appeared to be white-skinned, the British and Australian POWs captured by the Japanese that they had been told about. There were also dark-skinned Indians, and Sita wondered if this was where the men pulled from the scaffolding of the Ramakrishna Mission had been sent. She dozed again, but woke almost immediately with a start as the train stopped abruptly with a shuddering of brakes, throwing them all forward inside the wagon. The wail of an air raid siren was now heard, a thin bleating sound, far away.

'Out. Quick. *Hayaku*.' A Japanese soldier suddenly appeared before the open door, frantically gesturing for them to vacate the carriage.

'Run, run.' He ordered in English, pointing towards the surrounding jungle.

Grabbing their kit, they tumbled out of the wagon and, sliding down the embankment into the scrub below, ran into the hot tangled web of vegetation. Taking Muni by the hand, Sita pulled the girl down beside her. Flattened side by side in the sweltering undergrowth, they listened to the roar of approaching planes. Sita thought about snakes, but dared not move. About her the silence was broken by the buzz of insects, the cries of birds and the occasional yelp of monkeys high in the trees; mosquitoes and ants were everywhere. Head cushioned on her arms, the rich, earthy, rotting odours of the jungle floor filled Sita's nose.

Although she had given Shiva little thought since the last uncomfortable day together, her mind now flooded with images of him. If she died, how would he know? Where was he now? Had he reached Kohima or Imphal or was he somewhere else, in the unfamiliar country of Burma? A sudden, intense ache for her husband welled up in her. She remembered again those last hours together, and wished she could tell him she was sorry for whatever way she had displeased him, for she might die, and so might he.

The terrifying roar of low aircraft filled her ears and she closed her eyes, heart pounding. The explosion broke the world apart, the earth trembling beneath her. Clods of damp soil and vegetation cascaded down upon them, while above, the jungle canopy was ripped open, the sun streaming suddenly down upon them. The high-pitched screams of monkeys reverberated about them, clouds of birds soared up from the trees, a dark mass of frantic twittering. Sita covered her head with her hands. Eventually, the noise of the aircraft became a distant drone, and at last the all-clear siren floated faintly to them. The Japanese guards appeared again, calling them back to the train.

As they climbed out of the undergrowth and up the incline, they saw the train was untouched, but behind it the track they had just travelled over had disappeared into a gaping hole. As Sita stared at the bombed track she became aware of something on her arm, and looking down saw in horror that leeches clung to her limbs, moist black slugs, expanding by the minute. Nothing would dislodge them, and beside her Muni laughed.

'Like this,' Muni instructed, sliding her thumbnail beneath

one end of the creature, levering up its suckers and expertly flicking the slug away with a laugh.

'On the plantations leeches are everywhere,' she said in amusement.

Soon, they climbed nervously back into the train, aware of how vulnerable they were, settling back into the hot metal box of the wagon.

'This is your first real test as soldiers.' Prema remarked, but it was clear she too was battling terror.

'We are all in this together. If we die, we die together. We are sisters now.' Muni spoke up with unaccustomed determination.

Everyone turned in surprise, but Muni's face reflected the comfort she found in this thought and the truth of what she stated. In the weeks of training at the camp they had moved through experiences together, crossing over the boundaries that first divided them, of status and community, sharing the intimacies of flesh and thought, unknowingly nurturing each other. They had become a community, and their commonality cemented them together in an intangible way that they were only now, on this journey, beginning to recognise and depend upon. They sat down in the wagon again, heartened by Muni's sudden outburst.

When the train stopped next, it was at a sprawling encampment, a village that was now a labour camp. Once again they climbed out of the train and lined up, marching behind a Japanese officer to the huts where they would rest. It was clear the Japanese had some difficulty in evaluating them, for at each stop they were greeted with the same disapproving suspicion by the soldiers. They were not Japanese prisoners; they could not be manhandled, and as soldiers of the Indian National Army, they must be given respect. Yet, as women, they were dismissible.

The light was fading, and groups of prisoners were returning to the camp for the night from work sites along the railway line. Most of the prisoners were Caucasian men, tall, emaciated, underfed and exhausted, naked but for ragged loincloths such as common Asian labourers wore. They trudged wearily through the camp, some stumbling in fatigue, the sick supported by their companions, all of them wasted and skeletal. Sita stared in disbelief, distressed but also confused by the human misery before her. These men were the enemy she was supposedly fighting against, yet their wretchedness now in the shadow of death was hard to equate with Netaji's ringing words for battle, or Shiva's condemnation of the British. These men were no more than frail ghosts, as invisible to the world as she had once been in the *bhajanashram*. She followed their faltering progress, until they were lost from sight behind the mass of ramshackle huts.

Asian prisoners also crowded into the camp. Chinese and dark skinned Tamils, as skeletal and sick as the Europeans, were all whipped along like animals by the short legged, wide-jawed Japanese guards. Sita watched them herded into open-sided shacks that exposed them to the elements, snakes and wild animals. As she watched the crowd of men shuffling before her, she wondered again about the men pulled off the bamboo scaffolding outside the Ramakrishna Mission.

Unlike the prisoners' huts, the Ranis were given Japanese officers' quarters, structures raised up on stilts for safety and carpeted with clean rush matting. Once again villagers served them food, bowls of plentiful rice and vegetables. A short distance away, the prisoners lined up for a meagre cup of gruel dished out from large tureens. From where she sat on the wide wooden balcony of her accommodation, Sita looked down on the shacks of the Tamil labourers. In one corner of their accommodation she saw a small makeshift place of worship had been erected. A coconut shell garlanded with a plaited rope of grass, strewn with leaves and the petals of jungle flowers. These things were enough as a repository of hope. In her rucksack Sita carried the small picture of Durga on her tiger, and instinctively she reached in to touch it now, knowing the power of that unseen presence.

Later they were escorted to a stinking latrine used by the officers, open roofed but with rush walls for privacy. To get to this place they must pass the huts of the Tamil labourers. Heads down, the women hurried to the latrine, but Sita felt compelled to turn, as if to acknowledge that moment of witness, when men, who might be in this very camp, had been torn from their lives at the Ramakrishna Mission. That the Tamil labourers who now silently met her eye might not be those same men was of no importance. That she acknowledged her connection to them was all that mattered. The men eyed her curiously, and she turned away in embarrassment.

As the women sat on the open veranda of their sleeping quarters in the evening, conscious that they had an oil lamp while the camp now lay in darkness, there were low sounds. A small group of Tamil labourers crept towards them, looking fearfully about all the while for guards. Finally, feeling safe from the view of the Japanese, they crowded below the veranda, faces upturned towards the girls. They were men of small stature, wasted to the bone and naked, sores and wounds patterning their bodies. The oil lamp cast long shadows and lit up their faces so that their eyes, white against their dark faces, took on a luminous quality. One of the men began to speak in a low voice, while the others kept watch for patrolling guards.

'We come to thank you, sisters. We know you go to fight for us, to free India. It does our eyes good to see you. Whether we live or die here matters not, but we know you fight for us, for our children's future, for the future of India. If India is not freed, we will forever be imprisoned in our own land by a foreign power. We know now, white or yellow, all these great powers are the same. Fight, fight for us, fight for our children.'

'The guards will come if they see us all here like this,' Prema told them, pushing the girls back from the edge of the balcony, and leaning forward to speak to the men.

'Go back, brothers. It is too dangerous for you to speak to us. We thank you and will remember you.'

It matters little if we live or die; what matters is that India is free. Sita heard Netaji's words again as she looked down at the emaciated men, and knew some might not survive the coming day. In this camp, where the misery of death made men wretchedly equal, she saw more clearly than ever the commitment Shiva had made, and the reality of the cause

Netaji fought for. The men crowding below the hut had risked their lives to tell them this.

In the early morning when they awoke the camp was already empty, its skeletal inmates gone before daybreak to their unspeakable work. Soon, they boarded the train once again, to journey on, and Sita stared out through the open door at the fast flowing river winding beside the track. The sky was darkening behind grey clouds, heavy with the approaching monsoon. She settled down for the long journey ahead, and pressed against her, Muni gave a yawn, their sweat mingling where their bare arms touched.

The long journey eventually ended at a small dusty station at the Burmese border just as the monsoon was breaking. Trucks were waiting to take them on to INA headquarters in Rangoon. After a few days in the capital, they travelled on to Meiktila, then to Mandalay and at last to the military camp at Maymyo, several hundred miles north of the capital. As they travelled, an early monsoon shower rained upon them, the Burma downpour eclipsing even that of Singapore in its ferocity, thundering on the canvas roof of the truck, splattering copiously through its open sides. The terrain turned hilly, the road carrying them up into the Shan Highlands, the air becoming steadily cooler.

At last they reached the scenic hill station of Maymyo. The place had once been the summer capital for the British in Burma, and a military outpost. It had also been known as a centre of education, where the colonial British and wealthy Burmese sent their children to school. Now the many deserted schools provided bases and billets for the Japanese military, and also for the Indian National Army. The fresh invigorating air and leafy avenues of trees, the rolling views of green terraced land, the quaint English-style cottages and mock–Tudor houses, were a different world. Sita had seen nothing like it. The fresh air and sudden lack of humidity heightened the sense of entering a new world where anything seemed possible.

'Maybe Shiva is here,' Sita told Prema.

The small town of Maymyo was a centre of war operations and hummed with military activity, its sleepy village roads busy with armoured cars, trucks, and ambulances full of the wounded. Scanning the Indian National Army men who, with Japanese troops, swarmed about the town, marching along or crammed into army transport, Sita's heart lifted. Shiva had been unsure of where his regiment was going, so it was possible he might be here. At any moment she might turn her head and see Shiva, he might shout and wave to her from one of the crowded military trucks trundling down a road.

They also arrived to the startling news that Indian troops had crossed the Burmese border into India. In Manipur, they had raised the Azad Hind flag upon Indian soil, and were holding their position. The town fizzed with this jubilant news.

'I will ask about Shiva,' Prema promised.

Like most of the regiments crowding into the town, they were billeted in a deserted school, a large building with pseudo Tudor-style beams ornamenting its exterior. When they arrived, trenches were being dug around what was once the school playground. They were shown to the dormitories, airy rooms with high ceilings lined with rattan beds, topped by mosquito nets and mattresses and pillows stuffed with soft *kapok*. Precipitous views of wooded hills, stretching away in blue layer after layer filled the large windows. They rushed to look, breathing in the fresh air and the beauty of the sight. It was as if they were on holiday, not come to fight a war.

At night the rain coursed down again, drumming on the roof, hitting foliage and running off the leaves of fleshy vines in noisy rivulets. Once or twice Sita woke to the sound of thunder; a flash of lightning illuminated the sleeping girls about her, and Muni in the next bed. Sita stared up into the darkness and felt the strangeness of the place. When she thought of the long journey swinging away behind her, she imagined the silver trail of a snail. It was a relief to sleep in a bed again, and not doze in a moving train or a jolting truck, or beneath a thin blanket spread over the damp jungle floor, prey to ants, snakes, mosquitoes, leeches and worse. She seemed not to have slept for weeks. It was a relief just to reach a destination.

In Maymyo a new level of intensity impelled everything. The front was less than a couple of hundred miles away. The guerrilla warfare learned in Singapore was now relearned with a new intensity. They practised how to stalk their prey noiselessly, creeping forward on the ground, noses pressed to the dank moist earth, guns at the ready. They moved in small mobile units on long, tough route marches through the surrounding hills and stretches of jungle, depending on the local population for food and shelter, learning how to set ambushes and position bombs.

They marched the sixty-five miles from Maymyo to Mandalay, rested there at night and then marched back. There was sweetness in the fresh air, and they marched with new energy, ate the plain food they were served with new relish, flung themselves enthusiastically into the exhausting manoeuvres. The sudden immediacy of war filled them all with new vigour.

The town had a large military hospital and each day casualties were brought back from the front at Imphal and Kohima. In Maymyo life revolved around war, the talk of it, the thought of it, the sight of casualties coming in each day, the constant air raids. The proximity of the front line, to which sooner or later they would all make their way, to live or to die by its arbitrary choosing, heightened everything.

Shiva's 3rd Division was not in Maymyo, Prema told her, but possibly near Meiktila, or even already in Kohima; nobody knew for sure. Even though Sita had not expected Shiva to be in Maymyo, disappointment filled her. The news they got of the war was mostly through the nurses who cared for the wounded soldiers in the military hospital. These girls were also Ranis of the Jhansi Regiment and had received basic military training, but they had volunteered to be part of the nursing corps. The girls worked in the hospital, but returned to sleep in the camp and usually joined them in the evening at supper, and gave them the news of the day.

'The British are now fighting back, and the Japanese are not pushing forward like before,' one of the nurses told Sita.

'But the INA has crossed the border into India,' Sita protested.

'Well, now they have been pushed over the border again, back into Burma. The British are making new gains. A battle won, a battle lost, that is the way of war,' the girl replied, with a shrug of her shoulders.

Not long after they arrived they met Captain Lakshmi, who had just returned to Maymyo from visiting a hospital at Jiyawadi. As they finished breakfast, sitting at long tables in the school refectory, she entered the room, walking towards them, smart in freshly starched jodhpurs, the shoulder epaulettes of her shirt slashed by the stripes of her rank. She seemed even more striking than Sita remembered when she first saw her garlanding Netaji at the rally on the Padang. She commanded the room as soon as she entered. The warmth of her smile included them all as they crowded around her, eager to be noticed. Lakshmi's cap sat at a rakish angle on her head, and from a high window the clear morning sun spilt down, encircling her in a pool of light. She gave out a vitality that infected them all.

'Are you comfortable here? Is the food adequate? Are you warm at night? Do you need more blankets? It gets cold at this height.' Her smile and concern left them unprepared for what she said next.

'If casualties keep arriving at this rate in Maymyo, we will need more nurses, and I will have to call on you to help at the hospital.' Lakshmi's eyes were eagle bright beneath the thick eyebrows that dominated her face. There was a gasp of distress.

'We want to fight.' Sita said at last, shocked like everyone else around her at what Captain Lakshmi was suggesting.

'We are not nurses, we are soldiers,' Muni spoke up beside Sita, and behind her, everyone murmured approval. Lakshmi nodded but pursed her lips.

'I hope I will not have to call upon you, I hope casualties do not rise, but if they do, then the care of our men must be our first duty.' Lakshmi's voice was firm as she turned on her heel, and Prema hastened after her.

19
SINGAPORE, 2000

It was difficult to concentrate; the sun pressed hard against the window and fell in a fiery weight onto her left cheek and shoulder. Within half an hour the sun would have passed beyond the Arts and Social Sciences building, and Amita moved her chair slightly to avoid its blaze. She had a headache; most days now she seemed to get a headache, though she was not a headache type of person; it was the stress of living with the secret of Rishi. Whenever her nerves were frazzled, she found it best to focus on work. An early class was already behind her, and she had put aside the rest of the morning for preparing PowerPoint slides for the next lecture, and grading students' work.

With her undergraduate pupils, she was discussing an extract from a novel by a well-known Singaporean woman novelist about early Chinese immigrants to nineteenth-century Malaya. The extract concerned a young woman in a tin mining village in the state of Perak, bought cheaply from a brothel by her mother-in-law to be a wife to her idiot son. Married to a husband with the mental age of six, the young woman is soon accused by her Cantonese community of adultery with a man from a rival Hakka clan. Physically abused and vilified, she is thrust into a pig basket by the village men and brutally drowned in a nearby river. Amita began to speak into her Dictaphone, sorting out the main points she would later transcribe to the PowerPoint slides.

'We enter the narrative from the male perspective of Tuck Heng, who is a spectator along with all the villagers, while the woman, who is the spectacle, is pinned under the gaze of all the village men… Kneeling before a temple (note the symbolic attitude of supplication) she is positioned both in language and in social context in the *object positio*n — in other words, she is *objectified*. She is also under the gaze of the village women, who take a position of superiority over her, because they are not adulteresses like her. Figuratively, she is abused in language as *the whore, the bitch*. Literally, she is abused by being plastered with mud and dung, and bleeding from the beating inflicted upon her by the village men. Her identity is reduced to her sexuality and sexual parts as they yell, *cut off her cunt*. She is commodified; indeed, all women in that community are commodified. We are told, *A dagger is better than a wife in this jungle. A wife you can buy any time.* However, there is a resistance built into this narrative. At its centre is the silence of the woman. Why is this silence pivotal to the tale?'

Scanning the extract, Amita began marking words that would illustrate her points when she came to deconstruct it in the classroom, and then paused to check her watch. It was already eleven thirty. She needed to get to a doctor's appointment at twelve o'clock. The National University Hospital was part of the university campus and at the far end of Kent Ridge; it would not take her long to reach there by shuttle bus. She left her desk as it was, and hurried from the room, hoping she would not have to wait too long at the clinic. The thought of seeing Dr. Wong irritated her. He was a man, and she had hoped to see a woman who, she was sure, would discuss female issues with the right measure of sympathy. The American professor who suggested she take HRT had told her to see a woman doctor because, she said, a man was more likely to be obstructionist in anything that kept a woman vital, especially after menopause. And, she continued, it was even likely that an Asian male doctor might not agree to write a prescription for something that was an everyday thing in America; the professor had heard terrible things about the attitudes of male doctors in Japan.

As she feared, when she had laid her list of complaints before Dr. Wong a week back and suggested firmly that it was time for her to start hormone replacement therapy, he had refused to accommodate her without first taking a blood test to check her hormone levels, and also a urine test. With an effort she had controlled her annoyance; it was her body and she knew what it needed. There was no option but to go along with the process, and this forced compliance had put her in a bad mood. Now, on arrival at the clinic, she was relieved to see it was not too full. Her ankles were swollen and her feet felt tight in her shoes. She was glad to sit down to wait in the cool of the air conditioning. While she had struggled to endure the freezing cold of New York winters during the years she lived in that city, the heat and humidity of Singapore was no less easy to tolerate.

After so many years away, it had not been easy to return

to tiny Singapore, with its conservative ways. She was grateful to America; the time there was an awakening, for which her sheltered life in Singapore had offered no preparation. In the beginning, the intellectual choice and stimulation encountered was so heady she felt her sanity was being attacked. The freedom to pour out her views, to freely agitate and protest for a cause, was like nothing she had known in the subdued and politically correct environment of Singapore, where such openness of opinion was frowned upon. It was as if a different self had emerged from her, fully formed and waiting for that moment to materialise.

At Columbia University she was immediately pulled into the exciting rhetoric of feminist groups and, almost before she knew it, found herself an active agitator for women's rights. A floodgate opened within her, and she filled this new self with joyous abandon, seeking the most extreme positions. Sexuality, the family, the workplace, reproductive rights, legal inequalities, domestic violence and marital rape, changes in custody and divorce laws were what the women who befriended her were talking about. The importance of these issues fell about Amita in an entirely new and aggressive way, as if she woke from darkness into light. Suddenly, she saw everything differently and, as a token Asian presence in the midst of such heated debate, she was seen as a budding proselytiser who would take the feminist doctrine back with her when she returned to Asia.

Yet, on her eventual return to Singapore, she soon realised that the doctrines preached in the Western world were not readily adaptable to Asia. Her proselytising zeal was quickly muted. What had seemed normal in America appeared outlandish in Singapore, and she saw the need to dilute her views or keep them to herself. Even the women in Singapore whom she was prepared to fight for, did not always appreciate her strident arguments and opinions. Problematic questions of culture, cultural identity, cultural difference and cultural diversity soon made her aware that feminist issues in Asia needed to be approached on their own terms and in their own context. She swallowed down opinions, and tamed her argument to suit the role she was now called upon to fulfil as a teacher, while still devising subversive strategies to plant radical thoughts in the young minds around her.

Men too, she found, seemed unable to cope with the directness of her attitude. Those she took as lovers, seemed frightened of her capacity for fulfilment. Life narrowed, and she strove to rein in the instincts that she had so recently worked to release, adapting back to the familiar environment of Singapore, keeping her rage for her classes.

She remembered the number of men she had so easily slept with during those student years in America, throwing herself into every opportunity with a recklessness she looked back upon now in wonder.

In New York she had also volunteered at a local rape crisis centre, joining protests in the cold of winter and the heat of summer, agitating to keep threatened abortion centres open. She remembered the rush of adrenaline as she stood her ground against aggressive opposing groups, faced police cordons and the threat of tear gas, holding up a placard and shouting, 'Pro-

Choice. Pro-Choice.' She believed in all she stood for, defending Asian pragmatism where abortion was often used as a form of birth control. As she recalled her conduct at that time, it seemed she remembered a different person who had come into being for a specific purpose, and was lost to her now. It was as if she grieved for a dead friend.

The bus drew to a stop outside the hospital and Amita stood up and made her way down the aisle to the door. For some reason her mother now entered her mind, and she thought with a pricking of both pride and shame, that the access she had to her body must be something her mother had never known. Her mother might never have experienced an orgasm, nor even known that such pleasure might exist. The thought filled Amita with immediate discomfort and she thrust it away, climbing down from the bus and hurrying into the antiseptic depth of the hospital.

Dr. Wong looked up as Amita entered his small consulting room. A skeletally thin man with sucked in cheeks, he gave her a brief, assessing glance from behind his rimless spectacles. The hospital was government owned and, unlike private hospitals, where consultants filled their rented rooms with personal family photographs and memorabilia from grateful patients, Dr. Wong's room was bare of such accessories, reflecting the impersonal nature of government employment. Such austerity was both a relief and a disappointment, for while she was thankful the doctor's private life was not thrust at her, the lack of such hooks prevented Amita from making a cursory judgement of him in her usual way; she hoped he would not be obstructionist. She noticed he wore a wedding ring, and on the lapel of his jacket was pinned a small metal insignia with a cross. From this she deduced he was a churchgoer, and a family man, and this information did not reassure her.

Dr. Wong lowered his head and, opening her file, glanced at the paper of test results before fixing his gaze upon her. Behind his spectacles his eyes had a detached and glassy quality, it was impossible to know what he was thinking. Amita met his glance and prepared herself for argument, she could already see he might be one of those men the American professor had warned against, who might not easily give a woman the kind of medication she was asking for.

'Are you aware you are pregnant?'

Amita started in shock, her heart pitching in her chest.

'Impossible,' her voice was deep and fierce, the blood felt as if sucked from her body.

'You can't get pregnant at my age,' she heard the screech of her own voice. Her heart was fluttering about in her throat like a bird trying to escape its cage.

Dr. Wong's eyes remained upon her. Desperately now, Amita tried to remember the two times she had been with Rishi. He had worn a condom at the Bencoolen Street hotel, and in Amsterdam she was sure he had also worn one, but she could not be certain of anything that night. She had not even remembered the stumbled return to her own room. Steadying herself, she tried to think clearly about Amsterdam, but remembered little except an urgency of emotion that transcended everything else.

The last few years she had ceased to worry about pregnancy on those isolated occasions that might give her cause for anxiety. The occasional hot flush and the growing irregularity of her bodily cycle over the last year or more, and the blessed immunity from pregnancy that she thought menopause had brought her, was a house of cards collapsing about her now. Her heart beat in new panic.

'We verified it twice to be sure,' Dr. Wong confirmed in a detached tone of voice. 'And yes, it is rare to conceive at your age.'

'It's impossible.' Her voice was full of accusation before Dr. Wong's unemotional gaze.

'Most late pregnancies are due to IVF treatment, but it can also happen naturally, if rarely.' Dr. Wong continued to observe her with an interest she was becoming averse to.

'Not married?' he queried. She shook her head.

'But you can afford to keep the child?' His eyes never left her face, and his voice was detached.

'I don't want it. I can't have it.'

How would she tell people, what would she say to her mother, to Parvati, to anyone who knew her? Singapore was a traditional society that, as yet, had no place for even pre-marital co-habitation, leave alone single mothers of her kind. Everything inside her was collapsing; tears smarted in her eyes.

'I want a termination.'

The words sprang from her, and at once she knew that this was what she must do. She was desperate to smooth out her life, ease from it this wrinkle, to be as before. Dr. Wong looked up from her report to fix his gaze upon her again.

'It is not something I like to recommend. It is legal of course, and the option many women choose, but I usually advise patients in circumstances like your own, to consider well before making a decision. You can put the child up for adoption. We can offer you counselling.'

She caught an edge of censure in his voice and looked away, acutely aware that beneath the professional steadiness of his gaze he must be wondering about her. In his eyes she was probably what, in Biblical terms, he might call a loose woman.

Cut off her cunt! Drown the bitch! Slut! Slattern! Whore! The words she had transcribed to her PowerPoint just an hour ago filled her now with new force. She could not meet his gaze but sat in silence, looking down at her hands in her lap. Dr. Wong began to speak again.

'At your age, however, childbirth has many serious risks both of foetal abnormalities, and for yourself. I will give you a note for Dr. Tay in the obstetrics department. I'll see if they can fit you in right now for a preliminary examination, if you have time. They will then arrange a day and time for the termination, if you are sure that is what you want.'

Of course it is what I want, she wanted to shout the words out loud to him.

Dr. Wong picked up the phone and made the arrangement, then reached for a sheet of headed paper on his desk and began writing in a spidery hand, a note to take with her to Dr. Tay. Amita sat unmoving in the chair, relief pounding through her with an intensity equal to the desperation she had felt only moments before. Dr. Wong nodded as she stood up, but in her haste to be free of him she failed even to say an obligatory goodbye.

She made her way to the obstetrics clinic, following signboards with directions, wandering down the wide corridors of the hospital in a daze. People walking on the opposite track pushed against her, a gurney with an elderly patient hooked to a drip rolled past, accompanied by two nurses, an old man in a wheelchair approached and was gone, snatches of chatter filled her ears as people overtook her. She walked as if in a dream, but at last she found herself in front of the clinic and was obliged to push open the door.

'You'll have to wait. We'll try and slip you in between other patients,' the receptionist told her.

She did not want to wait. Waiting was time to think. She would have liked to do whatever had to be done, immediately. Then, she could put it all behind her and leave the hospital in the frame of mind she had entered it, and go back to transcribing her notes onto the Powerpoint presentation. She sat down on a chair and looked at the other waiting women, some in advanced stages of pregnancy, none of whom appeared to be in her own agitated frame of mind. They read magazines or watched the pictures flashing mutely over a television screen on the wall. All seemed calm; some even appeared to be bored. A young woman in the chair opposite occasionally stroked the prominent mound of her belly, caressing the child within, smiling gently. A drinking fountain stood in a corner and, on the excuse of getting a cup of water, Amita crossed the room to sit down on another chair with her back to the woman.

When at last her name was called and she entered the consulting room she found Dr. Tay to be a good-looking young man whose professional pleasantness filled the room. There was none of Dr. Wong's cool detachment; Dr. Tay leaned forward towards her over his desk, all briskness and compassion.

'Let me have a quick look, and then we will decide how best to go about this,' he reassured her, after reading Dr Wong's letter.

A thick head of hair rose from a widow's peak to crown his broad face. He showed no censure, no hesitation, and Amita warmed to him immediately, filled with hope that what had so suddenly descended upon her could also depart with equal alacrity. She stripped down as told behind a curtain and climbed up onto the examination table. A nurse appeared and placed a sheet over her nakedness, settling her feet into the cups on either side of the couch, pushing open her thighs and readying her for inspection.

While Dr. Tay prodded and pushed inside her, his shoes squeaked on the tiled floor. Legs spread wide apart, feet raised high and strapped into place on the stirrups, Amita turned her head away from him in distress and humiliation.

'It's all very healthy in there,' he announced, his shoes squeaking softly again as he turned discreetly away, releasing her.

'I'd say you are probably about four months pregnant. It would have been better to terminate earlier. Normally we would send you for counselling before making a decision, but at your age, in your circumstances, I am sure you know what you are doing,' he said, when she was dressed and sat again at his desk.

'I didn't know I was pregnant,' she mumbled. Dr. Tay nodded agreeably.

'Periods irregular? Early menopause? Then it's difficult to know. We'll take some blood for testing, and do a quick ultrasound. The hospital will call you with a date to come in, maybe early next week? The sooner the better.'

A leaden inability to think seemed to fill her. That she was already taking the necessary steps to recalibrate her life to its normal balance filled her with such profound relief that she closed her eyes in exhaustion. At last she lay back obediently on an examination couch as a young Filipina woman moved the transducer over the bare flesh of her stomach.

'Do you want to see?' the woman asked brightly, turning the computer screen toward Amita, continuing to slide the transducer over Amita's naked belly.

I don't want to see, she wanted to say, but instead felt compelled to turn her head towards the screen and its grainy fan-shaped image. Within that void a tide of black water swayed and swelled and gently moved, and at its heart she saw a dark grotto, sealed and silent, safe and dark. At its centre lay the manikin, the bulbous head, the upturned nose, an arm, a leg, the beating heart, the curvature of a spine; all were visible.

'It is still a bit early to be quite sure, but I would say it's a girl,' the woman announced with a smile.

'I didn't ask you,' Amita shouted, sitting up in anger.

The woman drew back in shock, hurriedly returning her attention to the computer screen.

'Listen. Heartbeat.' A soft thudding filled the room.

'I don't want to hear it. I'm having a termination,' Amita shouted again, pushing the woman's hand and the transducer away.

'I'm sorry, I wasn't told that, but we are finished now,' the woman apologised, giving Amita some paper towels to wipe the ultrasound gel from her body.

20
Burma, 1944–1945

In the dormitory, Sita struggled up through layers of sleep into consciousness and the wail of the air raid siren. Muni was already throwing off her blanket in the next bed and scrambling to her feet. Loud blasts shook the wooden building; flares of light from distant explosions illuminated the dark. Sita reached for her kitbag and her torch and heard an order shouted.

'Run.'

Jostling against each other in the narrow stairwell, they ran out into the night. The faint perfume of night flowers rose from the bushes in front of the building. The beams of their torches moved before them like an army of luminous eyes as they ran to the newly dug trenches. Sita glimpsed Muni a short distance ahead, then the banked earth of the trench was before her and everyone was stumbling and jumping down into the wet pit. Someone pushed against Sita and she fell awkwardly into the dark open grave, hurting her arm. Other girls dropped down beside her, falling on top of her, everyone squeezing into the crowded trench.

Almost immediately, an aircraft swooped low above them, spitting machine gun fire and dropping incendiaries. The detonations vibrated through the trench, each explosion throwing up fountains of soil that fell back upon them, burying them all beneath a layer of damp earth.

At last it was over, the bomber disappeared, and soon the all clear sounded, and as it ended, the noise of crickets was heard again. They began to clamber out of the trench.

'Muni,' Sita called, straining her eyes in the darkness.

Prema stood at the edge of the trench, flashing her torch over the girls, assessing the damage, taking a head count.

'Is everyone here, is anyone hurt?'

'I cannot find Muni,' Sita shouted.

As Prema's torch swept over the trench, Sita saw Muni struggling to free herself from beneath a mound of soil and debris to one side of the trench.

'The explosion came before I could get into the trench, everything came down on me,' Muni gasped, spitting out a mouthful of dirt, shaking earth off her body.

'Everyone is here, and no one seems to be hurt,' Prema announced with relief.

'The school is destroyed,' someone shouted and they turned to look at the building.

By the light of their torches they made out the flattened building, the piles of wood, plaster and smoke, and the fire spurting up within the collapsed shell where they had slept only minutes before.

New accommodation was found, another school, much smaller and not in such good repair, yet surrounded by tall trees that gave the building better camouflage. Sita was grateful that she had had the presence of mind to take her kitbag with her during the air raid. Along with her few possessions, the picture of the *devi* was still safely with her. Those who had left their rucksacks behind had lost everything, including their spare uniform, and had only the clothes they stood up in.

There was a great shortage of cloth in Maymyo and new uniforms could not be made, but the men's uniforms in the INA store were quickly altered to fit them. The stylish jodhpurs were gone, and instead they were dressed in the men's straight drill trousers or shorts, and shirts. Each girl was now ordered to keep a backpack with extra clothes and personal possessions beside her at all times. Air raid sirens blared all day and night as the bombing accelerated.

Finally, Netaji reached Maymyo from the front line. He would soon leave again for Singapore, to mobilise additional manpower, but the knowledge that he was in town energised everyone.

He came to visit them in the late afternoon. Captain Lakshmi arrived first with Prema, to alert them to Netaji's arrival.

'It was a spontaneous decision, he heard of the air raid and said, "Let me go and meet my girls, my Ranis, in their new accommodation." He was worried for you all after what you have been through.'

It began to rain just before he arrived, and Netaji climbed out of an armoured car into a puddle, splashing mud onto his high polished boots. Rain cascaded off the umbrella an attending officer held over him. The man's shorter height forced Netaji to hunch his shoulders and bend low beneath its shelter. Captain

Lakshmi and Prema were at the entrance to welcome him, and behind them the Ranis formed two long lines, standing to attention, saluting smartly as he stepped inside the building.

Netaji's cap had been knocked from his head as he ducked beneath the umbrella, and he held it in his hand, revealing his receding hairline above the deep arc of his brow. Stepping briskly towards the waiting girls, his face creased in a smile, his eyes alert behind heavy-framed spectacles. As he gestured for them to break ranks and come forward, he looked about him intently, taking in every detail of the scene around him.

'I wanted to see your new home. You are safer here than in the last place, with a good camouflage of trees,' Netaji remarked.

They clustered about him, silenced by his presence and nearness. His voice was detached yet gentle, as if he spoke to each one of them individually, as a father might speak to a daughter, in a low and intimate tone. The moment seemed unreal, and Sita fought the desire to reach out and touch him.

'You faced the ordeal of the bombing boldly, and I am proud of you. India is proud of you.' Netaji's smile embraced them all.

'*Dilli Chalo*,' they shouted.

'*Jai Hind.*' They pumped their fists in the air.

'The Rani of Jhansi's spirit is in you all.' Netaji chuckled, his full lips parting upon square teeth.

A smell of damp uniform, along with the perfume of boot polish and pomade surrounded him. Rain splashed his spectacles and he took them off to wipe them dry, lowering his head to blow upon the lens, before polishing them with a crumpled white handkerchief pulled from his pocket. Sita watched the glass cloud up as he breathed upon it. Devoid of spectacles his face appeared unknown, his round cheeks boyish and vulnerable. Then he placed the glasses on his nose again, and the familiar Netaji was before them once more.

Outside the open door rain fell in a curtain from the eaves, drumming on the roof, sliding off sodden trees. Netaji looked over his shoulder at the downpour and sighed.

'So much rain, and the monsoon is not yet properly here. This will be hard for our men. I had wanted the campaign fought and won before the rains began.'

"*Jai Hind*," they shouted at the mention of the campaign, but Netaji appeared distracted.

'You have heard of our setback at Imphal, that we were pushed back again into Burma? Rest assured this delay is temporary. Soon we will walk again on Indian soil.' He raised his hand for their attention, surveying them critically.

'As the battle heats up, so do our casualties increase. Your wounded brothers need your help. Some hours of your day must be given to nursing duties. Your military training will continue, but your work in the hospital is now of equal importance.' His voice was soft but firm.

About him the girls were silent, a low murmur of consternation was heard, but nobody spoke until Muni stepped forward suddenly.

'We want to fight.' An approving ripple of agreement was heard behind her. Netaji nodded patiently.

'*Beti*, as you know, I was under house arrest in Calcutta, but I slipped out of India in disguise and went to Germany, where I could fight better for India's freedom. I did not do this easily. It took me three months to decide if I had the strength to sacrifice myself for a bigger cause, to face death if necessary. If *I* could do this, and if so many of your brothers have sacrificed themselves for our Motherland, then, difficult as it is, this is the sacrifice I now ask of you. Remember, your military training will also continue. Your wounded brothers are only asking for a short part of your day.' Netaji threw his arms out wide in appeal.

'We want to fight,' Muni repeated, her voice falling to a whisper.

That night Sita dreamed of the *bhajanashram*. At the door Roop and the black dwarf, Motilal, waited for her with the palanquin, ready to ferry her to an unknown destiny. Then Billi appeared, pushing her aside, stepping into the litter instead of Sita.

'Go quickly to Old Maneka, she will help you escape,' Billi called as the palanquin moved away.

Sita ran and eventually found the old woman sitting by the riverbank.

'*Hare Krishna, Hare Krishna, Radhe, Radhe.*' Old Maneka's cracked voice rose as she swayed, eyes closed, lips bunched loosely over toothless gums in a gentle smile of devotion.

'Lord Krishna is there.' Maneka opened her eyes, and pointed across the river.

In the distance on the opposite bank Sita saw the handsome god, tall, muscular and blue skinned, playing his pipe, surrounded by a crowd of beautiful *gopis*. The cowgirls had left their cattle, to dance with the god. They swirled around him, bodies bending gracefully, eyes fixed upon him, full of longing. Then, suddenly, it was not the god Sita saw but Netaji, brass buttons and high polished boots agleam, broad belt buckled over his uniform, inclining his head with a bespectacled smile towards the yearning women.

Sita woke with a start to the dark narrow room, sweat pooling in the hollow of her neck, her heart pounding in her ears. In the next bed Muni breathed calmly.

From then on the day was divided, the larger part spent at the hospital. As the town was a military centre, there was always hope that news of Shiva would surface. The weeks went by and all the time in the hospital wounded men arrived. Each day Sita scoured the lists of new casualties, but Shiva's 3rd division never appeared. She asked about his regiment, but no one knew where it was or had heard of Shiva.

'We are fighting. We have no time to see who is there or who is not there beyond our squad, our own regiment,' one man told her, speaking grimly through his pain.

'Sister, we are dying there like flies,' another said.

'Dying in rain and mud, everywhere there is mud. Bodies cannot be cremated or buried, and swell up and turn blue. Crows peck out their eyes, and animals eat their flesh. The monsoon has washed away roads. Supply routes are cut; vehicles and guns are stuck in the mud. There's no transport, no food, no medicines. We are lucky to reach this hospital alive.' The man who offered this information had taken a bullet to the head and was swaddled in bandages, and he stared at Sita through his one good eye.

'Not even animals should die as we are dying at the front,' yet another man with no legs told her.

The sheet on his bed caved into nothingness over the stumps of his knees, and each time Sita sat with him she stared at the emptiness where his legs should have been, unable to control her horror. He reached out and grasped her arm.

'There is nothing to eat. Ants, lizards, jungle grasses, dead pack mules, we eat what we can. Tell them to send supplies or we will all die. We had only 38 mountain howitzers and 48 field guns; how can we hold a line with that?'

'Then, you do not know my husband?' Sita whispered.

'We do not know him, sister,' the man with the bandaged head confirmed, his voice full of sympathy.

The suffering they saw affected them all, and each night when they returned to the dormitory, they discussed the situation. Although the nights were cool in Maymyo, mosquitoes continued to plague them, and the room smelled of the citronella oil with which they now smothered themselves.

'We should be fighting with the men. That is what we are trained to do,' Sita said, thinking of Shiva, thinking of the legless man in the hospital.

She sat with Muni, Valli and Ambika, and soon Vasanthi and Shivani joined them. They crouched on the floor in the narrow space before their beds, and as they could not put on the electric light and did not want to waste torch batteries, they lit a couple of candles that cast long shadows on the dark walls. The flickering flame drew moths that blundered into their faces before flirting with the fire, dying with a sizzle and a singed smell.

'All the men have malaria or dysentery. The wards smell of diarrhoea,' Valli said, wrinkling her nose in distaste.

'Most die before reaching Maymyo,' Ambika added.

'We should be fighting with the men,' Vasanthi complained.

'Netaji is treating us like women when he has trained us like men.' Valli remarked.

'We must tell him he has to let us go to the front. We must write him a letter.' Sita sat forward, the thought leaping through her. If she reached the front line she felt sure she would find Shiva there.

'It must be a proper and serious letter,' Valli cautioned.

'We can sign it in our own blood.' Muni clapped her hands in excitement.

'Let's write before we change our minds,' Sita encouraged.

She lowered her eyes to hide her guilt. The girls beside her were prepared to die at the front for India and she was pushing them to do so, not for India but for Shiva, for her own private need.

They crouched together in the light of the candle. Paper, pen and ink were found, as was a razor and a teacup. It was judged that Sita was the most educated, and should write the letter. When she took up the pen and dipped it in the bottle of ink, she found her hand was trembling. With an effort she steadied the pen and began to write, the girls around her deliberating over each phrase.

Our training is complete, yet we are now denied access to the

front line. We are reduced to being nurses. You gave us the name
of the brave Rani of Jhansi. We beg you to send us to the front.
We have signed this petition in our blood, in order to prove to you
our determination to give our lives in the cause of freedom for
our Motherland.

'Now the blood for signing,' Sita pushed forward the teacup,
and Muni reached for the razor.

One by one they extended their hands, and Muni gave
each a quick prick on the soft pad of a finger. Sita closed her
eyes and held her breath as the razor sliced into her finger. The
blood, jewelled in the candlelight, dripped into the bowl as she
watched. With each drop she felt some part of her past trickled
from her, but what lay ahead was impossible to know. Finally,
they washed the black ink from the pen and dipped it in the
crimson liquid. Then, one by one, they signed the letter in their
blood and stared down in silence at the marks on the page.

Days passed and they heard nothing, but at last Netaji
summoned them. He had set up his headquarters in what was
once the home of a wealthy British official, at the end of a leafy
lane. The house was at the top of an incline, approached by a
path of flowering hedges, its heavy roof crowned by turrets, its
walls shrouded by thick creepers. Six of them had signed the
letter to Netaji, and it seemed appropriate they should meet
him as a group.

The door was opened by a male servant who ushered them
into a dark square entrance hall where they huddled together,
waiting uneasily. The odour of furniture wax and incense hung
in the air, along with the spicy residue of Netaji's lunch. Finally,

the door to Netaji's study opened and a Japanese general strode out, turning his head to glare unpleasantly at the uniformed women. One of Netaji's aides-de-camp hurried after the general, and once he had departed, beckoned them to come forward.

Netaji sat behind a large desk piled untidily with files and loose papers. A fan revolved in a corner, ruffling the documents momentarily as it swung about. The room was wood-panelled and sombre in spite of a large window with a view of the surrounding hills. As they entered, Netaji put down the file he was reading and clasped his hands together before him on the desk. Leaning back in his chair, he observed them silently with a sad expression, as if they were disobedient children. Through the open windows the scent of the creeper that smothered the house filled the room with an earthy potpourri. Netaji removed his spectacles and began polishing them with a handkerchief, concentrating silently on this task. They drew together, waiting nervously for him to speak. At last he put away his handkerchief, replaced his spectacles on his nose, and sighed deeply.

'You are all true daughters of India. The same feeling runs in your blood that ran through our Rani of Jhansi. What shall I do with you?'

'Please send us to the front,' Sita stepped forward, determined not to let this opportunity disappear, and feeling it her place to speak, as it was her resolve that had brought them here before Netaji.

Netaji was silent, doodling with a pencil on the leather bound blotter of soft pink paper. He drew a square and then another and another, linking them together in a geometrical tangle. Looking up at last, he spoke slowly, dropping each word into the silence.

'It is not my intention to send you to the front unless the war effort calls for the ultimate sacrifice of India's women. Only then would I consider it. At the moment the men are holding up, although the situation is difficult. There is no need for me to think of sending you to that hell.'

'The men are dying, there are no food or supplies, a man in the hospital told me.' Sita took a step forward, standing directly before Netaji's desk, apart from the girls behind her. The thought of Shiva filled her mind and gave her the courage to protest.

'War is about the shedding of blood; blood for blood. How many times have I said this? India cannot be free without the shedding of blood,' Netaji replied in a sad voice.

On the pink blotting paper, his design grew ever more complicated. Standing before him, Sita felt increasingly awkward with each passing moment as, deep in thought, Netaji concentrated on enlarging his architectural design. She was aware of the girls behind her shifting uncomfortably, even as she spoke for them all. At last Netaji looked up, his face heavy with the wretchedness of the decision they had placed upon him.

'Be aware of what you are asking of me. Yes, as you say, there is a scarcity of food, of clothes, of medicine and ammunition. Also be aware that at the front you must live like the men, under those same conditions, without any concession to your sex.'

They stood in silence as Netaji continued speaking in an increasingly sorrowful voice.

'Your families have sent you to me, and they have faith that I will return you to them safely. And that is what I will do. I cannot grant your wish to go to the front.'

He resumed his doodling, not raising his eyes, his gaze focused on the pink paper and his pencil. As he drew, Sita stared down at the growing conundrum of linked squares beneath his hand, a dense maze from which there was no escape.

'You are treating us like women, when you have trained us like men.' Muni stepped forward to stand beside Sita.

Netaji looked up in surprise, and after some moments of silence, sighed deeply once more.

'It is true. I have trained you like men and now deny you that equality. But if you go, no one else in the regiment must know where you have gone. Above all, I want you to know that if you die you will die, but if the enemy captures you, then I fear you will not be treated as men, but as women. I do not have to tell you what you might face in those circumstances.' Picking up his pencil, he continued in silence with his elaborate design.

21
BURMA, 1944–1945

The truck slipped quietly out of the Maymyo camp at 4am in the cool darkness before dawn, beginning the long journey to the front line. Sita did not look back as the town fell away behind them. The rasp of crickets filled the silence as the vehicle bumped over the rutted road, the harsh breathing of the engine filling the air with petrol fumes. Sita wondered if death already sat beside them in the truck, observing their wilful journey. Nobody spoke, and in the blackness little could be seen except what was illuminated in the sphere of the headlights, a hole in the night through which they moved. Beyond the boundary of this narrow tunnel, everything was unknown.

Netaji had ordered an officer from his own command to accompany them. Colonel Bahadur, a loud voiced man whose face was pitted by childhood smallpox, was accompanied by two *jawans*, Tamil men who had once worked on the rubber plantations of Malaya. The truck swung along precipitous mountain roads as it descended towards Mandalay. In the darkness the girls clung to each other as the vehicle careered around hairpin bends. Eventually, as dawn broke, the darkness eased and the sky turned a deep indigo, then ultramarine cut by pink and gold. At last, at first light they saw the forested slopes about them, plunging to the river far below, and the majesty of the view silenced them. They stopped for breakfast at a small village clinging to the side of a hill terraced by narrow rice fields, and climbed back into the truck, refreshed.

Soon, the mountainous terrain was left behind and they reached the flat land around Mandalay, keeping close to the great Irrawaddy River, driving beside it as the sun gathered strength. In places the opposite bank of the river, if they were able to see it, appeared as distant as a far country. Sita stared at the water, its fusty odour filling her head, and remembered the other river that had run so powerfully through her life. Fishing boats were returning to shore with their catch, and the sun, rising higher now, spread a mercurial light over the water. In the truck, Muni reached out to clasp Sita's hand as they held their faces to the cool breeze, blowing upon them as they sped along.

Soon they reached the town of Mandalay with its golden pagodas, and a palace constructed entirely of teak. Still following the huge river, they drove on until it met the wide tributary of the Chindwin. Here they left the truck to cross the Irrawaddy, ferried over on flat bamboo rafts by local fishermen. Their truck was also ferried across, lashed down tightly onto a raft. Once the river was forded they turned north along the Chindwin, driving up into the rough terrain of the Chin Hills. Here sporadic shelling had damaged parts of the road, slowing their progress. In places they left the truck as the driver negotiated the rutted ground, helping to clear any debris from their path. At last the truck drew to a sudden halt and the driver announced that water was leaking from the tank, and the engine had heated up.

'Cannot go further. Our soldiers are camped in this area, over that hill,' he told them.

They climbed out of the truck and prepared to walk. In spite of the cloudy monsoon sky the sun, when it broke free, spilled hotly upon them. Now at last they realised the value of the tough route marches and the tactics of guerrilla warfare practised so arduously in Maymyo.

'We are not yet near the front line, but Chin guerrillas are everywhere in these hills. We must be very quiet as we do not want to alert them to our presence,' Colonel Bahadur warned.

They looked about warily, keeping where possible to the cover of trees or bushes, searching to gauge how recently Chin soldiers may have passed the same way.

'Our own men have also used this road. The Chin don't move around with vehicles.' Colonel Bahadur pointed to the muddy tracks of boot and tyre marks that had dried in the sun, and stood out like plaster reliefs.

Within a short distance, the green vegetation ended abruptly. They found themselves in a basin of scorched devastation, the undergrowth burned to a mass of dark ash and the charred remains of trees, in stark contrast to the lush foliage in the distance. Colonel Bahadur bent to examine the ground, breaking off fragments of burned bark from the trees, poking the dried mud reliefs with a stick, inspecting the fired casings of bullets that littered the ground, along with the shrapnel of exploded shells and grenades.

'There's been a recent skirmish here. Our men must indeed be nearby in this area, but the Chin will also be around,' Bahadur cautioned.

'We must proceed carefully; there's always the danger of ambush. These Chin guerrillas are determined fighters; they know the hills well, and they've have been trained by British commandos.'

'Why are our forces fighting here and not at the front?' Sita asked, as they prepared to march on.

'The British forces have found new strength, and are pushing the Japanese back, along with our INA men. Skirmishes like this create diversions from the main thrust at Kohima and Imphal. It forces the Japanese and the INA to keep precious units of men in this area, away from where they are needed at the front. War is a complicated manoeuvre.'

As they walked higher into the hills magnificent views opened up, the silver ribbon of the river caught far below in the neck of green valleys. The stillness was only broken by the movement of their feet through the low scrub, the call of a bird, the buzzing of an insect, and the hard panting of their breath. They kept close together, Colonel Bahadur leading the way, the two *jawans* behind them at the rear of the column.

The image of Shiva was constantly in Sita's mind as she strode forward, the straps of the kitbag cutting into her shoulders, perspiration running freely off her. Was he somewhere in these same hills, lying in wait for the guerrillas? Had he been in the skirmish at that charred and bullet-strewn piece of ground?

They continued uphill through grassland, but as they approached the top of a slope Bahadur slowed his pace, gesturing suddenly for them to crouch down. At once they froze, pressing themselves against the ground, loaded guns thrust before them. Ahead, there was movement, and the sound of voices.

'They are our own men.' Bahadur stood up with a shout of relief.

As they appeared through the trees they were recognised, and welcomed into the camp. It was a small company of men, part of an INA guerrilla unit, commanded by a tall Sikh with a khaki turban.

'There are a hundred or more of us but we are split up into small groups in these hills. We have been camped out here for two days since we were ambushed in a skirmish, and lost two men,' Captain Govind Singh explained.

In the camp they were given hot millet gruel, and later sat around a fire. The day's march had been exhausting and they were grateful to relax and listen to the men's conversation. Muni leaned her head on Sita's shoulder, already half asleep. Valli stretched out, watching Shivani and Ambika playing a game of five-stones with some pebbles. The flames crackled in a blaze of hot light, sparks blowing up into the darkness as Govind Singh explained the situation.

'The Chin guerrillas are down there, at the base of this hill. The British are behind them and supplying reinforcements. Up here we are now cut off, but we plan another attack tomorrow and will try and push them back. We have these hills staked out.'

'We will continue our journey tomorrow,' Colonel Bahadur said, but the Sikh shook his head.

'You cannot go forward until we have cleared the way, and you can no longer go back because they will be in that area. You will have to stay here with our unit.'

'If you have to fight, then we will fight with you,' Valli burst out, interrupting the men's conversation.

Colonel Bahadur turned towards her as if about to say something, but fell silent. Shivani and Ambika dropped their five-stones and moved nearer the fire.

'That is why we are here, to fight along with our brothers,' Ambika insisted.

'You are women,' Captain Singh glanced in query at Colonel Bahadur, who averted his eyes and remained silent.

'Our training is no different from that of the INA men. We are soldiers.' Valli informed him.

'We are here with Netaji's blessing,' Vasanthi added.

'What they say is true,' Colonel Bahadur confirmed reluctantly when Govind Singh turned to him.

'Get some sleep while you can,' the captain said at last, still shaking his head in disapproval.

They slept in the open alongside the men, a guard keeping the fire smouldering to deter wild animals. Sita lay on her back, feeling the hard uneven ground beneath her, gazing up into the star-filled sky. She was sure Shiva was in these hills, camped out like her, staring up at the same great expanse of sky. She wrapped her blanket closer about her in the damp chill. A night bird shrieked and was answered by shrill calls across the forest, smoke from the fire mixed with the sweet scent of night flowers. Sita knew by the sounds of tossing and turning that none of the girls slept, their minds filled with the same thought that she was thinking, that this night might be their last.

Eventually, she fell into a fitful sleep, and when she opened her eyes the sky was already streaked by pink and her limbs were stiff and cramped. One by one they went to wash in a nearby stream and ready themselves for the day. A roll call was taken and a pledge to the Azad Hind flag repeated, the usual millet biscuits and tea were consumed. Captain Govind Singh stood before them, still clearly apprehensive of the idea of women going to war.

'It is my hope you will not be called upon to fight. You will take up positions at the top of the hill. Our men will be lower down the hill, nearer the enemy, and that is where I expect any fighting to be. Stay hidden. I expect our men to throw off the enemy, but fix your bayonets just in case of a charge. Over there, the British are waiting. They have shells and will fire them if necessary,' Captain Singh warned, gesturing into the distance.

The steep slopes about them were forested by broad-leafed trees, and draped richly with lianas. Large epiphytes clung to branches, and tall clumps of flowering rhododendron splashed the area with colour. Wild orchids were everywhere, nuthatch and laughing-thrush sang in the trees. It was too beautiful to be a battle site, Sita thought, touched by the peace of the place. The ground sloped up a short distance to a rocky outcrop of huge boulders, as if the earth spewed up its insides. The boulders provided better cover than the trees, with several shallow cave-like areas at their base, where it was possible to wedge a body. Sita beckoned to Muni, Shivani and Valli, and together they climbed up to the boulders, slipping into the narrow spaces between the stones, separate but not hidden from each other, able to signal and communicate. From this vantage point they had a good view of the slope beneath them, and also the surrounding hills where further INA men were camped. Tucked in amongst the boulders they waited.

This was the moment they had trained for, and in spite of the tension taut within her Sita did not feel afraid; everything was concentrated into the sharp point of waiting. The heavy boulder rose up in a smooth pillar above her, the trill of the white-headed laughing-thrush repeated from a nearby tree. All around her men waited silently to kill each other.

Taking out from her knapsack the small picture of the *devi* she always carried with her, she said the prayer she repeated each morning. From where she sat, a view down the steeper side of the hill opened up, and beyond it the green and blue folds of the mountain range, hazy already with the rising heat. From the small frame in Sita's hand the goddess smiled up benignly. In the picture, the landscape behind the *devi* resembled these very hills, Sita thought. The goddess too had waited upon a mountain peak, as Sita did now, ready for battle. As always, Sita took comfort from the amber-eyed tiger. It was a female tiger, inseparable from the goddess, and seemed to Sita to hold all the *devi*'s inner strength, her *shakti*. The goddess had not given in to fear before that great mythical battle at the beginning of time, and in the same way she too must be firm of resolve, Sita thought.

Under her hand the smooth cool stone, survivor of thousands of years, bore witness to the cycle of death and rebirth in these green hills. What would Shiva do if she died? What would she do if he were killed? She thought also of her brother, Dev. Many weeks ago a short note from him had reached her through the INA's postal network. Dev wrote that he was working again at Krishnaswami and Sons, which had reopened under a Japanese licence, and was now a senior manager there. He also told her he had married the daughter of one of the other managers in the shop. It has all happened quickly, he wrote, as things were inclined to do in war. His wife brought with her a small dowry that had enabled him to rent a room for them in a superior tenement. Sita tried to visualise Dev as a married man, but was unable to do so. As fast as she tried to pin down her thoughts they floated away, and seemed of no consequence. Within an hour she could lie dead upon the slope below. Everything, and nothing, was of importance now.

They waited, but no order came to fire, and a sense of anticlimax, then boredom, filled them. Nothing stirred but the birds in the trees and the whirring wings of passing insects, lean brown squirrels chased each other, leaping from branch to branch. The sun rose in the sky and was soon covered by clouds. A light shower of rain blew down upon them and they huddled wetly against the side of the rocks, damp and uncomfortable.

'Fire.' At last the order they had waited for came.

As they watched, INA men lower down the slope left their

wooded cover and ran forward at the command. Guerrillas were seen suddenly at the base of the hill. Men knotted together in hand to hand fighting, parted and knotted together again. Gunfire fractured the air. More Chin guerrillas appeared, running up the hill now towards them.

'Charge.'

The order floated to them from a distance, and for a moment they hesitated. Then, everything they had been trained for took over.

'Charge.' Sita heard her own voice echoing the cry.

Suddenly they were all shouting and running. They fired, reloaded and fired again. Everything was automatic; they did not think, they did not feel. The slope was steep and Sita raced wildly, rifle in hand, unable to stop if she wished. The breeze rushed in her face, her cap flew from her head.

'*Jai Hind!*' she screamed.

'*Jai Hind!*' Muni's voice was behind her.

They were all running. Out of the corner of her eye she glimpsed Valli, Shivani, Vasanthi and Ambika, their expressions fierce and warrior-like, eyes bulging, rifles thrust before them. They ran towards the INA men locked in hand-to-hand combat lower down the hill. Some fallen bodies were seen across the hill. There was the flash of bayonets, and the constant crackle of gunfire.

One moment there was nothing but the precipitous incline rushing towards her, and the next the man was before her, small and fierce, dressed in army fatigues, bayonet agleam at the end of his rifle. From his broad tribal features and weathered skin, Sita knew he was a Chin guerrilla. He moved up the slope towards her, uttering a fierce cry, lips drawn back upon his broad teeth.

She raised her gun and knew she must fire, that the moment to kill had come. In that split second her eyes met his and she saw his shock, saw the battle cry dry on his tongue as his eyes dropped to her breasts, checking the impossible, that he saw before him a woman. Although he had levelled his bayonet as if he would charge, he slowed to a stop before her, in disbelief. Sita stepped forward, knowing she had only this one moment her womanhood had brought her, and pulled the trigger, feeling the familiar recoil of the rifle against her shoulder as the bullet flew down the barrel of the gun.

Blood spread across the man's chest, and he stared at her in astonishment, his small eyes widening beneath his overhanging brow. Yet, even as the bullet left her gun, a shell landed behind him, and blew him up towards the sky in a fountain of dirt. She saw him twist and turn against the clouds, saw the grimace on his face as he descended, landing beside her, his body making the sound a sack of lentils had made when thrown onto the floor of her father's shop. Sita too was blown backwards by the force of the blast, a shower of earth cascading down upon her.

For a moment she lay looking up at the sky, at the drift of clouds above her, the noise of battle a distant sound. For a moment she wondered if she were dead, but soon found she was unhurt. Retrieving her rifle, she scrambled to her feet and stood gazing down at the man before her. Had she killed him before the shell landed? Blood coloured his left shoulder from the wound of her bullet. Then, to her horror, she saw that although the upper half of his body was intact, his legs had been blown off from the knees. As she stared down at the protruding white bones of his thighs, he opened his eyes. His gaze locked upon her, a great shuddering breath passing through him. In that moment she knew he died. Whether her bullet would have eventually killed him or not, she did not know, but she was now part of his death. His open eyes stared at her still, and would not let her free. She wanted to drop to her knees beside him, to tell him to forgive her, but more shots rang out and she remembered it was his life or hers.

As she began to run again, Muni sprinted past her. A deep boom sounded and then the high-pitched whirr of another approaching shell. Earth spurted up all around her again and she saw Muni fall, rolling down the slope, blood pouring from her. Sita cried out but could not stop, the steep slope pulling her on. The whirr of shells and bullets hummed about her, fountains of wet earth spewing up on every side. Then, unexpectedly, the slope was rising up toward her, dragging her down into blackness.

When she opened her eyes, the evening sky ran red above. The awkward jolt and sway of movement jarred her head. She tried to sit up.

'Lie back,' a voice ordered.

The familiar face of Colonel Bahadur peered down at her as she lay on a makeshift stretcher, carried by the two *jawans*.

'Muni?' Sita tried to sit up, images flooding through her.

'She's already safe in camp. Everyone is safe. You are the last one. We could not find you. You had rolled into shrub at the side of the hill,' Colonel Bahadur informed her.

'What happened?' Sita asked. Her head throbbed and blood soaked her shirt.

'We killed some Chin irregulars in hand combat, but then the British started shelling. Shells go a long way, the enemy doesn't have to move in close to fire, and we have only rifles with which to respond. We had to retreat, they've taken the hill and we've been pushed further back,' Colonel Bahadur told her.

'They were coming up the slope towards us,' Sita remembered.

'You girls never hesitated. You fought bravely.' Bahadur spoke with grudging respect.

When they reached the camp Valli, Shivani and Ambika clustered around her.

'A bullet grazed Muni's shoulder, but she is all right,' Valli informed her.

'Many INA men are dead,' Shivani added, walking beside Sita as she was carried into the camp.

Her head throbbed; voices and faces swirled around her. Colonel Bahudur appeared, and examined the wound on Sita's temple.

'A cut from a fragment of shell shrapnel, it seems superficial. You're lucky,' he told her, ordering Shivani, who stood nearby, to bandage Sita's head.

Beyond the open flap of the tent, Sita could see a number of *jawans* already digging graves, burying the dead. Muni lay on a blanket nearby, her shoulder swathed in a heavy dressing. In spite of her throbbing head, Sita moved to sit near her just as Captain Govind Singh entered the tent, striding up to Colonel Bahadur in a determined manner.

'As you know, we are being pushed back on all fronts. Conditions are chaotic. Food and medical supplies are low. Wounds that appear superficial can quickly turn septic and we have nothing to treat them with. Hundreds are dying needlessly like this. You must take these girls back to Maymyo.' He was unable to hide his wish to be rid of them, and Colonel Bahadur nodded.

'If our truck is repaired, we will leave tomorrow, and we will take any wounded men from this camp with us.'

'The way behind is clear now, so you will be safe, the Chin have all moved forward,' Captain Singh assured, visibly relieved that he would soon be rid of them.

In the night Muni developed a high temperature and, as they began the journey back to Maymyo the following day, tossed and turned in the back of the truck. Three wounded INA men also travelled with them. The weather was still bad, rain lashing the canvas roof of the truck.

Eventually they reached Maymyo, and found rain blanketed everything there too. Water sluiced off trees and roofs, cascading noisily along the open drains either side of the streets. They drove straight to the hospital.

It was some days before Muni was well enough to sit up and take some soup and light nourishment. Through the day Sita worked in the hospital, but looked in frequently on Muni. As the only woman patient in the hospital, a separate space was found for Muni, a cupboard of a room where files were kept and into which a bed was fitted.

Netaji was not in Maymyo to welcome them; he had left for Rangoon, but he sent an affectionate message congratulating them on their bravery, saying how relieved he was that they had returned safely to Maymyo.

'I hope you will now understand my fears for you in the harsh atmosphere of war.' Captain Lakshmi read out Netaji's words from the letter he had dictated to her only hours before, over a field telephone.

The bombing of Maymyo increased, air raids seemed almost continuous, but they took little notice, working on through the bombing. Casualties were now coming into Maymyo from the front at an accelerated rate. The wounds Sita dressed were distressing, gashes filled with maggots or shrapnel, limbs sliced off by flying shells, or emergency amputations because of gangrene. Medicines, anaesthetics and antiseptic dressings were low by now in Maymyo. Every man who arrived in the hospital was invariably suffering from malnutrition, dysentery, malaria or beriberi. With good food and nursing they improved, but as soon as they were well enough, they were immediately returned to the front. Men were no more than fodder for battle, Sita thought, trying to keep this thought from her mind as she remembered Shiva, wondering if he was dead or alive.

More weeks went by, shrouded by the interminable dampness of the monsoon. Pillows and cushions stank, mould grew on shoes and walls and the grouting of bathroom tiles. Insects, scorpions, rats and poisonous centipedes sought shelter in droves in houses and cupboards. Monkeys and snakes attempted to follow. The worst monsoon in decades, everyone said. In the hospital men told stories of the front, of the untenable conditions, the lack of food and supplies, the bodies that could not be cremated or buried, that were left to rot in a bog of mud.

Eventually, an order came from Netaji, who was now in Mandalay to discuss the war situation with Japanese generals. Captain Lakshmi had been at the meeting and when she returned to Maymyo, she faced the girls with tears in her eyes.

'Netaji has ordered me to evacuate the hospital here along with the patients, nurses and staff, and transfer everyone to the safety of the hospital at Jiyawadi. What was an offensive is now a defensive battle. The Japanese are retreating, and we are forced to retreat with them. Without Japanese support it is not possible for us to push forward alone. You will be leaving Maymyo for Rangoon, and will wait there for further orders. Maymyo is now too near the front and it is dangerous to remain here. It will be a temporary retreat. Netaji is working to regroup the troops and push forward again at a later date.'

They left Maymyo in a convoy of trucks, but when at last they reached Rangoon, the Japanese were already withdrawing from the place, and preparing to surrender the city to the advancing British army. Everywhere there was panic. In the centre of town columns of smoke rose from the compounds of government buildings as papers were burned and essentials packed up before the retreat. On Netaji's instructions the Rani of Jhansi Regiment was to be temporarily disbanded. Those girls who had joined the regiment from Burma and Thailand were now to be sent back home under escort. With great difficulty the Japanese were persuaded to supply vehicles for this purpose.

Of the remaining Ranis, only the girls from Malaya were now left in Rangoon and they were to depart on their homeward journey in the company of Netaji and the INA troops, as part of a general retreat. Anxiety mounted by the hour. There was also the fear that if Netaji were found in Rangoon when the British entered the city, he would be taken prisoner.

The monsoon rain lashed down upon them as they prepared to leave Rangoon, retreating to Bangkok in a convoy of cars and trucks. Those women of the Rani of Jhansi Regiment who had joined the force from Burma and Thailand had already been sent back to their homes, and the regiment was greatly depleted. The girls who still remained, from Malaya and Singapore, filled the first trucks of the convoy behind the vehicles that accommodated Netaji's personal entourage, members of his cabinet and an assortment of military personnel. Everyone was leaving Rangoon. Retreating INA troops from the battlefronts of Kohima and Imphal had already arrived in the town, and were following the convoy on foot.

Sita and Muni clambered into a truck, along with Prema and the remaining members of their squad. The vehicle was crowded, the usual downpour thrumming down on the tarpaulin roof, splashing into the gutter. Through the curtain of rain Netaji could be seen, hurrying up and down the convoy under an umbrella, two aides-de-camp by his side, intent on personally checking all details for the journey ahead.

As the shallow back flap of the truck was slammed into place Netaji suddenly appeared, peering into the vehicle, his bespectacled face anxiously assessing the women from under his umbrella.

'It will be a long ride. I know you are cramped in there, but the Japanese will not give us more trucks. Do you have enough water?' Behind his rain streaked spectacles Netaji's eyes were bloodshot with fatigue, but he exuded the usual energy, immediately hastening off to meet a Japanese military official who had just arrived at the scene.

In the unrelenting rain water buffaloes sheltered beneath the trees, old people and small children observed the convoy from *attap*-roofed shacks. As they were about to occupy the city, the British had ceased air attacks, the sound of enemy bombers had lessened over the town. Sita turned her head, staring through the curtain of rain at the view of tiled roofs, wooden houses and lush green vegetation. In the distance elephants worked through the deluge, pulling timber from the river, the golden spires of pagodas pushed up from the jumble of roofs, the majestic Shwedagon pagoda rising high above the town.

Then, suddenly, the convoy lurched unsteadily into action like a great creature lumbering to its feet, with a revving up of engines and a grinding of gears. At the jolt of movement Sita looked back and saw through the rain the thick body of men and vehicles, horses, pack mules, baggage carts and gun-carriages swaying behind them, everything moving as one entity. At the rear of the convoy marched the sodden ranks of infantry, rain streaming off their waterproof capes and metal helmets, the hundreds of starved and weary Indian National Army men who had come down from the Chin Hills into Rangoon. Although these men were not from Shiva's regiment, Sita knew that their physical condition could be no different from other INA units, all of which were retreating by alternative routes to Bangkok. If he were still alive, Shiva would eventually get to Bangkok, and she told herself to wait until she reached that city.

For a while they tried to doze but the rhythm of the truck, swaying and bumping over the rough road, the constant lashing of rain through the open sides of the vehicle, made this impossible. At times, there was the sound of aircraft high above. Eventually, they neared Pegu, where they were scheduled to stop, but the town had been bombed. Clouds of black smoke filled the sky, and fires were everywhere. The convoy drew to a halt, and Netaji sent an aide-de-camp, Captain Ahmed, a short man with a broad chest and long neck, to check on the women.

'We will have to go on to Waw, where the Japanese are gathering. It's the narrowest point at which to ford the river, and there are also ferries there. Now that we are clear of the city, it is dangerous to travel further by day; enemy aircraft will be looking for us. Although Pegu is bombed, we will rest here until dark and travel on through the night,' he told them.

The rain had stopped and the sun shone hotly again as they made camp under tall trees in a clearing of secondary jungle. Newly flooded rice paddies spread out beside the camp, a jigsaw of mirrors reflecting the sky. After the cool air of Maymyo, the lowlands were hot and steamy.

Soon the camp bustled with activity. A fire was lit and cauldrons of rice started cooking, into which would be added whatever scraps of dried meat, vegetables or edible jungle leaves they could find. The fire, made with difficulty from damp branches, gave off clouds of smoke and the smell drifting up from the pots of weevil-ridden rice was thin and unappetising. The INA men were camped together in a large area of their own, and the women settled themselves a distance away, near where Netaji sat beneath a tall tree with his aides-de-camp, Captains Ahmed and Sharma.

Soon a jawan approached with Netaji's shaving things, setting them out before him on a small folding table beneath a tree. Netaji stood up and turned to hang his shaving mirror on a protruding notch of trunk, and prepared to begin his shave. He took off his jacket, revealing a khaki shirt and green braces attached to his familiar roomy jodhpurs. The mirror hung low and Netaji was forced to stoop to view his chin while lathering up a beard of soap, carefully drawing a clean swathe through the foam with his razor. Before he had finished his shave bombers were heard again.

Sita jumped to her feet and with the other girls, prepared to run for cover as the planes droned low above the clearing. Under the tree Netaji did not move, continuing with his shave, peering unconcernedly into the mirror.

'Netaji.'

They called to him, hesitating to run when he stood as if deaf to the aircraft above him.

'Netaji.'

Captain Ahmed and Captain Sharma stepped forward, looking from the sky to their commander, disconcerted by his apparent indifference to danger, unable to determine if the planes were a threat or merely reconnaissance aircraft. Netaji turned to them impatiently, his face a strange sight with its soapy white beard.

'Please, all of you take cover, immediately. I shall finish my shave, nothing will happen. I am like a cat with nine lives.' He turned back to the mirror, picking up his razor again.

His aides at last retreated a short distance, to stand nervously at the edge of the clearing, refusing to seek full cover, and ready to dart forward if their commander appeared in danger. Netaji ignored them, fixing his eyes upon the mirror, drawing the blade through the foam on his cheek, clearing yet another furrow. Alone in his green braces beneath the tall tree, he absorbed himself in his task, taking no notice of the war.

Once the planes departed and the danger was over and his shave completed, Netaji relaxed with a cigarette, poring over a map his aides spread out on a table before him. A small and bloodied cut on his newly shaved cheeks remained as the only proof of any tension he might have felt during his shave.

At dusk the order to move came again, and they climbed back into their vehicles. When at last the convoy reached the main road they found it filled with retreating Japanese regiments from Rangoon, vehicles crammed with soldiers and weaponry. In the darkness a stream of lowered headlights rolled towards the town of Waw and the great Sittang River beyond. The growl of engines and the heavy tread of wheels filled the darkness. Although no bombers flew at night, Sita worried that the moving snake of lights must make them instantly visible to any enemy. Little could be seen in the blackness, and in the truck the women sat in silence. Muni coughed, weak with a chesty cold. Prema, who had earlier gone to speak to Captain Ahmed, now returned to run beside the slowly moving truck, and they pulled her aboard again.

'Captain Ahmed says enemy tanks are breaking through behind us. We must get across the river at Waw and then again across the Sittang River before they can catch up with us. The bridge at Waw has been bombed, but we have been allotted a ferryboat by the Japanese,' Prema informed them as they bumped forward over the muddy, potholed road.

'What about crocodiles? They say the rivers here are full of them,' Muni began to cough again.

'We will be on a ferryboat,' Prema assured her.

At last, at 2 am, they reached the first river and camped to wait for morning light. In the darkness it was not possible to cross the water, and once the sun was up enemy bombers would begin their sorties again. There was only a slim slice of time to ford the river during the first light of the breaking day. As the ground was wet the women remained in the truck, sleeping as best they could, propped up against each other. From the riverbank they listened to the noise of movement, to voices, the revving of an engine and the whinnying of a horse. Captain Ahmed soon appeared again with instructions from Netaji.

'We will cross the river at first light. There are some ferries, they are just bamboo rafts, but you girls will be taken safely over. Most of the men will swim.'

At last dawn lifted the edge of night, revealing a riverbank alive with activity. In the darkness it had been impossible to see the number of men waiting to cross the river. Thousands of sick and starving Japanese troops, retreating ahead of the INA men who had defended their flanks, had trekked down from the Chin Hills with tanks and jeeps, weaponry and horses, to reach the river before them. Everyone must cross the water in the brief span of dawn, or wait again for the same time the following day. As the sky lightened, Sita stretched and stood up in the truck and saw with relief that the river was narrow enough for the opposite bank to be clearly seen. The thick odour of the water moved through her, and it seemed to her that every river was but the same river.

Soldiers were already plunging into the water and swimming alongside horses and pack mules, men and animals forming one great splashing mass of bodies. Everyone was now awake, and the women jumped down from the truck, to await their ferryboat. A short distance away Netaji emerged from his tent, which was already being collapsed and packed up by his *jawans*.

Nearby, a group of Japanese commanders stood talking, observing the women in a critical manner as, one by one, they jumped out of the truck. Everyone knew the Japanese military's disapproval of the Rani of Jhansi Regiment, and their incredulity at Netaji's support of the women.

'Don't look at them,' Prema advised, turning her back on the Japanese officers.

Leaving his tent, Netaji hurried towards the Japanese, while glancing anxiously up at the sky. The commanders turned to him politely, but soon an argument developed and it was clear by the gestures involved that it concerned the waiting Ranis of the Jhansi Regiment. Eventually, Netaji broke away from the Japanese abruptly, and they heard his angry retort.

'Go to Hell. I will not cross until all the girls have gone over first.' Netaji's fury took the Japanese by surprise, and they glowered at the waiting women with open hostility.

Light was now edging out the darkness, and Netaji looked anxiously again at the sky as he hurried away to confer with his aides, his face contorted by anger. Soon Captain Sharma, a tall man with a flamboyantly curled moustache, made his way towards the waiting women.

'The Japanese have commandeered all the ferries, although one was promised for you girls. However, we cannot wait any longer. There's a place further up where the water is shallow. You will now have to swim across, as everyone else is doing. We will help you,' Captain Sharma assured them, as murmurs of consternation were heard.

'Give us your weapons. We will put them on one of the Japanese ferries,' Captain Ahmed ordered.

'What about the crocodiles?' Muni asked again, daring to voice everyone's dread. The danger of bombs appeared a modest peril compared to the snapping jaws of crocodiles.

'The river is shallow here but also fast flowing. Crocodiles prefer slow moving water; you will not find them here. It is the current you must worry about, it can sweep you away,' Captain Sharma replied.

'There is no time left, it will soon be light. We must hurry.' Captain Ahmed led them towards the shallow neck of the river to join the mass of men and animals wading into the water, everyone moving forward as fast as they could.

Sita turned to help Muni who stumbled under the weight of her heavy backpack.

'I cannot swim,' Muni's voice broke in terror.

'Hold onto me,' Sita ordered.

The muddy bank had been churned to a sticky soup by the crowd of men around them. One by one the women dropped into the river. Immediately, the water sank into their clothes, the heavy backpacks weighing them down. Muni clung to Sita as they waded forward, gasping in fear as the riverbed shelved and the water suddenly rose up to their chests. The river supported them and eased the weight of the backpack on Sita's shoulders, but as they pushed forward, they were suddenly out of their depth.

Muni's weight and desperate flailing about pulled Sita down. Treading water, she gasped and fought to stay afloat. The strong current now tugged like a rope about her feet, and she swallowed a mouthful of the foul water. Then, coughing and pulling the terrified Muni along behind her, she began to swim again. As she struck out, she recalled that other river in the village, in which she had swum as a child long ago.

She remembered how, holding her breath, she had plunged down, wanting to swim where no one had been before, to reach that mysterious place where she knew she would find her sister. Beneath the water a sense of limitlessness had filled her. The sun filtered down and in that glassy world she saw the silver flash of fish about her. Brown trout, snake-like eels and large carp glided past, the light catching in their scales. Deeper and deeper she swam, pliant as a fish, losing herself in a vast depth of silent nothingness, searching for that invisible space where she knew her sister lived in a secret river beneath the river, with the goddess Yami. She imagined a dark grotto, silent and safe, and at its centre her sister rested. The current gripped her limbs and pulled her along, as if her sister held her by the hand. As she swam deeper the light would begin to fade, and looking down she saw the darkness below, and terror always seized her. In the river's subterranean world lived monstrous, long whiskered catfish as big as a man with mouths that could swallow a child. She had seen one once in a fishermen's net. Then, her lungs ready to burst, she had spun upwards to break the surface, into the sunlight, gasping for air.

Now, as she swam forward in darkness across the Waw with the weight of Muni dangerously hampering her every stroke, she thought of the bottomless world of all rivers, where besides ugly catfish, crocodiles could also lurk, and she struck out in sudden panic. Stirred up by the army of men now fording the river, the water engulfed them in unstoppable waves. Horses swam beside them, the whites of their eyes rolling in fear, and a convoy of ferries travelled past with mounted guns and lorries tied to the flat bamboo rafts. The river appeared alive with men and animals and hardware, all moving forward as quickly as possible under the breaking light of the day.

There were other girls like Muni who, unable to swim, cried out in distress. Captains Sharma and Ahmed splashed into the water with a rope they had tied to a tree on the bank.

'Grab the rope and pull yourself forward,' Captain Sharma instructed, unwinding the twine, encouraging the girls to take hold of it, wading out of the water on the opposite bank to secure the rope to another tree. Over her shoulder Sita saw Valli, Vasanthi, Ambika and Shivani, all wrestling with the fast flowing water, gripping the rope held by the colonels.

Eventually, one by one, they reached the bank and staggered out of the river. Immediately, without the buoyancy of the water, the heavy weight of the knapsack cut painfully again into Sita's shoulders, water oozing freely from the canvas pack.

The Waw was crossed, but ahead of them the great Sittang River still waited. They rested through the day in a deserted village close to the riverbank. The rain had stopped and the sun emerged hotly again, quickly drying their sodden clothes. Enemy planes swooped low, but the heavy canopy of trees offered good protection for the convoy. Along with the others Sita unpacked the contents of her backpack, spreading things around her on the ground to dry, and was relieved to find her quinine pills were safe; she kept them in a small tin and not a paper box like so many of the other girls, who were now bemoaning this loss. They had only the clothes they stood up in, and the mud of the river now permeated everything, their uniform stiffening about them as it dried, perfumed by an unpleasant odour.

Early in the evening it began to rain again, but they could not delay, and left as darkness fell, clambering back into the trucks in their still damp clothes to press on towards the Sittang River. Soon, the road became a muddy track, littered with abandoned trucks and cars sunk deep in the mire. Eventually, it became impassable and an order was given to abandon their vehicles. Forming ranks and heaving their backpacks up onto their shoulders, they began to march again. Netaji was with them now, walking with the women at the head of his many regiments. Eventually, they reached the wide Sittang River before daybreak and crossed as planned at dawn, ferries plying them over the wide river, depositing them safely on the opposite bank. The Japanese troops occupied a village near the river, and Netaji and his army were allocated space and some shacks as a billet on the outskirts. Fires were lit, and from the Japanese encampment a smell of roasting meat floated to them. Everyone sniffed the air appreciatively.

'The Japanese have taken all the chickens in the village, but whatever is being cooked is only for their commanders. Everyone else is starving like us,' Prema reminded them.

Amita left the hospital and walked towards the bus stop. In the imaging department she had paid her ultra-sound bill in a daze, and then drifted, almost unseeing, through the hospital corridors towards the exit. It was only when she saw the bus stop ahead that she realised her intuition had guided her there; everything within her was blasted away. After a few minutes she saw the shuttle bus approaching, but as it drew to a halt she turned away suddenly, and walked on an impulse towards the taxi stand at the hospital's main entrance. It was the only day in the week that she had so many free hours between lectures and tutorials. With the morning class behind her, Amita had a couple of meetings with individual students in the late afternoon and a supervisory discussion with a PhD candidate in the early evening; there was no need to hurry back to the university.

It was not far from the hospital to the Botanic Gardens. The taxi took a route through Holland Village, stopping before a traffic light outside the shopping centre. The place was popular with the expatriate community for its many small boutiques selling ethnic items from the region, woven mats and wooden bowls, silver, jewellery, linen and chinaware. A group of young Caucasian women, pushing prams and holding young children by the hand, began crossing the road in front of the taxi. One of the women was heavily pregnant and at the sight of her Amita caught her breath, her pulse quickening uncomfortably. As the traffic light turned green the taxi jumped forward with abrupt acceleration, and to Amita's relief Holland Village was left behind.

She had not visited the Botanic Gardens for many years, but little seemed to have changed. The large iron gates stood open as always, and the lush green tranquillity of the place quickly enclosed her. The sky was darkening, already preparing for an afternoon squall. As a child, she had come here often with her mother, riding the bus away from the density of Serangoon Road with its press of noise, colour and odours. They always came in the late afternoon, when the soft yielding forms of the garden caught at shadows, and the evening deepened around them. Her mother said that here, amongst the embrace of tall trees and the jade water of the lake, she remembered the village beside the river where she was born, in far away India. Sometimes they walked around the gardens, between the manicured lawns and carefully trimmed bushes, to a bandstand where once Amita heard a man play a violin, the notes reaching the sky and dissolving the world. Sometimes they had fed the turtles that lived in the lake, bringing with them a bag of stale bread for this purpose, but mostly they just sat beneath the huge banyan tree beside the water, gazing into the murky depths.

'In my village, near my home and the river, we also had such a great tree. It was hundreds of years old and big, like a house. We climbed its branches and swung on its long roots.

Grandmother said Krishna himself always chose to rest in a banyan tree.' Sita told Amita the same thing each time, her voice wistful, her eyes moist with tears that could not be shed.

Now, as she walked towards the old tree beside the lake and the seat that still rested beneath it, Amita realised that each time her mother brought her here as a child, she must have been filled with unbearable nostalgia. Through the old tree and the lake she touched faded memories, rekindling a past lost to her forever. Amita had never before considered the pain of exile her mother must have endured, and the realisation sat heavily upon her now. She herself might look back with interest to her roots in India, like a scene glimpsed through a dusty window, but she did not feel emotionally connected to that country, did not suffer from a fractured identity, or the grief of loss as her mother did. She was a Singaporean, and her sense of belonging was only to this small island, a city-state. Although primarily a Chinese city for Chinese people, it still made room for her, an Indian, and for the other ethnic minorities that peopled it, including them all in its identity. She did not think of herself as Indian, but as an Indian Singaporean, which was an entirely different thing.

The lake was before her, and to her left the massive old banyan tree soared up. She strode forward as she would towards an old friend, her heart filling with gladness as its shadow fell upon her. A squirrel scurried up the trunk and along a branch and then stopped, its bright eyes fixed upon her for a moment, assessing her largeness and the potential danger. Then it skimmed lightly away over the branches and was gone. Unchanged over time, the old tree had waited for her, a repository of memory and emotion, holding in trust the sad yearning of her mother's heart and her own uncertain learnings. Under its huge skirt nothing grew, dry shrivelled leaves littered the gloomy floor. Sitting down on the seat, Amita looked up into the branches as she had when a child, and drew a breath of wonder. On and on, up and up, layer upon layer the tree ascended above her, like the vaulted roof of a great cathedral, until at last it reached the place where the sun broke through its canopy. A plaque near the tree told her it already stood there in 1877 when the Botanic Gardens were newly established, and no one knew how old it was. A beard of wiry aerial roots descended from its branches, touching the ground and growing back upwards again into the tree to prop up the central trunk, new streams of life merging with the ancient core. Glossy leaves cushioned huge boughs sweeping down about Amita, hanging low over the lake in a thick curtain. The branches almost touched the water, and were mirrored in its green face.

As Amita stared into the lake, a bubble of air disturbed the stillness, widening ripples circling over the water. As she watched, more and more bubbles appeared, then a quick splash as a fish broke the surface. Amita saw that she looked down upon the glass ceiling of another world, where dark sinuous shadows slipped through the murky depths below. A sudden breeze rustled the branches above her and lightning flashed through the sky. Looking back into the water, Amita met the eyes of a large fish staring up at her, unmoving. Sinking silently, the fish appeared to dissolve slowly, fading back into the gloom. In its place a dark-skinned catfish with ashen whiskers appeared, wheeled and turned and was gone. She heard another splash as a large water monitor, like a dark moving log, lizard head held above the water, began swimming steadily away across the lake. A jogger, an elderly man in shorts and singlet and a red cap, looked at Amita curiously as he passed. A woman with a small girl in a pink dress hurried by, the child pulling on the mother's hand and pointing to the turtles beneath the surface of the water, just as Amita had done as a child. The woman squinted up at the sky, struggling to open her umbrella at the imminent threat of rain. In the lake the fish had risen to observe Amita again.

Mirrored in the thick green water the banyan appeared to stand on its head, its great branches descending into the lake, the trailing roots pushing back into the sky. The ancient tree was but a shadow in the water, while the hidden world below the lake was the reality. There were, Amita saw, two worlds before her, the one that was hidden and the one that was known. In its mirroring, the truth of the tree could be understood, yet what she took as the reality about her was but a reflection to that other secret world. Perhaps life itself was a form of mirror-imagery, an upside down reality, she thought. Perhaps the world she could not enter, the spiritual world, was the true reality as all the old books said, and the material world in which she now sat beneath the old tree, a world of sensations, of pains and joys, was but a shadow of that hidden one. A sudden gust of wind lifted the branches again, stirring the shrivelled leaves at her feet, moving in the feathery banks of foliage bordering the lake. A fish broke the surface again with a splash.

The darkening sky was ripped apart by a sudden clap of thunder as rain abruptly drummed about her, churning up the surface of the lake. Amita retreated quickly to shelter beneath the tree, pressing her back against the trunk. Unmoved by the onslaught, rain rolling off its great spreading branches, the old tree kept her dry, just as it had when she had sheltered beneath it as a child. She marvelled at how completely she was enfolded and protected. At her feet the desiccated leaves beneath the tree's wide skirt lay dry and untouched by the rain.

Running her hand over the furrowed bark of the trunk, she felt again its rough and familiar caress. As a child, she had pressed her face against the old trunk, attempting to stretch her arms around it, embracing the tree as she would a friend, taking comfort from its ancient life. The original tree had rotted away long ago, enveloped and strangled by the thick mesh of its roots, to leave only a hollow core. Disregarding her mother's protests, Amita had delighted in climbing into that empty void as a child. It was like a gnarled and murky cave and crouching down within its damp confines, thick with the scent of rot and rodent droppings, she was at one with the old tree, protected within it by something she did not understand.

The floor about her, she remembered, was littered with a compost of rotting leaves, the moulted skins of cicadas, a dead mouse, a featherless hatchling; she never knew from one visit to another what she would find. As she watched, the corpse of a bee might be dismembered by an army of ants, and its parts carried away to nourish new life, or mulch the earth. Her presence did not disturb this endless process, the ants merely rerouting their path to avoid her, intent upon their task. She breathed in the deep rich smell of decay, an odour that was without end and that went on and on inside her.

Now, so many years later, she looked down again into the hollow where once she had crouched as a child, and experienced again its primordial scent, and the grief of loss. The small space that had so easily fitted her then in her innocence was denied to her now. The decomposing corpse of a squirrel, nestled amongst the damp rotting leaves, was black with a heaving mass of ants, intent on de-fleshing death. Here, nothing had changed over the years while she had grown and reached out to life; in the hollow of this old tree the process she had watched as a child continued, ceaseless and unstoppable, a continual transforming of death into life. She too, she saw now, was engaged in this same process, one version of herself changing into the next as she matured. She inhaled again and the scent of the past tunnelled into her head, resonating with her across a lifetime. She lived upon a narrow rope of time, waking afresh to each new morning, but she aged in an unseen experiential place. She was like the old tree, the original plant had rotted away but new streams of life grew back into the central trunk, thickening and texturing over the years. All the people she had been, the child hiding in the tree, the woman in America, the university professor, all merged with the timeless core of herself.

It was no longer possible to hide in the old tree; it could not protect her from herself. A frisson of panic ran through her. The future was unknowable, and already pressed upon her, and she did not know where it would take her. It seemed she had lived her life meeting the expectations of others, powerless even when she thought she had power, always seeking that power in the wrong places.

In her mind she saw the ultrasound screen again, the dark grotto of black water and at its centre the manikin growing within her, drawing its strength from her flesh and blood, female like herself, waiting to come alive. It was biding its time within her just as once she had waited, for what she did not know, within the hollow core of this ancient tree. She knew now that she wanted this child, and saw that she had unconsciously sought out a man to father it, and would keep it. She would not go ahead with the termination she had so resolutely planned just an hour earlier. While she pursued her external life, that other self which she was coming to realise lived deep within her with a will of its own, had arranged an alternative life for her, and she could do little to stop it. Across the lake she saw the child in the pink dress sheltering with her mother beneath a flimsy gazebo, and imagined how her life might one day bring her such a moment. Even as she thought these thoughts, a surge of joy ran through her.

24
BURMA, 1945

The train had only three carriages, and they boarded it for the journey to Bangkok as darkness fell. Netaji had developed bad blisters on his feet and had been persuaded to go ahead by car to Moulmein with some Japanese commanders, and from there to continue on to Bangkok. The railway carriages were dimly lit by a few low watt light bulbs that flickered unreliably. They were packed in so tightly that the girls were sitting in the aisles between seats. As always, for safety, they travelled by darkness. Valli sat with Sita and Muni, backpacks and guns between their feet. As Muni began to cough again, the lights went off and the train began to move, darkness blanketing the carriages. Sita stared through the open barred window, but nothing could be seen, the terrain outside was buried in the night, and at last she leaned back and fell asleep.

She was woken suddenly as the train lurched to a stop, and found they had been travelling for only an hour. Prema made her way hurriedly through the carriage to open the door, climbing down to determine what was happening. Sita pressed her face to the bars of the window, and the cool dank odour of vegetation filled her nostrils.

'The track has been bombed, we'll have to walk, but it's only

a few miles to the next station. Get your things together,' Prema
said when she returned to the carriage.

Eventually, by morning light they marched into the next
station, a sizable place with a roofed platform that provided
protection from sun and rain. The day was already upon them
and the usual drone of enemy aircraft had begun, like predatory
insects in the sky above. The station was occupied by a platoon
of Japanese soldiers, who were leaving for Bangkok that night.
The place appeared to be a depot, with a grid of lines fanning
out beyond the platforms. Carriages and goods wagons were
scattered haphazardly about over the rails, and a makeshift
bamboo shelter had been erected at one end. Prema stood,
hands on hips, surveying the strange arrangement.

'They've disengaged carriages from their engines, and pushed
them about at odd angles. From the air it will look like the
trains have been bombed and the blast has scattered the wagons.
See, that engine under the bamboo hideout. It's a clever trick.
They'll bring the engine out tonight for us and the Japanese
troops.' She went off to speak to a Japanese officer about the
onward arrangements to Bangkok.

An elderly Indian stationmaster with cheeks of unshaven
white stubble hurried up to advise the women on where best to
camp in the station.

'Beside tracks cool, and no Japanese here,' he smiled,
revealing nicotine-stained teeth, gesturing towards the soldiers
camped in village shacks some distance beyond the station.

Many of the girls took the old man's advice, depositing

their kitbags on the platform, settling down as comfortably as they could. Soon, a Japanese soldier appeared to check on them, walking the length of the platform, silently assessing the supine girls in unnecessary detail before returning to his squad. Bands of curious Burmese urchins from the nearby village also gathered to stare at the uniformed women. One small girl of five or six with filthy matted hair attached herself to Sita, Muni and Valli. Her bony shoulders protruded above a dirty green sarong tied under her armpits, and her cheeks were painted with pale yellow patches of cooling *thanakha*.

'We are also starving; go away,' Muni told her, beginning to cough again.

Sita beckoned to the child and from the depths of her backpack produced a millet biscuit, part of the precious rations they carried, and broke off a piece for the child.

A slight but welcome breeze moved between the platforms but, worried about Muni's cough, Sita led her and Valli over the rails to one of the uncoupled carriages. The wooden seats inside made a comfortable bed, and they stretched out in relief. Others followed them and soon the carriage was full, rifles and kit bags stacked everywhere. Sita turned, to find the child in the green sarong had followed them and was fingering the barrel of her rifle.

'No!' she snatched up the weapon, laying it beneath the seat. The child backed away and wandered about, staring curiously at the women.

At the back of the carriage Valli peeled a shrunken orange, and prepared to share it with those around her. Shivani, who had picked some branches of wild *longan* near the station, beckoned to the child and soon had her running up and down the carriage distributing the fruit to everyone. The child's eyes glowed with excitement in her dirty face. They were all hungry and set about peeling the thin shells from the fruit, relishing the white fleshy globes within. The child had taken a particular liking to Sita, who fed her an extra *longan*. She opened her lips to take the fruit into her mouth, the moist warmth of her tongue curling about Sita's fingers.

Later, Prema brought them a few bananas the stationmaster had produced, and these, with the *longans* and millet biscuits were a good breakfast. The day wore on, and one by one they fell asleep, the hot sun spearing the metal carriage, the heat blanketing everything. The child curled up on the bench, her body pressed against Sita, but in the silent carriage the sound of Muni's rasping cough was constant.

Sita seemed to have hardly fallen asleep before she woke abruptly to see the girl running up and down the carriage, shouting incomprehensibly while pointing out of the window. Still struggling to surface from sleep, and sticky with sweat, Sita reached out, taking hold of the child as she ran past.

'What is it?' she demanded.

The child continued her high-pitched yelling, pointing all the while at the windows. Sita peered out, but could see nothing untoward around the station. At last, pulling free of Sita's grasp, the girl jumped down from the carriage and ran off across the tracks, still shouting.

'Something is wrong.' Valli got up and pushed her way between the seats to the door.

'It's probably nothing. Let her go,' Sita advised, but Valli was already climbing out of the carriage.

From the window, Sita watched Valli sprinting over the tracks after the child, soon catching up with her and pulling her to a halt. As Sita watched, a shot rang out, and then another, and Valli crumpled to the ground, the child falling with her. Sita started up from her seat, and reached for her rifle. More shots were heard, nearer now, and there was the ring of metal as bullets bounced off the carriage. Muni, who had slept through the earlier commotion, awoke and began coughing again. Everyone in the carriage was now crouched down, grasping their rifles. Sita pulled Muni to the floor with her.

From where she knelt, Sita craned her neck to stare through the window at the unmoving forms of Valli and the child. A couple of men holding rifles could now be seen running into the woodland behind the station. Japanese soldiers quickly appeared and began firing into the screen of vegetation. Weapons at the ready, they checked the station for further snipers. On the tracks where they had fallen, Valli and the child did not move.

At last it seemed safe to leave the carriage. Sita ran across the railway lines to where Valli lay, sprawled on her back, an arm flung out, eyes open, and staring up at the sky. Blood pooled about her in a dark stain, as if she lay upon her own shadow. Beside her the child began to whimper.

'Valli,' Sita dropped to her knees.

'Guerrillas, Chin snipers,' Prema said, crouching down beside Sita, feeling Valli's neck for a pulse.

'It is too late,' she said quietly, withdrawing her hand and standing up.

Sita stared at Valli in disbelief. Sweat still moistened her neck and cheeks from the exertion of running after the child. Between her lips the edge of her wide front teeth could be seen. Sita was sure Valli would suddenly stir, and struggle to her feet. The faint smell of the orange she had peeled earlier drifted from her fingers. The child now scrambled up, and her whimpering became a terrified howl as she stared at the lifeless Valli stretched out on the ground.

Sita put an arm around the hysterical child, trying to draw her close, but the girl pulled away, screaming louder. At Prema's order, Sita gripped the child firmly by the shoulders, holding her still while Prema examined her, and found her to be without a scratch. Then the girl twisted free of Sita and ran off towards the village. Within a moment the stationmaster hurried up, four Japanese soldiers behind him.

He stared down at Valli's body, annoyance at the inconvenience of her death clear in his face. The Japanese soldiers glowered in equal impatience, muttering amongst themselves.

'Get all your kit off that carriage, and wait on the platform,' Prema instructed, trying to distract the girls, who were now crowding in acute distress around Valli's body.

Reluctantly, they trailed off towards the carriage but Sita found it impossible to turn away, and remained with Muni, who knelt beside Valli, sobbing and coughing.

What would they do with her body? How could they leave her in this place? Sita did not like to voice the thoughts that came to her now, and by her silence, she knew the same thoughts pressed upon Prema

'Guerrillas come back soon,' one of the soldiers said in broken English, staring down at the dead body.

'Snipers from the village have been watching this station; the villagers secretly harbour them,' the stationmaster commented, still gazing in frustration at Valli's body.

'Must bury quickly. Rain coming soon,' the English speaking Japanese advised, squinting up at the sky and the threatening clouds.

Muni gave another sob, and Sita placed a hand on her shoulder, as much to steady her own emotions as to calm Muni. Even Prema, now that a decision about Valli must be faced, was clearly troubled by the thought of leaving her in an unknown place.

'We must take her with us. Can you find a cloth to carry her in? We will cremate her in Bangkok. We must cremate her,' Prema told the stationmaster.

'Cannot cremate. We cannot make sufficient fire. All the wood is wet and also, no one nowadays is having so much oil. Nowadays everyone is being buried.' The stationmaster shook his head sorrowfully. As a Hindu himself, he understood the reluctance for burial, but continued to explain the problems.

'Sister, this is war. We cannot know if the next train to Bangkok may also be bombed and if it is, you must again walk a long distance. Then what will you do, how will you transport a body? You must bury her here, now.'

Above them the brooding sky was darkening with the

coming rain and approaching dusk. A distant crack of thunder sounded, and then a scream was heard. They saw the girls who had returned to the carriage for their kit running back towards them again.

'Shivani is also gone.' The words floated to them across the track.

In the carriage Shivani sat upright on her seat, head against the window frame, eyes closed as if asleep. On the bench beside her lay a remaining branch of *longan*, a few globes of fruit clinging to it still. Sita remembered the second burst of gunfire, and the metallic ring of bullets bouncing off the carriage.

Blood trickled from Shivani's temple, and ran in a thin line down her cheek and over her jaw, to be absorbed by the collar of her uniform. Even as they had sat around her, death had come and no one had noticed. They stood silently, muffling sobs of disbelief. Although they were trained for battle, nothing had readied them for death.

The stationmaster and soldiers climbed into the carriage, their voices filling the wagon. One of the Japanese lifted Shivani off the seat, throwing her lightly over his shoulder as if she were without weight. He climbed down from the carriage and Sita followed, keeping as close to the man as she could. One of Shivani's arms swung free of her body, and her head bobbed about against the man's back.

Already, on the orders of the Japanese soldiers, men from the village were digging a grave behind the platform. The stationmaster supervised the work, anxious that at such close proximity to his station, the job should be properly done.

'Both must go into one grave. No time for digging two graves before nightfall. More rain coming soon and then everything turning again to mud. If you are not digging deep enough, animals get to the bodies or the bodies are rising up to the surface in the soft mud. I have seen all this before.' He stared down at Valli and Shivani, who were both now laid out on the ground beside the half-dug grave.

The gravediggers had brought two old sarongs with them from the village to use as shrouds, and twine to secure the cloth about the bodies.

'You must hurry. They are making ready your train. Soon you must leave.' The stationmaster pointed to the camouflaged bamboo tunnel.

A large engine was already being pulled slowly out of the makeshift hideout by a crowd of village men, and pushed towards several carriages that were waiting to be coupled to it.

Together Prema and Sita lifted Valli, who seemed heavier in death than in life, onto a worn and faded purple sarong patterned with a scattering of yellow flowers. They could neither wash her clean nor take the bloodied clothes off her, but must roll her up in the hasty manner Sita had rolled up the sleeping mats each morning in the room off Norris Road. Beside them Vasanthi and Ambika were folding a green checked sarong about Shivani. Her face was calm, her long flat eyelids peacefully closed.

'Wrap it tightly, and take off their boots' Prema instructed, finding it difficult to wrap the shroud neatly around the heavy shoes.

Sita bent to untie the laces, pulling off Valli's boots. Her small foot lay in Sita's hand, the flesh still warm and soft, broad toenails in need of trimming. Sita remembered the ache Valli had endured with her flat feet. Inside her boot lay the moulded leather support the Bras Basah camp doctor had made for her, stained dark now with Valli's sweat. Even as she placed the boots side by side, the stationmaster was bending to snatch them up, tying the laces together to carry them over his arm.

'These things they will like in the village,' he remarked. He would sell them for a good price, Sita thought, although as far as she could see, the villagers all went barefoot.

Prema took the end of the purple sarong, and lowered it over Valli's face, securing the shroud with twine. The villagers had finished digging the grave and now leaned on their spades, looking at the women with interest.

'Wait,' Sita cried out.

The thought of Valli and Shivani being lowered into the wet earth and a weight of sodden mud shovelled upon them was more than she could bear. Reaching for her backpack, she pulled out the miniature of the *devi* she always carried. If she shut her eyes the *devi* was immediately before her, at a thought she could summon up her radiant face and the tiger with its burning eyes; Valli and Shivani had need of her now. Lifting the shroud, she pushed the picture into Valli's folded hands.

A distance away Muni sat sick and exhausted, leaning against a tree, and glancing at her flushed and pinched face, Sita was filled with fear for her. Dusk was already upon them, and the men were impatient. Two of them stood down in the grave while the other two lowered the bodies into the narrow trench, stacking one girl upon the other. Sita looked down into the pit with growing horror. The thin shrouds were no protection against the water that already seeped into the grave, but there was nothing she could do. The men clambered out and began impatiently shovelling damp earth back into the grave, packing it heavily down upon the corpses, anxious to be done with the task before night fell. All the while, the heavy clunk of metal could be heard from the station as the train was prepared for its journey, and the carriages were coupled together. At last, the gravediggers finished their job and quickly levelled off the earth, stamping it flat beneath their feet, before walking back to the village, shovels over their shoulders.

Around Sita the women moved forward to stand about the newly dug grave. It was difficult to know what to do.

'*Kadam kadam badhaye ja! Khushi ke geet gaye ja.*'

Sita began to sing their favourite marching song. As the words left her mouth, she heard again the sound of Valli's deep voice rising above the rhythmic tread of their boots. The others joined in and continued the verse. Muni also began to sing.

'*It's a long long way to Tipperary…*' She broke off coughing, and nobody took up the refrain or had the heart to continue.

'*Jai Hind! Jai Hind!*'

One by one, watched by the stationmaster, they gave a last salute at the grave, then turned to board the waiting train. Sita climbed into the carriage and sat silently with Muni on a hard wooden seat, her mind full of the image of the shrouded bodies, trapped for eternity in their waterlogged grave. She should have been more forceful, should have taken Valli's arm and dissuaded her from running after the child. If she had acted, Valli might still be alive.

The journey did not go smoothly. As they neared Bangkok they found the railway track bombed once again and were forced to march down the line to the next station. Muni was running a high fever, and they carried her in a hammock-like stretcher made from a sarong they begged from a village they passed through. By the time they eventually reached Bangkok they had been journeying for over a week.

Muni was taken straight to a hospital and her condition was cause for anxiety. Sita sat with her through the first night, refusing to leave her side. Her fever raged and she had difficulty breathing, each inhalation drawn in through painful rasps. Coughing racked her thin body, and much of the time she babbled deliriously. The doctors and nurses who came and went said little. Sita pressed a cool cloth to Muni's burning forehead, willing breath into her slight body; there was nothing she could do but wait. Finally, Muni opened her eyes, and asked where she was, and seemed to remember little of the journey to Bangkok.

After their arrival in Bangkok, things moved quickly. They were told the Rani of Jhansi Regiment was to be disbanded and soon after they arrived, they had to surrender their weapons. In the barracks they cleaned them for the last time.

Sita picked up the long bristle brush and passed it through the barrel of the gun until it emerged from the muzzle. Her weapon, she realised, had become a part of her, an extension of her being. Already she felt bereft, as though with the loss of the gun she would lose the person she had become. The acrid odour of the solvent and oil filled her nostrils as she drew the brush back and forth until the gun was clean, and then polished the soft patterning of the wooden butt, caressing its warmth, remembering that first powerful recoil that had thrown her to the ground and made her shoulder ache. With this gun she had killed the Chin guerrilla on that green slope in Burma. In her mind she saw the man again, saw him blown high, twisting and turning against the sky, his white thighbones protruding from his ripped flesh like a pair of ivory chopsticks, a sight she could never forget. Whether he had died from her gunshot or the exploding shell did not matter, she had pulled the trigger intending to kill him. Had she hesitated a moment longer, he might have turned away because he could not kill a woman, he might have moved beyond the shell and, like her, might still be alive. Nothing made sense to her any longer. The memory of Valli and Shivani stacked in their wet and muddy grave returned to her so forcefully that she sat down on a stool, the gun in her lap. She had been trained to kill; yet life and death appeared to balance on a knife's edge, observing laws beyond her comprehension, beyond the paltry power of a gun.

The next day, when she held out her rifle, surrendering it to Prema, who was in charge of collecting their weapons, her hand tightened about the familiar weight before it was lifted away from her and stacked with the other guns. Staring down at her empty upturned palms, it was as if an essential part of her had been ripped away.

There was some time to wait before they could be sent back to Singapore, and while they remained in Bangkok Sita volunteered to work in the hospital, in the hope of hearing news of Shiva. One by one units of INA men were arriving in Bangkok from distant locations, and at last the remnants of Shiva's unit arrived. They had journeyed across high mountains, through forests and jungle, marching for months and covering over one thousand miles. Suddenly the hospital was full of starved, ragged and emaciated men, but Shiva was not amongst them.

At last a stick of a man with an overgrown beard heard her asking about Shiva, and beckoned her to him. He raised himself on an elbow and reached out to grasp her wrist, staring up at her, his voice a painful rasp. Looking down, she saw the thin claws of his fingers, the uncut nails as long as talons, locked about her arm.

'I knew him. He told me his parents were killed in Jallianwala Bagh. That was why he was fighting this war. All he wanted was to set foot on Indian soil. He told me his wife was in the Jhansi Regiment; he was worried where she was, what was happening to her. One day he was there and another he was missing. We could not go back to search for him. Later I saw his name on a list of the dead.' He let go of her arm and fell back on the bed, breath twisting through his chest.

His words sank through her, and she realised she had known for a long time what this man was now telling her. At last she walked away, through corridors harsh with the smell of antiseptic and illness, and out into the street with its pungent odour of drains, incense, dried fish, rotting vegetables and the blossoms of the frangipani outside the entrance. She squatted down beneath the tree and stared up into the mass of flat-fingered leaves and soft white flowers. The dark tangle of boughs was embedded with a jigsaw of light, where small patches of sun shone through the gloom. She remembered the picture of the *devi* she had folded into Valli's hands, and wished she had it now. A fallen flower lay in the dirt beside her and she picked it up, cupping it in her hands, closing her eyes, seeing again the *devi* on her tawny tiger. To one side of the picture of the goddess, there had been a frangipani tree such as the one she now sat beneath, studded with flowers, bright as stars. What would she do now without Shiva? Once again she was a widow. This time, she vowed, she would never wear white, or shave her head again.

The petals of the frangipani were thick and soft as pieces of flesh, and she rubbed them between her fingers until the sweet smelling juice was moist on her hands. She had been a soldier, she had fired a gun and killed a man; she had lived the way of the warrior, careless of death. She had crossed the threshold into the world of men and written her name in blood. The force that drove her forward was without a name, but she knew it resided at the very centre of her being. She was one-in-herself, dependent on no one, and would find her own strength.

Before leaving Bangkok, Netaji called upon the remaining Ranis of the Jhansi Regiment. Standing before them, jovial as always, his high boots polished and gleaming, he adjusted his spectacles before speaking.

'The Japanese will surrender soon. The war is ending, and our position is no longer viable, but this is just a temporary disbanding. You must remain ready to regroup. Until then go back to Singapore, to your homes and families.'

Outside, the revving up of Netaji's car was heard. An aide approached, to remind him of the time and Netaji nodded, anxiously adjusting his spectacles once again. At the door he turned to wag a finger playfully at them.

'Promise not to go back and hide in the kitchen! Keep the fire of freedom burning in your hearts and pass it on to your children.'

Then he was gone. There was the slam of a car door, and the roar of the engine as he was driven away.

They could not sleep, worried now about a future they could not see clearly.

'I cannot go back to that plantation. They will force me to marry some old widower who wants a young girl for a wife.' Muni whispered to Sita that night, as if even saying the words aloud was to conjure them into reality.

Muni sat on her bed, hugging her knees, and Sita put an arm around her. Muni's fear brought before her the spectre of her first husband again, even though the experience was long gone.

'You need not go back. I am alone now. You can stay with me in Singapore.'

The idea flooded Sita's mind. Muni would share the room off Norris Road, they would work together, find some business to do. In the morning they went to speak to Prema, to inform her of the new arrangement; but Prema shook her head.

'The INA is responsible for returning all the girls to their families. We must have written permission from a family to send you to a different destination. Go back to your family first, and then with their permission you can join Sita in Singapore,' Prema told them, turning away quickly to another task, unaware of the effect of her words.

News that the war was over came at last. Soon Japanese soldiers were everywhere, moving out of the town with trucks of looted goods and weaponry, just as British troops began victoriously entering the Siamese capital. Muni and Sita, with the remaining Ranis from Malaya, were to accompany a regiment of INA men returning by train to Singapore. The girls were to begin the journey together, travelling over the Siam border into Malaya before going their separate ways. Those girls, like Muni, from up country estates in Malaya would be transported back home from there, and those whose destination was Singapore would travel on with the INA men.

Eventually, the train reached Alor Setar, a large railway junction Sita remembered passing through on the way to Burma. There, Muni and a group of other plantation girls climbed into waiting trucks that would take them to their respective estates, while Sita and the remaining girls stayed on the train. Even before the train drew to a halt at Alor Setar, Muni was sobbing uncontrollably.

Sita stood at the end of the platform as the distraught Muni was led away, and watched her climb up into the back of a truck.

She waved for as long as the truck was in view, remembering how, so long ago, Dr. Sen had waved to her on a station platform as she began her journey to Calcutta. Then, the truck turned a corner and was gone, while behind her the stationmaster blew his whistle, readying the train for its onward journey.

Sita sat in silence, listening to the other girls chat and laugh as the train ploughed through a lush green world. The bleat of the whistle sounded and Sita knew she journeyed towards yet another change of direction in her life. Once, as a small child her father had given her a book from his shop. The pages were blank except for some numbered black dots strewn loosely about on a sea of white paper. Dev had given her a pencil and showed her how to join one number to the next. She learned quickly, and it excited her how a picture would appear just by joining one dot to the next. It meant the picture was there all the time on the page, but she could not see it until she had journeyed with her pencil from one point to another. Her life seemed something like that, its shape invisible but already determined, waiting for her to find it.

Eventually, the train halted at a station, and at the stop everyone left the carriages and walked about the platform, glad of the break. Food hawkers appeared, and also sellers of hot tea and sticks of hard, chewy candy. The INA men relaxed, and a group of officers set up their field radio on the platform to listen to the latest military news. Soon the stationmaster appeared, blowing his whistle as always, and they began boarding the train to continue the journey. As Sita turned to climb into the carriage, one of the INA officers from the group around the field radio came running along the platform, waving his arms and shouting. People turned to the man with expressions of disbelief, and at last his words became clear to Sita.

'Netaji is dead. Netaji is dead.'

Everyone was shouting and crying at once. Those people who had already boarded the train began disembarking again, porters with bags stacked on their heads put down their loads in horrified incredulity, stray dogs began barking at the commotion. Up and down the platform people turned to each other in stunned disbelief, unable to absorb the news.

The officer continued to run wildly up and down the platform by the train, his voice collapsing then rising again.

'Netaji is dead. Netaji is dead. Killed in a plane crash in Taiwan.'

To Sita's surprise, Dev was at the station to meet her. He had made regular enquiries at the Bras Basah camp about her regiment and which trains Sita might possibly be returning on, and had gone to the station to meet each one. As the crowd of INA soldiers left the platform, Sita saw him standing alone at one end, anxiously craning his neck for a glimpse of her. She ran towards him, remembering his waiting figure at the dock when she first arrived in Singapore, and how she had not at first recognised him. Now, gaunt and prematurely balding, he had aged in a way that shocked her, but her heart lifted at the sight of him.

'I wrote many letters,' Dev protested when she commented on the length of time without news of him.

'I received only one, with the news of your marriage,' Sita replied.

From the station, waiting INA transport took Sita and others from her regiment to the Bras Basah camp. Everyone was nervous; no one knew exactly what would happen to them now, and the rumours swirling about were unsettling. The British were back in authority again in Singapore, and the INA was classed as part of the enemy. It was whispered that many of the civilian INA recruits had discarded their uniforms and melted away, returning unobtrusively to their former lives. However, the professional INA soldiers, who had once fought for the British but had been turned over to the Japanese as POWs at the time of the surrender, were now back with the British Army, but as their POWs. They were to be tried for treason in India, accused of 'waging war against the King'.

When at last Sita and the other girls arrived back at the Bras Basah camp, they found Major Pandey was still there, helping to officiate the handover to the British. She had not been harassed for her participation in the INA and was confident they would not be arrested like the men.

'The British are gentlemen; they look upon us as foolish women and don't really know what to do with us. Let them think what they wish, it frees us to regroup later if there is a need,' Major Pandey confided.

A British officer was at the camp to interview and assess the returning women of the Rani of Jhansi Regiment. He was a middle-aged man with a clipped voice and a fulsome moustache, who did not even bother to interview them individually, but hurried through the process, seeing several of them at one time, as dismissive as the Japanese military.

'I don't mind telling you that the British government sees you as misguided women carried away by romantic ideals. We are not a nation that likes to punish foolish women; some of you are no more than children. Go home to your families, get married, have children of your own,' he reprimanded, before continuing:

'This is not of course how we view the rest of the INA. Your men are a pack of traitors. They will be returned to India, to Delhi, to stand trial, and will get the hanging all traitors deserve.'

Along with the other girls, Sita was briskly discharged and stripped of all INA insignia. As she had no alternative clothes she was allowed to leave the camp in her khaki uniform. At the gate, Sita again found Dev waiting for her. He hailed a rickshaw and they climbed in for the journey back to Serangoon Road. So much had happened to her since they last met, and she waited for her brother's interrogation. To her surprise, after a few brief words of condolence, he avoided the subject of Shiva's death, eager instead to reveal the changes that had occurred in his own life. When Krishnaswami and Sons reopened under a Japanese licence, Dev had returned to work there, and was promoted to assistant manager. One of the senior managers at Krishnaswami, who had a young daughter, had approached him with a proposal of marriage.

'At that time all fathers were worried about their daughters. Japanese soldiers were roaming about, pulling young girls from their homes and using them as they wished. Many marriages were arranged quickly to keep girls safe,' Dev explained, as they bowled along in the direction of his new home.

'Rohini is a good wife,' he added with a self-conscious smile.

As they rode along Sita observed the ravaged town, strewn with bombsites and rubbish. People hurried about, heads down, a stance learned in their years of fear and deprivation under the Japanese. Food was still scarce and the ubiquitous tapioca still sprouted in the smallest space. Although she wore her INA clothes, Sita realised she was now a part of this crushed world, and must navigate her life within it.

Dev occupied a street-facing room in a tenement house near Krishnaswami and Sons. Rohini had been waiting at the window, and hurried down to meet them, throwing herself upon her new sister-in -law almost before she climbed out of the rickshaw. Sita extricated herself from Rohini's tight and clammy embrace, and saw before her a buxom woman in a purple sari, with a flat plain face and determined chin. Rohini appeared to be about her own age, but Sita met her sharp eyes and knew she must be wary. Rohini silently examined her, taking in the masculine military uniform, her eyes slipping from Sita's breasts to her belted waist, the crease of her crotch and the swell of her thighs beneath the crumpled cotton trousers. Her face appeared to close in disapproval, her voice becoming suddenly formal after the excited embrace, and Sita knew that in some way she did not meet Rohini's expectations.

The amount of light and air flowing into Dev's new home seemed to reflect his newly elevated prospects. Rohini boiled up tea on a primus stove, and unwrapped snacks purchased from the food stalls below to welcome Sita home.

'Eat, eat,' she insisted, pushing food before Sita.

As she bustled about, Dev talked of their wedding and his work in the shop, but glanced frequently up at Rohini, as if seeking her affirmation. At last, Rohini sat down and Dev smiled apprehensively, and after a nod from his wife, began to outline their plans for Sita now that she was back in Singapore.

'This room is big enough for three. It will be a help to Rohini to have you with her while I am at work.' Dev's voice was bright, but the hollowness of his feigned optimism sat upon them all.

'We have bought bedding for you,' Rohini announced, pointing to a new sleeping mat rolled up in a corner.

'I will stay here tonight, but tomorrow I will go home.' Sita answered firmly, after expressing her thanks.

'We bought that mat and other things for you only yesterday,' Rohini protested, full of muted affront.

'I am your brother, I will look after you now,' Dev's face creased in concern, and beside him Rohini nodded emphatically.

'You are a widow now, how will you live alone? What will people say?' Rohini reminded Sita, her voice low but determined.

'Tomorrow I will go home,' Sita repeated, controlling her irritation, equally determined, remembering how Dev had once before, many years ago, taken charge of her life on her arrival in Singapore. Things were different now; she was confident she could support herself and live her life independently.

Rohini gave a sudden grunt of exasperation and stood up to make more tea, her lips pursed in displeasure. Already, Sita sensed the rules for their lifelong engagement were being silently laid down. Dev would now have to make choices, and whether he liked it or not, his wife's opinion would inform his every decision.

The following day Sita returned home and Dev and Rohini accompanied her, advising repeatedly against her decision. They climbed the spiral metal stair and Sita turned the key in the heavy padlock, knowing it was Shiva who had secured the lock on that last day together. Stepping into the hot, trapped air of the room she breathed in the scent of mildew, and hurried to open the shutters of the window. Light and air flooded in and she glimpsed again the familiar view of the courtyard below, and at the top of the lane the Ramakrishna Mission with its roof of dome-shaped pavilions. There was the scuttle of geckoes amongst Shiva's books and papers. Everything was as they had left it on that last day. Dev and Rohini followed her into the room like adults pleasing a fractious child whose demands must run their course before common sense returns.

'This room is so small,' Rohini announced, hands on hips, looking around in a critical manner, clearly pleased that her own home appeared superior.

She inspected the kitchen arrangements, putting down the metal *tiffin* carrier of food she had cooked for Sita. Picking up a cushion and thick cotton rug, she shook them vigorously on the stairs outside, exclaiming at the dust.

'Now you are alone, you must see the door is always locked,' Dev warned.

'It is not right that you live alone. You are a widow, people will talk,' Rohini reminded Sita once again, returning to the room with the cushion and rug.

'It is the duty of a brother to look after his sister,' Dev reiterated in an aggrieved voice, taking the rug from Rohini and spreading it on the floor again.

'Being a soldier has made her more like a man,' Rohini observed with a short, hard laugh. Sita bit her lip and said nothing.

Rohini had found a woman to clean the room on a regular

basis and this old crone arrived as they stood talking, to be instructed loudly about her duties by Rohini.

'Where is your pail and cloth?' Rohini demanded, and Sita hurried to find these items.

'You will soon see this is not the way to live,' Dev announced sadly, as he prepared to leave at last, and beside him Rohini nodded, lips pursed in her customary manner.

Sita listened in relief to the metallic ring of their footsteps fading away down the stairs. Her brother seemed to have forgotten she had lived alone in this same room while Shiva was busy in the INA camp, and Dev was working at the far end of the island for the Japanese.

As soon as she was alone, Sita turned to the old clock on the wall, and wound up its rusty innards. Moving the hands to the right time, she remembered that it was Shiva who had last touched the key she now held. On the shelf, his shaving mug still stood as he had left it, the brush holding the faint perfume of his last shave. At the other end of the shelf the *devi* waited as always, perched upon her tiger, radiant in her metal frame. Sita found a stick of incense to light, and placed it before the goddess.

Alone at last, she had not realised how painfully memories would press upon her. The room was filled with the scent of burning incense, and she boiled up some water, remembering the copious amounts of tea Shiva drank and the ritual of making it for him. The food Dev and Rohini had left for her was still warm, and she ate it gratefully. In the weeks since Shiva's death was confirmed, she had found herself dry-eyed, everything

locked down inside her. Now, faced with Shiva's desk, and
the bedding roll upon which they had slept that last night,
realisation flooded through her, and she gave a cry of pain. The
memory of Shiva's displeasure on that last day, and his concern
for her the following morning as they prepared to leave, cut
through her anew, and she buried her head in her hands. On
the wall the old clock began to strike, coughing out its familiar
rusty chimes. The stick of incense burned low, the ash falling in
a worm of grey powder before the *devi*'s picture.

The next day she made her way to the Ramakrishna Mission.
At the corner of the alley Vishwanathan sat as usual at his stall.
He leaped to his feet when he saw her, looking about for Shiva.

'Be strong, sister, everyone is here for you,' he reassured her
when she gave him the news, turning sadly to select the usual
coconut and place it in her hands.

'Savitri also died. One day she just did not wake up.' He
looked down at his feet and fell silent.

Telling him she would pick up the coconut on the way home,
Sita turned the corner into Norris Road. The Japanese language
school was gone and the Ramakrishna Mission had returned to
reclaim its premises, and both the boys' and the girls' schools
were preparing to reopen. In place of Swami Baswaranada there
was now Swami Vamadevananda, a lanky man with no flesh
on his bones, who had recently arrived from India. He already
knew of Shiva's long association with the mission and the work
Sita had done before joining the INA. When she explained the
limits of her education, he listened patiently.

'We need all the help we can get at this time, there is much to rebuild and reorganise.' He was clearly pleased by Sita's wish for a role in the life of the mission, and respectful of her status as a Rani of the Jhansi Regiment.

'Our small girls need a teacher for games; with all your army discipline, you can do that. Also, we have had some enquiries for basic extra tutoring for beginners in reading and writing, and this also you can do,' Swami said, already looking for ways to help her.

He ordered some tea and as they drank it he told her about the many destitute children of dead Indian labourers, men who had been forcibly taken to work on the Burma Siam railway. Memories of the men pulled from the mission's scaffolding and those in the labour camp flooded back to Sita as she listened.

'We have established a boys' orphanage now on land we have been given at Bartley Road but, as we are pressed for space, we are moving our Girls' Home to the Ramakrishna Mission in Penang; they have very spacious premises there. I have one more job for you; will you help us escort the children there later? As an ex-soldier, everyone would feel very safe with you,' Swami Vamadevanada chuckled.

Her new life was not dissimilar to what it had been after Shiva joined the INA, and she had lived for a while by herself. The mission was once more full of children, and Vishwanathan again saved her a coconut each day. On Norris Road, even though food was not plentifully available, hawkers and stalls reappeared to sell whatever they could. The black market played a role in everyone's lives, and rationing continued.

Each day Sita went into the mission and organised sports of various kinds for the girls, on the land behind the building, where Shiva had once given cricket lessons and been photographed with his pupils. The children enjoyed the obstacle courses she set up, simplified versions of those she had trained on in the Bras Basah camp. Although she washed and ironed all her old saris, for sports lessons and as much as she could, she continued wearing her old army trousers and a long loose shirt, happy with such comfortable attire. After school, there was the tutoring Swami Vamadevananda had arranged for her. At first it was just one or two small children, but with recommendations and referrals, the list began to grow. The money she earned from the mission was small, but all she wanted was to be able to pay her rent and maintain her independence.

Soon, there was a routine to anchor her to her new life. In the schoolroom the smell of chalk, the shrill chirp of children's voices and the hum of rote learning floating from the classrooms, carried her through each day. Slowly, the months passed, and like a shadow dwindling as the light increased, Shiva's ghost in the room appeared less intense, until Sita understood there was nothing now in her life but herself. It disturbed her to find she did not clearly recall her husband's face, but could only remember him feature by feature. When she peered into Shiva's small shaving mirror there was only her own reflection, everywhere she turned she came up against herself. In the room shadows lengthened then lightened, then lengthened again, turning each day seamlessly into the next.

At the weekends, she visited Rohini and Dev, who was ever

anxious to do his brotherly duty. Sita understood his need to fulfil what he saw as his role in her life, and for that reason silently endured Rohini's unspoken condemnation. Something about her, she soon realised, must appear a threat to her sister-in-law. The thought surprised her for, widowed for a second time, what did she have in her life but the sum of bitter experience?

'Do not tell people what you did in the war,' Rohini warned more than once, her eyes narrowing.

'Even though you learned to shoot like a man, you could not bring us independence,' she added, unable to hide her satisfaction at Sita's failure.

'There is to be a big trial at the Red Fort in Delhi. The British want to hang our INA men as traitors,' Dev informed her quietly as they sat together one evening.

Sita said nothing, afraid to appear too knowledgeable of events in the world in front of Rohini. Alone in her room, she listened to Shiva's radio, and knew that all of India was ablaze with the impending Red Fort trial. Jawaralal Nehru himself was to defend the INA prisoners, and the British were apprehensive of the potential revolt this might inspire. On the radio it was said that the British were even considering giving India her independence. If this happened, then all Shiva and Netaji had fought for would come to be. She leaned forward to comment on this to Dev, but then fell silent, swallowing down her opinion for fear of upsetting Rohini.

At last, the Girls' Home at the Ramakrishna Mission was ready to close, and the children prepared for the move to Penang.

Besides Sita, four volunteers from the mission, the wives of local merchants, were to accompany the large group of small orphans. The route by train and bus retraced part of Sita's previous journey to Burma. Once again, surrounded now by a carriage-ful of small children, the lurch and swing of the train rocked through Sita as she stared out into the greenness of the jungle and rubber estates, the plaintive bleat of the whistle coming to her. Somewhere in that emerald world Muni lived her life, and what it may now encompass was impossible to know.

Now that the war was over and they travelled without fear of attack, the journey, although long, was smooth and easy, and the children were eventually deposited without incident at the Ramakrishna Mission at Penang. On the journey back they were to stop for a day and a night in Kuala Lumpur, and Sita knew what she would do. Muni's plantation was not far from the town, and as soon as they arrived at their accommodation Sita made enquiries.

'It is outside town, but not too far. A bus goes past that estate,' they told her at the hotel.

In the early morning, telling her companions from the mission that she was going to visit a friend, she boarded a bus, taking with her some bread and fruit in case the journey was longer than anticipated. At last she found herself at her destination, and stood before a set of rusty metal gates bearing the name, McCarthy Rubber Estate. The gate hung askew, and the letters above it that had once been emblazoned in gold were now faded and indistinct. Beyond the gate Sita glimpsed a green and orderly world of regimented rubber trees.

26

SINGAPORE, 2000

On her desk the computer screen glowed like a hole in the dim room. Amita did not bother to put on the light. The dark was comforting, and besides, she had one of her headaches. It seemed she had only to think of Rishi for a headache to begin. She wished she could climb through the glowing screen on the desk and disappear into another dimension. Outside, in the dusk, cars were starting up in the car park of the Arts and Social Sciences building, a headlight moved through the shadows; people were going home to their dinner. If she did not put on the light, Parvati would think she had also gone home. There would be no telltale glow beneath the door, and if she knocked, Amita would not answer. Rishi had come to collect Parvati, she could hear his voice in the corridor asking her if this bag was to go down to the car, or that one?

'Ready?' He spoke impatiently.

Amita imagined him standing in the doorway of the room, holding his wife's canvas bag of books, while Parvati picked up the empty flask of coffee from the desk and her handbag from the top of the filing cabinet, and reached to switch off the light. Almost as Amita imagined these moves she heard the click of the door shutting. Now, with a small movement of her head,

Parvati would glance towards Amita's door, see the darkness and turn away.

There was the sound of their footsteps in the corridor, the tap of Parvati's heels and the soft squeak of Rishi's rubber soles stepping in unison, growing fainter, then silence as they passed out of the glass doors before the lift. It was Friday night, the weekend stretched ahead and Amita would not have to think about either Parvati or Rishi until the following Monday. Parvati's interviews with her mother were over. Once Sita's narrative had reached the point of the disbanding of the Rani of Jhansi Regiment at the end of the war, Parvati's research was finished. Amita was relieved that she no longer need welcome Parvati into her home, and at the university also, she distanced herself in whatever small way she could. She had finally replaced her electric kettle, and splurged on a can of superior ground coffee as well as a glass cafetiere. It meant she now had coffee as good as Parvati's, and there was less need to go to her room.

Yet, for how long could she find excuses not to go to Parvati's office? And what would she say when loose clothes no longer hid her pregnancy? The thought of Rishi stirred through her more often than she liked, and she felt again the abrasive rub of his cheek upon her. These unexpected evocations of memory appeared unasked, like drifting spectres, invisible until they collided with her. She would never ever tell Rishi or Parvati about the child. Yet she already anticipated the problems ahead. Who is the father, Parvati would ask, as Amita grew bigger, looking up at her with a teasing smile. What would she say? What could she say? It was no longer a question of not wanting to hurt Parvati. The situation was now a conundrum of monumental proportions; it was a maze of dead-end avenues, and in each waited a ravenous Minotaur. There was also her mother; Amita had forgotten about her mother; what would she say to her? There was no way to survive the situation alive. Any sensible woman would have chosen the freedom of abortion, a freedom she herself had once marched for in America, angrily shaking a placard above her head. Amita placed a hand on her belly, seeing again the dark grotto on the ultrasound, and at its centre the manikin, and knew the decision she had made was the right one.

A day earlier she had called the hospital, and cancelled the appointment for a termination, speaking to the receptionist at the appointments desk, seeing no need to bother Dr. Tay directly. As soon as she put the phone down she was filled with joy and knew she wanted this child, her daughter. At first, in a rush of excited planning, she browsed through advertisements for vacant posts in American universities, but soon realised that by the time such a move could be arranged, half a year or more might pass. The object of running away before anyone knew of her condition was already defeated by the time lapse involved. And how would she move, looking by then like a ship in full sail, and trailing an ageing mother, for she could not leave Sita behind alone?

In the car park of the AS5 building a car door slammed and, as she listened to Rishi start the engine of his small second-hand Honda, the phone on her desk began to ring. It was Jennifer, one of her MA students.

'We're waiting for you in the seminar room. Is everything all right?'

'Sorry, got delayed. On my way now,' Amita hurriedly replied.

She had forgotten the evening class and the students waiting for her now in the department of Political Science, a short distance away.

The Faculty of Arts and Social Sciences was spread out across Kent Ridge. The older buildings on campus, often layered down hillsides and connected by walkways and endless flights of stairs, were not for the elderly or infirm; lifts were few and far between. Amita's headache and swollen feet added to her general discomfort and she was forced to rest on the journey to the seminar room, leaning against some railings along one of the walkways between buildings. As she was not going back to her room in AS5 after the class, but straight home, she carried with her a bag of books and her laptop, and these now weighed heavily upon her. As she paused to regain her breath she turned to look over the railing at the gathering shadows in the wide spreading branches of a raintree, and an idea came to her. The Delhi conference where she would be giving a plenary was only a few weeks away, and she had planned to visit her mother's village at that time. Perhaps she could take Sita with her and stay on, fabricating an emergency reason for not returning, such as some sudden illness for her mother. She could prepare lessons for a substitute teacher at the university, and be in email contact with her students. After the baby was born she would return to Singapore, saying she had adopted a child in India. It was a mad plan, but it might work. As she bent to pick up her bag and continue her journey, she felt the sudden sprouting of new hope.

At last she reached the seminar room and opened the door to face her post-graduate students. She was relieved to see there were only three of them grouped around the table tonight, two Indian girls, Shanti and Renu, and Jennifer, the Chinese girl who had called her earlier, the other two students in the group not having shown up.

Renu, a plump girl with an eagerness that endeared her to Amita and annoyed her in equal measure, had received funding to go to a conference in Manila to present a paper in a few weeks. In class the previous week Amita had agreed that tonight Renu would read her paper, and they would discuss it in class. Amita sank down on a chair in relief, immediately kicking off her tight shoes beneath the table, and plumped her bag down on the floor beside her. Not much would be demanded of her this evening, and for this she was grateful, as the energy she had to invest in the class was diminishing by the minute.

Renu's paper, *Discardable Daughters: Dowry Deaths in India*, was one she had personally steered the girl towards, yet now she was overcome by a deep need to hear no more on this subject or any other to do with Indian society's attitudes towards women. The girl's work was competent, but without the edge Amita expected from her students, and her papers were always long on quotes and short on argument.

As Renu began to read, Amita sighed and sat back in her chair, and although she could not close her eyes, prepared to quietly disassociate herself. She had only to listen and later to guide the discussion. Renu was not a good reader, her voice droned on in an unchanging tone, and Amita struggled to stay alert. Her head was thumping now in a sickening way. As she bent down to her bag to pull out the bottle of water she always carried, her head reeled. She was probably dehydrated, and had not drunk enough water, Amita thought. The bottle was still a third full, while usually it was empty by the end of the day. With an effort she straightened up and fumbled with the cap, lifting the bottle to her lips, but was suddenly aware that the water was spilling over her shirt. Her body had stiffened, her back and neck arched rigidly, and she found she could not move. When she tried to cry out, her voice was weighed down under a stone at the base of her throat, and it was difficult to breathe. Her hand began shaking and the bottle fell, more water spilling over her lap and onto the floor. Beneath the table her feet seemed to be jerking about uncontrollably.

'Prof...Prof...'

The girls clustered around her, she heard their voices calling to her as if from a great distance.

'Prof...Prof...'

'I'm all right. I'm all right.'

She struggled to sit upright as the girls fussed about her. Her feet were firmly on the floor again and the spasm in her back was gone. Whatever had happened to her, it was over. Her head was still thumping as if a rock inside it was bouncing around, but she had control of herself once again. About her the girls were trying to mop her wet clothes with tissues. Someone thrust a paper cup of water into her hands, and she sipped slowly. Although all she wanted to do was lie down on the floor and go to sleep, she forced herself to speak.

'Let's continue.' She insisted; she was weak and shaky, but she was all right.

When at last she arrived home her mother was pottering about the kitchen, taking out pans to warm the food she had cooked earlier in the day with the help of Joyce. The familiar aroma of spices drifted on the air, and Amita put down her bag and immediately took over the warming of the food. Settling her mother at the table, she placed the dishes of food before her.

'You shouldn't wait for me for dinner, especially on my late days. Tonight I'm not hungry, I had something to eat in the canteen earlier,' she lied, spooning food onto her mother's plate. She could not say that the smell of spices nauseated her, and pregnancy left her exhausted.

'The hospital called. You did not keep your appointment. They have given you another on Monday afternoon. Joyce wrote it all down.' Her mother pushed a scrap of paper across the table with the new appointment time and a phone number to ring.

Amita lay down on her bed, and stared up at the stain on the ceiling. The dark bruise of dampness could be imagined in many different ways, the fleshy profile of a face, a meandering map of China, anything one wanted, yet she could see nothing but an incubus hovering above her. If Dr. Tay had given her a new appointment for Monday afternoon, it seemed her message to cancel the termination had not got through to him. She would have to phone the appointments line again first thing on Monday morning.

At 9.30 am on Monday, as Amita settled at her desk with a mug of coffee made with her new electric kettle and glass cafetiere, and prepared to chart the day ahead, Dr. Tay's nurse called, to question the cancelled appointment.

'I left a message that I had changed my mind; I no longer want a termination.' Amita sounded as annoyed as she felt.

'Dr. Tay would still like to see you to discuss things with you, so please come in,' the nurse replied.

Monday was always a busy day with back-to-back classes until mid-afternoon, but she reluctantly agreed to the last afternoon appointment before the clinic closed. When the time came, she made her way to the hospital by shuttle bus and marched down the long corridor to the clinic, her feet swelling again in her shoes, thinking of ways to politely rebuke Dr. Tay for making her return for the formality of registering her decision with him.

Dr. Tay looked up from his desk as Amita entered his consulting room, and she noted he was not as young as she had first thought. Grey hair already flecked his temples, deep lines ran from his nose to his mouth, and even his affability, Amita decided,was no more than a professional ploy.

'I left a message that I had changed my mind. I have decided I want to have the baby.' She spoke firmly, in an effort to convey how inconvenient she found this visit.

Dr. Tay nodded absently and looked down at his notes, as if what she said was of little importance.

'It's not about your decision, it's about the result of your urine test. We found high levels of protein.' He looked up, settling his eyes upon her, leaning back to rest his elbows on the arms of his chair.

'What does that mean?' Amita frowned; she had had enough unpalatable surprises recently in this hospital.

'You have something called Preeclampsia. Any headaches, swollen feet or ankles?' Dr. Tay's eyes remained upon her.

'Isn't that usual when you are pregnant? What is this about?' Amita leaned forward in her chair. She disliked not knowing what Dr Tay was talking about, and the balance of knowledge being all on his side.

'It's also called Toxemia; the placenta doesn't function properly. We see it most often in first time pregnancies, and in women who have children later in life.' Dr. Tay spoke without emotion, conveying facts.

'What is the treatment?' Amita demanded.

'Any dizziness, muscle spasms, those sort of things; seizures?' Dr. Tay countered.

'Seizures? There was some dizziness and a muscle spasm the other day. What's the treatment?' she repeated impatiently; everything nowadays was treatable.

'As a temporary measure we can control the high blood pressure and hope to prevent another seizure, but this is a life threatening condition.' Dr. Tay spoke slowly, his eyes still upon her.

'I told you I have changed my mind. I will do whatever I have to do, to have the baby.'

She felt suddenly vulnerable, without any defence before whatever it was she sensed was now coming towards her. Dr. Tay rested his arms on the desk and began to speak again in a deliberate manner.

'I don't think you understand, this is a life threatening condition. All your levels are very high. Preeclampsia is fatal to the foetus; this may already have happened. And your own life is now in danger. Already you appear to have had a mild seizure.'

'Can't it be cured, or treated?' She heard the bleating plea in her voice.

'The only cure is to deliver the foetus.' Dr. Tay spoke without emotion.

Amita had the feeling she was unravelling, like a ball of string unrolling across a floor. Dr. Tay sat before her across the desk, giving her time to digest the things he was saying before he spoke again.

'In the beginning you wanted a termination, that was your first option; we even set the date. Now it is your only option. Stroke, liver damage, kidney failure, respiratory distress; this is what will begin to happen, and you could lose your life if you delay. I suggest you come in tomorrow for the procedure.'

She struggled to understand, staring blankly at him, meeting his detached gaze.

27

The gates to the McCarthy Rubber Estate stood open upon a narrow track leading to the gatehouse a short distance away. Sita made her way to the building, where a turbaned Sikh directed her to a Tamil supervisor working at a desk.

'No casual visitor is allowed into the estate,' the man told her, looking up with a frown from his papers.

'I have come from so far,' Sita replied.

'What is your friend's name?' The man asked impatiently.

'Muni…Muniamma…' She had no other name with which to identify Muni.

'Here all women are called Muniamma.' The supervisor lowered his head to his work again.

'We were in the INA together, in the Rani of Jhansi Regiment,' Sita added, seeking a way to identify Muni. The supervisor raised his head immediately, and his expression changed.

'You were with Netaji, you fought for India?' With a loud deferential scraping of his chair, he stood up.

'Do you know my friend?' Sita asked again.

'She is Muniamma Ramaiah, the wife of the *kangani* rubber tapper, Ramaiah.'

'How can I find her?' Sita asked, ignoring the man's now curious gaze.

'I will take you to her. I am Gopal,' he informed her.

Sita followed the man to an old jeep parked outside the guardhouse, and climbed into the vehicle beside him. With a grate of gears Gopal started the engine and they bumped forward over the rutted track. Turning to Sita as he drove, he offered advice in a confidential voice.

'I am a great admirer of Netaji, but do not tell anyone here you were with him in the war; it is safer nowadays to remain quiet. The British are back in charge of this estate, and they're not happy with the people who fought against them, or sided with the Japanese.'

Sita stared out of the window at the green and orderly world of the plantation. Rubber trees were planted so closely together that in places the dark tangle of branches deterred the sun, the ground dappled with fingers of light.

'I do not believe Netaji is dead. Soon he will return to lead us again,' Gopal speculated, as the jeep bounced over the uneven track deeper into the estate.

The constant sound of crickets and cicadas whirred in Sita's ears. Between the trees, crouching rows of women and children could be seen, clearing the ground of weeds, moving forward in unison on their haunches. On each tree a large cup was attached to the trunk, to collect the white sap bleeding from incisions in its bark. An unpleasant stench pervaded the place, and grew stronger the deeper they drove into the estate.

'It's the latex,' Gopal explained as Sita wrinkled up her nose in distaste.

'Muniamma Ramaiah should be in this area,' he said at last, slowing the jeep. Sita leaned forward expectantly, scanning the rows of weeding women, but could not see Muni. Finally, Gopal stopped the vehicle and jumped down.

'Muniamma Ramaiah. Muniamma Ramaiah,' He cupped his hand to his mouth and called loudly.

As Sita climbed out of the vehicle the labouring women and children looked up, sitting back on their heels, leaving their weeding to follow events. Slowly, a figure emerged, walking towards them through the trees, stepping carefully and carrying a metal pail. Muni wore a white blouse and a deep pink sari tied high above her ankles in a workman like way, and as she drew near, Sita saw she was pregnant. Soon she stood silently before Sita, hanging her head in the same dejected manner Sita remembered from that first day in the Bras Basah camp. Nothing about her indicated she was pleased to see Sita.

'I will come for you later at Ramaiah's house. The last bus passes by in the late afternoon, and if you miss it, there is nothing until tomorrow,' Gopal told Sita as he climbed back into the jeep and drove off.

The sound of the vehicle grew distant and the sawing of crickets and the whirr of cicadas filled Sita's ears again. The women and children continued to observe her with interest, the task of weeding forgotten.

'I have work to finish,' Muni announced in a low voice, picking up her bucket and turning away abruptly.

Sita stared after her, unsure if this was an invitation to follow
or an outright rejection. In the end she hurried after Muni, who
walked ahead, pausing before a tree to lift off the collecting cup
and pour the thick sticky latex into the metal bucket. Without
turning, her back still to Sita, she suddenly began to speak.

'The sun is high. I must collect the latex. The trees give sap
only until noon; they are cut early in the morning, for that
is when they will bleed. Only men do that cutting work; we
women collect latex and do weeding.'

'You're having a baby,' Sita interrupted, unable to stay silent
any longer.

'After I get the latex from all my trees, I have to take it to
the factory. There they roll it out through a big mangle, and
then they smoke and dry it. That is the smell you are smelling
everywhere.'

Muni continued with her work, walking off towards the next
tree, making no attempt to respond to Sita's observation. Sita
followed at a distance, staring at the bony nodules of Muni's spine
beneath the white blouse, her delicate neck and slight, sloping
shoulders. Everything that was familiar about her was made
unfamiliar now by the swell of her body and the child she carried.
The pregnancy was quite advanced, and the child must already
be kicking inside her, Sita thought, as she hurried after her. They
entered an area of deeper gloom, where the trees seemed larger
and more mature, their branches forming a tangled ceiling. The
gang of weeding women and children had been left behind and,
looking furtively around to check that no one was near, Muni
walked towards Sita and began to speak in a low tense voice.

'Just like I told you they would, my family forced me to marry. He is one of the *kangani* on the estate. They are the ones who recruit and control all the labour. Men come here from India to work, to make money and go home, but they become slaves to the *kangani*, because they are never free of debt to them; they never go home. For women it is worse,' Muni whispered.

Her hair had grown and was plaited in two stubby braids pulled forward over her shoulders. Sita stepped forward in concern, but Muni moved away.

'I am his third wife.' She spat out the words bitterly.

'Where do you live?' Sita asked.

Muni pointed through the trees to a line of dilapidated *attap* huts raised upon stilts, and a slightly larger but no less dilapidated dwelling set slightly apart from the others. Chickens roamed around at the base of the huts, a rusty bicycle was propped up against some steps, old buckets stacked up beside it. A clump of banana trees grew to one side and Sita remembered Muni's fear on the route march of the evil *pontianak* that supposedly lived in banana trees.

'Soon we break for lunch. I will take you there. He will not return until later when he is full of toddy, and before he returns you must go,' Muni insisted, turning back to her work, falling silent again.

Finally, when her bucket was full of the sticky white latex, Muni lugged the heavy pail to the factory. Sita gripped one side of the handle, walking silently beside Muni through the avenues of trees towards the low factory building. Muni's breath came in quick gasps and Sita's eyes kept slipping to the gentle swell of her pregnancy. She remembered her mother's swollen body silhouetted against the sun-filled doorway of the house in the village.

At last they reached the factory. The stench from the 'smoke house' coated the air with a reek that made Sita choke. They joined a queue of Tamil women, all carrying similar buckets of latex, all of whom turned to observe Sita curiously. Some of the women called out a greeting and Sita acknowledged them with a smile, while Muni frowned sourly. Finally, they reached the factory door and handed in the pail.

'Are those women your friends?' Sita asked as they walked towards the wooden huts where Muni lived. At Sita's question Muni turned on her angrily.

'I do not have friends here; those women laugh at me. They say, "You ran away to join the army! Thought a woman could be like a man! Went to bring us independence, but instead the British came back!" The other girls from this estate who joined the army have all gone away for one reason or another. I am the only one left here.'

'Gopal admires Netaji,' Sita replied in a low voice, remembering the man's advice not to mention the Rani of Jhansi Regiment.

'The women are jealous of what I did, and the men do not like that I can shoot and fight. If we had won the war and got independence for India, it would be different. The British manager sahibs are rude to me. They say if I were a man I would have been shot. My husband makes fun of me too. "You are no longer a soldier, now you are a wife." He laughs at me.' Muni's expression was fierce with the injustices piled upon her.

They reached the line of wooden huts and climbed the ladder to the door of the largest dwelling. A smell of old wood impregnated with the odours of stale food and creosol filled the dark hot house. At first Sita was blinded after the brightness outside, it took a moment to adjust to the dim interior. Muni wedged open the door and threw the window shutters wide, and light flooded in, illuminating a scuffed plank floor.

'Too many mosquitoes in this place! The manager sahibs give us quinine, but often the supply runs out and they don't bother to give us more. My husband's first wife died of malaria, the second in childbirth, and his children also died; they were both girls,' Muni looked down apprehensively at the swell of her body.

'If he controls the workers, he must be an important man,' Sita replied, trying to make conversation. The easy companionship she remembered with Muni had vanished, formality encased all that had been familiar between them.

'He was also once a worker on this estate. He is not an important *kangani*; he controls only a small number of men. He drinks and makes everyone terrified of him.' Muni's voice was bitter.

She walked over to an earthenware water jar, filled a glass and gave it to Sita to drink, while she heated the simple food she had cooked early in the morning on a small spirit stove. Sita waited, sitting cross-legged on the floor in a corner, sipping the tepid water. The room was depressing, the cheap wooden planks of the floor and walls were full of cracks, through which insects crawled and light edged in. A dirty mosquito net hung over a string bed, and two battered chairs and a table occupied a corner. The place could not throw off its threadbare melancholy, and as she stared out of the window at the broad leaves of the banana trees outside, Sita sensed the fear and despair Muni must feel.

After they ate, Muni sat down beside Sita and, reaching for a cloth bag, pulled out a ball of thread and a crochet needle, and began knitting in a concentrated manner, head bent to her work to avoid Sita's gaze.

'It's a jacket for the baby,' she whispered.

'Does he beat you?' Sita remembered her father's violence.

The words sprang from her as she searched for a way to shatter the wall Muni had built between them. Muni drew a startled breath and looked up.

'Does he?' Sita repeated, seeing again her mother's cowed face, remembering the force of her father's hand coming down upon her as a child, and the metallic taste of blood on her tongue.

'It is only when he has had too much toddy. Otherwise, he is …all right to me.' Muni stumbled over the words and Sita knew she wished she could say her husband was a kind man, but could not lie and yet did not wish to be disloyal.

'Come back with me to Singapore,' Sita urged.

'I cannot leave…not now.' Muni laid a hand upon her belly. 'He wants a boy from me,' she whispered.

'And if it's a girl?' Sita asked, a familiar dark feeling running through her.

'He says he will kick it out of me.'

Muni reached out a hand and gripped Sita's wrist, darting quick glances at the door, as if expecting her husband to return even as they spoke. From outside the calls of birds and the din of cicadas came to them. It was as if Muni's old world had risen up, animal-like, to claim her again, and she had retreated into that darkness from which, briefly, she had emerged to taste a different life. Perhaps, if Shiva had not died, she too might have found her old life waiting to reclaim her, just as it had repossessed Muni, Sita thought. Instead, with his death, Shiva had released her.

Soon, Gopal's jeep was heard drawing to a halt outside and Muni dropped Sita's hand, jumping up, her stress easing into relief now that she knew Sita would soon be gone. Sita too was filled with relief, impatient now to be free of the darkness she sensed about Muni. She had a little money and pressed this into Muni's hand.

'Use it for the baby,' she instructed as she climbed into Gopal's jeep.

She did not look back as the vehicle bounced away over the uneven ground. Gopal turned his head to glance at her, as if he understood her disappointment.

'Don't worry. She'll be all right. Ramaiah gets drunk but he is not a bad man, in fact he is better than many. If she has a boy he will be happy with her.'

'And if she has a girl?' Sita inquired.

At the wheel of the jeep Gopal shrugged, and sighed.

28

Amita let herself into the flat as silently as she could. In the kitchen she heard Sita talking to Joyce, the sound of onions being chopped on a wooden board, the clank of a pan, a gushing of water. Closing the door of her room, she lay down on the bed. A breeze blew in through the half open window, and she was grateful for its cool touch on her face. Above her the ghostly manikin gazed down from the ceiling as always, and she turned her head away. It was over. They had given her some anaesthetic and she had known nothing about it. One moment the child was within her, and the next it was gone. Afterwards, they kept her in a curtained cubicle for a few hours. Finally, Dr. Tay came to see her and told her to go home, and rest.

'Tomorrow is a national holiday, and then you have the weekend. By Monday you'll be fine. It will all be behind you.'

She began to cry, and seeing her tears he paused, a hand on the curtain, turning a kindly face to her.

'There was no option,' he reminded her.

Then, he was gone, pulling the flimsy screen back into place behind him.

No option. The words kept repeating in her mind. No option, and probable death for them both if she had done

nothing. In her distress she had not thought to ask about the
child's remains. On the ultrasound picture she had seen limbs
and a head. What had they done with that tiny body? Would
they have given it to her if she had asked, could she have
cremated it with some kind of rite? Instead, because she had
not even thought to inquire about her child, it would have been
tipped into the hospital incinerator along with other human
detritus. The thought troubled her painfully and would not let
her free, as if the child reproached her in an invisible way.

Some months ago she had seen a television documentary
about the practice in Japan of appeasing the souls of aborted
foetuses, or those miscarried or stillborn. Offerings were made
to a bodhisattva who was believed to protect these unborn
children. Statues of Jizo were often small with childlike faces,
and were adorned by bereaved mothers with red bibs and
caps for warmth in the afterlife. Such statues were everywhere
in Japan, and Amita knew now that they answered a need to
comfort not just the soul of the lost foetus, but the guilt-ridden,
grieving mother as well.

Somehow, she must find a way to hide what she was living
through from her own mother. She did not think she had the
strength to face the shock and distress Sita would feel at her
wanton behaviour, and its consequences. Her mother would
immediately light incense and say prayers before the *devi*, and
appeal to the goddess on behalf of her apostate daughter. To her
mother's way of thinking, Amita had now imperilled her karmic
progress by an act of violence, and also thwarted the karmic
evolution of another soul. In her present fragile condition,

Amita felt unable to argue her way out of the situation in the usual manner.

From the kitchen the clank of pans came to her. Whatever was being prepared must now have been cooked, for there was the clink of crockery as Joyce set the table and settled Sita to her lunch, then the echo of her goodbye and the shutting of the door. Amita closed her eyes and fell into a fitful sleep.

She did not know how long she slept, but a crack of thunder woke her. The usual tropical afternoon storm had arrived, and wind whistled through the flat, sweeping up the curtains at the window. The sky was dark and turbulent, rain drummed on the glass and splattered through the open pane. For a moment Amita, still struggling to surface from sleep, saw again the rain and lightning framed in a window in Amsterdam, but she shook the image away. From beyond the door there was the sound of her mother hurrying to shut windows she had earlier opened, and then her footsteps coming down the passage. The door to Amita's room was thrown open and Sita burst in, crossing the floor to close the window. Turning back into the room, Sita stared in shock at the sight of Amita on the bed.

'Came home early, not feeling well,' Amita hastily swung her feet off the bed and stood up.

Then, feeling the discomfort of dampness upon her, she looked down to see her slacks and the bed sheets were wet with blood. Her mother stared at her in alarm.

'I'm all right. Don't worry.'

Amita heard the brusqueness in her voice, and saw her mother's startled expression. Pushing past her, Amita paused before the cupboard to pull out clean underwear and trousers, then made her way to the bathroom.

When she returned, Sita was already changing the soiled linen, bent over the bed, frail and elderly, smoothing clean sheets into place, tucking in the corners with a military precision learned long ago in the army.

'What's wrong, something is wrong?' In her anxiety, Sita sounded accusatory.

'Nothing is wrong,' Amita heard the anger in her voice.

Her legs were weak, and a deep aching pain flooded through her to meet that other ache she could not define, but which was worse than any bodily wound. She needed to lie down.

'Come,' Sita hurried forward, taking her arm, helping her to the bed.

Amita shook herself free of her mother's touch, rounding upon her, taking no notice of her stricken face. In all the years they had lived together she had never raised her voice to her mother like this, but something had been released that she could not put back, and she heard her voice growing louder.

'It's nothing; leave me alone. What do you know of my life?'

Her mother stared at her in shock, lips parted and seemingly lost for words. Amita continued shouting, thrusting her face near Sita.

'I wanted it. That's what's strange, that's what I don't understand. I wanted to keep it. I didn't want this to happen, but we would both have died if I had not got rid of it. It was a girl, they told me it was a girl.' The words burst out, unstoppable, thrown up from deep within her.

Her mother sat down abruptly on a chair as Amita continued to shout, tears streaming down her face.

'It was my fault. I wanted this to happen. I didn't know I wanted it to happen, but I did. Only I didn't think it would end like this.' She could not stop the babble, or the sobs that shuddered through her.

Sita stared fixedly at her daughter, then, standing up, she placed a hand on Amita's arm, pushing her gently towards the bed.

'Rest,' she said.

'Go away. Leave me alone. How can I rest? What would *you* know?' Amita yelled.

'I do know,' Sita answered, her face filled with such raw emotion that Amita fell silent.

'I too lost a child. I wanted to be a good wife, to give him a boy, and I prayed and prayed, but it was a girl. He thought I had done it deliberately, but I did not. It just happened. Afterwards he would not speak to me.'

She remembered Shiva's expression as he looked down at her. She remembered the press of Uma's hand on her stomach, and the metal bowl of bloodied newspaper that held the remains of her child. Amita stared silently at her mother.

'I have never told this to anyone before,' Sita whispered, sitting down on the chair again.

'And then you had me? Another girl. What did he say to that?' For a moment Amita forgot her own grief and gazed at her mother.

It had never occurred to Amita that her father might not have wanted her, or that he would have preferred a boy. Something dense and suffocating seemed to be closing in about her. If the rain were not still drumming heavily upon the glass, she would have opened the window for air.

'That is another story,' her mother whispered, her eyes fixed upon her hands.

29
Singapore, 1948

When Sita returned from Penang, the routine of life at the Ramakrishna mission soon claimed her again. Swami Vamadevananda arranged for her to give evening classes to a group of women who had once worked on the rubber plantations. Their husbands had now found jobs in Singapore in the booming construction industry, as the city cleared up the damage of war. Although the girls' orphanage had moved to Penang, the boys' school remained, and Sita continued with her teaching and tutoring duties.

The year ended, and a new year arrived. As the weeks went by Sita thought of Muni growing and swelling as the birth of her child drew near. Muni's thin and fearful face was always before her, and she knew she must return to the rubber estate again. After a few months, she made an excuse to Dev and Rohini, cancelling her usual weekend visit to them, and instead took an overnight bus to Kuala Lumpur. The Ramakrishna Mission helped her buy a ticket, and along with food for the journey, she bought some packets of biscuits and a sari for Muni, plus a small dress and cotton shawl for the baby, and tied everything up in a carrying cloth.

The long distance bus was half-empty, and Sita settled down

for the night, stretching her legs out on the empty seat beside her. In the early morning the bus would halt in a town not far from Muni's plantation. From there a local bus would take Sita on to the nearby McCarthy Rubber Estate. Until that moment she had not realised how much the anticipation of the journey had tired her. Each sway and bump of the road rocked her deeper into sleep, and what she dreamed that night stayed in her mind, as a portal through which she passed into a new life. Nothing was ever the same again.

In her dream, she stood as her adult self beside the river in her childhood village, the muddy tide rippling past her. Gazing into the opaque water, she imagined she saw another river beneath the river, where her sister lived, still waiting for her after so many years. Stepping into the water, she plunged an arm beneath the surface, and grasped the hand she knew she would find stretched out to her there. Cold fingers gripped her own in a vice-like hold and, leaning back on her heel to better balance the weight that now dragged on her arm, she pulled and heaved until at last there was an abrupt lightening, like an anchor breaking free of its mooring. Then, in a great shower of water the body she clasped so tightly by the hand surfaced into the sunlight. Yet, instead of her sister's face, it was Muni she saw before her, laughing, dripping, and carrying a baby in her arms.

Sita woke with a start as the bus changed gear, her heart thumping in shock. Even as she struggled back into consciousness, the images rebounded through her, as if she had returned from visiting a strange and sinister landscape.

Morning light was already easing away the darkness in the bus.
Sita took a sip of water from the flask she carried, and tried to
keep calm.

Eventually, she arrived at her destination and changed to the
local bus that would take her to McCarthy Rubber Estate. The
bus was an ancient rattling vehicle crowded with Tamil labourers
travelling from one estate to another, or to the small kampongs
along the route. Sita found a seat next to an old woman with a
bamboo coop of chickens, her basket of birds crammed into the
narrow space of the aisle. The imprisoned chickens were piled
one upon another in three suffocating layers, unable to move,
and clucking in discomfort. The heat of the day seeped through
the metal roof of the vehicle as it lurched forward, but a breeze
blew on her face through the open windows, and Sita welcomed
it with relief. On either side of the road green walls of vegetation
pressed upon them.

Eventually, Sita stood again before the rusted gates of the
McCarthy Rubber Estate, but the Sikh guards at the gatehouse
told her Gopal was off sick.

'You were in the INA with Ramaiah's wife,' the man
remembered, pointing her in the direction of Muni's house, but
not offering to drive her there as Gopal had done.

Sita set off through the rows of trees, the emerald world
swallowing her again in its shadows. Wherever she looked,
identical lines of trees radiated out around her, so that at
times she stopped, unsure of her direction. In places the sun
speared the thick foliage, illuminating everything beneath with
a pale jade light. Once more the whirring din of cicadas and

crickets and the shrill cries of birds came to her. Then, at last in the distance she saw the line of the *attap*-roofed houses and, relieved, quickened her pace towards them.

The huts were raised up several feet upon stilts, for safety from snakes and wild animals. A group of women squatted below the houses, chatting and peeling vegetables, chickens picked the ground about them, a rooster crowed. Sita nodded a greeting to the women, and ignoring their curious glances, climbed the stair to Muni's house, knowing her progress was being silently followed. The door stood ajar and she pushed it open apprehensively, wondering in what condition she would find Muni, hoping her husband, Ramaiah, would be absent as before. As she stepped out of the bright sunlight into the dim interior of the house, she was momentarily blinded, just as she had been before. Searching the shadowy space for Muni, trying to adjust to the sudden transition of light, she saw a figure rise from a chair in a corner.

'Are you there?' Sita stepped forward in relief.

'You're late. Already one hour I am waiting here for you.'

Ramaiah moved angrily towards her. His thick muscular body had the energy of a coiled spring, and Sita stepped back in alarm. He gestured to the back of the room, glowering at Sita beneath his bushy eyebrows.

'Everything you need is there. I have work to do, I cannot wait here any longer, like a woman with nothing to do.'

He wore a stained white shirt, beneath which his belly bulged over a green checked sarong. He pushed roughly past her, and she saw the grey stubble of his cheeks and caught the smell of alcohol. As he descended the steps he called to the women peeling vegetables below.

'See that she does her job and gets out of here quickly.'

Sita stared after him in confusion, hoping to see Muni's slight form materialise from a dark corner of the room. The sour smell of the place settled about her again.

'Muni,' she called, but no answer came.

Instead, from behind her she heard a whimper, and turning, saw a cardboard box on the floor, within which something writhed and turned. Stepping forward, Sita bent to pull back an old sheet heaped up in the box and immediately a small face was visible. As she gazed at the child it began to scream, lips curled back over toothless gums. Sita stared into the dark hole of its open mouth and marvelled that something so small could make a noise so deafening. A fetid odour rose from the baby, and Sita turned away, wanting to retch. The child lay naked in its own filth, excrement encrusting her small buttocks, her delicate female parts sore and inflamed.

'Muni.'

Sita searched the room again, still hoping to see Muni emerge before her. As she stared down at the screaming child, unsure of what to do, the door opened and the women she had seen below, peeling vegetables, hurried into the room. A plump elderly matron in a green sari stepped forward.

'Take the baby away quickly. Ramaiah is angry, and when he is angry nobody knows what he will do. He says he will turn her face into the mud, or leave her in the jungle for snakes or wild animals. Already, he has tried to drown her in a bucket of water, but we came in at that moment and persuaded him to let her live. First that no-good wife of his gives him a girl, and then she dies on him as well. If the child was a boy he would not be so angry, he would keep a son with him, bring him up.' The women shook their heads sorrowfully.

'Muni?' Sita asked, bracing herself for what she must hear. A younger woman with a scar through her eyebrow spoke up.

'We tried to help her but nothing could save her. They cremated her body the day before yesterday. So many hours she was in labour. The child tore her apart to get out. The white manager sahib has told Ramaiah to put the baby in an orphanage. We were looking for a wet nurse, but no one wants to nurse a She-devil that killed its mother! No one will give their milk to her for fear she will kill them too.'

The plump woman stepped forward again to explain. 'Another woman from your orphanage came yesterday, she left some evaporated milk and a baby bottle and fed the child too before she left. Since then no one has fed her, and she is hungry. We are happy to help, but Ramaiah does not want it.' They stood in a circle around Sita, looking down at the screaming child.

'We'll feed her before you take her away to the orphanage,' another woman offered.

All the time the women talked, the baby continued to scream and Sita wondered again how so much distress could be voiced with so much gusto by something so small.

'Poor thing, she is so hungry. Ramaiah does not care and refuses to feed her. Let her starve to death, he shouted at us when we tried to help,' the woman with the scarred eyebrow remarked.

Another woman came forward with a bowl of water and, picking up the baby, began to sponge her. Yet another appeared with some oil to soothe her inflamed skin. Held against the warmth of a body and hushed and petted, the child quietened, the occasional sob still choking through her small frame. The women fussed about the baby, cleaning the fetid crust from her buttocks, finding a cloth to wrap about her hips. Sita hurried to untie her carrying bag, and gave the women the small dress and the shawl she had bought for the child.

'That Muniamma was strange. Went to war to fight for India like a man. Thought she was so clever, but what did she get, the British back here, and Ramaiah for a husband? Now she is dead, not like a soldier, but in childbirth like any other woman.' The plump woman gave a humourless laugh.

'A woman cannot escape her fate,' another sighed.

'We'll get the child ready, and make up the milk. That pitcher is full of boiled water. Muni always kept clean water ready. She's gone, but the water she boiled is still there for her daughter.' The plump woman sighed sadly.

Sita stood straight and still, swallowing each shock the women threw at her. She wanted to tell them she was not the woman from the orphanage, but something held her back. Instead, she moved to the where the earthenware water jar sat on a stool in a corner of the room. When she had worked in the first aid tent at Farrer Park there had been plenty of babies who had needed feeding, and she knew what to do. As she turned the tap on the water jar, diluting the evaporated milk, filling up the bottle, she was acutely aware that it was Muni who had filled the water she now drew, that the screaming child behind her had grown from Muni's own flesh and blood. As she straightened up, she caught sight of a pile of folded clothes in a corner, and saw the edge of the pink sari Muni had worn on Sita's last visit to the estate.

'This is what you want,' the plump woman laughed kindly, picking up the child, pushing the teat of the bottle into the baby's ravenous mouth. The child quietened immediately, sucking as if her life depended upon it. Sita stood behind the woman, and looking down at the child's tiny face searched for a glimpse of Muni, but saw only the squashed features of a newborn, its jaws clenched tight around the teat of the bottle. She put out a hand, and immediately the tiny fingers curled around her own with a determination that surprised her.

At last the baby would drink no more and fell asleep, and the woman thrust her into Sita's arms. The child slumped against her shoulder, replete, its slight weight resting in the palm of Sita's hand as she held its tiny body against her. The women were packing up the remaining bottles of milk, and the small squares of cloth to wrap about the child's tiny hips that Muni had cut and prepared.

I am not from the orphanage. She knew she must tell them now, but the words would still not form in her mouth. Against her neck she felt the dampness of the child's wet mouth, and heard the gurgle of a belch as she rubbed its back.

As she changed the child from one shoulder to another,

there was the sudden sound of hurried steps outside, then the wild shout of Ramaiah's voice.

'She's not from the orphanage,' Ramaiah flung open the screen door and burst into the room to stand before Sita, fury bristling from him.

'Take the child from her,' he ordered.

The plump matron, her face filled with confusion, hurried forward to lift the child from Sita's arms.

'Why are you here? Come to steal my child from me? Get out.' Ramaiah ordered, his voice roaring in Sita's ears.

He advanced towards Sita as the women cowered helplessly to one side. The baby began to whimper again, the noise quickly rising to a scream.

'I know who you are. They told me at the guardhouse. You're that INA friend who filled her head with no-good ideas. An army is for men, not for women. Get out of here.'

Sita backed out of the door, stumbling down the steps. Ramaiah stood above her in the open door, a tall thickset man in his fifties, throwing the gifts and food she had brought for Muni after her down the steps.

'I told her to give me a boy. What use is a girl, a rope round your neck waiting to hang you, with her need for dowry? I told her, if it's a girl, I don't want to see her, make sure she dies at birth.'

In her haste Sita tripped on the bottom step, and would have sprawled on the grass if she had not clung to the splintered wooden rail. Above her Ramaiah continued to shout, and behind him the baby screamed.

'Stop it, stop it screaming,' he yelled at the women, turning back into the house.

Sita scooped up her belongings, tying them together in the carrying cloth, and hurried away, her eyes blinded by tears, unable to control the sobs that rose up and burst from her. In her hand the bundle of food and gifts bumped against her knee. Her arms still carried the memory of Muni's child, the small head, the fragile bones. She walked forward in a daze, past the guardhouse and then out of the rusty gates, arriving at last at the bus stop. The road was deserted, and she sat down on a rough wooden bench to wait, not knowing or caring now when the next bus would arrive. The heat of the day pressed upon her. An emerald green tree snake moved sinuously across the road towards her, and she stared at it unmoved, feeling nothing as it slipped into the undergrowth behind the bench.

30

Sita dared not ask her daughter the exact nature of all she had just experienced, but clearly she had had a miscarriage, or even an abortion. This knowledge released such a rush of buried emotion in Sita that she gripped the chair to steady herself. The past swung powerfully before her, and she knew she could not ignore where it was leading her. Obeying an inexplicable impulse, she started up from the chair and hurried out of the room. Amita stared after her, already regretting the things she had disclosed, and filled with discomfort at her mother's own revelations.

From Sita's bedroom Amita heard the sound of drawers opening and shutting. Soon her mother returned with a small, shapeless brown paper package held loosely together with string, and placed it in Amita's hands. The package was soft, the wrapping paper old and creased, limp from a life of repeated use. Amita frowned, impatient with whatever game it was her mother now wished to play. She had had enough for one day; all she wanted to do was sleep.

Sita waited in apprehension, listening to the rustling of paper in her daughter's hands. Everything was whittled away before her now, only the truth was left to tell. And she must tell it now, before courage deserted her again.

'What's this?' Amita demanded in exasperation, pulling the limp string off the package, too exhausted to humour her mother any further.

'Open it,' Sita ordered, her voice breaking as she spoke.

The paper fell apart to reveal a soft knitted article, and Amita lifted up a tiny white crocheted jacket, yellowed with age. A sudden spurt of rage rushed through her. This must be a jacket she, Amita, had worn as a baby, or something Sita had knitted for her own miscarried child. Her mother had no sense of timing. At this moment it was enough just to process her own experience; she could not carry the pain of others. She turned to her mother, her mouth full of harsh words, but fell silent before Sita's stricken face.

As she held the jacket out before her, trying to make sense of its tiny arms, the flared skirt and the ribbon threaded round the neck, something slipped from the paper onto the bed beside her, and fell to the floor at her feet. Amita bent to retrieve a small drawstring bag, and held it out to her mother, but Sita shook her head.

'Open it.'

Amita pulled apart the string and tipped out from the pouch a thin gold chain with a tiny pendant. A fleck of a ruby, no bigger than a teardrop, sparkled at its centre.

'What are these things?' Amita turned to her mother in frustration.

The chain lay weightlessly in her palm, and she looked down at it with foreboding. Yet, she thought at first that she misunderstood the words her mother breathed out with such difficulty.

'These things were left for you by your mother.'

'My *mother*?'

Sita sank back into the chair, feeling suddenly weightless. Her voice drifted from her, the words she spoke almost soundless after the painful compression of years. The secret they carried floated free in the room and hung suspended, birthed and immovable, lodged openly at last between herself and her daughter. All Sita had dreaded would happen when Parvati began her interviews was happening now. Layer by layer, the cruel unwrapping of experience had brought her to the thing she had so carefully buried, the one thing she wished Amita never to know. Once the unravelling began, she had sensed there would be no way to stop until the end was reached and Amita knew the truth. Perhaps this was what she had wanted all along, to tell Amita the truth.

As Sita began to speak her voice grew stronger, and Amita listened, her eyes locked upon her mother's face.

Sita was not sure how long she sat on the bench at the bus stop before Ramaiah arrived. He stood a few feet from her in his green *lungi*, his shirt hanging open, his dirty cotton vest sodden with perspiration, sweat glistening on his muscular limbs from his hurried pursuit of her. She drew back on the bench before the raw urgency of his expression, apprehensive now of what he might want.

'Come back to the house,' Ramaiah demanded. He appeared calmer, his anger dissipated.

She thought she heard a plea in his voice, and meeting

his eyes, was surprised at the distress in his face. Reluctantly, she rose from the bench to follow him. In the distance a bird shrieked, and the sound of Ramaiah's laboured breathing filled the silence between them as they walked back into the estate. When they reached the house he went before her up the steps, to where the baby lay quietly in the room, sleeping now in her box. He motioned Sita to a chair.

'Whatever I could do for her, I did,' he pushed out his lower lip defensively. He was a balding man, grey haired and with round, fleshy features and deeply pouched eyes.

'You beat her,' Sita reminded him, her eyes settling again on Muni's pink sari folded up in a corner. The baby began whimpering once more in the box.

'What man does not beat his wife? I told her to be sure to make a boy.' Anger spat out of him again.

'You killed her,' Sita shouted, unable to control her rage.

For a moment Ramaiah appeared about to lunge at her in his fury, but as suddenly as it welled up, his anger evaporated and he sat down abruptly on the remaining chair, gazing down silently at his bare feet. From the opposite chair Sita sat staring at him. He was not a bad man, she saw the sadness beneath his anger, and her own rage died as she observed his contrition.

'The child took too long to come. She was not strong.' He spoke in a low voice, his head bowed, his gaze still fixed upon his feet.

'Did she see the baby? Did she know it was a girl?' Sita asked. Ramaiah nodded, his face creasing in unexpected grief.

'Yes, she saw her, held her. I am not a bad man. Sometimes

I get angry, but it is only when I am full of toddy.' The words barely rose above his breath.

For a while they sat in silence, Sita twisting her hands in her lap, not knowing what was expected of her, yet all the while aware of the child stirring restlessly in her box.

'She often spoke about you.' At last Ramaiah lifted his head to stare curiously at Sita.

'She knew I could not manage a child on my own. She knew because it was a girl, I would put an end to it or send it to the orphanage. If I die, give her to Sita, she told me. That was the last thing she said, the last thing. So, now I must give her to you. Bring her up with your family, with your own children.'

'I have no children. I am a widow.' Sita told him stiffly, meeting his gaze, her heart beating.

'Then keep her for me, for her. I will pay you; I have some money.' His voice was heavy and tired.

'I do not need money.' Sita's head was a whirl of disconnected thoughts.

'Then it is all right. The orphanage woman will come soon. They will take care of her.' Ramaiah sighed, shrugged and stood up, nodding his acceptance of Sita's decision.

Sita rose from her chair and faced him squarely, knowing suddenly the words that now left her mouth had shaped themselves at the moment she first saw the baby, when she realised Muni was dead. The dream on the bus came back to her and she saw again Muni, breaking free of the water, laughing and dripping, the child in her arms. This was all Muni's doing. It was Muni's wish that she should take the child. The knowledge that she must grasp this moment before it slipped away flooded through her.

'If I take her, I will adopt her. She will be my child, to bring up as I wish.' Sita announced.

Ramaiah nodded his agreement, his face already filled by growing relief that this dark episode might soon be behind him, and he would be free. He bent to pick up the milk bottles and the nappies the women had earlier packed in a jute bag, pushing them towards Sita.

'Go quickly then, before that orphanage woman arrives,' he said, walking towards the door.

Holding the child and the bulging jute bag, Sita descended the steps of the house, the child cradled in her arms, holding her close, careful not to put a foot wrong. Ramaiah stood at the top of the stairs and watched her, and she was conscious of his eyes upon her.

'Wait,' he called suddenly, and disappeared into the house as she turned to look back up the steps.

Soon he reappeared, climbing down towards her, his big body filling the narrow stairway, his grubby white vest stretched tight across his loose paunch. He stood before her and seemed lost for words as he thrust a small soft package towards her. Still gripping the child, the weight of the bag pulling on her arm, Sita freed her hands to pull apart the string on the brown paper wrapping.

'She knitted it for the baby.'

His voice broke as he stared down at the tiny white crocheted jacket Sita now held, as if moved by the sight of its

smallness and delicacy. Sweat collected in the folds of his neck
and dampened the rough grey stubble of his unshaven cheeks.
Staring into his face, she was surprised to see his eyes were moist
with tears. Extending an arm towards her, he opened his closed
fist to her gaze. In his fleshy palm lay Muni's good luck pendant
on its thin gold chain.

'It is right that her daughter should have this. Keep it for her.'

Sita took it from him and gazed at the pendant, no heavier
than a drop of water, the fleck of ruby sparkling uncertainly
in the sun. She closed her fingers around it, holding it tight in
her hand.

'Go quickly now, before that orphanage woman comes,'
Ramaiah urged, turning to climb back up the steps.

Once free of the house, Sita walked as quickly as she dared,
afraid of falling on the uneven ground, surprised at the weight
and solidity of the tiny sleeping bundle she carried. It was
as if she walked in a dream, nothing seemed real. Fate had
pounced suddenly upon her, sweeping her up in a way she was
powerless to resist. She tightened her grip on the child, aware
all the while of the light rise and fall of its breath beneath
her hand.

At last she reached the gatehouse. Through the open window
she glimpsed a stout woman in a navy blue sari, whose stance
was full of officialdom, and knew this was the woman from the
orphanage. A Sikh guard was already directing her to Ramaiah's
house. Sita slipped through the rusty gates of the estate, walking
quickly to the bus stop a short distance away. As she waited for
the bus she rocked the baby gently. Above her the sky, empty

of cloud, arched over the green mesh of the jungle. A group of Brahminy Kites wheeled up, soaring higher and higher, gliding seamlessly on the wing, far above the world. Then, at last, in the distance the faint rumble of an engine was heard. Already the outline of the bus could be seen, drawing nearer, becoming clearer as it broke free of the hot haze of the surrounding vegetation.

Sita climbed up into the bus and found a seat. The baby slept on her shoulder, unknowing of the journey they took together now, away from the ancient griefs of the past. The future waited, as yet insubstantial, but Sita knew it would be a future of her own making. She had already decided she would call the child Amita, for it meant *boundless; without a limit*, and would set her firmly upon the path she must follow if she were to fashion her own special universe. Sita leaned back in the seat and drew a deep breath. Beyond the window a flock of green parrots rose from the trees in an emerald cloud, forging patterns of mystery in the deepening light of the afternoon. Upon her shoulder the child slept.

'I don't understand.' Amita pushed out the words, numb with shock.

'It is not the right moment to tell you. But if I do not tell you now, I may never tell you. I was wrong to keep it from you for so long,' Sita whispered.

'Then my father is also not my father?'

The thick-haired man in that cherished photograph, who stood beneath the tree with his students at the Ramakrishna

Mission, was not the man Amita thought he was; he was not her father.

'Shiva never knew you, he never saw you. He died in the war before I returned to Singapore. I saw him last on that day before we left for Burma,' Sita admitted.

'Are you telling me that my father is the man who tried to drown me in a bucket of water?' Amita stared at Sita, trying to comprehend.

There was nothing left of her that was still intact. First, they had sucked out her innards with a vacuum cleaner, killing her child, and now her mother had taken a pickaxe to her to shatter her soul and mind. She was locked into a nightmare, and any moment now she must wake up. There was the sound of the fan turning above, round and round, the same small precise revolution, on and on; on and on.

'Muni gave you to me. Please understand, she told Ramaiah to give you to me, and he fulfilled her wish.'

'That man, is he still alive?' Amita asked. She could not call him, father. Sita shook her head.

'He died some years ago. Gopal, on the estate, wrote to me.'

'He never came to see me? Never sent you money?'

'I adopted you. Everything was legal; the Ramakrishna Mission helped me. You are my daughter.'

'Do I look like him, or do I look like her?' She had to ask the question.

'Like him,' Sita was forced to admit.

'I look like the man who tried to drown me in a bucket of water!' For once Amita was lost for appropriate words.

Sita was silent, gazing at her daughter and then down at her hands, as if they were a place of refuge. There was nowhere in the room to hide.

'What is this, then?' Amita asked savagely, staring at the pendant in her open palm.

'It was Muni's good luck charm. She wore it always. Her mother died when she was small, of malaria; it belonged to your grandmother. And Muni crocheted that jacket for you. The last time I saw her she was knitting it for you.'

'This is crazy,' Amita shouted so loudly Sita drew back.

'Why did you not tell me all this before? Why are you telling me now, on this day of all days?'

Amita wanted to scream and laugh at the same time. She was entering a madness she would never be free of, a madness she feared she might not even survive. The chill of it filled her, and she found she was trembling. She could hear the chatter of her teeth.

'It's a lie. It's all one of your lies,' she shouted.

'If you were my biological daughter, you would be older than you are. The war was already finished and Shiva some years dead when I adopted you,' Sita replied, speaking carefully, holding on to the facts.

Amita paused for a moment to calculate, and she saw this was true. Why had she never seen this blatant discrepancy in her age before? Had she not wanted to see it, or had she just accepted as children accept without question, the circumstances of her life?

'Go away. Just go away.'

'I *wanted* you; I *love* you. I wanted a *daughter*,' Sita pleaded. 'Go away. Go away.'

Amita slept and could not seem to wake up, leaving her bed only for the bathroom. At times, as she tossed and turned, she was conscious of Sita opening the door and peering in at her. Sometimes, she entered with a tray of food, a sandwich or a cup of Milo. If Amita woke up hungry she ate the food her mother left there, and when next she woke she found the snacks had been replenished. She lost count of time, waking with the expectation of day, only to find it was night. In the distance she heard the hoarse chime of her mother's old clock, striking again and again, marking unheeded hours. Each time she woke she thought the nightmare was over, but surfacing into consciousness, she found that the bleak reality remained.

The balance of her life was changed. It had been tossed up into the air, as if a great weight had suddenly been placed upon one side of the scale of her existence. She drank the Milo and ate the sandwich, but nothing stopped the pain of being forced to recognise that her life was an aberration. She tried not to think about it, and yet she could not stop thinking about it. It was a grotesque injury she was forced to examine, like a wounded soldier must face the sight of his own guts spilling from his ripped belly. That was how she felt. She slept again, and did not know if hours or days passed her by. Strange dreams wrapped about her, moving through her, leaving within her an unpalatable residue.

Eventually she awoke, and although the same sickening reality was still before her there was a sense that the weight had lessened, like an over rich meal she had partially digested. Beside her on a tray was the usual vacuum tumbler of Milo and a sandwich wrapped in cling film. She sat up in bed and drank the hot Milo, and for the first time ate hungrily, tasting the sandwich filling of egg mayonnaise with an edge of satisfaction. Beyond the curtained window it was dark, and in the depths of the flat the clock struck eight. A faint smell of food and incense drifted into the room. Her mother would have heated the food she had cooked with Joyce's help in the morning, and earlier in the evening she would have lit a stick of incense before the *devi*'s picture. Even as these images came before her Amita corrected herself — the woman whom she called her mother but who was in fact not her mother — the confusion was making her ill. Sleep once again drew her under, and she gave herself to it gratefully. All Amita wanted was oblivion.

Once again strange dreams floated through her. Amita stood by the river in her mother's village; behind her was the banyan tree Sita had climbed as a child. Although she had never been to this river, Amita felt she knew it well. Squinting across the broad channel of glinting water, she saw the white shapes of temples on the opposite bank, the thick smell of the river filled her nose. The water was glassy clear and she could see right down to the river bed, to the dark waving tangle of weeds, where fish darted and wheeled in flashes of silver. The river appeared to be alive with the sinuous movement of thousands of fish. Yet, when she looked again she saw it was not fish the river held, but the lithe and mercurial souls of a missing multitude of girl children, jostling and swimming together as one. The sacred waters shimmered and glowed and she saw then that it was no ordinary river, but the river of consciousness from which all life drank.

She woke with a start and found she was sweating, her heart pounding in her chest. The images of the dream were fading fast and she sought to hold onto them as they weakened and broke apart. Soon they were gone, but one truth stayed with her. She had been saved from a bucket of water, and fished from a river of souls. And with the dream came another conviction. Perhaps in claiming her, Sita had reclaimed the lost soul of her own sister. These strange thoughts filled her with confusion; tears welled up in her eyes, tears for herself and tears for Sita, and for the unknown woman who had been her birth mother. For an instant, the image of the river's mercurial water filled her mind again, lithe with jostling souls.

Then her mind was filled by another image. She imagined the bucket of water, and herself, newly born, pushed down head first, her lungs heaving and spluttering as she struggled to live. She lay back on the pillows, her heart still thumping with the vividness of the scenes passing through her mind.

When next she woke, she sat up in bed, put on the light and reached for the soft package upon the bedside table. Lifting the tiny jacket from the paper, she held it up before her. The woman who had knitted it had fashioned it for her and nobody else, and had formed each stitch in an anticipation of love. Then, picking up the pendant on its thin chain, Amita stared at it as it lay in the palm of her hand. The light from the table-lamp warmed the dull gold, and the tiny grain of ruby glowed, the eye in a needle whose thread guided her back through the generations of women whose blood she shared. The gold in her hand had absorbed the very essence of the woman who had given birth to her, whose flesh she had fed off and grown upon, who herself might have escaped the fate of the river or a bucket of water by a narrowness of margins Amita would never know.

Sita's slow shuffling steps could be heard coming down the corridor. They paused before Amita's door as Sita pushed it open a crack to check on her daughter.

'Come in, Ma.' There was no place left in her now for anger.

'Did you drink the Milo?' Sita asked.

She stared hesitantly at her daughter, who sat gazing down at the chain in her hand and the knitted jacket spread out on her lap. Picking up the tray, Sita took a step towards the door, but then turned back again to Amita.

'She loved you. She wanted you. She died to give you life.'

However Amita would respond, Sita knew she must risk her daughter's wrath and say the things that had been repeating in her head through the hours Amita had been asleep.

'I know,' Amita whispered, tears filling her eyes.

Surprised that Amita did not attack her with the usual shower of jagged words, Sita was emboldened to continue.

'When she knew she was dying she told him to give you to me, to protect you. She knew what he would do to you if she did not tell him that. Those were her last words, he told me. She rescued you. And you rescued me.'

'I know,' Amita repeated, almost under her breath.

'Muni and I, we have both loved you; we have shared you. She grew you and I have looked after you. You have us both, you have two mothers.' Sita's voice gained strength as she saw Amita was listening to her.

'More Milo?' she asked as she turned towards the door, and Amita nodded.

Lying back again on the pillows, the pendant warm in the palm of her hand, Amita stared up at the stain of the incubus on the ceiling above her. Through the open door the scent of incense drifted to her again. On a shelf in her mother's room, snug in her metal frame, the *devi* sat upon her tiger, flowers and offerings spread before her. Amita wished she could pray with the ease of her mother, wished she had the gift of humility. Instead, she stared up at the incubus.

'Tell me what to do,' she entreated.

As her mother's footsteps sounded again in the corridor, the image of the river flickered before Amita, fleeting fragments of her dream returning like formless spectres, only to vanish before she could grasp them. Her heart stirred in a way she now recognised, when that other woman within her decided to emerge and take hold of her life. How many versions of herself had she travelled through to disembark at this unexpected place? How did one become the person one became, she wondered? Had she now arrived at herself, or were there still further versions of this person to journey through before she reached a destination? Would there ever be a destination?

Sita entered the room with a new cup of Milo and an extra

cup for herself, and sat down apprehensively on the chair, uneasy about the damage her revelations had initiated. Before she could speak, Amita turned, her face firm with new resolve.

'Soon, I'm going to a conference in Delhi and afterwards I plan to find your village, Sagarnagar, and see the river where you played.'

'Everything will have changed,' Sita warned, sipping the hot drink cautiously.

When she gave her plenary in Delhi on the 'missing' girls, Amita decided, she would tell them how she sought to personally balance a terrible practice in her own way.

'I've decided, I'm taking you with me. We will go back to that river together,' she told her mother.

Already, she smelled the thick scent of the water, and saw the endless spiral of souls in its depths. Just days ago, in desperation, she had planned to go to Delhi and stay on to have her child in India, and to later return to Singapore with news that she had adopted an orphaned girl. And that was what she would do now. Her own child was gone, but just as she had been saved from a bucket of water, she too could fish a being from that river of souls.

A full life required embracing, not running away, and she was free to choose her own narrative. Like the *devi* on her tiger, she too could be both woman and warrior, one-in-herself and answerable to none. If people talked in the conservative town she lived in then she would let them talk, for it mattered little to her, and her mother, she knew, would support her. She saw at last that this woman who was not her mother and yet was her mother, who had nurtured and guided her, had voyaged a similar path to her own. The bond of blood may not hold them together, Amita was not made in Sita's image, but she had grown up within the rhythm of her spirit and found her reflection mirrored within herself.

'We will go back to the river together,' she repeated, and a surge of joy rushed through her.

GLOSSARY

Aie Bhagwan! – Oh God!

akka – elder sister

angrezi – English

attap – palm leaf

ayurvedic – traditional Indian medicine

bidi – a type of cigarette

beti – daughter

bhaiya – elder brother

bhai – brother

bhajan – Hindu religious song

bhajanashram – ashram for widows

chai – tea

chapati – unleavened bread

dal – lentils

devi – goddess

didi – elder sister

Dilli Chalo! – Onwards to Delhi!

dhoti – lower garment worn by many male Hindus

dosai – rice pancake

gharry – carriage

ghats – steps on bank of the river

gopis – cow-herding girls

harijan – untouchable caste

Jai Hind! – Hail India!

jawan – infantry soldier

kala pani – black water

kangani – supervisor who organised labour on an estate

karanguni man – recycle collection man

kurta – loose Indian shirt

ladoo – sweetmeat

lota – metal water pot

lungi – sarong

mais – women

manga – japanese comic

mangalsutra – wedding necklace worn in some Indian communities

mehendi – henna

matka – earthenware pot

nataraja – figurine of god Shiva

pallu – end of the sari

peon – errand boy

paratha – unleavened bread, cooked in ghee or oil

pujari – priest

shaitaan – the devil

shakti – divine feminine power

sati – widow victim of ritual *sati*

thanaka – cosmetic paste, commonly used in Myanmar

tawa – griddle

sindhoor – carmine mark denoting marriage for Hindu women

tonga – horse carriage

tongawallah – carriage driver

varna – caste

ACKNOWLEDGEMENTS

My deepest thanks to Dr Cynthia vanden Dreisen for her invaluable help and support over the many incarnations this book has been through, before it arrived at its final embodiment.

This novel owes its genesis to work done at the University of Western Australia, and I thank the university, and particularly the English Department, for their kindness and support during my time in Perth.

I am grateful to both Richard Cohen in New York, and Gretchen Liu in Singapore, for their reading of the manuscript and their comments.

Thanks also to Prof. Chitra Sankaran of the National University of Singapore for making me a guest student in the Integrated Virtual Learning Environment (IVLE) of her Gender Studies Class.

Suchen Christine Lim allowed me to use and quote from an incident in Chapter One of her novel, *A Bit of Earth* (2001), and I appreciate this.

The novel mentioned on page 118 is *Rich Like Us* by Nayantara Sahgal (1985), London: Heinemann.

Both the late Padmashri Puan Sri Datin Janaky Davar Nahappan, and Bharati Choudhry (nee Asha Sahay), gave generously of their time to share with me their recollections as recruits in the Rani of Jhansi Regiment of the INA.

My thanks to Swami Satyalokananda and the Ramakrishna Mission, Singapore, for help in my research.

I appreciate the assistance of the Oral History Department of the National Archives of Singapore for the use of material regarding the Indian National Army.

My thanks also to the National Heritage Board of Singapore for giving me special access to the Oral History video interview with Capt. Lakshmi Sahgal.

Quotes in Chapter 5 are taken from Barbara D. Miller's paper, *Female Infanticide and Child Neglect in Rural North India* (1987), and from Rajeswari Sunder Rajan's book, *Real or Imagined Women* (1993).

Quotes in Chapter 8 regarding the practice of *sati* are from Gayatri Chakravorty Spivak's *A Critique of Post Colonial Reason* (1999), and Julie Leslie, ed., *Roles and Rituals for Hindu Women* (1992).

I also appreciate the information found in the following papers:

- *Discarded Daughters: The Patriarchal Grip: Dowry Deaths, Sex Ratio Imbalances & Foeticide in India* by Aysan Sev'er, University of Toronto (2006).
- *Female Foeticide and Infanticide in India: An Analysis of Crimes against Girl Children* by Sneh Lata Tandon and Renu Sharma, University of Delhi (2006).

Last but not least, grateful thanks to Tara Dhar Hasnain for all her help, and for pulling me up over so many important details.

ABOUT THE AUTHOR

Meira Chand is of Indian-Swiss parentage and was born and educated in London. She has lived for many years in Japan, and also in India. In 1997 she moved to Singapore, and is now a citizen of the country. Her multi-cultural heritage is reflected in her novels.

Also by Meira Chand:

A Different Sky

A Far Horizon

A Choice of Evils

House of the Sun

The Painted Cage

The Bonsai Tree

Last Quadrant

The Gossamer Fly